WANTING A KISS

"Please."

"Please what?" he asked, his breath spiced with wicked promise. "Please go away?"

"Please kiss me," she whispered, hating herself for pleading. But he made no further comment.

He lowered his head until his lips grazed across her skin, slowly, teasingly, devastatingly, from the hollow beneath her ear along the line of her jaw until he reached the trembling pulse on the other side.

His lips brushed across hers, once, twice, thrice. He was toying with her. Tempting her. Teasing her with desire for his withheld kisses until she could stand it no more. The next time he slid his open mouth over hers, she allowed her tongue to edge just far enough between her parted lips to taste him.

Everything changed . . .

BOOK YOUR PLACE ON OUR WEBSITE AND MAKE THE READING CONNECTION!

We've created a customized website just for our very special readers, where you can get the inside scoop on everything that's going on with Zebra, Pinnacle and Kensington books.

When you come online, you'll have the exciting opportunity to:

- View covers of upcoming books
- Read sample chapters
- Learn about our future publishing schedule (listed by publication month *and author*)
- Find out when your favorite authors will be visiting a city near you
- Search for and order backlist books from our online catalog
- Check out author bios and background information
- Send e-mail to your favorite authors
- Meet the Kensington staff online
- Join us in weekly chats with authors, readers and other guests
- Get writing guidelines
- AND MUCH MORE!

Visit our website at
http://www.kensingtonbooks.com

TOO WICKED TO KISS

ERICA RIDLEY

ZEBRA BOOKS
Kensington Publishing Corp.
http://www.kensingtonbooks.com

ZEBRA BOOKS are published by

Kensington Publishing Corp.
119 West 40th Street
New York, NY 10018

All Kensington titles, imprints, and distributed lines are available at special quantity discounts for bulk purchases for sales promotion, premiums, fund-raising, educational, or institutional use.

Special book excerpts or customized printings can also be created to fit specific needs. For details, write or phone the office of the Kensington Special Sales Manager: Attn.: Special Sales Department. Kensington Publishing Corp., 119 West 40th Street, New York, NY 10018. Phone: 1-800-221-2647.

Zebra and the Z logo Reg. U.S. Pat. & TM Off.

ISBN-13: 978-1-4201-0993-1
ISBN-10: 1-4201-0993-6

First Printing: March 2010

10 9 8 7 6 5 4 3 2 1

Printed in the United States of America

ACKNOWLEDGMENTS

This story would never have made it out of my imagination and into bookstores without the help, guidance, and encouragement of many individuals. Heartfelt thanks go to my critique partners Darcy Burke and Lacey Kaye, my early readers Kelly Remick, Amanda Freebourn, Jackie Barbosa, and June Bowen, my agent Lauren Abramo, who is chock-full of awesome sauce, and to my editor John Scognamiglio and everyone on the Kensington team who helped make this book a reality. Super big hugs go to my friends Diana Peterfreund and Karen Rose, who are always willing to talk shop or talk me down from a ledge, depending on the circumstance. (They're not just good people—they're great writers, too. Go buy their books!)

I would never have made the transition from aspiring author to published author without the amazing resource of RWA, the support of my local writing chapter TARA, my plotting pals PCubed, and the advice and encouragement from Julie Leto, C. L. Wilson, and Virginia Henley. A special thank you goes out to Carrie Ryan, Phyllis Towzey, Carrie Friedauer, and Janice Goodfellow, for believing in me even when I was convinced my calling was writing madcap romantic comedies about a would-be tooth fairy.

The biggest thank you of all goes to my grandma and one-time librarian, Bettie Igney, who has always thought being an author was a fine career and never once suggested I give up my dreams in order to pursue a "real" job. You'll never know how many times your unswerving faith helped me through the rough patches. I cannot thank you enough.

Chapter One

October 13, 1813

Evangeline Pemberton's head slammed against the carriage window, jarring her from another nightmare. For a moment, she thought she was still stuffed in a tiny, airless mail coach. No. She was almost free. She even had elbow room and a clean dress, thanks to the two scowling women seated across from her.

Lady Stanton, a narrow, angular woman with approximately the same shape and warmth as an icicle, stared down her nose at Evangeline with the same glacial expression she'd worn when Evangeline had appeared on her doorstep last evening. Then as now, Lady Stanton's thin, bloodless lips pressed tightly together, stretching the single black mole hovering below her left nostril. A pale lavender gown the color of snow in shadow swathed her sharp, bony limbs. Blond hair so limp and lifeless as to appear almost white coiled beneath her bonnet like the sloughed dry skin of a snake.

Evangeline clutched her too-small pelisse around her shoulders and averted her gaze to Lady Stanton's daughter. A pair of spectacles and a mint green hair ribbon softened the harsh pale beauty Miss Stanton—or Susan, as Evangeline had been bade to call her—shared with her mother, but the easy smiles she'd bestowed upon Evangeline earlier today had long fled from her face.

Susan's hands fell by her sides in loose fists to rest atop the crimson seat cushion. She wore mitts, long and tight as most gloves were, but without closed tips to cover the ends of her fingers. Perhaps she was immune to the harsh autumn chill.

Evangeline straightened the blanket across her lap and tried to ignore the carriage window's mocking reflection. Her borrowed dress was now wrinkled beyond all hope. Her stubborn hair refused to stay clasped to her head, choosing instead to cling to her neck and cheeks in damp curls. Grooves from the window frame left uncomfortable lines down her face.

"Thank you again for the invitation," she said, hoping to coax into the chilly confines of the carriage at least the pretense of a pleasant atmosphere. "This is my first time to London."

Lady Stanton turned her nose to the other carriage window, apparently preferring the lengthening shadows to idle conversation. Her thin fingers worked a delicately painted fan near her perfumed neck, filling the carriage with the cloying stench of unwatered roses left to wilt in a forgotten room.

Wait. Shadows. "How long was I asleep?"

Susan nudged her spectacles with the back of a gloved hand. "Hours."

"Hours?" Evangeline repeated, staring out the window in confusion. It had taken hours and hours to flee from her home in the Chiltern Hills all the way to London, but how could it possibly take hours to go from Stanton House to a local soiree? "Where are we?"

Susan glanced at her mother, who was still pointedly focused on the setting sun disappearing behind the skeletal gray arms of leafless trees stretching their knobby limbs toward the heavy sky. Perhaps Lady Stanton was worried the impending storm would delay their travel. But their travel *where*?

"Braintree," Susan whispered at last, as though wary of speaking the word aloud. "We're almost there."

The view from the dusty window dimmed with the setting of the sun, tinting the thick forest surrounding them from pink to purple to gray, until the only light came from the exterior carriage lamps.

Evangeline's flesh began to prickle. "I thought the house party was in Town."

"I believe I said 'outside London,'" Lady Stanton corrected without removing her gaze from the window.

From ten in the morning to twilight meant more than a little "outside" London but having thrown herself on the Stantons' mercy, Evangeline doubted she could complain and still expect shelter. A single day's drive was far preferable to the living hell awaiting her at home. If her stepfather *let* her live. At this precise moment, he was either whipping his servants for allowing her to escape from the pantry or well on his way to finding her and bringing her back.

"Your fiancé lives in . . . Braintree?" she asked Susan, seeking to replace memories of small dark rooms with a more pleasant topic.

"Actually," Lady Stanton answered, "he's not her fiancé."

"Actually," Susan echoed without making eye contact, "he's never met me."

An uneasy tremor rippled through Evangeline's stomach. That was not precisely the same story they'd told her back at Stanton House when they'd loaded up the carriage and set off for a "local" party.

"I must have misunderstood," Evangeline said slowly, although she was certain her ears were as sharp as ever. "I thought you said you were going to marry him."

Susan adjusted her spectacles. "I am."

"That's where you come in." Lady Stanton closed her fan with a snap. Small hard eyes much paler than the blue of her veins glittered like a matching pair of hard, colorless diamonds. "To help her win his hand and his pocketbook, by fair means or foul. After all, recluses cannot spend their wealth alone. A simple compromise should do the trick. Merely get them alone, then 'accidentally' stumble upon them, screaming for all the world to hear. I'll take care of the rest."

"What?" Evangeline stared openmouthed at the Stanton women, momentarily abandoning her intention to appear calm and biddable. "I'm to entrap an innocent bachelor into marriage with a complete stranger?"

"He's no innocent," Susan said darkly, her gaze finally meeting Evangeline's. "Quite the opposite."

Meaning what? Evangeline focused on the two women before her. Something wasn't right. Something worse than saying "outside London" when one truly meant "a desolate stretch of uninhabited country." Something worse than saying "join us for a delightful party" when one truly meant "force a total stranger to the altar."

She shook her head, unable to believe the people she'd trusted to provide her shelter had abducted her in a mad scheme to win an unwilling husband. "Why not seek marriage in a more . . . traditional way?"

"Would that we were able." Lady Stanton cast a quelling glance at her daughter. "Desperate measures must be taken now that the impertinent baggage is no longer welcome in London. Or by anyone who knows anyone who *is* welcome in London."

"If I were, we wouldn't be caught dead anywhere near Blackberry Manor." Susan smiled, but the humor didn't reach her eyes. "Of course, we might be caught dead anyway."

"What do you mean?" Evangeline fought the frisson of cold slithering between her stays and her spine. "Has there been an accident?"

"Not at all." Susan straightened her perfectly straight bonnet. "Lionkiller strikes on purpose."

"Lion*croft*." Lady Stanton rapped Susan's knee with the fan. "Don't bait the beast with that horrid nickname, or I shan't be surprised to see your body join the others."

Evangeline froze, unable to tear her gaze from Lady Stanton's hard, colorless eyes. "What others?"

One hand rubbing her knee, Susan glared at her mother. "Just his parents. Perhaps mine are next."

Lady Stanton returned her attention to her window. "Your father won't be attending the party."

Susan's eyes narrowed. "Pity."

Evangeline's gloved fingers dug into the squab. Such jests were never funny. "May I remind you," she said quietly, "I've just lost my mother."

"Five days ago." With her thin nose held high, Lady Stanton flapped a gloved hand toward Evangeline's face like a frantic bird unable to take flight. "If that's long enough to leave your home, it's long enough to ensure we return to ours with a betrothal contract."

Five long, long days of unspeakable grief. Five equally long nights of sleepless terror. And one desperate attempt to escape with her life. Evangeline's damp shift stuck to her skin as she rolled back her shoulders.

"No matter what you think, I am still in mourning. Nothing will change that."

"Nobody's asking otherwise." Her lip curled at Evangeline's still-shaking head. "You can mourn your mother and help Susan win Lioncroft at the same time. It's not as if he'd prefer whiling away his time with *you*."

Susan adjusted her hair ribbon. "Do you dance?"

No. But how humiliating to admit such a lack. Evangeline hesitated before replying, "When I'm not in mourning."

The eerie cries of unseen animals rose in harmony with distant thunder.

"She doesn't *look* like she's in mourning," Lady Stanton informed her daughter, sotto voce.

"That's because she's in my castoffs," Susan murmured back. "And I've never mourned anything."

"I'm grateful for your generosity." Borrowed silk scratched

against her skin as Evangeline shifted uncomfortably. "But I can't condone tricking a man to the altar just to get his money, nor do I think locking ourselves up with a murderer for two weeks is in any of our best interests."

"Increased coffers are always in one's best interest," Lady Stanton countered. "But if you feel otherwise, so be it."

Evangeline's eyes widened. "Truly?"

"Of course." Lady Stanton's crystal eyes turned calculating. "Have a delightful walk back home."

A sudden burst of lightning lit up both the carriage and the countryside seconds before heavy drops of rain pelted the rattling windows.

Evangeline shivered as an icy breeze snaked through the cracks. "There's nowhere to walk to. Not even an inn."

"And you have no money," Susan put in, casting a pointed gaze at Evangeline's borrowed gown. "Which means you're dead either way, so you might as well help."

"Just so," Lady Stanton fanned her pale neck. "Miss Pemberton must do as she's told. As do you."

"Only because it's the lesser evil, I might remind you." Susan turned to Evangeline, her tone apologetic. "It was this or stay confined to the town house until summer. I'd rather wait until the end of the party to trap him, but Mother wishes to get the compromise over with first thing. Either way, we do need your assistance."

"To win the hand of a murderer?" Evangeline rubbed the gooseflesh prickling her arms. "Why wasn't he sent to the gallows?"

"Nothing was ever proven," Lady Stanton said with a snap of her fan. "Lioncroft's quite clever."

"And both reclusive and exclusive." Susan leaned forward, eyes shining. "We wouldn't even be invited if Mother wasn't a close personal acquaintance of his sister, Lady Hetherington. Just think—Lioncroft's first social engagement since he killed their parents. Scandal sheets would pay *dearly* for first-hand accounts of this party!"

"I do apologize," Evangeline said, although she felt like she should be listening to an apology rather than making one of her own. "But this is a bit too much intrigue for me. I would've preferred to work in your scullery than come along on this trip, had I known what you planned."

"Of course you would've." Lady Stanton arched pale eyebrows at Evangeline. "That's why we didn't tell you."

"I must insist I be left out of any schemes to—"

"Too late," Susan interrupted, tapping the window. "We're here."

Evangeline craned her neck for a better view and nearly broke her nose on the glass when the carriage jolted across yet another deep rut.

A castle rose in silhouette against the stark light of the moon. The house, if one could call it that, was a massive, sprawling mansion with three stories and a circular tower, all made of wide gray stones. Two wings jutted forward from either side, forming three sides of a square, with a large gate in the center. Darkness enshrouded the whole, for few candles burned at the windows. Heavy clouds gathered over jagged eaves. Two hulking guardsmen heaved open thick wrought-iron gates. Thunder growled across the sky.

"Blackberry Manor," Susan breathed, and straightened her spectacles. "Black, like Lionkiller's soul, and berry because he's going to bury us back in the garden with the rest of the bodies."

"Not until after your wedding," Lady Stanton snapped. "Coffers first, coffins second." She pointed her fan toward Evangeline. "And you'll do exactly as I say, Miss Pemberton, or you won't have a bed to sleep in."

"Then I'll just wait in the carriage," Evangeline muttered, her breath steaming against the window. She cleared the glass with one sleeve. Fat droplets splattered against the rain-streaked pane as she stared at the looming mansion. Stone beasts glared at her from their crouched positions upon the roof.

As they neared, more and more orange light flickered in the windows. A flock of ravens settled atop each tower. She could never live in such a dark, lonely place.

She wasn't even certain she could survive a fortnight.

As the heavy iron doors closed behind her with ominous finality, Evangeline came to a dead stop inside the entryway to Blackberry Manor.

Despite the tall arched ceiling with its bowed wooden beams curving at the creases like so many rib bones, the air was thick, heavy, oppressive, as if she had not stepped into the foyer of an aristocrat's mansion, but a long forgotten sepulcher untouched by anything but death.

At Lady Stanton's unveiled glare, Evangeline forced her feet further into the echoing anteroom. The cold marble floor spreading from her battered boots to the edges of every wall might have been ivory or alabaster or cream in color, had there been more light than the occasional flickering sconce. Instead, the murky pattern was a foggy, swirling gray, as though a thundercloud had hardened beneath her feet.

Were there no windows? Evangeline craned her neck to peer upward, just beneath the rafters. Ah, yes. Several. But not the kind to let in light.

The narrow slashes high above her head were the sort suited for medieval castles, for skilled archers to aim their deadly arrows at those who would trespass below, not for illuminating entryways for members of Polite Society. This evening, no archers crouched at the ready, just as no sun hung in the sky. Only the slipperiest, blackest of shadows filtered through the thin cracks to fall upon her upturned face like the cool caress of ghostly hands. The wisps of damp hair on Evangeline's neck fluttered nervously, touched by a breeze she could not feel.

Lady Stanton, for her part, was momentarily nonplused. Gone was the calculating gleam in her eyes, replaced by . . . not fear, precisely. Wariness. As if she would cleave to her stratagem as planned, but was no longer convinced of its wisdom.

Susan stood in the very center of the room, perhaps determined not to edge too near to the shadows seeping from the corners. Her wide, quick eyes took in the ceiling, the staircase, the narrow slits of lightless windows, and then her trembling hands were at her pale face. She snatched off her spectacles and shoved them in a pocket. Evangeline had the terrible suspicion Susan did so because she had no wish to see just what they'd gotten themselves into.

A gaunt, wizened butler stood silently against one wall, the sputtering candle above his head doing little to illuminate his expression. His gnarled face remained impassive when whispers came from an adjacent hallway, then footfalls, followed by a beautiful blond lady, four spindly-limbed footmen, and three cowering maids.

The lady did not look at home in the mansion, despite her fancy dress. She looked frightened. After a jerking peek over her shoulder at the vacant marble staircase curving up from the anteroom's furthest shadows, she hurried into the foyer to greet them.

Lady Stanton moved forward, her steps hesitant. "Lady Hetherington."

"Good evening." Lady Hetherington exchanged an indecipherable glance with the butler before facing her guests. "Lady Stanton, Miss Stanton, Miss . . . ?"

"Pemberton." Evangeline joined the trio and gave her a tentative smile.

The regal lady did not smile back.

"That's Lionkiller's estranged sister," Susan whispered to Evangeline. "The countess."

"The footmen will see to your trunks," the lady continued, her voice low and hushed. "You must be exhausted after your journey. Hot water is on its way to your rooms." She gestured to the three girls still hovering by the doorway. "Molly, Betsy, and Liza will be happy to—"

"We have our own maids," Lady Stanton interrupted stiffly. She appeared wounded the countess would even offer to supply such a common staple as ladies' maids, but the crack in her voice suggested she was floundering for any sense of control.

The countess did not appear affronted. If anything, she seemed to have forgotten she'd been speaking. Rather than continue her welcome, the countess glanced at the staircase again and bit at her lower lip.

"I have no maid," Evangeline said into the silence. Hollow echoes of her voice whispered from the recesses of the high-ceilinged chamber.

Lady Stanton shot her an acid glare, but Lady Hetherington's mouth relaxed into a brief but grateful smile. Susan murmured a question and both ladies stepped closer to assuage some concern. Evangeline did not. She could not. A sudden chill descended upon the room and her every sense tingled with danger.

Impossibly, she felt him before she saw him.

Although she seemed to be the only one affected thus, she didn't doubt the prickling sensitivity along her bare neck for a single moment. While the three ladies conversed quietly, gesturing now and again at a maid or a footman, Evangeline lifted her gaze upward once more.

And there he was.

He stood at the landing above the spiral stair, cloaked in shadow. Tall. Unnaturally so. Was it the angle, the skewed perspective of being so far beneath him? Or was his towering stature undeniable, evident in the width of his shoulders, the muscular length of his legs, the long pale fingers curved around the banister?

The shadows made discerning features difficult. Evangeline could not tell if he were truly as savage as he appeared, or if a trick of the light—or lack thereof—caused the slatted darkness to undulate across his form. Almost without realizing it, she began to back away.

He continued down the spiral stairway, silent, sure, the leather of his boots making no noise on the cold marble. Although shadow obscured his face, his eyes glittered like those of a wolf loping alongside a lonely carriage. Thin fingers still curled lightly around the gleaming banister, he took another step forward. When there were as many steps behind him as there were before him, a brief flicker from a nearby sconce lit his face.

Evangeline swallowed a gasp.

Not because of the obsidian eyes framed by equally black lashes. Nor because of the angry slash of cheekbones, the flash of bared teeth, or the scar just above the edge of his jaw. Those things, though separately terrible, together formed a face of cold, cruel beauty. A face for statues, for frescoes, for—

Another flutter of orange light as he reached the final stair, and Evangeline could no longer breathe.

He was angry. Horribly angry. Livid. Enraged. Furious. His eyes glittered like a wolf's because he *was* a wolf, a beautiful, powerful, violent wolf, prowling toward his unsuspecting prey. His dark hair slid across his face, snapping Evangeline from her trance just as his long, gloveless hand fell atop the countess's shoulder.

The countess started, froze, paled. Her fingers touched her bare neck, grasping at her bare throat. Her shoulders curved inward, her spine slumped, as though his mere touch had the power to melt her very bones, deflating her from countess to servant in the space of a breath.

"Gavin," she said, the name almost a whisper. "You've come to meet our guests."

"Have I?" He jerked his hand from her shoulder. His lip curled, as though a rancid stench filled the chamber.

She winced, but continued on, louder now, her voice infused

with false gaiety, as if she were an ordinary hostess greeting ordinary guests, and not a shell of a countess with her unprotected back toward her parents' killer.

"This is Lady Stanton," she said. A brittle smile stretched her mouth until the words came out unnatural and strange. "This is her lovely daughter, Miss Susan Stanton."

Trembling, Evangeline waited to hear her name. It was not forthcoming.

In light of their host's murderous expression, she was more pleased than offended by the omission. But then Susan—still without her spectacles—gave a weak wave, indicating the edge of the room where Evangeline had stood to watch the wolf's descent.

"Miss Pemberton," Susan squeaked. "Miss Pemberton is also with us."

The wolf's gaze snapped to Evangeline's, his face turning so fast she'd barely caught the motion. Trapped, she could neither breathe nor blink.

His shoulders rolled back, his lips hardened, his muscles flexed. No—not a wolf, but a lion. Twice as dangerous.

His eyes were black, recessed, hollowed as though he hadn't slept well. For decades. His gaze, however, was dark and quick, as if nothing so trivial as a sleepless night would stop him from tracking her down, should she be foolish enough to flee.

She couldn't flee. She couldn't move. She couldn't speak. Evangeline could only stare, wide-eyed and helpless.

He returned the scrutiny, made her the object of his sole and endless focus. The sheen fell from his eyes until they were flat and hard. Even candlelight no longer reflected on their surface. The corners of his lips quirked in a smile that was more ferocious than friendly.

"Guests." The single word, a belated echo of the countess's earlier statement, seemed to scatter the charged air, prickling them all with a hint of unleashed fury. "So I see."

This time, the countess did turn to face him, although her

gaze did not meet his. "May we discuss our private matter privately?" The unsteadiness of her voice belied the reproach in her words.

He turned toward the countess. Released from his stare, Evangeline desperately sucked in air. He stiffened, as if he could hear her uneven breaths above the pounding of her heart, but his gaze stayed on the countess. "Be assured, madam. We will."

After an uncertain moment, Lady Hetherington angled her body to one side, gesturing with one gloved arm. "Lady Stanton, Miss Stanton, Miss Pemberton. May I present my brother, Mr. Gavin Lioncroft."

Ignoring both mute Stantons, Lioncroft's eyes fixed on Evangeline once again. In one fluid movement, he gave a sweeping, mocking bow. The murderer, it seemed, had both elegance and grace.

Mechanically, Evangeline dipped in an answering curtsy— or, at least, tried to. Her blistered heel gave way beneath her. Her boot slipped across the slick marble, pitching her forward.

At first, she thought her dark-haired tormenter had moved closer, as though to catch her before she toppled to the ground. But then she was being righted by a footman, and Lioncroft seemed to be laughing at her with his black glittering eyes and beautiful unsmiling mouth.

He looked, Evangeline realized, like someone accustomed to having commoners like her faint dead away at the sight of him. And why not? He was an aristocrat, a murderer, an animal.

A man perhaps even worse than the monster she had fled.

Chapter Two

Gavin Lioncroft, outcast and killer, caged himself in his office until he was certain his sister had deposited the "guests" safely in their rooms on the opposite side of his aging mansion. Only then did he take the shortest path to the west wing, using the unlit corridors between the walls.

The murky interior was as dark and cold as the rest of the house. The edges of his shoulders brushed against the sides of the dank, narrow walls as he prowled through the blackness, taking a sharp turn here, another there. He had no need for map or candle when memory served him just as well.

Centuries ago, the secret passageways had been built for a far deadlier purpose than avoiding the pathetic quivering of unwanted visitors. But it was better for Gavin, and better for the uncertain futures of the guests themselves, if they did not chance upon his company while his blood still steamed with fury.

It had taken all of his willpower not to roar at them from atop the stairs, and send them fleeing into the night from whence they came. Somehow he'd restrained himself. The past had passed, and his solitude was already ruined without adding death to the evening. Dangerous to tear off down the pitted roads at twilight.

He pivoted at another intersection. Light. There, at the end of the passageway. Just a tiny flickering crack. The guest wing, where his unwelcome visitors were housed.

Lady Stanton, a ridiculous birdlike woman with a pointed nose and a tremulous mole perched above pursed lips, her claw-like hands clutched about a hideous painted fan as though it possessed the power to save her from evil. Her daughter, the unfortunate Miss Stanton, a portrait-perfect waif dressed and coiffed and painted just so, as though she were nothing more than a lifelike doll for her mother to play with.

And the other one. Miss Pemberton. Not anyone's doll. She looked like a wild thing, with her dark mass of flyaway hair, sun-bronzed skin, and censorious eyes. She looked no less terrified than the rest of them, but in a different way. As if she saw straight through his exterior, and judged the real man twice as frightening.

Gavin was not in search of his guests, however. And the time had come to make a few things clear.

He swung a secret panel and stepped into the hallway right behind his sister. The painting-adorned panel closed silently, sealing the passageway from prying eyes until the landscape in the gilded frame looked no different than the dozen others lining the hall.

"Evening, Rose."

To her credit, she did not scream. Instead, she froze, just as before in the foyer when he'd caught her welcoming the un-welcome arrivals.

"How do you do that?" she whispered, shooting a nervous glance down the otherwise empty corridor.

"I am nowhere and everywhere," he answered with a little smile. "You cannot hide from me."

"I wasn't hiding," she said, the protest weak and uncon-vincing. "I wanted to make sure the chambers were ready for the others."

"Ah. The others," he growled softly, stepping forward until

he could see her face. "To what do I owe the pleasure of such unexpected company?"

By the twisting of her hands, Rose did not mistake his meaning. "We—they—" She coughed and started anew. "I didn't think you'd mind a few extra heads overmuch."

"No?" Gavin kept his voice low, smooth, modulated, the snarl hidden beneath the words. "Am I so welcoming?"

After an interminable pause, she mumbled, "Never. That I know of."

Never was right. Solitude was much preferred over those who tolerated his company only to get closer to his pockets.

Gavin moved closer, purposefully crowding her until she backed against the closest wall and shivered. People tended not to feel safe when he was near. They sensed his inability to suffer fools. He stared at her until she blinked and looked away.

"And yet," he said then, "you are cavalier with my good-will. Does the role of elder sister grant you leave to act as mistress in my house, even while I am at home?"

"I . . . No, of course not, I—" she broke off, unable to say more. She glanced down both sides of the shadowed corridor before returning her nervous gaze to Gavin's face.

"You," he said, "have done enough. All guests leave tomorrow morning."

"But the house party," she stammered, fixing him with watery puppy dog eyes. Gavin was unmoved by beasts with watery eyes, especially those who used them to manipulate. "You said they could stay a fortnight."

"Nonsense," he corrected softly. "I said 'family'."

Her cheeks leeched of color. "N-not *our* family."

"I see." And he did. He saw it was the height of foolishness for him to think his siblings could forgive a murderer, even after more than a decade had seeped away. And twice as foolish to believe that his sister's sudden interest had been anything more than a ploy to use him for her benefit. Gavin clenched his teeth. He had known better. "Whose family should I be expecting?"

Rose's lip trembled. "Mine, any moment. My husband's brother and sister-in-law, Benedict and Francine Rutherford. And their cousin, Edmund Rutherford."

He raised his brows. "And the Stantons? Whose cousins are they?"

"No one's," she admitted, tugging at her bare fingers.

He slammed his palm against the wall. Paintings jumped. So did his sister. "Then why are they here?" He spun to face her, eyes narrowed. "You dare to match-make under my roof, madam?"

Her response was a vivid blush and a violent shake of the head.

"How convenient for me," he mocked, stroking a finger along his jaw as though pretending to consider the possibility. "Which chit is fit for a killer? The prim, vacant-eyed one with the blue eyes and yellow ringlets, or the unfashionably bronzed one, with the wild hair and clumsy curtsy? Perhaps I'll have the former for my days and the latter for my nights. How kind of you to sacrifice such innocent creatures."

"They're not for you," Rose blurted out, horrified. "Leave them alone."

Gavin stared at her with a ghost of a smile. "Why invite them, if not for the master of the house?"

She slumped against the wainscoting lining the shadowed hallway. "I'm not matchmaking *them*. I'm matchmaking my eldest. Mr. Teasdale has expressed some interest in Nancy but I couldn't very well invite him alone."

Nancy. He hadn't been a welcome caller ever since his parents' fateful ride the night he'd—

Gavin glared at his sister, realizing now how she'd managed to turn his dark sprawling mansion into grounds for a house party. How dare she use the past against him, dangle forgiveness as a lure? The stratagem had worked. He had been enticed. Eager. But no longer. He would send them *all* home at dawn. Not just the Stantons.

"I needed other guests here to make it seem . . ." His sister's voice faded to nothing, but he somehow still heard her final word. "Respectable."

That much was true, at least. His company could hardly be seen as respectable.

"Why come at all, then?"

A sudden draft accompanied his words, setting the wall sconces to popping. Shadows flickered across the whorls and swirls of his papered walls, giving the dark gray pattern the appearance of movement.

Rose's shoulders shook. "You mean . . . who would accept the invitation of a known . . ."

He inclined his head, his expression hard.

"I—I've known Lady Stanton for years and years." Rose nibbled at her lip, as if deciding whether a breach of confidence would occur if she told a secret to a man with no one to pass it on to. "Her daughter got into a scrape last Season and is most likely not welcome back. I knew they would jump at a diversion." Rose tossed him a nervous glance as she clenched her fingers together so tightly the knuckles went white. "Where *did* you come from?"

Gavin lifted his brows. "Meaning what, heaven or hell? Hell, of course."

Her pale forehead furrowed. "I was utterly alone in the hallway, I would swear it. And then there you were. I even looked over my shoulder to see if . . ." Her words trailed off as another crimson stain spread up her throat.

"Ah," he said, allowing his smile to turn predatory. "You worry I'll sneak up behind you and snap your neck. Tempting, but not my preferred method."

"As I recall, your method was sabotaging carriages." Although the words were bold, she did not meet his gaze.

"Exactly so," he agreed, despite the tightness in his jaw. She started and blanched and looked as though she wished she'd never mentioned carriages in the first place. "Make no mistake, you'll be getting in yours tomorrow morning. You all will."

Her eyes widened. First dry, then damp. She looked away, eyelashes quivering, and he could smell the unease in her sweat. "Can we not start anew, brother? Nancy marrying well is of the utmost importance to me. I cannot stress that point enough. She'll be eighteen soon, and the sad truth is we cannot afford a Season. We've already sold our town house, our best horses, let go most of the servants. The jewels I wear are paste. Please. Just let me have one fortnight."

A very pretty speech, but he didn't believe a single word from her lips. After all, Rose had just admitted that only the outcast and the destitute were willing to risk their lives and reputations beneath his roof. "May I ask what you have planned for tonight, madam?"

"Supper," she said instantly, as though her mind was focused solely on her next meal. Perhaps her husband's pockets held even less than she'd intimated. "And then dancing. Do you . . . ?"

His jaw clenched. "I do not dance."

With guests I did not invite, he might have clarified, but the blatant relief bathing her face at the thought of spending some of the evening without his company changed his mind.

"Tonight," he continued with a lift of his brow, "I shall make an exception."

Chapter Three

With her back flush against the closed door, Evangeline stared at her bedchamber in horror. She was supposed to *sleep* here?

To one side stood a cavernous fireplace, its embers glowing and crackling. Despite the feeble light cast by the dying fire, the room was as dark and foreboding as the rest of the house. Evangeline inched forward to nudge at the charred logs with a poker. Sparks spit at her. Sinuous shadows danced across the murky walls as the flames lengthened.

On the other side of the fireplace was a single wooden door. According to Lady Hetherington, this led directly to Susan's bedchamber. Near as Evangeline could determine, proximity to another living human was the sole redeeming quality of her assigned quarters.

The gray swirls above the wainscoting matched those in the outer corridors, lending all the walls of the mansion the alarming appearance of swarming with snakes. The flickering shadows caused the serpents to teem, to undulate, until Evangeline was certain she could hear them hiss. She resolved not to edge too near, lest they bite.

Chiding herself for the unease tensing her muscles and chilling her skin, she crept cautiously around the room.

The wall with the hallway door was bare of all decoration, save a small cracked mirror. The long snake-covered wall on the opposite side of the room was unbroken by door or window. Diabolical, Evangeline decided, that neither sunlight nor fresh air could find its way in. That wall corresponded with the rear of the house and should face a forgotten garden, perhaps, or even the forest. Instead, she saw nothing but seething shadows. She should beg for a room with windows—unless, of course, whatever lurked behind the mansion was something she'd rather not see.

Much like the bed.

The four-poster monstrosity stretched from the interior wall to well past the center of the room. The foot of the bed faced the fireplace. She supposed the fat little forms carved into the oak were supposed to be frolicking angels, but the artist had made them tiny naked trolls instead. No matter where she stood, their eyes followed her, their stubby fingers beckoning, their smiles ghastly and overstretched.

The thick velvet tester hung in heavy crimson folds about the perimeter of the bed. Evangeline edged closer. Dark scab-colored material lined the canopy. At least while she slept, the covering would block the ceiling from view, where the same macabre artist had frescoed another army of pale winged trolls, dancing and frolicking and beckoning overhead with their too-small eyes and terrifying grins.

To the right of the bed was a tall wooden door, leading not into another guest room, but rather, a dressing chamber. Between the windowless wall and the length of the bed lurked a short, squat series of waist-high bookshelves, the tops still several inches short of the sculpted molding where serpents met wainscoting.

The only other object in the room was a single wingback chair, its upholstery the mottled hue of an old bruise. Beneath her shift, Evangeline had many that would match. She dragged the chair as close to the fireplace as she dared and was just about to sink onto the seat cushion when the hallway door swung open.

"Oh! Excuse me, mum," said a small, frightened maid, her dark gaze darting about the room as if the serpents might leap from the walls to her person.

Evangeline could certainly empathize.

"Come in," she said, motioning with one hand.

"I mustn't," said the maid as she stepped inside. "Gor! He'll kill me for sure."

"Who?" Evangeline asked, then blanched at the stupidity of her question. Lioncroft, of course. The only murderer present. She changed her query to, "Why?" and gazed at the maid until the latter sighed.

"I've lost summat, that's why. And I'll be sacked by morning, I will."

From long habit, Evangeline was at her side, tugging off a glove as she walked. The maid froze in either sheer terror or utter confusion as the back of Evangeline's cold hand pressed against her forehead, her cheek, her forearm.

What did you lose? her pale fingers demanded. *Remember. Remember.*

With each touch, Evangeline's surroundings disappeared as visions of the maid's memories enveloped her. And as usual, each touch brought renewed pressure to Evangeline's skull until the pain dimmed her eyesight and roared in her aching ears. Sometimes she succeeded in conjuring the right images. Sometimes she failed. But she always, always tried.

Show me what you lost today. Show me.

"A handkerchief?" she asked over the throbbing in her temples. At the maid's startled expression, Evangeline nodded. "You dropped it next to a dressing bureau when you read the letter."

"When I read the—" the maid broke off, paled, and gaped at her.

"You were crying," Evangeline said apologetically, knowing the maid hadn't meant anyone to see her secret pain. "You were holding a pile of soiled linen beneath one arm, and the handkerchief fell behind you as you stuffed the letter back in your pocket."

Sudden clarity flashed in the maid's eyes.

She did not thank Evangeline, however, nor hug her or smile at her or heap praise upon her, or anything else Evangeline had come to expect from the grateful servants back home who'd considered both she and her mother to be angels from heaven. Instead, the maid's nervous gaze darted about the chamber once more before she edged backward from the room. She bolted down the hall without bothering to close the door behind her.

It was then that Evangeline realized not only was she as far as possible from home, but that "home" was something she couldn't duplicate, even on a small level. Hopefully the maid hadn't run off to tell her master of their guest's obvious madness—or worse, of her exploitable talent.

Evangeline touched her trembling hands to her temple as her brain raged against her skull. She could usually avoid the headaches by limiting the number of her visions. Why had she been so determined to help the maid? To recapture a small sense of normalcy? Or to prove to herself she had a higher purpose than merely being Lady Stanton's puppet?

Never trust Polite Society, Mama had said. Evangeline would be wise not to trust their servants, either. At least not until she'd had a chance to better observe the situation.

She made it to the bruised wingback chair before being interrupted again. The new disruption was blond, thin, and bespectacled, and barreled into the room by way of the connecting door.

"There you are," Susan said, as if Evangeline might be anywhere else. "I wondered where you got off to."

"I'm here." Evangeline rubbed the tension from the base of her neck with cramped fingers. "Against my better judgment."

"Two weeks is all. Nothing to it." Susan peered at her closely. "Have you got a headache?"

"Something terrible," Evangeline admitted, then remembered not to take any new individuals into confidence. Mama had regretted telling Lady Stanton about her own visions when they'd been children. Evangeline wouldn't make the same mistake with Susan. Not after she and her mother lied to her, abducted her, and expected her to blithely hoodwink a killer. "How is your room?" she asked politely, hoping to change the subject.

"Oh, dreadful," Susan answered cheerfully, gazing around Evangeline's chamber. "Easily as dismal as this one. No windows, same hideous painted babies with their odd little hands and misshapen heads, blood-colored décor splattered about the chamber . . ." She leaned a hip against the closest bedpost, running one finger along the ferocious grin of a tiny troll. "I say, but there has never been a man more in want of a wife than Lionkiller. First thing I shall do is sell this oversized mausoleum. And if he won't let me do that, at least I'll have windows put in every single room. Then sconces. And paint. Buckets and buckets of bright yellow paint."

Evangeline stood, rearranged her chair to face her guest, and sat back down. "So," she began slowly, unsure of how to respond to any of Susan's statements. "You still wish to go through with it, then? Marry him, I mean?"

Susan laughed without humor. "Do I wish to? It's the lesser evil, I'm afraid. Though I'd prefer to marry a title, I could do worse than marry a murderer."

"You could?" Evangeline echoed, still rubbing her neck. "How?"

"Staying at home with Mother, for one." Susan's eyes lit with mischief. "I'd sooner marry a chimney sweep as commit myself to a lifetime of *that*."

Evangeline could see her point.

"Lioncroft is the younger son of a viscount," Susan continued. "What with his brother's six or seven potential heirs in line first, there's not much chance of inheritance. Except . . . With a man like Lionkiller, who knows how many people could turn up dead." Susan wiggled her eyebrows above her spectacles. "I could be a viscountess yet."

Evangeline gripped the edges of her chair. "You cannot possibly condone—"

"No, no, don't be silly. I'm just having a bit of sport, is all. He hasn't killed in years. I doubt he'll start the habit back up again on my account, even if I say 'please.'" She shrugged, as if this lack of action meant Mr. Lioncroft had become quite dull. "And now we—" A staccato knock interrupted whatever Susan had been about to say. She leapt from the bedpost to the door, twisting the knob as though it were her room, not Evangeline's. "Why, good evening, Mother. I was just about to discuss you quite rudely in your absence."

"Impertinent chit," Lady Stanton said coldly, sweeping into the room without giving her daughter a second glance. "Miss Pemberton," she said instead. "I am here to discuss strategy."

"Huzzah," Susan cried, slamming the door shut behind her. "How I love strategy!"

Lady Stanton ignored her.

"For Mr. Lioncroft, you mean?" Evangeline asked, rising to allow Lady Stanton the sole chair.

"Of course." Lady Stanton sank onto the cushion with a scowl. "We begin tonight. Now, what's the best motivator for a man to propose?"

"Love?" Evangeline suggested at the same time Susan said, "Money?"

"Scandal," Lady Stanton corrected. "Although 'money' is a very good guess, Susan. The simplest method to bring a man up to scratch is to find oneself in a compromising position with him."

"I don't want him to ravish me," Susan blurted out. "Not until after we've wed."

Lady Stanton's jaw clenched. "Compromised, not *ruined*. Perhaps a kiss—"

"No kisses!"

"—or an embrace—"

"No embraces!"

"—or even simply being caught alone together should do." After successfully ignoring her daughter's many outbursts, Lady Stanton nodded to Evangeline. "That is your task. Be sure to appear both horrified and scandalized. As a gentleman, he will have no choice but to propose at once."

"Except he's not a gentleman," Susan put in. "What if he doesn't propose? Won't I be ruined anyway?"

"You've already ruined yourself with your silly Town antics," Lady Stanton snapped. "I have no doubt Lioncroft will do as he ought. You simply have to catch him alone, and Miss Pemberton will do the rest." Susan and Evangeline exchanged a wordless glance as a chime sounded from outside the door. "That's the supper bell," Lady Stanton said. "Don't dawdle, Susan. Tardiness does not become a future bride."

With that, Lady Stanton rose, tossed a frigid glance about the room, and strode out the door.

"Tardiness does not become a future bride," Susan mocked, dropping into Evangeline's chair before Evangeline had an opportunity to do so. "Be honest. What do you think of Mother's stratagem?"

Evangeline swallowed the word "mad" and tried to formulate a safe response. Much as she hated to admit it, the Stantons were right about one thing—only death awaited her if she walked away now. She only hoped Lady Stanton didn't suspect Evangeline had inherited her mother's visions. "You don't think the plan will work?"

"Of course, it will work. Half the *ton* marriages are based on business decisions, the other half on indiscretions with bad timing." Susan shook her head, a grin toying with her lips.

"Aren't you frightened of marrying a murderer?" Evangeline asked, unable to imagine toying with such a man. "Or his reaction, once he realizes you have tricked him?"

Susan's cheeks colored. "Ideally, he won't realize that part. Mother believes the events will unfold naturally. Young ladies are compromised all the time, accidentally or otherwise. As to being frightened—well, of course I'm frightened. After all, he might kill me."

"Then what makes this plan the lesser evil?"

"Invitations have all but dried up for me." Susan looked genuinely miserable. "I must marry at once or die a spinster. At home. With my mother."

Evangeline stared at the crackling fire. "Mr. Lioncroft is a last resort, then?"

Susan shrugged, although her eyes were cloudy. "You don't see anybody else chasing him, do you? I'm sure to be his last resort as well. And just think: the idea would never have occurred to Mother had Lady Hetherington not stopped by with an invitation."

"One of the many things that makes no sense," Evangeline murmured. "Why would he want to host a house party in the first place?"

"I don't suppose he wanted one at all. The look on his face when he first saw us . . ." Susan shivered delicately. "I thought surely he'd kill us all, right there in the anteroom."

"So did I." Evangeline didn't want to imagine what he would do if he knew what the scheming Stantons had planned. "He seemed . . . powerful. Watchful. Deadly. Like a coiled snake or a crouched wolf or a lion about to pounce upon his prey."

"That about sums it up," Susan admitted. "It's also why I don't wish to be compromised until the very last day. No matter what Mother says, you won't rush things, will you?"

Evangeline shook her head. She wouldn't participate in their schemes at all. She wasn't eager to play games with a lion. Besides, to catch the two of them alone she would have to be present as well. And she was fairly certain two young ladies were no match for a monster like Mr. Lioncroft.

"There's the bell again," she said aloud. "Shall we dine?"

In fact, now that suppertime was upon them, perhaps she ought to see what else she could learn about the man and his house, to better prepare herself against him. She reached for her reticule on the floor next to the bed and pulled out two matching gloves of lace and silk, hemmed to allow her bare fingertips through.

"Oh!" cried Susan from right behind Evangeline, causing her to jump. "Your mitts are ever so gorgeous." She wiggled her fingers. "You'll make mine look positively boorish. Where did you get them?"

Evangeline smoothed the thin material up over her forearms without responding. Mama had worn these very gloves the night Evangeline's father exercised his marital right to lock his wife in a tiny moldering attic. Evangeline shuddered. There was nothing she hated more than being locked in small dark spaces. Nothing.

"My mother gave them to me," she answered finally, unable to avoid Susan's curious gaze any longer. "These mitts were hers."

"Then they're lucky gloves." Susan slapped her hands together. "How lovely."

Lucky? They'd accompanied her mother through two husbands, one who took her freedom, and one who took her life. Could scraps of silk carry such "luck" with them?

"I hope not," Evangeline muttered and followed Susan into the hallway toward Lady Stanton's chamber. The door banged shut behind them, extinguishing a nearby sconce. Evangeline shivered, nervously rubbing her mitts.

The last thing either of them needed was luck like that.

Chapter Four

"I have no sense of orientation," Susan announced as she strode from Evangeline's chamber. "All the endless hallways and twisted corridors vanished from my head within seconds of Lady Hetherington pointing them out. I shall die of hunger before I recall the location of the dining room."

Evangeline felt in control of her surroundings for the first time since their arrival.

"Follow me," she said, and set off down a series of spidering passageways, each as dark and ill-lit as the last.

Evangeline had been born with an innate sense of direction, and being left to her own devices in a sprawling country village for hours at a time had eradicated any fear of finding her way on her own. In fact, the serpentine corridors of Blackberry Manor did not instill alarm at the thought of becoming lost, so much as a general dread of stumbling across someone or something she had no wish to find.

At one shadowed intersection, she stopped so suddenly that Susan barreled directly into her.

"What is it?" Susan asked, peering over Evangeline's shoulder. "Dead body?"

Evangeline shook her head. "Voices. I'm positive we're

to turn left, but I think I hear Lady Hetherington down the hallway to the right."

Before Evangeline could stop her, Susan darted down the hall and peeked around the corner. She glanced over her shoulder, motioned to Evangeline, and then returned her focus to whatever Lady Hetherington was up to.

With a sigh, Evangeline followed. Susan reached out one gloved hand and yanked Evangeline closer until they were huddled together like frightened rabbits.

At the other end of the darkened hall, Lady Hetherington was deep in discussion with an elderly man turned out in expensively tailored clothing. Although his spine curved and his cane trembled and his thinning hair sprang from his head in dry white curls, the scowl etched in his wrinkled face gave Evangeline the impression of someone very, very angry. She wished Lady Hetherington's back was not to them, so they could gauge her expression.

"Is that her husband?" Evangeline whispered once she'd ducked back out of view.

Susan snorted. "Lord Hetherington's about forty years younger. Maybe that's her grandfather. Or Father Christmas, arriving a little early this year."

Hmmm. Somehow Evangeline doubted Father Christmas shook his cane at cowering countesses while hissing heaven-knew-what under his breath.

Tugging Susan along with her, Evangeline turned around and headed down the correct corridor, only to find another couple standing in the center. Whether they too were arguing was anyone's guess, for their conversation died the moment they caught sight of the two young women.

The man, a rotund ruddy individual with a spotted complexion and a wan smile, melted against the wall to allow them passage. His companion, an over-rouged woman bedecked in a lime green gown, flaxen curls, and a pink plumed hat, stared at them with heavily kohled eyes.

Neither spoke.

At the last possible moment, the man inclined his head in greeting. Evangeline dipped into an awkward walking-curtsy, causing Susan to collide with her for the second time that evening. And then they were around the corner and out of both eyesight and earshot.

"The Rutherfords," Susan murmured, answering Evangeline's unasked question. "Benedict Rutherford is Lord Hetherington's younger brother and next in line for the earldom. Francine Rutherford is his wife. Theirs is not a happy marriage."

Whose was? Evangeline thought, but aloud she asked, "If you know them, why didn't we stop?"

A flush crept up Susan's neck. "Lady Rutherford despises me. She's a petty social climber who never forgave herself for settling on second best. I'm sure Lady Hetherington would never have invited me if she had the slightest inkling we—"

This time, Susan was the one to come to a jarring standstill.

Evangeline, having chosen to walk alongside Susan rather than behind her, did not stop, and in fact continued another step or two forward. Until she saw the two things looming directly in front of her.

The first was the dining room. Beyond an open doorway was a long, beautifully carved table adorned with elegant bone china and sparkling crystal goblets. Evangeline had never seen such finery. And she was meant to eat and drink from them?

The second thing to catch her attention was the dark-haired, dark-eyed man lounging negligently against the dining room doorway, wide shoulders leaning against the frame, thumbs hooked casually into his waistband, one polished black boot crossed over the other.

Lioncroft.

He had not failed to notice Evangeline's proximity, if the sudden heat darkening his eyes was any indication. His gaze slid down her body like warm oil over bare skin, gliding past her unruly mane, to the helpless widening of her eyes, to the erratic pulsing in her throat, to the odd constriction in her bodice, to the flowing silk of her borrowed gown, to the tips of her slippered feet.

And then his gaze retraced its path back up, just as slowly.

Just as *insolently*, Evangeline reminded herself, for no gentleman would dare to stare so boldly, to allow his eyebrows to lift in blatant appreciation, to quirk his lips in obvious amusement at her consternation.

The corners of his eyes crinkled slightly. He made no attempt to look away. Was the beast *laughing* at her?

Vexed, Evangeline decided to give Mr. Lioncroft a taste of his own rude behavior. She arched her brows in acknowledgment of his smirk before letting her own gaze drink in every facet of his appearance.

The soft hair tumbling across his forehead and down the back of his neck was not black, as she'd first thought, but rather a rich, glossy brown, much the same shade as freshly tilled soil in springtime. Or, she corrected herself darkly, like the sinister hue of a recently dug grave.

His eyes were the same deep brown, although his long lashes and thick brows were both a shade darker. His nose was straight, his chin strong. His skin was smooth, pale, and unblemished, excepting the faint shadow of hair along his jawline, not quite masking the long thin scar she'd glimpsed earlier. No doubt a memento from a duel, or some other such devilry.

A skillfully creased cravat flowed at his neckline, just above a cream-colored shirt made of a material so smooth and soft it fairly begged for her to run her bare fingertips across its surface.

Not that Evangeline wished to touch Mr. Lioncroft's chest, to feel the beating of his heart beneath her palm. If he even had a heart.

A perfectly tailored jacket hugged his powerful form just so, emphasizing both his impressive height and the breadth of his shoulders. Breeches stretched over long limbs, outlining the strength and musculature of his legs before disappearing into spotless Hessians.

When she glanced back at his face, he lowered one eyelid in a knowing wink. His smile was slow, lazy, devastating. The wicked promise in his gaze had her lungs gasping for air and her skin tingling in anticipation. Her flesh felt heated, her breasts heavy, her stays laced too tight.

Even if he hadn't been a murderer, Evangeline realized with an involuntary gulp, Gavin Lioncroft was exactly the sort of man from whom mamas everywhere protected their virginal young daughters. And the quirk of his full, wide lips suggested he well knew it.

"I'm not ready for a betrothal yet," came a frantic whisper from somewhere behind Evangeline's back.

Susan. Good heavens. For a moment, Evangeline had completely forgotten Lady Stanton's stratagem. And, if Evangeline were honest, Susan's presence at all.

Luckily for Susan, the rapid heartbeat raging in Evangeline's chest prevented her from breathing properly, much less screaming like a madwoman about Susan allegedly being compromised before a dining room doorway after the bell had been twice rung. In fact, all Evangeline could do was continue staring helplessly at Mr. Lioncroft.

Who hadn't yet ceased staring right back.

"My word, mum, I didn't expect to run into you so soon," came a small, shaky voice, arresting both her and Mr. Lioncroft's attention. The maid who'd been in Evangeline's room earlier was now at her elbow, staring up at her with wide blue eyes. "It's me, Ginny. I got no idea how you did it, but thank you ever so much for helping. I hope I got it before she chanced upon it, because if not, he'll—" The maid broke off midsentence as voices spilled from the hallway behind them. She seemed to catch sight of Mr. Lioncroft for the first time and flinched. "I'll find you later, if I'm not sacked between now and then. I must know—"

But whatever Ginny had to ask was swallowed by the buzz of conversation as Benedict and Francine Rutherford strode down the hall, laughing and chatting with the cane-wielding man from earlier. Evangeline frowned. Where was Lady Hetherington? She'd been talking to the elderly man only a few minutes ago. Speaking of which, if the white-haired man wasn't Lady Hetherington's husband, who was, and where was he?

Evangeline turned back to Ginny, only to discover the maid was no longer there. She'd disappeared into the blackness of the passageway like one of the many shadows.

Conversation sputtered and died by the end of the first course.

Across the table, Gavin's sister placed her spoon next to her empty bowl and refused to meet his eyes. When she'd first been seated—later than all the rest—she'd been oddly pale, her cheeks rouged with a heavy hand. By the time the bowls of steaming soup appeared, so had the reason for the face paint. Her delicate skin had always bruised easily.

His houseguests slunk nervous glances from her face to his, as the pinkness of Rose's left cheek purpled and spread to the size and proportion of a man's hand. There was no doubt she'd bear the horrible mark for the rest of the party, just like there was no doubt in anyone's mind who had struck her.

Except . . . Gavin hadn't.

Considering the crimes in his past, one might think he wouldn't mind being saddled with the occasional misplaced lesser crime. After all, of what import was the implied accusation behind a mere bruise, compared to the greater sin of patricide? Nonetheless, the ease with which he was cast in the role of villain rankled. Such presumption of guilt was precisely why he chose to avoid the company of so-called Polite Society in the first place.

Gavin couldn't deny the presence of his temper, a rash thing, a recklessness, an ever-simmering rage. When at Cambridge, how often had he been chastised for neck-or-nothing phaeton races ending with blood and bruises, or for the myriad fights that would break out afterward over who had won and who had lost? But he'd been a boy then, not more than seventeen. And while his anger might still be quick to surface, he now had at least a tenuous hold on something he'd never possessed before: self-control.

He didn't discipline his servants with his fist, although doing so was perfectly legal. He'd never hit a woman in his life, no matter how provoked. And he certainly hadn't struck his sister for no reason at all, despite the accusing glances surreptitiously sent his way from all corners of the table.

But who had?

Her husband, a slimy pompous rat of an earl, would've been Gavin's first guess, had Rose not taken her place beside him with a buss and a smile.

What about Lord Hetherington's brother? Benedict Rutherford, heir presumptive to the title, coughed discreetly into his napkin. A charming, bedimpled wastrel, yes, but hardly one to go about slapping other men's wives. Nor his own. His wife Francine Rutherford was a plumed ostrich of a woman, her costume and manner fit more for the stage than a drawing room. The silver lining to the shocked glances was a blessed halt to the woman's shrill, forced laughter.

Gavin's niece, Nancy, sat between her father—the only person still eating, as though he'd somehow missed the coiled tension thickening the air—and her intended, the elderly William Teasdale. If Teasdale raised his palsied hand to anyone, he'd likely lose his balance and tumble directly to the floor, arms and legs flailing in the air like an overturned cockroach. The old codger couldn't see well enough to slap his own face.

That left Edmund Rutherford, Hetherington's tawny-haired cousin and second in line for the title. Now, *there* was one who spent more time in his cups than in his right mind. He was even now motioning a footman for more wine. But as far as Gavin knew, Edmund got more pleasure from dallying with other men's wives than striking them. Edmund, as usual, merely appeared drunk. Was drunk. Gavin, seated next to him, had the misfortune of smelling Edmund's rancid, humid breath.

As Rose stared at her brimming soup bowl, the scarlet stain spreading up her neck suggested she was beginning to realize powder and rouge hadn't masked her injury as well as she'd hoped. She appeared ready to bolt at the slightest provocation.

The only other guests were Lady Stanton, then Miss Stanton, then Miss Pemberton, none of whom Gavin suspected of striking his sister.

Lady Stanton, for her part, seemed far too frigid an individual to even be capable of the passion necessary for anger. Her veined skin was almost as pale a blue as her gown, her colorless eyes close-set and narrow. If it weren't for the trembling mole on the edge of her upper lip, her entire person would be as unremarkable as an icicle in winter.

The daughter was a noisier, more colorful version of the mother. Although the same general size and shape in body, the eyes behind Miss Stanton's spectacles were bluer, her hair more yellow, her skin less transparent. And her mouth— Gavin was fairly certain the chit hadn't closed the damn thing since the moment she plopped down next to Miss Pemberton, who even now was feigning interest in Miss Stanton's hushed whispers.

Feigning, Gavin was convinced, because out in the hallway he'd seen *true* interest widen those long-lashed eyes. Eyes that now refused to meet his. Miss Pemberton ducked her head, giving him a view of an undulating mass of unruly, dark caramel hair straying from its binding in random, wavy locks. Gavin's fingers twitched against the tablecloth, aching to bury themselves in all that luxuriant softness. Such disarray lent her the appearance of a woman recently tupped. He couldn't help but wish he were the man doing the tupping. Perhaps he was in luck. By her manner in the hall, Miss Pemberton was no simpering debutante. Her bold gaze along the length of his body ignited his flesh until he could barely restrain from trapping her between the wall and his heated limbs to devour her in a kiss. The very thought made Gavin shift in his seat, the elegantly carved woodwork suddenly awkward and uncomfortable.

How many years had passed since he'd been with a woman he hadn't had to pay for? Perhaps, if he were to let the so-called "party" continue, he and the delectable Miss Pemberton might share an entirely different variety of dining experience.

She sat much too far away for Gavin to speak to her, which was just as well given the libidinous direction of his thoughts . . . and the ever-present hiss of the Stanton chit's incessant tongue. She was no doubt regaling Miss Pemberton with the very suspicions no other guest dared put to words—that the murderer at the head of the table couldn't be bothered to contain his violence even for a single evening.

Gavin returned his gaze to his sister, unaware he was scowling until she caught his eye and flinched.

"So tell us," came Edmund's loud voice, the words slurring together until they were barely decipherable. His amber eyes blinked several times as if he found focusing on Gavin's face a difficult task. "Why'd you plant your sister the facer?"

Without bothering to respond to the grinning sot, Gavin leaned back in his chair until his weight balanced on the rear legs. He knew he gave the impression of perfect boredom, and why not? No point defending oneself when judgment had already been made.

The furtive glances shared between the other guests confirmed this suspicion.

Nothing was quite as cock-shriveling as fear moistening the eyes of a woman. Gavin was pleased to note Miss Pemberton was one of only two females not currently pale with terror. Unfortunately, her expression bordered on rage, as though she were more disgusted with his apparent lack of self-control than worried she might be the next to feel his wrath.

The other woman unafraid of him was Rose herself, as she alone knew the true culprit.

"He didn't hit me," she mumbled now, her eyes meeting neither his nor Edmund's. Had there been any other sound in the dining room, she might've gone unheard. In the silence, however, her words were cannon blasts.

Skepticism graced the faces now peering in her direction. All save one. Hetherington lifted his dun-colored brows and cast his wife a look of such unmitigated scorn that her bruised cheek nearly disappeared beneath the force of her blush.

"*You,*" Gavin seethed between clenched teeth.

A few of the guests startled to hear his first word of the evening.

Lord Hetherington's brows merely returned to a relaxed position, dismissing Gavin's snarled accusation without a word. Rose trembled when her husband raised his hand near her face, but he simply reached for a basket of fresh-baked bread—and smirked.

It was the smirk that did it.

Gavin leaned forward and leapt to his feet. He landed with his legs at shoulder width and knees slightly crouched, ready to spring across the table and tackle Hetherington in his seat. The chair toppled over behind him, clattering to the hardwood floor. Gavin ignored it. His sister had reentered his life after over a decade of absence. Violence against his family had taken her from him before. He would not allow it to do so again.

"Outside," he ordered her husband, fists ready, voice hard. "Now."

Rose paled. Edmund motioned for a footman to refill his wineglass. The rest of the guests watched, breathless and twitching, as if they were debating the wisdom of diving for cover beneath the table.

Lord Hetherington's lip curled as he sneered his rejection of

Gavin's command. Were it not for the tremor in Hetherington's hand as he replaced the basket of bread upon the table, Gavin might have thought him unmoved. Everyone else apparently witnessed the same tremor, and their gazes swung in uniform terror from Hetherington's shaking fingers back to Gavin's furious scowl, as if quite certain now, *now,* he would leap across the table to snap Hetherington's pale neck.

Gavin was certainly considering it.

"Stop." The word was soft, a mere breath, but came from Rose.

A footman righted the fallen chair. After a moment, Gavin sat. The wary guests did not look convinced of his harmlessness.

"My—my daughter," Rose stammered, making a small gesture toward Gavin's wide-eyed niece. "Nancy was just getting to know Mr. Teasdale when the supper bell rang."

Gavin stared at his sister. What the hell did Teasdale have to do with anything?

Nancy gasped, as if a sharp elbow had just connected with her ribs. "Er, yes," she said loudly, casting an over-bright smile around the table. "Splendid weather we're having. Didn't you say so earlier, Mr. Teasdale?"

Gavin forced his fists to relax as he belatedly realized she was attempting to diffuse tension. Based on the half dozen pair of eyes refusing to meet his, no one at the table would be surprised if Gavin drew a pistol, shot Hetherington in the face, and continued with his meal. Pity he didn't have a pistol handy.

Rose cast him a beseeching look. It seemed she was hoping for an evening a bit less bloody than the one Gavin now had in mind, so that her daughter could catch the eye of the white-haired sack of bones snoring softly in his seat. Very well. For the sake of his sister and his niece, Gavin would allow the farce of normalcy to continue. For now.

"I said nothing of the sort," came Mr. Teasdale's quavering nasal voice, as if Nancy's words had only now reached his failing ears. "Too cold outside and too hot inside. Can't get a good grip on my cane with the way my hand sweats so."

A very unladylike snort came from either Miss Stanton or Miss Pemberton, both seated on the opposite side of the table. Edmund gave a drunken laugh, shook his head, and motioned for more wine. Apparently, Gavin wasn't the only one who found the old coot a ridiculous match for his young niece, no matter how full Teasdale's coffers might be.

Lady Stanton shot an icy stare in the direction of the stifled snort.

"Why, yes, delightful weather," came the rapid-fire speech he now recognized as belonging to the Stanton chit. She must've been the snorter. "Bitter wind and endless rain is just the thing for a house party. Don't you agree, Evangeline?"

"Hmmm," came a soft, warm voice that could only belong to the mysterious Miss Pemberton, whose hot little gaze and enticing body were tucked safely out of view.

She probably thought she'd shocked him by mimicking his appreciative stare. As it turned out, he'd managed to shock himself with his body's instantaneous reaction. Even the sultry timbre of her voice had him thinking about tasting the curve of her red lips, instead of avenging his sister's bruised cheek.

"I do find autumn leaves beautiful," his siren was saying now, "but the trees here have gone gray and barren. As they were at your home as well, Lady Stanton. Do you miss the changing colors?"

Lady Stanton sniffed, as though displeased at being addressed by Miss Pemberton. "I despise nature," she said dismissively and turned to face Gavin, the first of the dinner guests to openly do so since the handprint had first made its appearance. She fixed him with a strange, calculating gaze. "You have a lovely estate, Mr. Lioncroft. Susan was just telling me how pleasant she found her accommodations." From the startled gaping of Miss Stanton's curiously wordless mouth, Gavin deduced she'd said nothing of the sort. Lady Stanton pursed her lips, as if all too cognizant her daughter's expression had given the lie to her words. "In any case, I am sure you kept the weather in mind and planned plenty of indoor activities."

Gavin stared at her small glassine eyes and chose not to respond.

For one, he hadn't planned for a single activity besides evicting everyone from his premises at the earliest possible moment. For two, he was disappointed at having the conversational ball tossed back into his court so quickly. Couldn't the fops and fribbles spout off about the weather amongst themselves and leave him in peace?

A trio of footmen arrived with platters of fresh fish and tiny pots of cream and sauces. Gavin turned his focus to his supper plate, ignoring Lady Stanton's question and Lord Hetherington's continued smirks. The latter would get Gavin's "response" later, when no one was around to witness it.

Chapter Five

Evangeline didn't take her first easy breath until the men and women went their separate ways after supper. Yet even in the ladies' withdrawing room, something was not quite right.

The walls were crimson in this wing, which would've been a welcome departure from the seething snakes, had the color not given the feel of a room awash with fresh blood.

The servants setting the tea were as ubiquitous and unobtrusive as ever, but seemed to dally with their tasks longer than necessary. They darted quick little glances toward Evangeline when the aristocrats weren't looking—which they never were, as Polite Society rarely noticed their staff unless they required something—and exchanged meaningful looks with each other as if an irresistible but forbidden curiosity had been placed just out of reach.

Evangeline had a terrible suspicion the curiosity in question was her. How could she have forgotten to tell Ginny not to mention her help to others?

"I knew it," whispered Susan, dragging her to a quiet corner.

"You knew what?" Evangeline glanced around to make sure they were somewhat private. Only the servants were still watching.

"I knew he'd as soon kill us as dine with us. He didn't utter more than three or four words during the entire meal, but the evil in his eyes spoke volumes. Did you see his expression when Lord Hetherington lifted his hand as though to strike the countess anew? Lionkiller positively smoldered. I'd wager they're brawling on the floor in the other room right now."

"I can't imagine Lord Hetherington in a brawl," Evangeline said, deciding to concentrate on Susan's patter and pretend she was unaware of the servants' relentless scrutiny.

"Oh, Lioncroft would thrash him, no question there. I heard he's always been a rough-and-tumble sort. Infamous for his quick temper even when at Eton and Cambridge. Mother says to this day, the only two attractions capable of luring him from his home are pugilism clubs and brothels."

Fighting and whoring. Splendid. Evangeline well knew the sort of man who delighted in such things, as fighting and whoring were her sotted stepfather's primary activities when not at home beating his womenfolk. There wasn't much to recommend Mr. Lioncroft in the first place, but further proof of his similarity to Neal Pemberton was the final nail in his coffin. Evangeline would rather stow away to India than be caught alone with such a man.

"And what about the handprint on Lady Hetherington's cheek?" Susan continued in a hushed whisper, her eyes alight with the excitement of scandal. "I cannot imagine the ignominy of walking about with such a mark. During a party, no less. What do you suppose she did to deserve it?"

"What makes you think she deserved it at all?" Evangeline snapped, suddenly hyperconscious of her own fading bruises beneath her gown. She had no wish to see unnecessary pain inflicted upon someone else.

Susan shook her head. "Don't be silly. Husbands don't hit their wives for no reason."

Evangeline strangled on an outraged reply. Was "because Mama happened to be standing there" a good enough reason for fists to fly? Or "because he was drunk" or "because he was

hungry" or "because his horse threw a shoe that day?" Neal
Pemberton might think so. Evangeline did not. But in the end,
she decided not to share her opinion aloud. Perhaps Susan was
better off not knowing how the world really worked.

"Shhh, here she comes." Susan leapt to her feet. Evangeline followed suit.

The countess approached with wary eyes and a hesitant
smile. She'd reapplied her face powder, somewhat masking the
redness of her cheek. "Are you ladies game for some dancing
later?"

"Oh, yes," Susan gushed, clasping her hands together. "I
love dancing."

"I'm afraid I am to be a wallflower," Evangeline said. There
hadn't been much time for dancing in their little village,
though she'd always wanted to try. But with less than a week
gone by since her mother's funeral, dancing seemed wholly
out of the question.

"Just as well," Lady Hetherington said with a relieved expression. "We are an uneven eleven, but ten is well-suited for
dancing."

Although Lady Hetherington appeared neither angry nor
resentful for their skewed numbers, Evangeline was well
aware her uninvited presence was the cause. She didn't
belong at a house party. She didn't belong in the world of
the *ton*. She belonged in a simple little shire off in the country, where the townsfolk actually needed her. Somewhere she
could put her Gift to use without fear of repercussion.

At that thought, the weight of the servants' furtive stares
upon her back finally proved too much for Evangeline. She
needed to find Ginny—*now*, while all the others were guar-
anteed to be occupied in their separate after-dinner rooms—
and discover if there were any way to undo whatever damage
Ginny's gossip had done.

"If you'll excuse me," Evangeline murmured, making an

awkward expression she hoped translated as, "Don't mind me—I'm off to find a chamber pot."

"Of course," Lady Hetherington demurred. She linked her arm with Susan's and turned to stroll about the room. "There's Nancy," she said as they walked away. "Shall we join her?"

Evangeline, quite used to being dismissed, made a swift exit. Two servants raced to be the first to swing open the door for her, as though Evangeline were royalty and not a runaway orphan. At home, she didn't mind such attention from the villagers. In this house, however, she preferred anonymity. The *ton* was far too dangerous for her to be openly different.

As she stepped into the hall, she turned to smile her thanks at the servants because to do so was hopelessly ingrained upon her personality. And because her head was facing a different direction than her feet, she wasn't watching where she was going.

Which was how, not two steps from the closing door, Evangeline found herself belly to groin with Gavin Lioncroft.

"It's been a while since I had a woman hurl herself into my arms," came a low, deep voice.

With the side of her face plastered against his chest, each syllable rumbled from his body to hers, sending an unfamiliar sensation skittering across Evangeline's flesh. The heat from his breath tickled the flyaway hair atop her head in a sensual, intimate manner. She sucked in an indignant breath, only to fill her lungs with the heady scent of expensive port and fresh soap and virile man. Her eyes closed, just for a moment, to better allow the combination of scent and proximity to invade her senses.

And then Evangeline remembered exactly whom she'd collided with.

She pushed away. Or tried to, but his warm strong arms were still locked tight around her, likely to prevent her from toppling over when she'd first crashed into him. As she was no longer in danger of falling, he should let her go.

He did not.

"What are you doing?" she asked, the words coming out breathy and muffled against the hardness of his chest and the softness of his cravat.

"Holding you," he answered, his tone droll, as if the situation was ridiculously obvious.

Which, she supposed, it was.

"What are you doing *here?*" she demanded. As defiantly as one could, with one's breasts flattened against a muscular male torso and one's legs tangled with long, lean limbs.

"I live here." His nose glided along the top of her hair. He inhaled, shuddering slightly as if her scent affected him as much as his affected her. "What are *you* doing here?"

Before Evangeline could form a sharp retort about being unable to do much of anything, what with him crushing her to him in the middle of a darkened corridor, he abruptly released her. The withdrawal of his support was somehow more damaging to her equilibrium than his audacious presumption in the first place. In attempting to regain her balance, she stumbled. Very briefly, but in that moment, he caught her to him again.

And this time was different.

Instead of enveloping her body in a steadying sort of hug, now his arms were bent and loose, his shoulders relaxed, his fingers resting lightly above the curve of her hips. His legs intertwined with hers. And with his back leaning against the wall opposite the (thankfully) still-closed door, his body was at just enough of an angle that she straddled his strong, hard thigh.

His entire frame was pressed against hers in the most shocking, scandalous, *provocative* of places.

And this time, her breasts were not flattened against his chest, nor was her face smashed against the ruined creases of his cravat. This time, her shoulders were just far enough back that only the tips of her nipples pushed the silk of her gown into the starched perfection of his shirt. Her face tilted upward, bringing her mouth within inches of his. Instead of tickling against the top of her head, his port-spiced breath steamed against her cheek, her nose, her lips, causing the latter to part involuntarily.

"Perhaps," he said softly, never taking his heated gaze from hers, "you came out here to be kissed."

"I—" Evangeline stammered, violently shaking her head. At least, she hoped she was shaking her head. She might've just been staring at him, breathlessly awaiting his next move.

It wasn't until he lifted a dark brow and murmured, "No?" that Evangeline was assured she'd shaken her head after all.

And it wasn't until he still hadn't let go that Evangeline realized he wasn't even holding her against him. The tips of his fingers burned through the silk of her gown and the cotton of her shift to the shivering flesh beneath, but he was in no way preventing her from quitting his embrace.

In fact, she was the one whose fingers clutched at the hard muscle of his upper arms. She was the one who leaned against him in wanton abandon, turning his indolent pose into something shocking and lascivious. She was the one with her face still tilted toward his, lashes lowered, lips parted, throat dry.

Heaven help her, if she didn't get away from him right this very second, *she* might be the one to close the distance between his mouth and hers, sweeping her tongue across his in a manner she'd only seen in visions, discovering for herself whether he truly tasted as hot as he felt and as wicked as he looked.

Evangeline jerked out of his grasp, tripping over her own feet and righting herself with a palm to the wall. Still clutching the wainscoting, she peeked over her shoulder at him, half-afraid of what she might see.

He was right where she'd left him, lounging in the shadows, with his shoulders braced against the serpentine walls. One leg stretched slightly before him. The other was bent at the knee, the sole of his boot against the footboard. His thumbs hooked into his waistband, giving him the same careless pose as when she'd first run into him outside the dining room door.

Then, her eyes catalogued the curl of his dark hair, the smart cut of his clothes, the arrogance of his manner. This time, she couldn't help but notice the way his gaze heated as he looked at her, the way his chest shifted with each breath, the way the curving of his fingers seemed to point directly at the unmistakable interest evident in the tight fit of his breeches.

Evangeline spun away, simultaneously gulping and blushing and pretending she hadn't seen what they both knew she'd seen.

Please, God, she prayed silently. *Don't let him mention it, for I think I might die.*

"I'll be here," came Mr. Lioncroft's sinful voice from the shadows, "if you change your mind about the kissing."

She shivered, turning to face him despite herself. Why was the idea so tempting? Perhaps the man truly was the devil himself.

"What are you really doing out here?" she stammered, hoping to change the subject to a far safer topic than kisses.

He gazed at her for a moment, as if her feeble attempt at distraction amused him.

At first, Evangeline thought he didn't plan to answer. After all, he'd already spoken more words to her here in the silent corridor than he had during the dinner hours and the anteroom introductions combined.

But then he shrugged, kicked off from the wall, and took a step closer. She flinched, but held her ground. He smiled.

"I'm here," he said, motioning to an open door some six or seven yards down the hallway, "because were I in there, I would find my fist in Hetherington's face."

Well. Evangeline swallowed. That was certainly a straightforward response. And just what she needed to remind herself that he was no dark prince to be kissing in the corridors, but a savage wolf, fully capable of attacking in anger. Had she not compared him to her stepfather just five minutes prior? Thank heavens she hadn't been foolish enough to let her lips brush against his. All skin-to-skin contact sparked visions, and she'd seen plenty of violence from her glimpses into her stepfather's mind. She had no wish to witness whatever Mr. Lioncroft had done to his poor parents, and everyone else who'd crossed him in some way.

"Besides," he continued with a surprisingly boyish grin. "It's Edmund's turn now."

"Edmund's turn?" Evangeline echoed, reminding herself that a heart-melting smile did not make Mr. Lioncroft a trustworthy man.

"We'd been in the library not two seconds when Hetherington's brother pulled him aside. Between coughing fits, Benedict managed to rail at Hetherington for a good ten minutes before Edmund lurched betwixt, swearing and stumbling and drinking my best scotch like water." He grimaced. "All of that was perfectly tolerable compared to being subsequently trapped by Teasdale."

"Mr. Teasdale trapped you?" Evangeline bit back an involuntary laugh. "How is that even possible?"

"One word," Mr. Lioncroft said with a melodramatic sigh. "Nancy. He's contemplating an offer, according to my sister, and I'm to facilitate the match as best I can. But there's no way I can condemn my niece to a wedding with Father Time, especially now that I know he'd never even laid eyes on her before this evening. All that girl needs is a Season or two. She's bound to collect a slew of better suitors."

"I agree," Evangeline said slowly. "W-why are you telling me?"

"Because you seem different," he answered after a moment's reflection. His steady gaze still focused on her face. "Intelligent. Self-sufficient. Alone." He drew in a breath, then let it out slowly. "Like me."

"I'm not like you." Evangeline recoiled in horror. "I'm nothing like you."

A flicker of something indecipherable crossed his face, but she stalked away from him before she could identify the exact emotion. How could he possibly compare himself to her? She wasn't a violent beast of a man like him. She had a soul. She had a talent. She used her Gift to help others. Which made her *good*. Nothing like him at all.

He reached her side before she rounded the first corner.

No matter how fast she walked or how many corners she turned, he was right there beside her, silent, brooding.

Evangeline gave up on her illogical hope of losing him so she could find Ginny when she realized the only person she'd managed to lose was herself.

Although this narrow, empty hallway had the same dark wainscoting and undulating paper as the rest, she didn't recognize the series of closed doors before her. In fact, she realized as she glanced over her shoulder at the branching corridors beyond, she wasn't even sure which intersection led back to the drawing room.

"I give up," she admitted, and blinked when he started, as if he'd forgotten her presence beside him. "Where are we?"

"By the nursery." He motioned up ahead toward a shaft of light flickering beneath a wide door. He stared at her for a long moment. "Do you care to meet my nieces?"

"I . . ." Evangeline stared at Mr. Lioncroft. Nieces. She'd been so fixated on him being a heartless killer, she'd quite forgotten he was also an uncle. "All right."

He smiled, that eye-crinkling, teeth-flashing grin, but his eyes showed surprise, as if he'd fully expected her to shove her nose in the air and storm off, turning her back on both him and his innocent nieces.

Evangeline followed him into the room, and curtseyed at each wide-eyed little girl as Mr. Lioncroft introduced them.

"Jane, this is Miss Pemberton," he said, addressing the

tallest of the three. "Miss Pemberton, this beautiful young lady is Miss Jane Hetherington, whose very favorite game is pall-mall."

Jane turned shining blue eyes to Evangeline. "My birthday is in three days, and Uncle Lioncroft says the children and adults can play together. Oh, and we're to have kite-flying," she added, slanting him a coy look. "You promised."

"If it doesn't snow," he confirmed before crouching to introduce the other two girls, each as fair and blond as the other. "These two troublemakers are Rachel and Rebecca, whose birthday is not for several months."

"Twins," Jane said with a roll of her eyes. "Twice the terror."

Mr. Lioncroft rose to his full height again and stared at all three girls, as if he wasn't quite sure what to do next, now that the introductions were over.

After a moment, the two younger ones wandered back to a porcelain doll. A sudden, fierce ache twisted in Evangeline's gut as she stared after them. As a young girl, she would've given anything to have had friends, to be normal, to link arms with another child without her head exploding in an onslaught of unwanted visions. As a woman . . . She glanced at Mr. Lioncroft through lowered lashes. As a woman, the yearning to touch and be touched had not waned. She'd simply become old enough to realize a true relationship would always be an impossible dream. After all, her mother had tried—and failed.

Clearly bored with the conspicuous absence of conversation, Jane crossed the room to tease the twins, and an immediate row broke out.

Rather than interrupt the argument, Mr. Lioncroft seized their distraction as an opportunity to escape, backing up to the doorway and holding the door open for Evangeline without another word.

Men. They never did know what to do around children. She supposed he'd done as fair a job as anyone, considering he'd been shuttered in a childless mansion for more than the past decade.

"Well," he said after they'd regained the hallway and the door had closed behind them, "now you've met my nieces."

"Yes." She could hardly believe those adorable girls were related to their violent, sneering father or their violent, reclusive uncle. But aloud, all she said was, "They're darlings."

"Indeed," Mr. Lioncroft uttered, his voice oddly hesitant. "They're the only people in this house not frightened of me."

Not frightened of a murderer?

"That's because they're not old enough to know better," she said without thinking—and then *started* thinking. Thinking about just whom she was alone with, in a darkened passageway so far from the others. She spun away from him and headed back the way they came, her footsteps pounding as rapidly as her heart.

Evangeline hadn't gone far before her back slammed against the wainscoting, her breath whooshed from her lungs, and Mr. Lioncroft's strong hands pinned her gloved wrists to the wall on either side of her head.

He loomed over her, blocking out the flickering sconce light and filling her nostrils with his unmistakable scent. Her traitorous body reacted just as it had before. By the heat smoldering in his dark gaze, she was sure he hadn't missed the quickening of her pulse or the stuttering of her breath.

When she struggled against him, he leaned closer, pressing his chest to her breasts, his thighs to her hips, until she was trapped motionless beneath him. And then he said the most surprising thing.

"I apologize," he muttered, the words coming out hot and moist and strained. "For earlier, when I first held you in the hallway."

Evangeline twisted in his grasp and merely succeeded in rubbing her aching body even more fiercely against his. "For attacking me?" she panted, glaring up at him. "Like the brute you obviously are?"

"I wish I'd kissed you then," he said softly. "When I thought you were different." His lip curled with an expression bordering on disgust. "I was clearly mistaken."

He released her and pushed away in a single movement, leaving her wrists bruised, her flesh overheated, and her body off balance once again. She fought for both her breath and her footing.

This time, he didn't bother to help her. He strode down the hallway without another word or a backward glance. Within seconds, he had disappeared into the teeming shadows.

Evangeline stared at the empty corridor, hugging herself and cursing him. He *left* her. Alone. And lost.

With no one to blame but herself.

Chapter Six

When Evangeline finally found the other guests, they'd reconvened in a large room devoid of carpet and filled with candelabra. A lone musician thrummed at an ancient pianoforte, but the guests' feet leapt and thumped across the hardwood floor as though dancing in the thrall of a full orchestra.

Evangeline slipped in as stealthily as she could, considering eleven people didn't quite constitute a crush and her appearance would no doubt be noticed.

She made her way to a row of tall wooden chairs lined flush with one wall and lowered herself to a cushioned seat to watch the whirling gowns.

As the music segued from country dance to waltz, the dancers divided into couples. Mr. Lioncroft's attention was concentrated on someone else. Someone far more appropriate than a country miss with a sharp tongue and a borrowed dress.

He spun Susan about the floor with elegance and grace, his movements only occasionally hesitant—as might be expected in someone who hadn't stepped foot in a soiree in over a decade.

Try as Evangeline might to catch his eye, his gaze stayed focused on his partner's face. Susan, who claimed to want neither his touch nor his kiss. Susan, who would marry him for his money, to appease and escape her mother. Susan, whose steps even now were stiff and jerky, plainly displaying her discomfort at being in such close proximity.

Why, if Evangeline were dancing with him, she'd—

Evangeline swallowed a self-deprecating laugh. She'd what? Press her body close? Beg forgiveness for her sharp tongue? Use that tongue to lick those wide, firm lips?

She could do none of those things. She couldn't publicly apologize for her rudeness, since nobody present even suspected they'd spoken. Only if they danced would she have a moment to whisper anything at all. But she'd already indicated her preference to remain a wallflower for the duration of the party. And Mr. Lioncroft seemed perfectly willing to leave her alone and unnoticed.

While he danced with Susan.

Susan, who flinched when he touched her, whose averted gaze missed his strained smile, who tripped over his feet with her inability to match his rhythm.

Evangeline's fingers clutched at her gown. She was not jealous of Susan. She was *not*. The curdling in her stomach was no doubt a reaction to the baked fish, not to the striking couple swooping and gliding together across the hardwood floor.

No matter how Evangeline stared, Mr. Lioncroft managed to avoid her eyes. How could he not see her, when all she could see was him? She gripped the sides of her chair and continued to watch him, unable to tear her gaze from the whirling bodies.

Where Susan was delicate and thin and fair, Mr. Lioncroft was big and muscular and darkly handsome. Susan's opposite in every way, although just as striking.

His jaw was firm, angular, shadowed with a hint of dark stubble, a perfect backdrop for that pale jagged scar. The mark made him overlarge, impossibly real. Human. Vulnerable.

A loud clatter interrupted her thoughts. Evangeline jumped.

Mr. Teasdale fell heavily into a seat near hers before leaning over to scoop up his fallen cane from the floor. His arm stretched. His hand shook. He managed to miss the cane altogether.

Evangeline leaned over to fetch it for him. He reached out at the same time, and she was unable to avoid the pads of her fingers coming in contact with the spotted skin of his wrist. In a flash, she found herself just outside the open door of a strange bedchamber.

> *"What do you mean, French tutor?" Mr. Teasdale demands, the quaver in his voice more pronounced than ever.*
>
> *"I'm just as appalled," Lord Hetherington replies, looking far more bored than appalled. He stifles a yawn. "But it changes nothing."*
>
> *"Nothing?" Mr. Teasdale brandishes his cane with one speckled hand. "It changes everything. The deal is off."*
>
> *Lord Hetherington's eyes narrow and the ennui vanishes from his demeanor. "My good man, honor dictates—"*
>
> *"Honor!" Mr. Teasdale shrieks. "There's more honor in my arse than in your daughter. I'll not waste my fortune on a chit more interested in giving her charms to a common tutor than a respected member of Society. I leave in the morning."*
>
> *"Now, look here, Teasdale—"*

Evangeline jerked her hand back to her side. She shouldn't have worn her mitts after all. She touched her bare fingertips to her temples, hoping to massage away the headache before it could overpower her. She winced, shut her eyes, scrubbed her temples harder—and then Mr. Lioncroft was right there before her.

"What happened?" he asked, bending on one knee to better see her face. He lifted her chin with the curve of a gloved knuckle. "Are you all right?"

"I . . ." Evangeline stared at him. Tendrils the color of dark chocolate fell across his furrowed brow, his eyes wide and the lines of his mouth taut. He was *worried* about her. And had left Susan standing by herself in the center of the dance floor.

"Dance," Evangeline hissed, catching sight of Lady Stanton's malevolent stare. "You're making a scene."

"I don't care," he answered, but his face softened as if having her glare at him again was a more assuring indicator of her well-being than just her word alone. "Come," he said and tugged at her wrist. "Dance with me."

"I can't," she stammered. "You have Susan, and besides, I—"

"They're already playing a different melody," he interrupted. "Listen to the melody. It's a country dance. For everyone." When she continued shaking her head, he added, "Mr. Teasdale is throwing our numbers off by snoring in his seat. You *must* dance."

"You don't give a fig about dancing," Evangeline muttered, positive the force of Lady Stanton's glare was singeing holes in the side of her head. "I saw your face when your sister mentioned it."

But he pulled her to her feet and onto the floor, murmuring, "If I have to, you have to," smiling at her as if they were friends conspiring against a common enemy.

And she was so pleased at the return of both his rakish grin and his good favor that despite her protestations, she found herself in line with the other couples just as they started to move. She quickly discovered country dances were not at all the sort of thing one could figure out as one went along, and spent a good deal of time hopping in and out of line and tripping over others' feet, spinning the wrong direction and flailing to regain lost balance. All of which, luckily, seemed to restore her tenuous position in Lady Stanton's good graces, as Evangeline's clumsiness made her a perfect foil to Susan's poise and confidence.

Unluckily, however, Evangeline stumbled into one person after another, and the constant contact kept up a steady barrage of visions until she was sure her brain would explode from her pounding skull.

Within a very few moments, Evangeline knew Edmund Rutherford had fathered yet another bastard child, Nancy had permitted Pierre Lefebvre several stolen kisses, Lord Hetherington had severed the relationship with his mistress immediately before the party, blood had been appearing in Benedict Rutherford's handkerchief when he coughed as of late, Francine Rutherford was in an Interesting Condition, Lady Hetherington had been forced into a "good match" against her will at seventeen, Lady Stanton had been frightened of Evangeline's mother throughout her childhood, and country dances were impossible to execute with any degree of competency while suffering from a savage headache.

Evangeline utterly regretted removing her kid gloves in favor of her mitts.

She took Mr. Lioncroft's arm for the next turn and stopped breathing when she realized she'd suffered visions about every single person present—except him. Not now, and not in the hallway earlier.

How could this be happening?

She'd known such things were possible, although instances were rare. Her poor mother had been unable to glean visions from Neal Pemberton when she'd arrived pregnant and penniless in his small village, and had interpreted the odd immunity as an indication of True Love. The miscalculation had cost Mama her life.

When Evangeline was a child, Mama had pointed out that the visions were always of emotional moments in people's lives. She'd said Neal Pemberton didn't care enough about anything or anyone to *have* emotion. After all, he prided himself on his cruelty and indifference. But unlike her mother, as Evangeline grew older she'd endured horrific visions with every strike of her stepfather's hand. His endless trips to the taverns where he'd rut in nearby alleys with a serving girl, his perverse pleasure in beating her mother for her "witch-like" ways. The occasions when he drunkenly confessed to his cronies what he most wanted to do to his stepdaughter was— No. Best not to think of such things.

But what could it mean for Gavin Lioncroft's skin to be so relentlessly silent? A twist of fate? Or more proof that he was even more like her monster of a stepfather than she had at first feared?

Before she could come up with a satisfactory hypothesis, the music ended. Evangeline stumbled from Mr. Lioncroft before he could do more than toss her a quizzical glance.

Just as quickly, Lord Hetherington inclined his head to his wife, bowed to the rest of the party, and excused himself for the evening with a murmured explanation of "business matters."

Still slumped in a wooden chair, Mr. Teasdale awoke, blinked at the non-dancing people standing awkwardly before him, and tottered out the door, his cane clomping with each step.

Lady Hetherington frowned after him. "Now we're six women and three men. This won't do at all, if we're to continue dancing." She glanced at the pianist, the open door, and then her brother. "Gavin," she whispered, "Would you please ask them to return? I'd go myself, but I . . ."

Mr. Lioncroft made eye contact with Evangeline for a split second before inclining his head to his sister and disappearing through the door. She had the sudden suspicion he'd gone to bludgeon his brother-in-law to death, not beg him to continue dancing.

With a loud bark, Benedict Rutherford erupted into a vicious coughing fit. When he regained control, he mumbled, "I've had enough music for one evening." Before Lady Hetherington could coax him to stay, he bowed and left.

Francine Rutherford affected a huge yawn, covered her red-painted mouth with a chartreuse-gloved hand, and said, "I ought to retire with my husband." She followed shortly behind him.

Evangeline was afraid Lady Hetherington might burst into tears.

"Mama." Nancy tugged on Lady Hetherington's arm. "If there's to be no more dancing, and Mr. Teasdale isn't even here to talk with me, may I go, too?"

"Fine. Go." A muscle pulsed in Lady Hetherington's temple above her bruised cheek. "Get some sleep, and I'll see you at breakfast."

"In that case, I'm going back to the library." Edmund Rutherford inched toward the door. "I believe I abandoned a delicious port." Within seconds, he was gone.

Evangeline glanced about the almost empty room. All that remained were Lady Hetherington, whose hands clenched at her sides, Lady Stanton, who stood cold and unmoving, and Susan, who appeared thrilled with the entire debacle.

Lady Stanton gestured toward the dance floor. "Will Lioncroft be right back, then?"

Lady Hetherington's face crumpled. "Tonight was a disaster. You might as well go to your rooms. We can save the dancing for next time. If there is a next time."

"Tonight was lovely," Evangeline assured her, when neither Stanton spoke up.

"Thank you, dear." Lady Hetherington reached over to pat Evangeline's arm and once again the room disappeared, replaced with the same bedchamber as in the vision with Mr. Teasdale. Except this time, Mr. Teasdale was nowhere in sight.

Lord Hetherington sits at a small desk, scrawling on parchment. His head snaps up as Lady Hetherington comes into the room. "What now?"

"I saw your handkerchief."

"What the hell are you talking about?" He turns his attention back to his scribbling.

"You said you lost it weeks ago, and then there it was. With rouge stains."

His pen falters. "What are you implying, Rose?"

"I don't have to imply anything! Red stains on white linen speak for themselves." She places one hand on her slender stomach, the other on his stiff shoulder. "Must you really—"

Lord Hetherington stands so quickly his chair shoots backward. The sudden movement sets his wife off balance. Rather than right her, he sets a palm to stinging the side of her cheek. She collapses to the floor in a heap.

The supper bell rings. Without bothering to help her up, he steps around her crumpled form.

When she lifts up her head, he is gone.

Lady Hetherington removed her hand from Evangeline's arm in order to give little hugs and cheek-busses to Susan and Lady Stanton. She then turned, chin down, and trudged from the room.

Evangeline gazed after her, half-wishing Mr. Lioncroft really would plant his fist in Lord Hetherington's face.

Lady Stanton harrumphed behind her painted fan. "Well, Susan spent time with Lioncroft, and that's what's important. But what in the world were you thinking to join the dancing, Miss Pemberton? You are not one of us. Forget yourself again and I'll have half a mind to toss you to the streets. You're to be encouraging an engagement with Susan, not angling for attention of your own. Not that he'd be interested in the likes of you."

Evangeline's jaw clenched. Lady Stanton had no idea what kind of attention Evangeline had managed to garner on her own.

"Oh, Mother," Susan said with a sigh. "Leave her be. I told you I don't want to get compromised until the end of the party. I'm not used to him yet. Just dancing with him was horrible enough."

Horrible! Evangeline stared at her in disbelief. She'd never waltzed before, but she was quite certain if Mr. Lioncroft had whirled her about the floor like he whirled Susan, it would've been anything but horrible.

"Get some sleep, Susan," Lady Stanton commanded, snapping her fan closed. "You want to look your best in the morning."

And with that, she too strode from the room.

Susan and Evangeline exchanged a look, but by the time they reached the doorway, Lady Stanton was already down the hall and around the corner. Other than a few servants tidying the music room, they were alone.

Susan's face twisted into a pout. "I suppose Mother left us unchaperoned for me to more easily be compromised. She no doubt believes Lioncroft is on his way back here at any moment, and that victory is at hand. I'd better find her fast and disabuse her of the notion. I said I wasn't ready yet, and I meant it."

"You think he's coming back?"

"Suppose not. Even if he does, Lady Hetherington specifically requested he bring her husband with him." Susan gave a little shudder. "I don't intend to sit around chatting with that one, to be sure. He might start slapping me." She squinted at Evangeline over the top of her spectacles before blurting out, "How *did* you do it?"

Evangeline blinked at her. "Do what?"

"Draw Lioncroft to you without so much as a word. One moment he was swinging me in the most nauseating of circles, and the next I was quite alone and watching the two of you from a distance."

"Oh," Evangeline said, hoping the flickering candles hid the heating of her cheeks. "I don't know. Perhaps he just noticed me there and wanted to say good evening."

"You jest." Susan stared at her as if she'd gone mad. "First of all, Lionkiller doesn't deign to say 'good anything' because he's far too occupied being dark and brooding and deadly. Second, he knew the very moment you snuck through the door."

"He did?" Evangeline fought a flattered smile. Despite her sharp tongue, he'd only pretended immunity to her presence. Or, perhaps, because of it. Her smile faded. She couldn't blame him for ignoring her, and she still owed him that apology.

Susan nodded. "It was the only time his steps faltered the entire evening. Oh, and when he nearly spun me into a wall after you made that odd grimace and rubbed at your head. You do seem to get a lot of headaches."

"True," Evangeline agreed, wincing anew. "It's a curse."

"Rather like this party is cursed." Susan shoved her spectacles up the bridge of her nose with the back of one hand. "I say, I've never seen such an ignominious disbanding of a dance set in my entire life. It's as if not a single person present wanted to be here."

"I certainly didn't." Evangeline muttered, frowning at her lacy mitts.

Guilt plagued her. She hadn't meant to dance. Watching Susan with Mr. Lioncroft had been uncomfortable enough. When he'd come and pulled her to the floor, Evangeline hadn't thought twice. For a brief moment, she'd even forgotten she was in mourning. How had one man filled her entire world for the space of a song?

"Oh, I know *you* didn't want to be there. You told Mother as much. But everyone else? Dancing at a house party is as common as breathing, Evangeline. Something isn't right." Susan flicked a glance into the music room then down the empty hall. "This place gives me gooseflesh. I'm heading back to our quarters." She started to walk, then glanced over her shoulder at Evangeline. "Aren't you coming? I have to catch up with Mother before I'm compromised."

"I—I will in a moment," Evangeline hedged, belatedly remembering she never did have a chance to find Ginny. Perhaps now was as good a time as any. "Go on ahead. I'll retire soon."

Susan frowned, shrugged, and sprinted down the hallway, leaving Evangeline to wander the dark mansion alone.

* * *

Gavin burst into his candlelit office. The heavy oak door banged against the wall. A shiver rippled among a cluster of paintings, jostling several of them askew.

Blackberry Manor was his home, and this his most private domain. No one with any sense would dare encroach upon his territory without first requesting permission. And even if the oily snake seated behind Gavin's desk had bothered to ask, Gavin would have refused.

"Get. Up." He advanced toward the desk, biting out the words through clenched teeth. A fire sizzled behind the grate, filling the shadowed room with the stench of acrid smoke.

Hetherington glanced up from a stack of papers with ill-concealed annoyance. "Lioncroft. I wondered if you would drop by."

With the sweep of an arm, Gavin knocked the contents of the desktop to the floor, papers and inkwell and all. Both hands splayed on the now-bare surface, he loomed over the desk until his face was inches from Hetherington's. "I expect you didn't wonder long. From the moment you struck my sister, you knew you'd have to answer to me."

"Did I?" Hetherington leaned back in Gavin's chair, but made no attempt to reclaim the scattered pages. "I'm afraid there you're mistaken. I answer to no one."

"Because you're a peer?" Gavin infused the word with mockery and contempt.

"Not because I'm a peer. Because she's my wife." Hetherington smirked. Gavin itched to smash his fist through it. "I own her, Lioncroft. She's my property. And as such, I can do with her what I will."

Gavin's fingers spasmed as he vaulted over the desk. Within seconds he had Hetherington by the throat. He lifted the earl by his worthless neck, kicking the chair out from under him and sending it spinning perilously near the fireplace. As he tightened his hold, Gavin contemplated slamming the whoreson's head into the rock solid table.

"Watch yourself," Hetherington choked out, his pallid face empurpling. "Whatever you do to me, I can do to Rose."

"Not if I kill you," Gavin growled. He gave Hetherington a violent shake, and smiled when the snake's hallmark smirk twisted into panic.

The blackguard's continued violence to Rose, however, was a valid threat. Unless Gavin took Hetherington's life, right here and now, there was little he could do to protect his sister from further abuse.

He glared at the arrogant earl, aware of nothing but the blind fury thrumming through his veins.

After a moment, he loosened his grip just enough to allow the saucer-eyed tyrant to draw in a shaky, wheezing breath. Damn. Gavin had to let him live. But he didn't have to tolerate thoughtless cruelty. Just because the courts sanctioned Hetherington's use of physical strength against his helpless wife didn't mean that Gavin couldn't wield his fair share of raw power while the knave was here in his home.

A knave who, above Gavin's unyielding fingers, continued to smirk.

"Rose hasn't forgiven you for killing her parents," Hetherington rasped after several gasping breaths, "And even you must realize she'd hardly forgive you for murdering her husband in cold blood." His smile was pure malice. "The father of four children."

Gavin gave Hetherington's throat another taunting squeeze before hurling him at the nearest wall in disgust. Gavin's favorite oil painting tumbled down after, scraping the side of Hetherington's face with its heavy gilded frame.

After touching his cheekbone, Hetherington's fingertips came away wet and crimson. "I knew you'd never do anything to hurt your darling sister." He fingered his bruised throat with trembling fingers before adding in a sly voice, "On purpose, that is."

Gavin's fists twitched. Hetherington wouldn't be able to do much smirking with a broken jaw, or much slapping with broken fingers.

"My sister," Gavin said over the roaring in his ears, "had better receive no more wounds by your hand. You will answer to me before you answer to the law. The courts may be on your side, but I am on hers. And you," he spat as he straightened to his full height, "are in my home, imposing on my ever dwindling goodwill." He rolled back his shoulders. "Stand up, collect your things, and return to your quarters immediately. Rose and the children are welcome to remain as long as they please, but *you* will be gone by first light."

Hate and rage warred in the blue of Hetherington's eyes as he struggled to a kneeling position in order to gather up his scattered belongings. Although his lip curled, he made no attempt to strike out with his fists.

Gavin stood beside the kneeling earl, arms crossed and feet spread, half-tempted to plant his boot on Hetherington's ass. Only a coward ignored the man at his ready in favor of beating his helpless wife. And after being vilified and feared for over a decade, Gavin had no further patience for cowards.

"You crumpled my papers," Hetherington muttered, sending Gavin a black look.

Gavin shrugged and arched a brow. "You bloodied my painting."

Hetherington slapped a sweaty palm against the side of Gavin's desk. Unimpressed, Gavin knocked him face down with a well-aimed boot to the shoulder.

"Get up," he commanded the still-writhing snake. "And be gone."

"But I haven't all my things." Hetherington's scratchy voice was more petulant than malevolent. Typical of a pampered peer more used to giving lashes than receiving them.

Gavin glanced at the papers. Copies of Nancy's betrothal contract to Teasdale. That'd be a marriage made in hell.

"I will burn whatever remains." Gavin gave a slow, deadly smile before gesturing toward the open doorway. "Remove yourself from my sight. Now. Before I regret allowing you to leave alive."

Cheeks pale and throat purple, Hetherington rose to his feet with an armful of ruined parchment. He cast a last livid glare over his shoulder before lurching from the room and careening down the hall.

Chapter Seven

The first doorway Evangeline stepped through in her search for the loose-tongued Ginny was the one Mr. Lioncroft had pointed out earlier. The men's after-dinner room turned out to be a large, well-stocked library, with a half dozen wingback chairs, a smoldering fire, and row after row of leather-bound volumes.

The maid wasn't there. Nor was Edmund Rutherford, who'd mentioned returning for his glass of port. The only person present besides herself was a tall, sallow footman silently refilling a decanter on the sideboard.

"Pardon me," Evangeline said, careful to keep her voice soft so as not to startle him.

The hand pouring burgundy liquid into the crystal vessel never faltered, as if the servants of Blackberry Manor were quite used to being dropped in on unexpectedly. The footman capped the decanter before turning to Evangeline, his dull eyes devoid of curiosity.

"How may I assist you?"

Evangeline offered him a small smile. His expression did not change. "I'm looking for a maid by the name of Ginny. She's perhaps a few inches shorter than me, with a slender frame, quick blue eyes, hair the color of—"

"I know no maid by that name."

Evangeline blinked at him. Back home, the servants in any given house were not only familiar with the names of all those who worked under their roofs, but also knew the faces and histories of every other servant in the village. But, she reminded herself again, Blackberry Manor was not home.

"Perhaps you could tell me where to find the footmen who worked in the music room earlier," she suggested hesitantly. "One of them might be more familiar with the staff, and better able to help me find—"

"The footmen," came the pointed reply, "returned the dishes to the scullery as the gentlemen left to rejoin the ladies. They are no doubt settling themselves in for the night. I assure you, no maid by that name works in this house."

A frustrated sigh hissed softly between Evangeline's teeth. Granted, she was hardly one of the aristocracy, but this footman's tone and demeanor were a far cry from the solicitousness his fellows had shown in the music room. But perhaps . . . for the same reason?

"Sir," she began, and paused when the salutation made him blink. "Are you displeased with me for some reason?"

The footman hesitated, but when at last he spoke, his words were honest. "I do not trust witchery."

Her jaw dropped. "Then you do know Ginny!"

"I know only rumors." His expression went cold. "And my master has had enough trouble in his life without adding more from you." When Evangeline proved momentarily speechless, he murmured, "If you'll excuse me," and strode out the door, leaving her in the library alone.

"Well," she huffed to the empty room, following up with a muttered, "Damn."

The only thing her stepfather had given her—besides the back of his hand—was a colorful vocabulary for use when dissatisfied. And what could be more dissatisfying than being unable to locate the maid responsible for turning half the

Blackberry Manor staff into conspicuously attentive fools, and the other half completely against her?

Evangeline was sorely tempted to select a novel from the many shelves lining the library. She longed to curl up in one of the dark crimson chairs and ignore all thoughts of Ginny's hinged tongue and Neal Pemberton's ready whip and Lady Stanton's threats of tossing Evangeline back into the streets.

Unfortunately, the dying fire offered little light and even less warmth. With a defeated sigh, Evangeline plucked a book at random from the shadowy shelves and crossed quickly to the hallway in order to head back to her bedchamber in the guest quarters. She hoped the fire there would burn bright enough for her to read.

Not two steps down the sconce-dotted passageway, an odd noise froze Evangeline where she stood. A slow but steady *drag . . . thump! drag . . . thump!* came from one of the myriad connecting corridors, a sound too eerie to be human footfalls.

Was Blackberry Manor haunted?

With dread slithering in her stomach, she clutched the dusty book to her chest and did her very best not to move so much as an eyelash.

The dragging and thumping grew closer.

Evangeline dashed back to the relative safety of the darkened library, just as the cause of the noise crossed the intersection not six feet from her.

Mr. Teasdale, his wrinkled face twisting into a grimace, limped across the hall, his palsied hand bearing down heavily on a gold-tipped cane as he dragged his lame leg behind him a few inches at a time.

He didn't look like a doddering, sleepy old man. He looked . . . furious. Ducking out of sight into the library was no doubt a far better choice of action than to interrupt him on his journey.

After the eerie sounds receded at last, Evangeline stepped from the shadows, once again intending to make her way to her chamber in the guest wing. She had no sooner turned toward the same corridor into which Mr. Teasdale had vanished when a horrid series of wracking coughs barked from down a different hallway.

Only one guest present had lungs like that. Since Evangeline had even less desire to explain her unchaperoned presence to Benedict Rutherford than she did to Mr. Teasdale, she sprinted down a random sequence of passageways—and almost found herself face-to-face with a distracted-looking Francine Rutherford.

Fumbling for the handle of the closest door in order to hide herself from the quickly approaching woman, Evangeline twisted the knob and fell backward into blackness just as the plumed and rouged blonde glided past with a frightening feline smile. After a moment, Francine Rutherford disappeared around a corner with a swish of her lime green skirts.

Good heavens. Was *everyone* skulking about Blackberry Manor tonight?

Evangeline slumped against the blessedly solid doorframe. She rested her head against the wooden frame until her breath and her pulse returned to normal. Once assured of both her calmed nerves and her renewed solitude, she pushed off to step back into the hallway.

"Leaving so soon?" came a deep voice from the shadows behind her.

She shrieked and spun about, one hand clapped to her chest. Mr. Lioncroft's eyes glittered somewhere in the gloomy murk. So much for the calm state of her lungs and heart.

"What are you doing here?" she managed, the words tumbling out frantic and breathless.

"I live here."

Evangeline closed her eyes as she realized this was the second time tonight he'd been forced to remind her of that fact. She was a ninny. Her breath faltered as her eyes flew open. A ninny once again alone in the darkness . . . with the wolf.

"Lost again, my little lamb?" came his low, droll voice.

She shivered. Definitely a wolf.

From somewhere in the black, a chair scraped across the floor, followed by slow, relentless footfalls. Evangeline edged backward into the relative comfort of the vacant hallway.

He caught her before she had a chance to run.

Once again, she was up against a wall, her spine to the wainscoting. This time, however, she was not pinned by the wrists but rather by the heat in his gaze. Glowing and darkening with each flicker of candlelight, his eyes focused on hers, without moving, without blinking.

By the time Evangeline realized Mr. Lioncroft was very, very angry, it was too late. His palms were flattened to the wall above each of her shoulders, his feet planted on either side of hers, trapping her in place.

"I didn't mean to startle you," she stammered, helplessly staring back at him as she gulped for scraps of air.

He smiled. Darkly. Wolfishly. Alarmingly. But he said nothing.

"I—I'll just head back to my chambers now, then." She meant the words to be decisive and firm, but they sounded fearful and tentative even to her own ears.

"Will you?" he asked, his face dipping closer to hers, his intent clear. "When the night is just getting interesting?"

Evangeline pressed her lips together and the back of her head against the unyielding wall.

"Don't kiss me in anger," she whispered. Her visions had explicitly illustrated the level of damage lust from a violent brute like her stepfather could do. She had no wish to be ravished—or ravaged—by any man under the influence of drink or rage. Ever.

"In anger?" Mr. Lioncroft repeated softly, lowering his head until his breath coasted across her cheek. Her nerves prickled, as if she could feel that moist heat tickling against every inch of her flesh. He smiled again. "But I'm quite pleased by your presence, little lamb. I'm hoping your sweet kisses will make me forget my anger."

Evangeline's mouth gaped. She clapped her jaw closed before he had a chance to sweep his tongue inside her mouth. His smile widened, as if he'd correctly interpreted her action and found it amusing . . . but not the least bit daunting.

Although the threat of visions had kept Evangeline from kissing or being kissed for over twenty years, she had the distinct impression that deficiency would be corrected within the next few moments.

Even worse, a restless, burning ache spreading from her belly to her heated limbs made a small part of her wish he would quit teasing and start kissing.

As if reading her mind, he leaned even closer, until his hips tilted at hers and the tips of her breasts rubbed against the bleached linen of his shirt. The borrowed book fell from her fingers to the floor. If Mr. Lioncroft noticed, he gave no sign.

Instead, he coasted his open mouth just above her flushed cheek, his breath steaming against the curve of her cheekbone, the dip below her earlobe, the length of her exposed neck.

Her traitorous body writhed between the hard wall and the even harder man before her. A sudden urge to force his lips upon her thrummed in her veins, but her dimming sense of self-preservation cautioned her to flee while she was still able.

As the warm air from his lips traced the same heated path across the other side of her upturned face, she let out a slow, shuddering breath. She would not flee. She could not. She wanted his skin touching hers perhaps even more than he did.

Finally, his mouth returned to its original position, a mere finger's breadth from hers.

Evangeline's lips parted involuntarily, but she kept them parted on purpose.

Victory flashed in his eyes. A rakish grin transformed him from darkly mysterious recluse to triumphant seducer. She blushed at the sudden, frustrated moan she hadn't meant to make. He had won. He knew he had won. But still he didn't kiss her.

Her pulse pounded in her ears. *"Please."*

"Please what?" he asked, his breath spiced with wicked promise. "Please go away?"

"Please kiss me," she whispered, hating herself for pleading. But he made no further comment.

He lowered his head until his lips grazed across her skin, slowly, teasingly, devastatingly, from the hollow beneath her ear along the line of her jaw until he reached the trembling pulse on the other side.

Still no visions. But Evangeline couldn't make herself care. She couldn't make herself do anything but wiggle against him, until his hips swung forward to trap her more firmly against his frame. Her aching, swelling breasts flattened against his chest. She gasped to realize she could *feel* the pounding of his heart, leaping and skittering with the same fevered excitement as hers.

His lips brushed across hers, once, twice, thrice. He was toying with her. Tempting her. Teasing her with desire for his withheld kisses until she could stand it no more. The next time he slid his open mouth over hers, she allowed her tongue to edge just far enough between her parted lips to taste him.

Everything changed.

With a growl, his mouth was upon hers. Hot. Wet. Insistent. His fingers still splayed against the wall on either side of her head, but the muscles of his shoulders trembled as though it required all his willpower to keep his hands on the walls and off her body.

His mouth moved against hers, recklessly, desperately. He devoured her in hungry kisses, suckling her tongue, her lower lip, seizing her every breath and replacing it with his.

More than his hips jutted against her. Something long, hard, and unmistakable pulsed between them, sending a frisson of danger up her spine.

She found his sides with her fingers, intending to thrust him from her trembling body, but instead found herself gripping his hips to pull him even closer.

He was everywhere, his mouth bruising hers, his chest chafing her nipples, his molten thighs rubbing against hers, and that throbbing hard length of him stroking a place no other man had touched.

Evangeline shook with the forbidden pleasure of such delicious contact. She gripped him closer, delighting in the heightened sensitivity and half-wishing she could widen her legs to better allow the exquisite, tantalizing friction. He set her flesh afire with every kiss, with every caress, with every breath.

Without warning, he ripped his mouth from hers with a tortured gasp.

"Go," he rasped. His ragged panting sent shivers across her skin.

She caused him to struggle for breath, to fight for control, to throb between her thighs. The realization that desire could be mutual made her long for his touch even more. She rubbed her body against him slowly, seductively, and reveled in her first taste of feminine power. He groaned. Shuddered. She smiled and licked at his lips.

"Go now," he repeated, his expression pained but his tone desperate. "Unless you want to experience more than mere kisses, right here in the hallway."

Evangeline's smile froze as she realized the peril of stoking such an unpredictable, dangerous fire. He viciously jerked an arm back to his side, as if the last thing on earth he wanted was for her to escape the intoxicating heat of his embrace.

With his burning gaze still locked on her lips, she removed her shaking hands from the hard warmth of his sides. His eyes closed. She hesitated. His heat throbbed against her belly.

She fled.

* * *

Before Evangeline could complete the mere half dozen steps between the dressing room door and her looming bed, the narrow door opposite the smoldering fireplace flew open and Susan Stanton burst into the room.

"There you are," she announced, flashing a delighted smile before crossing directly to the rack of brass stokers next to the fireplace. "Were you lost? You took so long returning, I thought Lionkiller had perhaps struck again."

Susan laughed at her own jest. She might not have done so had she been aware Mr. Lioncroft had in fact been up to wickedness—although not in the sense Susan intended.

Belated guilt frosted over the warmth of remembered passion as Evangeline stared at her companion in horror.

Heaven help her. She was supposed to be entrapping him with Susan, not rubbing her belly against—well. Evangeline's cheeks burned, and she hoped when Susan turned from the flames, she'd attribute any flush of her face to heat from the now-crackling fire, rather than shame.

Only a wanton trollop kissed another woman's intended in shadowed passageways. When had Evangeline turned into a wanton trollop?

After a final jab with the poker, Susan returned the brass instrument to the rack and flopped into the sole wingback chair. "Well?" she demanded, arms crossed and feet outstretched. "Where did you go? I've been ever so bored without you. Pacing up and down one's room is no fun by oneself."

"I . . ." Evangeline began, and then faltered. She glanced around her room for inspiration. Her gaze lit on the row of hip-high bookcases along the rear wall. "I went to the library," she finished truthfully, "and picked out a novel."

At least, she thought it was a novel. As dark as the library had been, she might have grabbed a treatise on the history of mercantilism in India. And . . . oh, no. She'd left the book lying on the floor in the middle of the hallway, forgotten because of an exquisite forbidden kiss.

Susan's eyes widened with interest. "What book did you select?"

Evangeline started, broke eye contact, and turned to the bookcases. She lifted a hand to the closest set, intending to tug a volume free at random, and almost groaned when every book on the top shelf proved immobile. Only the twisted mind who'd designed her bedchamber's nightmare-inspired décor would display something so diabolical as a row of false books. Splendid.

She rested an elbow atop the bookcase as she fished for an alternate avenue of conversation. "Do you read?" she settled on, when a better topic failed to present itself.

"Of course. But real life is ever so much more interesting. Some people might think nothing could be stranger than attending the house party of a reclusive blackguard like Lioncroft, wouldn't you agree? Yet, every guest here is equally odd in his or her own way. Except, perhaps, for Mr. Teasdale. He's just old. I wasn't at all surprised when he left the music room in favor of his bedchamber."

"Except, he didn't," Evangeline mused, forcing thoughts of Mr. Lioncroft's delicious heat aside as she recalled the fury distorting Mr. Teasdale's wrinkled face. "I saw him hobbling down a corridor with his cane. His leg seemed to trouble him something awful, no doubt due to all that dancing."

"Or worse," Susan intoned darkly.

"Worse than what? Dancing?"

Susan rolled her eyes. "Of course, worse than dancing. He lied about going to sleep, didn't he? He might be up to evil after all."

"You said you were going to sleep, but here you are in my bedchamber, seated before my fire."

"I never sleep, so if I say so, then of course, I'm lying. Old men sleep all the time. I would've thought I could at least take Teasdale at his word." She shrugged deeper into the chair. "Well, there's still Hetherington's worthless cousin, Edmund

Rutherford. He's an easy enough sort to read, wastrel that he is. I imagine he's still in the men's after-dinner room, drinking Lioncroft out of port."

Evangeline shook her head. "The men's after-dinner room was the library, which was absent of both port and Mr. Rutherford. The footman refilling the decanter said they'd cleared up the glasses as the men left to rejoin us."

"I knew it," Susan cried, jerking upright in the chair as she clapped her hands together. "Scandal is afoot!"

"It is?" Evangeline fought another blush. It most certainly was, but she had no intention of discussing *her* scandalous behavior. She hadn't even meant to come upon the sinfully handsome man, let alone shiver against him as he devoured her with kisses.

"Yet another liar," Susan crowed. "Edmund must have known there was neither port nor glass to drink it in, and invented his mission back to the library as a cover for some other, more dastardly deed."

"Maybe he simply tired of dancing," Evangeline suggested.

"Ha. A reprobate like him? No doubt he was en route to or from an assignation. Besides dancing, assignations are house parties' primary allure."

"*What* is?"

"Love-making with other guests," Susan clarified matter-of-factly. "Secretly, of course."

This time Evangeline couldn't staunch the sudden rush of blood to her cheeks and neck. Had she been a baser sort of woman—or Mr. Lioncroft a less considerate sort of man—she herself might've been one of that number earlier tonight.

"Bah, don't be missish," Susan scoffed, thankfully misinterpreting Evangeline's blush as something other than guilt. "Assignations are a *ton* staple. I only wonder who was lonely enough to rut with a rotter like Edmund. A servant, perhaps? Surely not a guest. Did you see where he got off to?"

"I never saw him at all. I didn't actually see Benedict Rutherford, either, but I heard him coughing down one of the halls."

"Aargh," Susan groaned, startling Evangeline from her perch against the useless bookshelf. "If it's to be my house, too, can't I skulk about like everyone else? The only person I saw up to any mischief was Nancy, trying to sneak into her bedchamber and being laughably noisy about it. Although I suppose stealth hardly matters if she plans to marry a deaf old mummer like Teasdale." Her shoulders shook in a dramatic shudder. "Next time you wander the corridors alone, you absolutely must invite me to accompany you. Where was Francine? By her husband's side, as she claimed?"

"No, she was . . ." Evangeline thought back. "She was outside Mr. Lioncroft's office, I think. I'm not quite sure."

"Yet another assignation," Susan breathed, eyes alight behind her spectacles. "I suspected as much."

Evangeline's stomach twisted. "Another . . . what?"

"Assignation. If you recall, I mentioned the Rutherfords and I have some unfortunate history. Trust me when I say I am not the least bit surprised to discover Francine taking her pleasure with Lioncroft. She can't resist the scent of power, and Lioncroft positively reeks of it."

Ice slid beneath Evangeline's skin, covering her arms with gooseflesh. Had Mr. Lioncroft left the hallway where they'd kissed, only to make love to an over-rouged Francine Rutherford? Or, worse, had he already done so before she'd unwittingly entered his office in the first place?

Gagging, Evangeline thrust a fist to her lips and shuddered. She was the worst kind of fool. Her initial suspicion that Mr. Lioncroft was no better than her philandering sot of a stepfather was correct after all.

"Oh!" Susan leapt from the chair and rushed to Evangeline's side. "You look like you're going to be ill. Truly, you must learn not to be so missish about who does what with whom. *I'm* not upset she's the secret paramour of my fiancé-to-be. He can keep her as his mistress even after we marry, as far as I'm concerned. The less he forces his husbandly attention upon me, the better. A woman can only do so much closing of her eyes and thinking of Mother England."

Evangeline bit at the knuckle of her first finger until she drew blood, certain now she would regurgitate her meal all over those ugly wooden trolls. How could she have been so stupid?

She'd liked his attention. Encouraged him. Participated wantonly and willfully.

Hadn't she learned from her mother's example that just because a woman was unable to experience visions of a man's misdeeds in no way implied the man in question was absent of them?

Neal Pemberton was a vicious brute, sotted or sober, who cared little for his servants and even less for his womenfolk. Heaven knew the mercurial Mr. Lioncroft was no doubt even worse a profligate, and capable of equally unspeakable cruelty.

She would never again be so foolish as to find herself alone with an animal like him.

"Truly . . ." Susan patted Evangeline's shoulder, her voice uncharacteristically concerned. "Are you quite all right? Mother says I never know when to curb my tongue. I should like to be friends with you, not send you into a fit of the vapors after only a minute or two of my conversation."

Evangeline dropped her fists to her sides and forced a wan smile. She opened her mouth to assure Susan of their continued friendship when a series of loud staccato screams ripped across the silent mansion and echoed through the chambers.

"Aaahh!" Susan bounced on her heels like a pony itching to race across a field. "Something's happening! Come, come, I shan't miss it!"

"Go without me." Evangeline backed up until the bookcase

dug into her spine. Screams were never good. They brought back too many memories better left buried.

Susan goggled at her, as if staying put was hardly an option. "What did I just say? If we skulk, we skulk together. Whyever would I leave without you?"

"Because I don't want to go. Besides, I'm in my night-clothes."

"We're all in our nightclothes, goose. It's well after mid-night." Susan heaved on Evangeline's linen-swathed arm, haul-ing her toward the door with the exaggerated force of a circus strongman. "What if someone needs our help? What if—what if—" She gasped, managing to look simultaneously thrilled and horrified. "What if Lioncroft has killed *again?*"

Chapter Eight

Icy sweat froze the tiny hairs on the back of Gavin's neck as he raced through the hidden passageways to the bedchamber his sister shared with her husband.

"Rose?" he shouted as he burst from behind a concealed access panel and into the deserted corridor. "Rose?"

He slammed into the closed chamber door and fumbled with the handle. The door swung open from within. Rose stood silent, wooden, bloodless. She didn't move. She didn't speak.

"What happened? Are you all right?" With trepidation doubling the rhythm of his already-pounding heart, Gavin fought the urge to reach out for her, to touch her. If she'd had a bad dream or saw a spider, he was not one she'd turn to for comfort. Over a decade had passed since the last time he and his sister had embraced, and he was not yet ready to accept more rejection.

His sister's dull, sightless eyes stared right through him.

"Hetherington." The hollowness in Rose's voice sent chills rippling along the muscles of Gavin's back. "He's dead."

Gavin staggered against the doorframe. "He's what?"

"Dead." She stepped backward, away from the hallway, away from him, granting him access to the chamber's shadowy interior. "See for yourself."

Not entirely certain he wanted to see for himself, Gavin inched further into the darkness until he could make out a motionless lump beneath a pile of blankets.

Hetherington, all right. Not that he'd expected to encounter anyone else in his sister's bed. Gavin edged closer. No sound. No movement. Not a good sign. He leaned over the prone body until his ear brushed against the earl's cold, parted lips.

One second passed in silence. Two seconds. Three. After a long moment, Gavin stopped waiting. He straightened, ripped his gaze from Hetherington's waxy face, and turned to his sister.

"I'm sorry, Rose. He—he's not breathing."

She nodded, her head jerking like a marionette on a string. "He's dead."

"I'm sorry," he said again, involuntarily transported back in time to another dark autumn night, another pale motionless figure, another face forever frozen in death. An irreversible horror for which he could never be forgiven. He took a halting step toward his sister. Had he ever apologized for what he'd done to their parents? He hadn't seen her, hadn't spoken to her . . . until now. "Forgive me, Rose. I'm so sorry. I didn't mean for—"

A chorus of gasps crackled from the corridor.

Gavin whirled to find the rest of the house party, in various stages of undress, stacked in the doorway. They tumbled into the room like bone dice from an overturned cup, their faces pallid, their manner frightened, their eyes judging.

Edmund clutched a glass of whiskey with pale fingers, the stench of alcohol on his breath overpowering in the close quarters. His cousin Benedict stood to the left with one hand clapped to his mouth, although whether to hold back coughs or bile, Gavin couldn't guess. Benedict's wife Francine hovered behind him, still coiffed and over-rouged. With both spotted hands balancing his weight atop his gold-tipped cane, Mr. Teasdale stared past Rose to the figure half-covered with blankets. Nancy swayed next to him, her eyes closed and her lip quivering. Miss Stanton, right beside her, stared wide-eyed and slack-jawed, not at Hetherington's corpse, but at Gavin, as though half-expecting to find him drenched in blood. Her mother stood behind her, one blue-veined hand fluttering at her throat.

The only one paying more attention to his sister than the body on the bed was Miss Pemberton. She stood next to Rose, one gloveless hand upon her arm. After a moment, she lifted her fingers and turned to face Gavin. Gone was the heightened color her cheeks had held less than an hour earlier, replaced now by a vast and horrible emptiness. She met his gaze, unblinking, unmoving, unspeaking.

He swallowed, unaccountably feeling like he owed her an explanation for the tableau before them, even though he had no better idea than anyone else what caused Lord Hetherington's demise. Or whom.

Edmund Rutherford broke both the silence and the stillness by downing the rest of his whiskey in one gulp and drawling, "Caught with another body, eh, Lioncroft?"

Gavin growled and stepped forward.

"Ai!" Edmund leapt backward and bumped into Francine Rutherford. "I'm just pointing out the coincidence."

"Get off me, you oaf." She gave him a shove and he stumbled forward a few feet. "Don't touch me."

Benedict Rutherford doubled over with a coughing fit and smothered his face in the crook of his elbow. When he straightened, his face was even whiter than before. With a small shudder, he turned to Rose and asked, "What happened?"

She didn't respond.

All the nervous gazes returned to Gavin. Miss Pemberton was the first to speak.

"Did somebody . . . hurt him?" she asked, her voice soft but steady. "Or did he just pass?"

A choking laugh escaped Rose's throat, startling everyone.

"When I came in," she said, the words as dull and lifeless

as her expression, "I thought he was sleeping. After dismissing my maid, I crawled into bed next to him. I bid my husband good night. He said nothing. I thought he was ignoring me again, to be cruel." The tips of her fingers rubbed idly against her still-bruised cheek. "I hadn't forgiven him for striking me, nor for the cause of our argument. So I poked his arm with my finger. When that had no effect, I shook his shoulder. When *that* had no effect"—her voice trembled—"I slapped him like he slapped me. He deserved it!" She turned her wild gaze from her husband to the houseguests. "But he didn't feel it. He didn't say a word. He didn't even breathe, because he was dead. *Dead*." Her fingers clutched at her elbows. "So help me, I slapped a dead man. When I realized . . . When I—"

Rose fell in a sudden faint. Miss Pemberton's arms flew forward to catch her. She grimaced, her eyes squinting as though blinded by a bright light. She staggered to one side. Gavin stepped forward to take his sister from her. Benedict intercepted the move, slipping his hands under Rose's flaccid arms and taking her from Miss Pemberton. With Rose's dead weight clutched to his chest, he half-carried, half-dragged her toward the bed.

"You can't put her on a pillow right next to her dead husband," came Miss Pemberton's pained voice, stopping Benedict in his tracks. "She'll faint again the moment she comes to."

Benedict froze, frowned, coughed.

Gavin rescued his sister's limp body from the wheezing man. With little effort, he scooped her into his arms and stalked right into the throng of horrified faces. His houseguests parted like the Red Sea, melting against the walls to allow him passage.

"Where are you taking her?" came Teasdale's quavering voice.

"I don't know," Gavin muttered, his footsteps halting. "Away."

"Put Mother in my room," Nancy said, her eyes glassy with shock. "I don't want to sleep alone tonight."

Gavin nodded and continued his path down the dim corridor. Sconces scattered shadows across old paintings and nervous footmen. The procession of houseguests and servants followed him like rats behind the Pied Piper of Hamelin.

He laid his sister in his niece's bed and instructed a handful of maids to keep an eye on them both. With a final glance at Rose's ashen complexion, he strode back through the crowded hallway to the Hetherington guest chambers.

As before, the guests followed.

"What now?" Francine asked, once they came upon Hetherington lying precisely as they'd left him.

"I don't know," Gavin said.

"Now," said Miss Pemberton as she stepped forward, "We're going to take a closer look at Lord Hetherington."

Lady Stanton ducked behind a painted fan. "Why?"

"Because Lady Hetherington was unable to . . . tell me," Miss Pemberton answered, "whether or not she thought his death was accidental." All gazes locked on Gavin's. Miss Pemberton's was the only countenance tinged with something other than suspicion and fear. Her methodical, cool-tempered responses made her seem oddly capable and eerily resigned, like a surgeon approaching a blood-soaked battlefield. "That is, if we may?"

Gavin inclined his head in acknowledgement.

"You think foul play is a possibility?" Francine asked.

"Foul play is a probability," Edmund corrected. "I'd wager someone in this very room offed the arrogant fop."

From the weight of so many stares, Gavin wagered he could suppose who his guests assumed had done the killing. "I'd like to prove that false."

He motioned the servants into the room. They scurried about the perimeter, lighting tapers until every wick sputtered with orange flame.

Slowly, Gavin approached the bed. Now that candlelight chased the shadows from the chamber, he could make out more than Hetherington's general form. A white handkerchief wrapped around the top of the earl's head. The portion above his left temple was encrusted with dried blood. Gavin glanced over his shoulder at Miss Pemberton, who sighed.

"What is it?" The Stanton chit called from the doorway. "A gunshot? A knife wound? Snakes?"

Miss Pemberton shook her head. "Blood—"

Everyone gasped.

"—but the injury has been bandaged. We've no way to know when or how he got the wound. He may have tripped, fallen, and bandaged himself before retiring for the night."

Or he might've had an oil painting land on his head.

Gavin stared at the woman kneeling in her nightrail next to the bed. Would she defend him to the others? Their expressions broadcast their unwavering belief that if anyone had murdered a man tonight, Gavin was no doubt the villain.

Miss Pemberton was the first person in the last eleven years of his acquaintance to turn to logic before rumor when determining guilt. Thankfully, she was unsure about the source of the wound. He did tidy up that frame afterward, didn't he? Perhaps they'd all assume Hetherington had injured himself. As long as there were no other signs of foul play, Gavin would not have to fear being relabeled a murderer.

"Wouldn't he have rung for a servant to tend a blow to the head?" Lady Stanton asked from just behind her daughter. "I would've done so."

"A fine suggestion," Gavin said. He gazed at Miss Pemberton, willing her to look at him. She did not. "They shall all be questioned first thing in the morning."

A silence fell. No one seemed eager to exchange glances with each other, much less look too long at the corpse upon the bed. Even Miss Pemberton was not scrutinizing the earl's body as she'd first suggested—not that Gavin blamed her— and was instead biting her lip and gazing at the carpeted floor as if she'd rather be anywhere than where she currently stood.

"I heard you, by the way," Edmund slurred from his perch against a wardrobe. "I heard you apologize to your sister for killing him."

"No," Gavin said. "You heard me apologize for killing someone else."

His clarification failed to ease the tension.

Perhaps impatient with Miss Pemberton's reluctant perusal of the lifeless earl, Benedict at last strode forward and tugged the pile of blankets from Hetherington's still form.

Two things became quickly apparent. One was a mottled bruise surrounding the left side of Hetherington's throat, matching the shape of Gavin's left hand. The other was a corresponding bruise covering the other side, matching the shape of Gavin's right.

Benedict gasped. A surplus of air sent him off into another vicious coughing streak.

No one spoke.

Miss Pemberton's eyes dipped closed for a long moment before reopening. "I'd have to wager," she said at last, "Lord Hetherington did not strangle himself with his bare hands after settling into bed."

Lady Stanton sucked in a shocked breath. "*Strangled,*" she repeated, clutching her bespectacled daughter by the shoulders. "We need to call for the constabulary. Immediately."

Gavin tried very hard not to react. The last thing he needed was the constabulary. Given his questionable past and his outburst at the dining table, they'd have him condemned to the gallows within a week. Unfortunately, he could think of no good reason to deny Lady Stanton's request. Devil take it.

Careful to keep his expression neutral, Gavin slid his gaze about the roomful of onlookers and waited for their response.

They said nothing.

The Stanton chit and her mother exchanged an indecipherable look. Edmund stared into the bottom of his empty glass as though hoping more whiskey would magically reappear. Benedict dropped the blankets he'd yanked from Hetherington's body, as if the woven wool had scalded him. Francine clutched her belly with both hands, giving the impression she was a moment away from vomiting. Teasdale fidgeted with his cane, eyes downcast.

"Well?" Lady Stanton demanded. "Is someone calling for the constabulary or not?"

"Apparently," Edmund said as he slammed his empty glass atop a dressing table, "not."

"Useless bunch," Francine put in, the dip of the orange plume atop her coiffed head suddenly garish and out-of-place.

"Volunteers," her husband Benedict agreed, dabbing at his mouth with a handkerchief. "Fools, every one of them."

Teasdale examined his cane as if he had just noticed its presence in his hand. Conversation strangled to a halt.

"What time is it?" Miss Pemberton asked after another excruciating lull. Everyone stared at her as though she'd spoken in tongues.

Gavin fumbled for his fob. "Half past two."

"Then it's late." She squared her shoulders. "We're all tired, we've had a shock, and none of us are thinking clearly. Now is not the time to make accusations." She took a deep breath. "Why don't we reconvene in the morning, as planned?"

"For breakfast?" came Lady Stanton's cold, incredulous voice. "Who can eat at a time like this?"

"Hell, I can. Drink, too." Edmund jerked his head toward Hetherington's motionless body. "Just because he's dead doesn't mean I am. Breakfast sounds like a fine time to make accusations."

The Stanton chit tittered hysterically and clapped both hands across her mouth.

Teasdale waved his cane toward the bed. "What are you going to do with Hetherington in the meantime? Seeing as how we're not penning a note to the local constabulary."

"I'll pen one to the rectory instead." Gavin ran a hand

through his hair too harshly, pulling a few strands from his scalp. "We'll still need a funeral."

God help him, not a funeral. He hadn't attended one since he was seventeen. His nieces were much too young to have to throw dirt atop the casket of a parent.

He swallowed, forcing old memories from his mind. "Clear the chamber." The others started when his words came out too loud, but he suddenly couldn't stand to be in the same room as another lifeless body. "Return to your rooms. I'm returning to mine. Breakfast . . . breakfast will be ready by eight."

Slowly, they shuffled out of the room and dispersed into the corridor.

"Well, I for one shan't sleep a wink," said Lady Stanton as she preceded her daughter down the hall.

"Lioncroft will sleep like a baby," came Edmund's slurred rejoinder. "He's used to family members popping up dead in mysterious circumstances."

Gavin took two quick strides out of the room and into the hall, prepared to have it out with Edmund then and there.

Before Edmund even registered his approach, however, Gavin's footsteps faltered. Thrashing a sotted Edmund lost its allure the more distance Gavin put between himself and Hetherington's cold, bruised body. Whether Edmund deserved a fist to the face or not, Gavin had had enough violence for one day.

Tomorrow would come soon enough.

Evangeline jerked awake from yet another nightmare long before a maid arrived to open the bed curtains. She staggered out of bed and over to the small washbasin in the corner, hoping the freezing water would splash the memory of her mother's broken body from her mind. As usual, the shock of icy wetness sent gooseflesh shivering across her skin but did little to dispel the images trapped in her head.

Another day, another death.

Eventually, a slight lady's maid slipped into the room with a candle clutched between her rough hands. She used the orange flame to light the tall tapers dotting Evangeline's chamber before disappearing into the connecting dressing room to gather new garments and undergarments.

"Your morning dress, mum," the girl murmured, returning with an armful of borrowed silk.

Evangeline winced. What should have been a *mourning* dress was instead a flowing mass of palest green, trimmed beneath the bodice by a strip of satin the deep hue of pine. Soft, gorgeous, and a mockery to her mother's memory with its bold color.

She forced herself to hold still as a shift, stays, and the mint-colored gown replaced her nightrail.

What now? Now that Lioncroft had killed again? Surely Lady Stanton didn't mean to proceed with her machinations, no matter how badly they'd all secretly wished someone would avenge the cruelty done to Lady Hetherington.

While Evangeline suspected most of the guests wouldn't much miss the late lord, the earl's four children couldn't help but suffer at the loss. Her heart twisted in empathy. She could find the nursery, could she not? As soon as she could excuse herself from the breakfast table, she should make her way directly there to check on the children.

"You should've seen it coming," the maid muttered under her breath as she fastened the last of the buttons on the back of Evangeline's neck.

"I—what?"

"Should've seen it coming," the maid repeated. "Or did you, an' you just didn't see fit to tell anybody?"

Mouth agape, Evangeline whirled to face the young girl.

The maid's complexion was more or less the same shade of pale green as the borrowed morning dress. Nonetheless, she stared up at Evangeline with shaking hands and a determined gaze. A strand of red hair fell from her bonnet to her

face and she shoved the offending lock away without breaking eye contact.

"I heard what you were," she insisted, the faint quiver in
her voice giving away her fear of speaking out, even to a
nobody like Evangeline. "All of us know."

"Us" no doubt meant the staff of Blackberry Manor, just
like "witch" was no doubt the word that went unspoken.

Back home, servants had been Evangeline's staunchest sup-
porters. Here, they were . . . not. She could expect neither un-
derstanding nor tolerance under the best of circumstances. A
dead body abovestairs was not the best of circumstances. Especially for a runaway suspected of witchery. And after helping Ginny, Evangeline could hardly deny her visions.

"I didn't know," she said at last. "I swear."

The maid flinched, as if she'd half-expected Evangeline
to toss her bodily from the room rather than respond to a mere
maid. Was such skittishness because she was used to violent
treatment from Mr. Lioncroft? Or because the maid feared
Evangeline herself?

"What's your name?"

"Molly."

"You're a smart woman, Molly. You're right about my visions. But what you may not know is that the only way I can
attempt to guide the content of my visions is by concentrating on a single question as I touch another person. And even
that fails more often than not." Evangeline paused. How
much did she need to reveal in order to keep her biggest secrets? "I had no reason to anticipate Lord Hetherington's
death. Accidental visions are useless at best. Were I to touch
you now, I'd be just as likely to see you toddle behind your
mother in leading strings as to see you snuggled before a fire
with your husband and three children."

The girl blinked. "I'm to have three children?"

"I have no idea. That's my point." Evangeline met and held
the girl's nervous gaze. "More importantly, I hope to keep

my . . . talent in the strictest confidence. I've no wish to be thrown to the streets, or into Bedlam, and I do not hold the openness of the *ton*'s collective minds in particularly high esteem."

"My master doesn't hold toffs in any esteem," Molly scoffed. "He says they're all self-important rotters with lukewarm lemonade for brains."

"Yes. Well. I'd tend to agree." As Evangeline hugged herself, the lace of her mitts scratched against her dry skin. "Wait . . . Mr. Lioncroft doesn't—you haven't told him about my visions, have you?"

The girl's chin jerked up. "For all his troubles, he's a good master. If he asks if you're a witch, any one of us would tell him the truth."

Normally, such staunch loyalty would bring a smile to Evangeline's face. In this case, however, her words sent ice along Evangeline's spine.

"But if he doesn't ask?" she insisted.

After a long moment, Molly shrugged. "He's not one for idle chatter. There's many haven't once heard him speak. I doubt he'll mention you at all."

Evangeline supposed the unlikelihood of her name crossing Mr. Lioncroft's lips should make her feel better, but instead— Evangeline straightened her shoulders. Best to not analyze her illogical emotions. She'd be long gone before he caught wind of any witchery afoot.

After doing her best to twist Evangeline's unruly curls— which had never suffered pins for more than a few minutes before, and showed no signs of doing otherwise today—into some sort of looping plait, Molly gave up, curtsied, and left.

Within a moment, a brisk knock rattled the connecting door to Susan's chamber. Evangeline twisted the handle and welcomed in her neighbor.

Susan's gown, a powder-blue confection with indigo accents, elegantly complemented her cerulean eyes and pale skin. Unlike Evangeline, Susan wore both a portrait-perfect chignon and a delighted smile.

"I'm surprised you answered so quickly," she said, sweeping past Evangeline to warm her hands by the fire. "I half-suspected you to be a slugabed."

"I'm surprised you knocked," Evangeline muttered as she closed the connecting door. "I didn't think you knew how."

"Oh, don't be shrewish. It's much too fine a day."

"How do you know? There are no windows."

"Not outside, goose. Inside. I haven't had such excitement in ages." Susan threw open the hallway door and grinned. "Are you coming or not?"

Seeing no recourse, Evangeline joined her in the corridor and led the way to the breakfast table. As it happened, Lady Stanton had not yet arrived. Neither had Lady Hetherington or her daughter Nancy.

Mr. Lioncroft sat at the head of the table, brooding over a plateful of untouched eggs. Francine Rutherford was to his left, toying with a slice of toasted bread. Her husband Benedict sat on her left, showing no trouble consuming his kippers. His cousin Edmund was next, with a full glass of wine and only a few crumbs remaining on his plate.

Nobody occupied the two seats to Lioncroft's immediate right.

Mr. Teasdale occupied the chair following the gap, his cane dangling between the curved wooden slats.

Although they'd surely heard Susan and Evangeline approach, not a single guest so much as glanced up at two young ladies hesitating in the doorway.

"Well, we're here," Susan whispered behind a gloved hand. "You want Teasdale or Lioncroft?"

Evangeline wanted to go back to bed. Sleep, however, did not await her there. "I don't care," she murmured. "I'm not even hungry."

Susan fished one hand in her pocket. "Heads or tails?"

"Just go in and sit down." Evangeline nudged her forward. "We can't stand here whispering."

"Fine." Susan removed her empty hand from her pocket and began to tug off her gloves. "You get Lioncroft, then."

Evangeline took a step into the room, and then paused. "He's your future fiancé. Don't you want to sit by him?"

Susan clutched the doorframe. "I will when we're married and not a moment sooner."

"If he frightens you so," Evangeline hissed behind her cupped palm, "why marry him?"

"Lesser evil. He's a good catch now that I'm ruined, remember?" Susan's brow furrowed. "Well, he was before he started murdering people again. He might hang for it this time. And I can't marry a dead man. If I'm lucky, Mother will have given up on the whole idea."

"I should hope so. Now is not the time to trap anyone into false comp—"

"Ladies." Mr. Lioncroft's deep voice boomed into the stillness. "There's plenty of provisions yet on the sideboard."

Evangeline dropped her hands back to her sides and flashed an embarrassed smile at five pairs of curious eyes. Susan crossed to the sideboard, scooped meat and eggs onto her plate, and plopped down next to Mr. Teasdale, across from Benedict Rutherford. Evangeline laid a single slice of toasted bread on hers before taking her place between Susan and Mr. Lioncroft.

"What were you discussing in the doorway?" Edmund Rutherford slurred over a glass of wine. "Which one of us will be the next to be throttled in our sleep?"

He laughed at his own jest. Neither Evangeline nor Susan bothered to reply. During the awkward silence which followed, however, Evangeline finally risked a glance at the silent man seated next to her. Mr. Lioncroft's glare singed the air between him and Edmund, warning him without words. Edmund returned his gaze to his glass. Evangeline couldn't tear hers from Mr. Lioncroft.

Like her, he appeared not to have slept well.

His shirt was pressed, his breeches clean and snug, but his cravat appeared to have been tied without aid of candle-light. Dark whiskers shadowed the hollows below his cheek-bones and the line of his jaw. The jagged scar stood out bold and pale. Tousled locks curled about his neck and ears and tumbled forward into dark brown eyes. The pale skin visible beneath the blackness of his lashes was tinged with a faint purple, as though his nightmares were no less consuming than hers.

"I say," Edmund said, breaking the silence. "I'd wager the lot of us sleep with scarves about our necks tonight."

Francine Rutherford shoved her untouched plate across the table. "Tasteless, Edmund."

Benedict laid his hand atop hers. "He's a drunk."

"He's an ass," she countered.

"And you," Edmund put in, "are the new Lord and Lady Hetherington. Very churlish of Benedict, I'd say. He was already next in line without pushing things along quite so violently."

"See here," was all Benedict managed to get out before erupting into a bout of barking coughs.

"And now you're the heir, Edmund," Francine pointed out. The plume from her bonnet dipped and swayed above her forehead. "Very neatly done. Do I have to guard my husband in his sleep?"

"Perhaps, perhaps." Edmund downed the last of his wine and motioned for a footman to refill the glass. "Although I suppose we should turn to the head of the table for a glimpse at the true villain."

All eyes swiveled toward Mr. Lioncroft.

He lifted a dark brow and stared back without blinking. "What are you implying?"

"I'm not implying anything. I'm *saying* it." Edmund wiped sweat from his lip with the back of one hand. "Where were you last night when Hetherington blew out his last breath?"

A silence descended.

"In my office." A muscle twitched near Mr. Lioncroft's temple. "I could call you out for suggesting otherwise."

"Nobody will call anybody out," Mr. Teasdale interrupted. He peeled the crust from his toast with trembling fingers. "One untimely death is enough for now."

Francine sent a quelling gaze at Edmund. "No matter how much some people might deserve theirs."

Edmund winked, as though the desirability of his demise was none of his concern.

"Where were you last night?" Evangeline asked him before she could stop herself. "In the library as you claimed?"

"Why, yes, you saucy thing. I was." He toasted her with his empty wineglass. "I had a glass of port. Several of them. Spent hours there, just as I said I'd do."

Evangeline frowned.

Susan, however, sucked in a loud gasp. She dropped her knife to the table with a clatter and turned wide blue eyes to Evangeline. "Didn't you say—Ow! What the dickens, Evangeline. Did you just kick me?"

"Yes," Evangeline hissed, half-tempted to kick her again. "Be quiet."

Mr. Lioncroft stared at them both, but said nothing.

"Where were the rest of you?" Edmund asked as he swirled his newly filled glass. "Dancing into the wee hours?"

"In bed," Benedict answered.

Francine nodded. "And I with him."

"I retired as well," Mr. Teasdale added, his voice cracking.

Liars, all. Evangeline could hardly believe her ears.

Susan's jaw dropped. Evangeline gave her a preemptive kick beneath the table. No wonder they hadn't been eager to summon the constabulary. They all had something to hide.

If the rest of them saw no need to admit their nocturnal wanderings, why should she? For all she knew, neither Lady

Stanton nor Lady Hetherington nor Nancy Hetherington had been in their quarters, either.

"I was in my bedchamber," she said aloud.

"As was I," Susan added. "In my bedchamber, that is. Not Evangeline's."

Mr. Lioncroft shot Evangeline a quick, wry glance as if to say *he* would not have been opposed to spending the evening in Evangeline's bedchamber rather than just a portion of it up against the wall outside his office. Arrogant blackguard. She should never have kissed him.

"I interviewed the servants," he said calmly, as if he spent most mornings questioning his staff about inconvenient homicides. "They saw nothing."

Edmund toyed with his silver flask. "Well, somebody strangled Hetherington."

"Perhaps the marks on his neck have nothing to do with his death," Mr. Lioncroft suggested softly. "Those could easily be a relic of an earlier altercation."

"That's true." Evangeline glanced at him from the corner of her eye. She'd be willing to wager Mr. Lioncroft had been an active participant in any earlier altercations. "Lord Hetherington was also bandaged about the head. Perhaps that wound was the fatal injury."

For some reason, Mr. Lioncroft appeared no happier with her alternate explanation. No doubt the violent brute was the cause of both. And she'd rubbed herself against him in pleasure a scant hour beforehand. No doubt he gloated over that conquest as well.

"Botheration." Susan's arms crossed below her bodice. "I suppose we shall never know the truth."

Evangeline sipped her tea and wondered if Susan was right. Last night's vision with Lady Hetherington had only shown what the lady herself had recounted.

"Convenient," Edmund put in, with a sly glance toward Mr. Lioncroft. "Much like last time."

Mr. Lioncroft leapt to his feet so fast Edmund started, spilling burgundy liquid down the front of his shirt and into his lap.

"The primary question," came Mr. Teasdale's quavering voice, "is why anyone would murder Hetherington in the first place. I can only imagine two motives."

Still standing, Mr. Lioncroft slid his dark gaze to Mr. Teasdale. "Only two?"

"First, and no offense to the new earl, but any time a title-holder is killed, we must generally take a look at the next in line. The most obvious reason for bloodshed is personal gain."

Personal gain? Evangeline stared at her toast. Maybe that seemed like a reasonable motive to sheltered rich folk who'd never met a man like Neal Pemberton. Where her stepfather was concerned, violence was sport, not strategy.

Benedict coughed, scowled, crossed his arms. "And the other reason?"

"Anger, of course. Rage makes us capable of the worst possible things."

"Well, the old codger's right," Edmund drawled. "And nobody had more to gain than the new Lord Coughs-A-Lot."

"Point your greasy finger at someone else, or I'll—" Benedict began, but the rest of his warning was lost in a barrage of hacking coughs, which only served to send Edmund into a fit of drunken laughter. When Benedict regained control of himself, he took several sips of tea before speaking again. "Don't you think I know a suspicious death would bode badly for me, precisely because of primogeniture? I'd rather *never* bear the title than to earn it through such catastrophic means. Rage, not the title, was the motivator in this instance."

"Not only that," Mr. Teasdale said after a moment, "in most cases where some dastardly cousin or unscrupulous younger brother sought to usurp his brother's place, the death was made to look accidental. There's nothing accidental about being clubbed on the head and strangled. Whoever did that was angry."

Benedict and Francine Rutherford shot Mr. Lioncroft considering glances. His gaze remained hard and inscrutable.

"The angriest," Edmund drawled, "would have to be Lioncroft. Murderous past aside, we all knew from the very moment he saw the handprint on his sister's face that there was a man who could kill."

Once again, all eyes faced the head of the table.

Lioncroft's jaw flexed. "I. Did not. Kill him."

Evangeline struggled to keep the skepticism from her face. Men like him never owned up to their actions.

"Right, right," Edmund agreed with patronizing cheerfulness. "We believe you. Excuse me, there, old boy." He gestured for a footman. "Splash a little more wine into my glass, would you?"

"I admit . . ." Francine slanted a glance toward Lioncroft. "You did look angry enough to throttle Hetherington."

"I *was* angry enough," Lioncroft admitted in a low growl. "But I let him live."

With one hand cupped over her mouth, Susan leaned close to Evangeline. "He's going to have to polish his alibi," she stage-whispered. "Not very persuasive, as such things go."

Evangeline silently agreed. "I could've, but didn't," was not the strongest defense.

"Hetherington slapped his wife, not Lioncroft." Francine's words were low, smooth, insidious. "Perhaps . . ."

"The countess did him in herself?" Edmund chuckled. "Of course. Who would suspect her?"

"Not me," Susan said in awe. "She looks so timid. I say, you never can tell."

Mr. Lioncroft's gaze turned fierce. "The lady isn't present to defend herself, and has suffered quite enough already without being judged a murderess in her absence."

"To be honest," Edmund said with a swish of his wine, "my money's still on you."

"Then you would do well," Mr. Lioncroft bit out, "not to prick my temper further."

A startled gasp sounded from the open door. All heads swiveled toward the entryway of the breakfast room, where Lady Stanton stood frozen. One pale hand clutched her throat.

"Did I just hear you confess your guilt?"

"I assure you, madam" Mr. Lioncroft said. "You did not."

"Why, good morning, Mother. We were just saying how unfortunate it was that we shall never know what—or who—perpetrated Lord Hetherington's death."

"Of course we shall." Frost coated Lady Stanton's tone as she glared at her daughter. After Susan dropped her gaze, Lady Stanton turned an arched brow to the rest of the table. "Just have Miss Pemberton feel him."

"*Feel* him?" Benedict Rutherford echoed. "Why on earth would she do that?"

Lady Stanton blinked. "Why, because she's a—"

"I'm a . . . religious person," Evangeline interrupted, leaping to her feet. Her breathing sounded overloud. Rushing blood echoed in her ears. "As you may know, many religious people lay their hands upon each other for . . . religious reasons."

As their expressions ranged from confused to suspicious, Evangeline half-wished she'd gone ahead and let Lady Stanton label her a witch. At least she wouldn't have to fear a murderer on the loose if the aristocrats carted her off to Bedlam. Then again, she'd rather flee through the countryside on foot than be incarcerated in a small, windowless room for the rest of her life.

After a long disbelieving silence, Edmund was the first to find his voice. "What's Miss Pemberton going to do, *pray* on him? Surely he's a bit beyond the point where he'd rise from the dead."

Francine grimaced. "Pardon my rudeness, but that is a bit ridiculous."

Lady Stanton sniffed. "I hadn't wished to divulge the shocking truth, but she claims to—"

"Hear voices from God," Evangeline blurted out. She nodded vigorously when several doubtful faces gazed her way. "Heavenly conversation is not at all the sort of thing one brags about. Isn't that right, Lady Stanton?"

She fixed Lady Stanton with a desperate stare. The lady was unmoved.

"If I say yes, will you 'pray' about it?"

"Yes!"

"Then, yes." Lady Stanton waved a disdainful hand in Evangeline's direction. "She hears voices from God. Shall she go touch Hetherington now?"

Evangeline closed her eyes, but not before she saw the baffled expressions bounce from her, to Lady Stanton, back to her again, then on to Mr. Lioncroft.

Of all the times for Lady Stanton to start hinting at her secret, why volunteer her to touch a corpse during breakfast? The way things were going, at least if she got sent to Bedlam, Lady Stanton would be coming with her. Angels above. Perhaps Evangeline *ought* to get religious.

"Fine," Mr. Lioncroft said at last.

Evangeline opened her eyes. His level stare contained more mistrust than curiosity. Splendid. As her mother before her, Evangeline strived to keep mistrust out of other people's eyes. Especially since such an emotion tended to accompany threats of violence or demands to perform on command. In the case of her stepfather, she'd suffered both. Who knew what Mr. Lioncroft would make her suffer.

"F-fine?" she croaked. The last thing she wanted to do was touch the earl's dead body. Her mother had been the first and last victim of violence Evangeline had touched with her bare hands, and that episode—that episode was one she had no desire to relive. She still bore the marks of that folly. "Truly," she managed, "I don't mind *not* touching him. In fact, should I be given the choice, I'd have to say I—"

Mr. Lioncroft pinned her with the intensity of his gaze. "Far be it for me to prevent the good Lord from speaking to devout disciples like yourself, Miss Pemberton. And since *I didn't kill him,* what do I have to lose?" He glared around the table. Evangeline gulped. No one spoke. "In fact," he said, "I'll take you there myself. Right now."

Susan jumped up, eyes shining. "I'll go, too."

Lady Stanton snapped open a painted fan. "You'll do no such thing, young lady. You're coming to my quarters with me, where we'll have a nice chat about appropriate decorum."

"I thought you wanted me to take advantage of any opportunity to—"

"Not *now,* Susan. Use your head for once."

"But, Mother . . ." Susan glanced about the breakfast room as though searching for a logical reason to revisit the late earl. "I—I don't want to leave Evangeline alone. Like you always say, proper young ladies cannot gad about unchaperoned. And with *Lioncroft,* at that. Who knows what could happen?"

Mr. Lioncroft's voice tightened. "I am not going to kill her."

"Plenty else you can do with an unchaperoned chit," Edmund said with a grin.

"For the love of God," Mr. Lioncroft exploded. "I'm not going to kill her and I'm not going to ravish her in the same bed as my dead brother-in-law."

Edmund snorted. "Some other bed, perhaps?"

Despite herself, Evangeline blushed. And dared not meet Mr. Lioncroft's eyes, the devil. If only he hadn't touched her.

"Most ladies," Francine Rutherford put in as she got to her feet, "don't go about feeling corpses, chaperoned or otherwise. The very thought makes me nauseous."

"Nauseous a lot lately, isn't she," Susan muttered to Evangeline. "Lionkiller moves fast."

"Susan!" Lady Stanton snapped. "Come now. This conversation is not for your ears."

With a groan, Susan pushed away from the table and reluctantly followed her mother out the door.

Francine touched her belly with one hand and her throat with the other. "I, for one, have no wish to lay eyes upon Hetherington again before the funeral."

"Nor I," Benedict said with a shiver, rising to join his wife. "True gentlemen are equally as averse to such morbidity as the ladies."

"Agreed," Mr. Teasdale quavered. "Besides, servants crawl over every inch of the property. We're never truly alone, nor would Lioncroft and Miss Pemberton be. Surely a maid or two could be present?"

Mr. Lioncroft nodded. "Of course. An army of them."

Edmund slammed his empty wineglass to the breakfast table and lumbered to his feet. He clutched the back of his chair with both hands.

"It's settled, then," he said, swaying slightly. "You two run along, feel Hetherington's dead body all you like, and meet us later to fill us in on God's message."

Evangeline stared weakly as the breakfast room emptied of its last few occupants, save for she and Mr. Lioncroft.

"Well, Miss Pemberton?" came his low, deep voice.

She turned to face him, but words failed her. For a moment, the tortured expression darkening his eyes was so fierce, she could almost believe him innocent of the crime.

But then, Neal Pemberton had mastered the art of appearing blameless despite his culpability. Such looks were not to be trusted. Particularly those from men she could not read with a simple touch.

Mr. Lioncroft's gaze was equally unreadable as he said, "I must admit the truth."

Evangeline blinked. He would admit to killing Lord Hetherington?

"I don't believe for one second that any celestial deities speak to you. In fact, I don't even believe that you believe it."

He rose and held out a palm, as though to assist her to her feet. Although for the first time in her life she could touch and be touched without being overcome with visions, she did not place her hand in his. She wished to touch a murderer even less than she wished to touch the lifeless body of his victim.

She hoped she wasn't next.

Chapter Nine

"Are you ready?" Gavin asked once he and the reluctant Miss Pemberton reached Hetherington's guest quarters. He paused, one hand on the brass doorknob, and waited for her reply.

Miss Pemberton hesitated, neither nodding nor shaking her head, careful not to meet his eyes.

Why? Because touching Hetherington's dead body was an elaborate ruse designed to—to—to what, exactly? Gavin could think of no good reason—or even a bad reason—for a young lady to lay her hands upon a corpse. Reasons for Lady Stanton to suggest such a charade likewise escaped him. Whatever her agenda might be, Gavin doubted Miss Pemberton heard voices from God.

There was no God.

Or if there were, He was a capricious, vengeful God, delighting in sending loved ones to the grave before their time, and destroying the lives of those who remained behind. If such a God could speak to them through Hetherington's cold body, Gavin had no wish to hear the message. He already knew he was damned.

Without waiting for Miss Pemberton to decide whether or not she would enter or flee, Gavin twisted the handle and thrust open the door.

The guest chamber looked much like it did when they'd gathered there a few hours before. Same oil-on-canvas landscapes, same rotting furniture, same stiff body stretched across the mattress.

A few items, however, were different.

The smell, for one. Gavin's lungs seized in protest. The cluster of crimson roses decaying on the nightstand couldn't mask the unmistakable stench of death pervading the still bedchamber. He would have to remove Hetherington soon before the entire mansion stank of his corpse.

Fewer candles flickered now than in the middle of the night, but Hetherington's prone form was clearly visible. The thick scarlet curtains had been pulled back and tied with frayed golden ropes, allowing warm shafts of sunlight to fall upon the bed. Dust motes glittered in the stale air above the big bay windows, casting a sheen across the lumpy cushions and an unnatural glow across Hetherington's sunken cheeks.

No fire burned behind the cold grate, just as no blood pulsed beneath the dead man's waxy skin.

Gavin strode into the room, into the patch of shimmering dust. His back blocked the sun, blocked the light, sending his odd, elongated shadow scuttling across the untouched bed.

Miss Pemberton remained in the doorway, eyes tightly closed.

He couldn't blame her. As much as he'd despised the earl's company when Hetherington was still alive, spending the morning with his corpse was even less appealing.

The mottled handprints stretched around the earl's pale neck stood out bold and incriminatory against skin the color of snow and ash, announcing Gavin's infamous inability to control his temper. He stared at the marks his hands had bruised into the earl's skin. To tell the truth, Gavin hadn't *wanted* to control his cursed temper. He'd wanted to wring the earl's bloody neck.

And then he'd wanted Miss Pemberton—who showed

no signs of remembering their interplay. At least not with any nostalgia.

She stood in the doorway, dark lashes fanning against pale cheeks, arms clutched tightly beneath her bodice, curls springing from their pins as if they, too, would rather flee than enter.

The dead man's jaw hung open, as if he'd died while snoring. How *had* he died? He'd left Gavin's office with nothing more than a sore throat and a bruised ego. Well, and a scrape on his temple where the portrait had struck him. Was Gavin once again a killer, after all? Could that glancing blow have somehow caused Hetherington's death?

Gavin knelt beside the bed, allowing the insistent sun to shine above his head across the earl's lifeless face. A folded handkerchief tied snug around the motionless skull, blood crusting the linen above the earl's right ear. Gavin frowned. The earl's *right* ear? The gilded frame had struck the opposite side! Look. There. A patch of raw skin scratched across his left cheekbone where the painting had glanced off the earl's face.

Hetherington may well have died from a blow to the head, but it wasn't *Gavin's* blow. Someone else had struck him and left him to die. Someone else murdered him. Someone else had stood silent and allowed accusation and innuendo to surround Gavin once again.

He began to wish Miss Pemberton really could converse directly with God. Perhaps she could ask Him for a hint as to who had dealt the killing blow. Gavin glanced at the doorway.

Miss Pemberton was no longer there.

She was crossing the room with short, quick strides, her slippered feet silent against the square of plush carpet, her hands fisted beneath the flowing silk of her gown, her full lips pressed together in an expression of fierce determination.

"Move," she said. Then, "Please."

Gavin moved.

He rose to his feet, stepped backward to the bay window

and sat on the lumpy crimson cushion. He immediately leapt upright again.

"Wait."

She did not wait. She strode directly to the spot he had just vacated beside the bed. And began peeling off her left glove. Slowly, slowly, the delicate leather rolled down her arm and off her fingers, revealing pale skin covered in gooseflesh.

"Wait," he said again.

The sight unsettled him, although he was unsure why. He glimpsed her bare fingers every time they gathered to eat, so his unease did not stem from the soft whiteness of her hands. Perhaps his pulse skittered in fits and starts because of the still-visible gooseflesh rising on her skin, because of the trembling of her slender fingers, because of the pained resignation lining her eyes as though she faced something even worse than the sightless eyes of a dead man.

"What's wrong?" she said now, her palms paused a few inches above the earl's gaping mouth. "Besides coming here to touch a dead man."

"I—" *Hell.* Gavin stared at the back of Miss Pemberton's head for a long moment, unable to move toward her and unable to retake his seat. Her hands shook. "I forgot to summon the maids," he said at last, remembering why he had spoken. "I promised an army of servants, not none. Just allow me a moment to tug the bellpull, and we'll have—"

"I prefer to be alone."

Her words cut through the stillness, cut through his speech, cut through the thick air, cold and heavy with the scent of death.

"You . . . wish for me to leave?"

She glanced over her shoulder, meeting his gaze for the first time since reaching the guest quarters. "No," she said softly. "Stay."

"All right."

He stayed, but did not sit. For some reason, his muscles

warned him to remain tense, alert, at the ready in case some unknown danger lurked nearby.

Miss Pemberton nodded slowly. Her eyes were large, dry, weary. She turned back toward the man on the bed and squared her shoulders. "I doubt anything will happen, but if it does . . . if it does, you are the only one who can bring me back without making it worse."

Gavin frowned. He also doubted anything would happen, but . . . as before, something was off. Something in her tone, her manner, her words. She did not sound like a disciple about to commune with God. She sounded . . . anxious. Nervous. Frightened.

But if not of being alone with him, the supposed murderer, then what?

"Back from where?" he asked, recalling her odd choice in words. "Where are you going?"

"Nowhere. Here. I'll be right here."

Her answer was logical, but a strange tremor distorted the words. Gavin had the distinct impression she was lying, but that made no sense. Perhaps she, too, believed in a fickle, vengeful God. Perhaps she feared He *would* speak to her. Or that He would smite her for daring to summon him like a common beast, leaving her as cold and dead as the corpse before her.

Gavin was gripped by the sudden urge to stop Miss Pemberton from touching the earl's dead flesh. To protect her. To tackle her to the floor if need be, anything, *anything*, to keep her from laying her trembling fingers atop Hetherington's flaccid gray skin.

But the thought came too late.

Her palms flattened against the earl's pale cheeks. A quick inhalation whistled through her teeth. And then she froze.

For several long moments, Gavin watched her, unnerved by how still she held herself, how statue-like she posed. Her body was as lifeless and beautiful as an ivory sarcophagus molded in her image.

She stood so quiet and unmoving he might well have been in a room with two dead bodies. The unwelcome sensation of watching a pair of corpses had his muscles twitching in trepidation.

Gavin shifted his weight, uncomfortable in his own skin, even less comfortable with the motionless woman a few feet before him. Her fingers no longer shook, so frozen did she stand. He could not hear her breathing, even in the unnatural silence of the dank chamber. Her breasts no longer rose and fell. Even the folds of her gown held no ripples, no motion, as if they too were carved of stone and impervious to both breeze and life.

Feeling more nervous than foolish, he edged closer until her profile was a mere foot from his face. If she breathed, she did so silently. He heard nothing, smelled nothing, felt nothing. *His* breathing was rapid, erratic, overloud. She did not seem to notice. Her eyes were vacant. Glassy. Sightless. She didn't move. She didn't blink.

Gavin passed a hand before her face. She gazed right through it. At nothing. He tilted closer, until the scent of her soap clashed with the stench from the bed. She didn't move. She didn't blink. He leaned in until the tip of his nose brushed the icy skin of her forehead. She jerked.

He jumped.

"Hhh. Hhh. Hhh." Loud, frantic gasps choked from her throat. She sucked air into her lungs with shallow, wheezing breaths.

Her eyelids fluttered closed, then back open. The irises rolled back into her head. Palms still flush against Hetherington's pallid face, her arms trembled once before her entire body erupted into violent shaking.

Whether or not she wanted him interrupting, Gavin had seen enough.

He reached both arms around her hitching chest and

yanked her to him. Fingertips still grazing Hetherington's sunken cheeks, her body convulsed against Gavin's.

"Hhh. Hhh. Help. Hhh. Hhh. Help me." With a series of shallow, staccato gasps, Miss Pemberton's head jerked from side to side, clipping Gavin's chin. His jaw snapped closed with enough force to bring tears to his eyes, but he only gripped her tighter.

Her limbs twitched and flailed as she struggled for breath. The graceless jerking of her body reminded Gavin of the one and only time his father had taken him fishing. The fish—so beautiful and full of life before they'd hooked its lip and flung it from the water to the shore—had reacted in just such a way, gasping and convulsing on the dirt by Gavin's feet until the last of its life leeched from its bulging eyes.

He'd had nightmares for months.

Gavin flipped Miss Pemberton around until she faced him. Her fingers slipped from the corpse's face. He gripped her by the shoulders, ripping one of her sleeves in the process. She'd recover from that shock later. First, she had to breathe. A bluish cast tinged the whiteness of her skin. Phantom bruises cast a faint shadow about her neck. Terror widened her eyes, and no doubt his as well.

"Miss Pemberton! Miss Pemberton!" Not knowing what else to do, he shook her. She sagged in his arms as lifeless as a doll. Gooseflesh raced along his skin. "Breathe-breathe-breathe-breathe-breathe. *Please*. You're scaring the devil out of me." Again, he shook her. Again, her limbs flopped, offering no resistance and no response. "Breathe, damn it!"

He sucked in great lungfuls of air and pressed his open mouth to hers, forcing the breaths into her body. He was certain that was wrong, that shared breathing was only for victims of drowning, but he knew no other way to help her. For the first time in eleven years, Gavin prayed.

And as before, God ignored him.

Miss Pemberton's head twitched to one side. A drop of

blood trickled from her unbreathing nose. She fell against Gavin's chest with a thud.

"*Damn* it." He tossed frantic glances around the empty chamber. "Please, please, don't die on me, too."

Gavin scooped up her limp body and stared in horror at the gray pallor of her face. He stumbled over to the window seat. He fell onto the cushion and hauled her into his lap, his arms still locked around her motionless chest in a desperate embrace.

Her skirts fanned out across his legs. Her head lolled against his shoulder.

He pressed his ear to her lips, much as he had done that cold autumn night so many years ago, when his mother had been thrown from the pitching carriage before it tumbled off the embankment to the unforgiving river below. He'd reached his mother too late. He hadn't been able to reach his father at all.

Unlike the ghosts who haunted his nightmares, Miss Pemberton was not yet a corpse. Her breaths were faint, shallow, uneven. But at least she breathed.

"Miss Pemberton," Gavin whispered, his nose brushing against hers. "Miss Pemberton, wake up."

She did not.

He held her, hoping to warm her with his body, to share his very breath.

Her eyes flew open. They both stifled screams. Gavin jerked his head back with an odd, choking sort of laugh. She stared at him with panicked eyes.

"L—Lioncroft?" she managed, her voice raw and unsteady. Her pupils dilated, then contracted. Her breath came stronger. "I mean . . . Mr. Lioncroft," she corrected weakly, color returning to her pale cheeks.

"Mister, hell. After that, call me Gavin." He pulled her to him in a sudden, crushing hug. "Thank you, thank you, *thank* you for not dying. I don't know what I would've done."

His cravat muffled her reply, but he thought he heard her say, "Thank you for not allowing my death."

As if he'd had any control over whatever the hell had just happened.

Once he convinced his arms to loosen their grip on the trembling woman in his lap, Gavin leaned back against the window and fixed Miss Pemberton with his most dangerous glare.

"What," he demanded, "was *that?*"

Wariness reentered her eyes. "Nothing. Nothing."

"Don't insult me."

"I don't mean to. It's . . . complicated. I don't know what to tell you."

"Tell me everything." He fought the urge to shake her again. "For God's sake, woman, I thought you were going to die."

Rather than smile or call him melodramatic, she shivered in his arms.

"Me, too," she whispered.

The admission did nothing to calm his frayed nerves.

"Well?" he said, when Miss Pemberton showed no signs of explaining further.

"Well," she echoed softly. Her gaze slid toward the body on the bed. "He was definitely murdered. I don't know about the blow to his head, but someone . . . someone smothered Lord Hetherington. With a pillow." Her gaze snapped back to Gavin, her eyes round and huge. "He couldn't breathe."

Her breath hitched again, as if in remembrance. Her limbs twitched. Gavin pulled her closer, so that he leaned against the cold glass of the windowpane and she nestled atop the wrinkled linen of his shirt and the crumpled pillow of his cravat.

Was she insane? Was *he* insane for half-believing her?

Half-believing her, hell. After what he had witnessed, he absolutely believed her. He remained unconvinced God whispered the secret into her ear, but no skill at playacting could slow her heart to a standstill, render her lungs incapable of motion, and leech the pallor of death into her cold skin.

Whatever had just happened with Miss Pemberton, he believed Hetherington had been asphyxiated. Gavin cast his own fleeting glance toward the bed. So much for his hopes of death by natural causes. Someone suffocated the sanctimonious bastard with his own pillow. Not a crime in Gavin's book, except for one thing.

Gavin was still the primary suspect.

Chapter Ten

Miss Pemberton's breathing had calmed, her limbs were now warm and steady. Her gaze still fixed on his. She seemed to be awaiting a response.

"All I know," Gavin said at last, "is that you didn't get that news from God."

She shoved his arms, knocking them from their loose hug.

"But I believe you," he said softly.

She paused in the act of rising from his lap. The tight muscles of her bottom still perched on his thigh, as though she were one heartbeat from taking flight. She turned, slowly, her parted lips mere inches from his. "You do?"

"I do."

Before he could say more, a gasp and a chuckle clashed in the corridor. Dread encasing his stomach, he dragged his gaze to the doorway at the source of the noise.

The gasp came from his sister, the chuckle from Edmund.

"Guess the Stanton chit was right, eh, Lioncroft?" Edmund wiggled thick eyebrows. "Reckon we should've sent up a chaperone after all. What happened to the army of maidservants? They defect?"

With a strangled cry, Miss Pemberton leapt from Gavin's lap and staggered forward. She glared at him over her shoulder as she found herself trapped between two pairs of curious eyes, a murder victim, and the suspected killer lounging across the window seat.

"Don't be a bore, Edmund." Lioncroft infused his voice with as much disinterest as he could affect. "As any young lady might do faced with mortality, Miss Pemberton merely fainted. I couldn't very well lay her next to him until she recovered, so I made do with the window seat."

Edmund snorted, retrieved a silver flask from his pocket, and saluted Gavin with it.

Rose shook her head. "Miss Pemberton, I'm not sure you realize how uncomplimentary . . ." She swallowed and pierced Gavin with her gaze. "I just came to see . . . to see that he was still dead. That I hadn't imagined it."

Edmund smirked. "And instead, we came across you. God impart any good gossip before you wound up in Lioncroft's lap, Miss Pemberton?"

"Edmund!" Rose snapped, her face draining of color. "Enough."

She pushed past him, striding forward until she reached the foot of the bed.

Miss Pemberton closed her eyes. She breathed slowly, deeply, as if to do so required every bit of her concentration. When her eyes reopened, she focused them on Edmund.

"Yes," she answered, one hand on the mattress as if for balance. "He did."

Edmund choked on a mouthful of whiskey. From the shocked expression on his face, Gavin half-expected him to expire of apoplexy.

"What?" Edmund staggered against the doorframe. "What did He say? I mean, what did God say?"

Miss Pemberton trembled slightly, as if her limbs were not quite ready to hold her upright again.

Gavin rose from the window seat. "Leave her alone."

Edmund tipped back his flask with a shrug. Miss Pemberton glanced at the bed, winced, swayed. Gavin leapt forward.

Rose reached out one hand to steady her. "Ignore Edmund. He's a drunk and a fool. You look—"

But the moment Rose's bare fingertips brushed against Miss Pemberton's still ungloved wrist, Miss Pemberton dropped to the floor in a dead faint.

Evangeline awoke in her windowless bedchamber with the worst headache of her life.

A low fire crackled in the hearth, filling the room with flickering light and the faint stench of burning logs.

Anything but the scent of death.

Never again. So help her, she'd never step near that cursed chamber again. Let Lady Stanton do her worst. Evangeline far preferred the poverty of life on the street to death by the fickle hand of her dark Gift. Was that why Mama made her swear to always use her talent to help those in need? Because the possessor of the Gift was doomed to a short life of violence, loneliness, and betrayal?

Not for the first time, Evangeline wished she were a typical girl from a typical family. Even if her family were atypical, they'd at least be atypical in a typical way.

Like Susan, whose mother was determined to matchmake her to the first available bachelor. Susan, whose dearest desire was to escape her mother. Susan, who . . . was seated before Evangeline's fire, flipping the pages of a small book.

Evangeline no longer questioned Susan's presence in her room, but she couldn't help but wonder how Susan had managed to pry a real book from the false shelves.

"What are you reading?" Evangeline croaked. She grimaced, swallowed, tried again. "What are you reading?"

The book tumbled from Susan's fingers. "You're awake! Oh. This?" Susan's head dipped as she bent to retrieve the fallen book. "*De Re Metallica*, a hideously boring treatise on the history of metallurgy in the sixteenth century. You would know better than me. Lioncroft says you dropped it by accident." Susan made a face. "I'd drop it, too. Into the nearest river."

Evangeline bit back a laugh. The "novel" she'd filched from the library was a treatise on metallurgy? Mr. Lioncroft was no doubt as confused by her selection as Susan was, although it was kind of him to bring it by.

Kind. Kindness wasn't a quality she suspected the average murderer to possess. Nor was empathy or thoughtfulness. Although, from the first, Mr. Lioncroft had been anything but average. She would've died right along with the earl had he not been there to save her. He'd offered comfort. Ordered her to breathe. Bade her speak his name.

Gavin.

Evangeline shivered. She could not. She would not. Not even in her mind. Kindness did not outweigh violence. Although . . . his kindness did give her pause. Her stepfather—another murderer—was not a kind man. He terrorized her and her mother, just like he terrorized the simple folk in her hometown, just like he terrorized the poor creatures slaving for him in his Spital Fields factories.

Gavin—Mr. Lioncroft, rather—did not seem to thrive on terrorizing others. He seemed to expect others to be terrified on their own. And used his reputation to his benefit. But did he seek to act upon the fear of others by striking out with vicious cruelty against innocents? No.

Lord Hetherington was hardly an innocent. Evangeline would never say anyone *deserved* to die, but hadn't she herself hoped Mr. Lioncroft would teach him a lesson about fear and revenge?

Of course, she hadn't expected murder.

Susan yanked back a curtain and loomed over the side of the bed. "Ew. You look all pale and clammy. Are those bruises on your neck? Lionkiller didn't try and strangle you, too, did he?"

Evangeline struggled to sit up, failed, and sank back down. "How long have you been here?"

"Ever since Lionkiller brought you in."

"And when was that?"

"I don't know. Perhaps an hour ago? Time flies when reading sixteenth century treatises on metal extraction techniques. Truly, Evangeline. A novel would've been better."

"Thank you for the suggestion."

Susan settled on the edge of the bed and met Evangeline's eyes. "Will you please tell me what happened?"

What *had* happened?

Evangeline had been in some kind of trance, reliving the final, panic-stricken moments of Lord Hetherington's abbreviated life. The next thing she knew, she was tucked in Gavin Lioncroft's strong arms. Warm. Safe. Protected. Evangeline frowned at the realization. In her entire life, her mother had been the only other person who had attempted to protect her. And in the end, she'd died. At the hands of a violent brute. In this case, Mr. Lioncroft *was* the violent brute—and also the protector.

At the very least, the man was an enigma Evangeline had no clue how to solve.

"I don't know," she said aloud, unsure whether she was addressing Susan's spoken query or her own unvoiced questions.

"What do you mean, you don't know? You were there! Did you learn whether Hetherington died peacefully or not?"

Evangeline nodded reluctantly.

"Well? Did he kick off in his slumber? Or was something more sinister afoot?"

"Something more sinister, I'm afraid."

"Aaahh! I insist you divulge every detail. What happened? Who killed him?"

Evangeline sorely wished she could tell her about her vision and how badly the experience shook her. For years, she'd ached for a friend, someone she could discuss her Gift with, someone who could be trusted. But Mama said the *ton* could never be trusted. Susan was nice, but also *ton*. And Susan's mother, the very woman Mama had entrusted to keep her daughter and her secret, had been willing to inform a houseful of strangers of Evangeline's visions over the breakfast table. Mama was right. The *ton* was not to be trusted.

So Evangeline just shrugged, and winced as the motion pulled at her sore shoulders.

"What?" Susan cried. "How don't you know? You should know everything. And then you should tell *me!*"

If only life were that simple. Just the very thought—the sensation of laying atop her mattress, just as Lord Hetherington had lain across his mattress—the soft cushion of the feathers beneath her head just like the pillow beneath the earl's, just like the pillow that covered his face, stealing his breath, stealing the air, stealing his life—

"Evangeline! Evangeline! Are you all right? You're scaring—"

The moment Susan's warm knuckles pressed against Evangeline's forehead, the bedchamber disappeared. Instead, a wide flat plain rolled out before her, a never-ending field filled with row after row of wilting plants. A strange, dead farm Evangeline had never seen.

Susan races down one of the soil paths, sweating, panting, skirt hiked up to her shins so she could run even faster.

"Evangeline!" she yells. "Evangeline! Come back! He's out there! He'll kill you!"

Susan clutches at her side with one hand. The scrawny bushes scratch at her skirts.

"Evangeline," she pants. "No. Wait. Come back."

Up ahead, the neat rows of scraggy bushes ends. A pair of scarred brown horses chew at the closest plants. Stiff leather tethers the beasts to a small black carriage with dirty windows. An all-too-familiar driver perches aloft, holding the reins.

Her stepfather's driver.
The vile blackguard bursts from an adjacent path. A
kicking and biting version of herself flails in his arms,
trying desperately to escape.
As always, he silences her with his fist . . . and laughs.

Susan lifted her fingers from Evangeline's forehead.
"Good Lord. You look worse now than when you arrived."

Evangeline *felt* worse than when she'd arrived. Worse,
even, than when she'd arrived at Stanton House just three
days before. Then she'd believed she had a chance of evading
her stepfather until her twenty-first birthday. Now she knew
her efforts would be futile. Wherever Susan was in the vision,
so would Evangeline be—and Neal Pemberton right behind
her. But where were they? And *when* were they? How much
time did Evangeline have before her stepfather found her? A
year? A month? A week?

Now more than ever, she yearned for a friend.

Which might be why, instead of saying nothing, Evangeline said, "Don't touch me." At Susan's stricken expression,
Evangeline added, "It's better if you don't. I-I get visions
when people touch me. And headaches. Awful ones."

Evangeline expected Susan to laugh off the assertion, or at
least to ask if Evangeline had just received a vision from their
brief touch, or whether she'd gotten a vision from Lord Hetherington's cold flesh.

Instead, Susan's forehead creased. "I was just feeling for
fever. How else can you feel for fever? Has no one ever
touched you? How can you live without being touched?"

"My mother touched me. She felt for my fevers."

"But she's dead. Who will feel for your fevers now?"

Pain gripped Evangeline's heart. "Nobody."

"What about children?"

"I won't have any."

"No, I mean other children, when you were a child. However did you play Fox and Hounds or Sardines or even learn to sew without touching anybody?"

"I never did any of those things."

"You cannot *sew?*" Susan clapped her hands to her chest. "You are so *lucky*. If I never see another sampler as long as I live . . . but then, I don't have visions to contend with, and I can touch anyone I please. Although, to be honest, I doubt I'd touch many corpses if it were left up to me. Did it not work?"

"It worked," Evangeline admitted. "But I didn't see who did it."

"Lioncroft, of course. No question. How did Hetherington die?"

"Smothered with a pillow."

"A *what?*" Susan stared at her, mouth agape. "Well. I admit, that hardly sounds like Lioncroft's style. He seems much more forward with his aggression. For example, had you said he strangled Hetherington to death, I wouldn't have blinked an eye. Likewise, had you told me Lioncroft bashed in his head with a large rock. Rocks can be vulgar and deadly. But a *pillow,* of all things. No . . . I wouldn't have guessed that."

"What are you saying? You think him innocent?"

"Well," Susan said again. "Well. I guess I'm saying, now I don't *know*. He's probably the villain, but—a pillow?"

For some reason, this small concession made Evangeline more unsettled, rather than less. The situation seemed so much more straightforward when everyone was convinced of Mr. Lioncroft's guilt. Doubt . . . doubt made things murky.

Evangeline tried never to doubt.

"A pillow seems cowardly," Susan was saying now. "Lioncroft may be many evil things, but he doesn't strike me as cowardly. He seems the type to hurl Hetherington from the closest balcony window or impale him on a rapier, not the sort to sneak in on him when he's sleeping and smother him with a pillow. Perhaps even Lady Hetherington's pillow. She might've *lain* on it, not even knowing. How positively dreadful!"

Susan clapped a hand to her throat as if she couldn't wait to share this possibility with the lady in question. Evangeline would just as soon spend the rest of the house party sequestered in her room. She had far worse to worry about— Neal Pemberton's relentless pursuit. She'd never heard of anyone outwitting an event foretold in a vision, but heaven help her, Evangeline hoped to do the impossible.

"May I ask a favor, Susan? Two of them, actually?"

"Of course."

"First, I must beg you not to mention my visions to anyone. Speaking to God may not be any more believable, but at least people rarely make waves against things having to do with the Church."

"As long as you'll keep me informed of whatever visions you experience," Susan said with a laugh. "Truly, you have my word." She drew a cross over her bodice with one finger. "And the other thing?"

"If you—If I—" Evangeline paused, unsure how to phrase her request. "Should you catch even the smallest whisper of my stepfather's presence, would you warn me immediately?"

"Where? Here? He's invited to Blackberry Manor?"

"No, not here. Perhaps we'll be on a farm, but I'm not sure where or when. Just if you *would* catch wind of my stepfather, please alert me as soon as possible. His name is Neal Pemberton. Stay as far away from him as you can. He's dangerous."

"All right." Confusion ebbed the good humor from Susan's face. "I think you may still be overtaxed. Try to sleep some more. I'll check on you again before lunch."

She reached out to pat Evangeline's arm, checked herself midair, and returned her hand to her side with an embarrassed smile.

"Forgive me," she murmured. "I'm far more used to touching than I realized."

Without waiting for a response, she pivoted on one heel and strode from the bedside. She dropped the small leather-bound book atop the bookcase before slipping out the door, closing it firmly behind her.

Save for the crackling of the fire, silence filled the chamber. And yet, Evangeline knew she would not sleep. Had no wish to sleep. Only nightmares awaited her there.

She rose from the bed and crossed to the row of bookshelves lining the large, windowless wall. As before, she tugged on the books overflowing the top shelf. As before, they did not budge. She moved to the next shelf and pulled at one of the books. It flew into her hands, almost knocking her off balance.

What in heaven's name . . . ?

Evangeline hunched before each of the bookstands, jerking titles at random from each shelf.

Volumes fell into her fingers from every shelf—save one.

She returned to that first shelf, crouching until she was eye level. The books *looked* real enough. Perhaps they were just stuck?

Her fingertips ran across the dusty spines, gliding up to where the binding met the pages, letting the uneven paper rub against her skin. With as much force as she could muster, she yanked at the biggest book on the top shelf.

It did not budge. Not only did it not budge, the effort threw Evangeline off-kilter, rocking her back on her heels. Arms flailing like windmills, she pitched forward in a frantic attempt to regain her balance. She fell hard against the bookcase, crashing her shoulder against the immobile top shelf. The entire bookcase swung inward. Inward—into the *wall*.

And Evangeline tumbled with it.

After a helpless sneezing fit, she picked herself up, smacked the dust from her gown, and stared in wonder.

No wonder her room had no windows.

The secret passageway—for, of course, it was that—hid all the windows. Small circles of glass dotted the wall above her head, much like the portholes of a passenger ship. Evangeline wished she were tall enough to peer through them, to see what lay behind the mansion. Undoubtedly, the windows had been positioned to prevent just such an action, so that whoever lurked between the walls could skulk about undetected.

Had she truly begun to doubt Mr. Lioncroft's guilt? Of course, he was a murderer. What other kind of man dwelled in a mausoleum like Blackberry Manor, creeping about betwixt the walls? Had he—had he spied on her? In her bed? As she slept?

Gooseflesh rippled up her arms. As she hugged herself, her hip bumped against the open bookcase.

And the concealed door swung closed.

The thick walls swallowed Evangeline's cry as she flattened her palms against the dirt and cobwebs, scrabbling her fingernails for purchase. Nothing. How could there be nothing? The door swung inward, so certainly there must be a knob, a handle, some mechanism by which to reopen access to her chamber. Still nothing. She banged with her fists, screaming for someone to help her.

No one came.

She scratched at the cracks until her fingers bled before finally admitting defeat. This was even worse than being locked in the cursed pantry. She sagged against the wall, her back to the unyielding surface, her face tilted toward those tiny round windows high above her head.

Even if she could leap high enough to reach the glass, the circular frames were much too narrow to climb through. Trapped in the walls. Oh, God. Oh, God. She hated closed spaces. She hated dark, closed spaces. And she hated being *trapped* in dark, closed spaces the most. No solution presented itself but to continue on the passageway and hope to find an exit.

With a tiny, distressed moan, she inched down the dusty corridor. How did Mr. Lioncroft fit inside the narrow passage without his shoulders scraping against the sides? Evangeline had to be careful not to keep grating her knuckles against the rough walls. She would've put her gloves back on if she'd known she was about to tumble through a bookcase. In fact, she would've fled the manor altogether.

After walking no more than five minutes, the path diverged. She could either continue straight, following the feeble light cast by the small windows overhead, or she could turn right and venture into darkness.

Evangeline chewed her lip, then grimaced when her skin tasted like dust. She assumed straight led further along the guest wing. As hers was one of the last occupied chambers, she doubted much help lay in that direction. So darkness it would be.

She squared her shoulders and strode into the shadows.

Evangeline hadn't gone more than a dozen paces into the dark, musty corridor before running into the first cobweb. By the time she'd clawed sticky strands from her cheeks for the third or fourth time, the idea of a secret passageway had gone from distressing to hellish.

The only silver lining to the pure blackness was her inability to tell whether any spiders still lived on the webs. She squinted into the shadows, not to see better, for the blackness was too thick and perfect to see through, but to keep the gummy fibers from her eyes.

Dust clogged her nostrils with each footstep. The dank passage narrowed, at times causing her to twist her arms before her stomach or edge sideways with her heels to one wall and her toes touching the other, pressing in on her the further she went, like the unforgiving walls of a casket.

Briefly, she considered turning around, but for what? There was nothing to return to but more dust and shadow and spiders. Her fingers still ached from scratching at the swinging door.

Inside the walls . . . walls which grew taller, thicker, closer. They loomed overhead, mocking her, squeezing her.

She drew a shaky breath. One would think years of her stepfather locking her into cramped, dark places would lessen the impact of such an environment, not fill her with instant terror. The vile pantry he preferred to keep her in was almost large enough to lay prone upon the floor, arms outstretched. Here in the walls, she barely fit upright and wouldn't dare to lie upon the floor. At home, enough feeble light flickered around the edges of the pantry door to illuminate the shelves, the jars, the occasional rat. Nothing but blackness filled the sliver of space between the walls of Blackberry Manor. Blackness and cobwebs and spiders.

Her fluttering heart was edging closer and closer to panic.

Hot tears stung at Evangeline's eyes when she found herself at a crossroads. Which way should she go? She was lost. Trapped. Helpless.

She stood in the center of the intersection, reaching blindly with both hands. The opening straight ahead was as tight and narrow as the one she had just escaped. She refused to select that path. The passages to her left and right were wide enough to let her stand with her hands on her hips without fear of her elbows scraping against the rough walls.

Think, she commanded herself over the roaring in her ears. *Right or left?*

Eyes squeezed tight against the oppressive blackness, she did her best to picture the guest quarters in her mind. Behind her was her own room, an impossible distance away. To her left lay the furthest bedchambers, empty of guests. Before her was another passage too narrow to risk entering. To her right must be the other guest hall, leading to the Hetheringtons' and Rutherfords' chambers—and possibly a murderer.

Evangeline turned right.

This passageway was not only wider than the previous one, it seemed friendlier. Less dusty. Less dank. No cobwebs. Although she was grateful for that small favor, something was amiss. What could make one secret passageway cleaner than another, but recent use? Had Mr. Lioncroft slipped into Lord Hetherington's chamber through a false bookcase in order to smother the earl as he slept?

Light. She gasped, and choked on the musty air.

Pale, flickering orange glowed through four skinny cracks, forming a perfect rectangle against the wall up ahead. Evangeline sprinted forward. She hurled herself at the dark expanse in the center. The door flew outward, flinging Evangeline with it. She tumbled to the ground in a jumble of bruised elbows and knees. The door swung closed as she rolled to a stop. She untangled herself and stood, facing the spot where she'd emerged. A large oil painting stared back at her. She tugged on the gilded frame. It creaked and eased forward, awarding her with a glimpse of the darkness beyond. She jumped backward. The painting clicked into place. The painting . . . seemed vaguely familiar. Oils on canvas hung along the entire corridor, just like they did . . . where?

Evangeline cocked her head. Voices. Female voices. Young female voices. She was near the nursery!

She swiped her forearm across her face and grimaced when her arm came away smeared with dust. No way to tell whether the dirt had come from her face or if she'd just managed to transfer it *to* her face.

A glance at her gown revealed the borrowed dress to be in no better condition. Smudges and tears marred the flowing silk, as if she'd spent the morning tumbling down hills and gullies. A stray spider web clung to her slipper. When she tried to rub off the strands with her other shoe, she merely succeeded in spreading the sparkling cobweb to both feet.

Splendid.

She was in no condition to drop in unannounced on Lady Hetherington's children. Nonetheless, the music of voices sounded impossibly dear, and she found herself creeping down the hall to listen outside the closed door.

"Gimme!" came a small voice.

"Mine!" came another.

"*Girls!*" That one belonged to Nancy Hetherington. "Shhh. This is important."

"I don't see why," came a bored voice. Jane, the middle child. "Nobody talks to us anyway."

"But if they do," Nancy insisted, "you are to say that Mother and I both were in the nursery with you all night."

"Why do I have to be in the nursery at all? I'll be thirteen in two days. When will I be old enough to—"

"My dolly!"

"Jane! Jane! Rebecca won't—"

An ear-piercing shriek interrupted any further conversation.

Evangeline stepped away from the door when the shrieking continued unabated. Definitely not the best moment to visit.

She turned back to the false painting, shuddering at the knowledge of what lay beyond the canvas. Except the painting wasn't false, was it? It was well-crafted and beautifully done, making it as perfect a disguise as her bookcase had been.

Under no circumstances was she interested in revisiting the hidden passageway beyond. Instead, she faced the sconce-lit corridor and hurried away before Nancy Hetherington fled the cacophonous nursery and caught her in the hallway. A moment later, Evangeline froze before an open doorway.

Lord Hetherington's bedchamber.

She had no wish to revisit it, no wish to peer inside, but somehow her eyes disobeyed her brain and she found herself gazing upon the bed where the earl had died.

Empty.

He was gone. The body was gone. The bed was freshly made. Somebody had been cleaning. The room smelled of lemons and vinegar instead of panic and death.

Despite herself, Evangeline stepped forward into the chamber. A bonneted maid crouched along one wall, straightening the earl's collection of fancy swordsticks. She glanced over her shoulder as if sensing the presence in the doorway. Evangeline gasped.

Ginny. With her face covered in bruises.

Evangeline rushed forward. "What happened?"

Ginny blinked, touched her face, and struggled to her feet. "M'master happened, mum. 'Twas the handkerchief."

Mr. Lioncroft had beaten a maid over a lost handkerchief? He was truly a beast. She'd been right not to trust him.

"Oh, no." Evangeline bit at her lower lip. "I thought you found it before he discovered it was missing?"

"That I did, mum. But not before m'mistress come upon it."

"Your . . . what?"

"Mistress. The lady of the house."

"There's a lady of the house?" Heat rushed to Evangeline's cheeks. Of all the arrogant, dastardly things for him to do, Mr. Lioncroft had kissed her while his *mistress* slept beneath the same roof?

"Yes'm. Although I don't guess she still is, now that he's dead."

"Now that he's . . . what?"

"Dead. Weren't you just in here this morning to lay your hands upon his corpse?"

"I—I—what?" Evangeline stared at her as the realization set in. "You work for the Hetheringtons?"

"Yes'm. That I do."

Evangeline closed her eyes. No wonder the footman claimed no Ginny worked with them. No Ginny *did* work with them. Not only that . . .

"Lord Hetherington hit you?"

Ginny nodded. "Better me than m'mistress, although he gave her a good one, too. If you don't mind me saying so, you don't look so fine yourself, covered in dust as you are. Haven't you got a maid to do the cleaning?"

"I—yes, I suppose so. Why aren't Mr. Lioncroft's servants doing the cleaning in here?"

"They did. Everything except for my master's swordsticks, that is. He was always real particular about them things. Cost a pretty penny, I suppose. Hope m'mistress sells every last one."

"Me, too," Evangeline agreed, still reeling from the combined shock of Ginny's battered face and the knowledge Lord Hetherington, not Mr. Lioncroft, put the bruises there. "I . . . I apologize for not helping you sooner. Maybe I could've saved you both."

"How could you help sooner when I hadn't met you sooner?" Ginny pointed out reasonably. "Besides, if he hadn't beat me for that, it would've been for something else. Probably for looking at him wrong, or letting one of his swordsticks get dirty. Some men are like that."

Evangeline couldn't help but nod. Most men were like that. Maybe *all* men.

Ginny resumed cleaning. Evangeline hurried back into the hallway. She needed to get back to her room—and changed—before anyone else saw her.

Unfortunately, she was not so lucky.

No sooner had she rounded the next corner when Edmund Rutherford swaggered out of an adjoining room, a tumbler of whiskey clutched in one hand.

"Well, well." He blinked at her, then grinned. "Why, it's Miss Pemberton. For a moment there, I thought I'd discovered a new maid I hadn't yet tried."

Evangeline bit back a grimace. All men *were* like her stepfather. Edmund Rutherford was a shining example.

"Why the long face, darling? I'll try you, too, if that's what you want. I've never minded a bit of dirt before." He lumbered closer. The alcohol from his breath burned Evangeline's nostrils.

"No, thank you." She ducked under the arm holding the whiskey and headed down the hallway.

His free hand grabbed for her, ripping a bit of the lace from her back. "What's the hurry, Miss Pemberton? You've got nowhere to be. Everybody thinks you're asleep in your chamber." He leered at her. "I'll be glad to give you something better to do with your time."

"If you touch me," she ground out, "I'll scream."

"Kind of like you did when Lioncroft pulled you into his lap? Oh, wait. You weren't screaming then. I doubt you'll scream for me, either. Except in pleasure."

"You're disgusting."

"Some women like it that way." He winked, tipped back the rest of his whiskey, and stumbled to stay upright.

Evangeline took advantage of his momentary imbalance, and took off down the corridor at a dead run.

Within seconds, Edmund lumbered right behind her.

"I love a chase," he called out drunkenly. "Makes the capture so much sweeter."

She ran faster.

Up ahead, a door creaked open. A familiar cane poked through, followed by a yawning Mr. Teasdale. "What's the meaning of this ruckus? Good Lord, Miss Pemberton. You look like a dust rag."

Evangeline slowed, then flew forward when Edmund crashed directly into her. His empty tumbler shattered against the wall.

"Rutherford, what is the matter with you?" Mr. Teasdale held out a trembling hand toward Evangeline. "May I help you up?"

She shook her head and scrambled to her feet before Edmund could grab her.

"Nothing's the matter with me," he said from the hallway floor. He met Evangeline's glare with laughing eyes. "Miss Pemberton and I were just having a friendly chat, that's all."

Mr. Teasdale harrumphed. "About what?"

Evangeline crossed her arms and raised an eyebrow at Edmund.

He grinned. "About her tête-à-tête with God, of course. She

was just saying how she can't wait to tell us all about it . . .
once she has a nice hot bath, with lots of sweet-smelling soap
all over her wet—"

"Rutherford, really." Mr. Teasdale shook his cane at Edmund
before turning to Evangeline. "Will you be joining us for lunch,
Miss Pemberton? You can recount your story to us all at once."

She glanced at Edmund out of the corner of her eye. He was
on his feet now, and swaggering closer.

"I may take a tray in my room," she answered. Forever, if that
meant she could avoid men like Edmund Rutherford.

"Very well, child. You can join us after lunch, since we certainly won't be bothering you in your chamber."

"I will." Edmund's eyebrows wiggled. "If she says please."

She glared at him. "Over my dead body."

The cocky smile vanished from his face.

"In this house, Miss Pemberton, you'd better mind what you
wish for."

Chapter Eleven

When Evangeline finally reached her section of the guest quarters, a dark figure lounged against the wall outside her door, thumbs hooked in his waistband, eyes closed as if asleep. She tried to slip in her room without catching his notice, but the creak of a loose floorboard betrayed her.

His eyelashes lifted. "Miss Pemberton. How do you feel?"

"Much improved, Mr. Lioncroft. Thank you for asking."

"I meant it when I said you could call me Gavin."

"I'd rather not." She stepped past him, ducked her head, and reached for the doorknob.

"Did you forget something?"

Her fingers clutching the cold brass of the doorknob, she glanced at him over her shoulder. He hadn't moved. He hadn't changed. He still stared at her with the most intense gaze she'd ever encountered, his posture tense but casual, the soft tumble of his hair carelessly rakish, the familiar lines of his warm mouth—no. She wasn't forgetting anything. She only wished she could.

"No," she said at last. "I plan to stay in my chamber for a while."

"You plan to—" As his eyes finally quit their focus on hers long enough to take in her tangled hair, her tattered dress, her ruined fingernails, his words simply stopped. He blinked once, twice, again. And then, "What happened?"

What could she say? *Oh, I've been skulking between the walls, just like you?*

"Nothing."

"Nothing? Look at you. Where the hell have you been?"

"Your favorite place, no doubt."

"What's that supposed to mean?"

"It means, go away. I'm not in the best temper, and I don't want conversation. I want a bath."

"I'll call for one." He strode forward, intent on entering her bedchamber.

"You stay right there! I can operate a bellpull myself."

Mr. Lioncroft paused. He leaned back against the wall, his demeanor not quite as relaxed as before. "All right."

Evangeline's hand fell from the doorknob. "What are you doing?"

"Staying here."

"I said go away!"

"You also said to stay right here," he pointed out reasonably. "I chose to follow the latter directive."

"I meant 'go away' both times." She glared at him. He didn't move. "Why were you lurking in the shadows?"

He lifted a shoulder. "I wanted to make sure you were all right. You frightened me."

"Well, you can't just—Oh. That's very kind of you. I frightened me, too. But I'm fine now, so you can—"

"You don't look fine. You look . . . dirty."

"Why, thank you, Mr. Lioncroft. That's why I'm calling for a bath."

"And call me Gavin." When she made no effort to do so, he just grinned. "Are you going back to bed?"

"Not if you plan to sneak in and smother me."

Evangeline regretted the snappish words the moment they flew from her lips.

Mr. Lioncroft, however, seemed neither stung nor perturbed by her waspishness. Because he was guilty? Or because he was simply accustomed to being presumed as much, and expected no preferential treatment from her?

She opened her mouth—to say what, exactly, she didn't know—but in one smooth step, he stood between her and the safety of her bedchamber.

"I'm here because I was worried about you, Miss Pemberton. And because I'm attracted to you."

"I—" The protest caught in her throat as his dark gaze burned into hers.

"As to your imminent death . . . Did you see me smother anyone?"

She backed up a step. "I wasn't there."

"Did God tell you I smothered Hetherington before He sent you that attack?"

"Don't be ridiculous. The Lord didn't send me an attack."

"What did happen, Miss Pemberton?" He studied her face as if he'd spent the better part of two hours trying to solve that particular riddle.

"Nothing happened. Much." She glanced down both sides of the deserted corridor. "I truly don't wish to talk about this."

"No? Or not out here? I'll gladly follow you into your chamber."

Evangeline swallowed. At this rate, she'd be the one compromised with Mr. Lioncroft, not Susan. And the last thing she needed was to be the legal property of yet another murderer. "You'll do no such thing."

He smiled, leaned forward, brushed his fingertips down the curve of her cheek, along her neck, to the hollow of her throat. He lifted his fingers away just before they could slide across the lace of her bodice. Gooseflesh raced down her spine and along the bare flesh of her arms.

"Why not?" he asked softly. "You don't trust yourself alone with me?"

"I don't trust *you*."

"Why not?"

"You know why."

"Tell me anyway."

He wanted the truth? Fine. She'd give him the truth. "Because you're a known murderer," she said through gritted teeth. "Lord Hetherington's death was no mysterious accident—he was clearly murdered. And none of us will be safe while the crime goes unpunished."

Heavens above. Had she just blurted out all that to the killer? Mr. Lioncroft crossed his arms over his chest, but his gaze never fell from hers.

"Hmmm." He slanted her a considering glance. "If you're convinced of my guilt, why explain your reasoning to me instead of screaming for help?"

"Because I—well, because—I don't know." She stared at him for a moment, speechless. "I guess that's not very logical of me."

"On the contrary. Thus far, you've proven yourself the most logical of all my uninvited guests. Unfortunately for me, I happen to be the most logical suspect."

"Fortunately for you, nobody summoned the constabulary."

"Ahhh." He smiled. "Perfect. Use your logic, Miss Pemberton. What does that mean?"

"You're a blackguard with devilish powers of persuasion?"

"I like to think so, yes. Nonetheless, would I have been able to shoo away the constabulary had an angry mob arrived to string my neck from a gibbet?"

She stared at him for a moment, at the seriousness of his expression, the furrow in his brow, the white slash of his scar against the stubble of his jaw. Would he be able to escape punishment by fleeing through his labyrinthine mansion? If he used the secret passageways, perhaps. For a time. But would he ever be truly free?

"No," she answered grudgingly. "I suppose not."

"Then why aren't they here? If everyone present was as

convinced of my guilt as you are, surely by now one of them would have put ink to paper and demanded my capture."

Evangeline had no response. She stormed forward, intending to shoulder past him by force if necessary. When he stepped aside to let her pass, she half-stumbled, half-fell into her chamber. She turned, positive his expression would be smug, his wide lips curved, his eyes mocking her.

But he was gone, leaving only his subtle masculine scent behind.

During her bath, Mr. Lioncroft's words echoed in her mind. Later, as her lady's maid attempted—and failed—to fashion a chignon from Evangeline's heavy curls, his words kept repeating themselves to her. By the time Susan Stanton burst through the connecting doorway, Evangeline was dressed, somewhat coiffed, and sick unto death of her mind replaying Mr. Lioncroft's parting words.

He had a point.

She couldn't fathom why most of the guests seemed equally averse to constabulary intervention. She was right to label him a blackguard with devilish powers of persuasion. He almost had her considering the notion he—but, no. He was no doubt the villain. Because if he wasn't . . . who was?

"You look better," Susan observed from her position in the sole chair, "but still deathly pale. Are you certain you're feeling quite the thing? Have you eaten anything?"

"Yes," Evangeline said, choosing only to respond to the latter. "Molly brought me some bread and fruit."

"Who's Molly?"

"My lady's maid. That is, my borrowed lady's maid."

"You talk to Lionkiller's servants? Maybe that's why you're so pale. You were supposed to be sleeping, not talking. Couldn't you sleep?"

"I—no." Evangeline frowned at Susan, who was too busy warming her feet by the fire to notice. Of course, Evangeline talked to the servants. She understood them. They tended to be more straightforward, friendlier, *safer* than Polite Society aristocrats. She didn't expect Susan to feel the same. They came from different worlds. "Where are the others now?" she asked. "Dining?"

"No, they're in the Green Salon. Well, those who remotely believe in the possibility of you chatting with God are."

Evangeline glanced around her crimson chamber. "There's a Green Salon?"

"Don't look so hopeful. Not green like dandelion leaves and lime ices and grass in the springtime. Green like decaying moss moldering atop a tombstone. Gray is the only other color. Well, and brown. Made me long for scab-colored furniture again. Lionkiller is in dire need of a bride. And a shopping excursion."

"Who is in the Green Salon? Your mother?"

"Of course." Susan selected a poker from next to the fireplace. "She's not going anywhere until the matter is solved, one way or the other."

"I don't understand why she doesn't want to escape while we're all still alive. Does she think him innocent?"

"Lioncroft? Lawk, no. But he got away with murder last time, didn't he? History may repeat itself. In which case, he remains rich and eligible, and with his neck intact."

"You'd marry a murderer?"

"I was already planning to do so," Susan pointed out, nudging the fire with the poker. "If he escapes the noose again, nothing of substance will have changed."

Not true. Plenty had changed.

Evangeline leaned against one of the cavorting-troll bedposts and frowned. For one, "Lioncroft" was no longer a faceless name. She'd met the man himself. Argued with him. Danced with him. Kissed him. Watched him threaten a man . . . for laying a hand to his sister. He admitted being angry enough to kill. And he didn't deny having done so in the past.

What was wrong with her for being attracted to him in spite of herself?

His weren't mere character flaws. Dangerous, violent, unpredictable. He shared many of his worst traits with her stepfather, a man of no redeeming qualities. A vile man she'd never understood why her mother had remained with, even if—as Mama claimed—she'd only done so for Evangeline's sake.

What if Mama had felt a similar . . . *attraction* . . . to Neal Pemberton? A quickening of the pulse, a tingling of the skin, an undeniable awareness from deep within?

Evangeline shuddered. Revolting idea. But suddenly, horribly, humiliatingly plausible. Understandable. Relatable. Oh, God. Had her mother's attraction to her second husband's pretty exterior blinded her to the evil inside? Evangeline would not make the same mistake. Would *not*.

"What's wrong?" Susan asked, one hand on her hip, the other gripping the poker. "You made the most horrid face of revulsion I have ever seen in my life. What were you thinking about?"

"Mr. Lioncroft."

"And he merited such an expression? I'm the one to marry him, not you."

That's right. Evangeline would never marry. She stared into the crackling fire. The carved trolls scaling her bedpost dug into her back. "Don't you—that is to say, *do* you—find him attractive?"

Susan shrugged. "Perhaps, if you're the sort to find Satan himself attractive."

"How would you know what Satan looks like?"

"Obviously, like Lioncroft." Iron clanked against iron as Susan shoved the poker back in its stand. "At least the man's been tarrying outside your door instead of mine."

Evangeline pushed away from her bed. He had, but how would Susan know? He'd disappeared long before she'd sailed through the connecting door.

"You saw us?"

"'Us'? You mean him. Of course. He took root right there in the hallway and said he planned to wait until you woke, just to make sure you were all right. Disturbing. If I should sicken after we marry, I hope he leaves me well alone."

Evangeline crossed over to the cracked mirror next to the doorway. Disturbing? Only because it was Mr. Lioncroft. In any other man, such an act would've been sweet. Charming. Kindhearted.

"You didn't tell me he was out there waiting."

"I did so. I said he came by with that horrible treatise on metallurgy."

After trying and failing to poke her flyaway curls back into their coil, Evangeline glared at her reflection. "You didn't say he *stayed* by."

"I figured he'd get bored and leave. Why, is he still there?"

"No."

"There you are. Passing fancy." Susan strode to the doorway, nudged open the door, and peered through the crack. "He's long gone."

"What if he hadn't been? What if he'd slipped inside my room and killed me? You weren't concerned about my safety?"

"I'd hear you scream."

Evangeline crossed her arms. "Not if I was smothered in my sleep like Lord Hetherington."

"Well, I'd know Lioncroft was the villain because I saw him around. He'd be sure to hang. But you're still alive, and guests are waiting for you in the Green Salon. At least, they were." Susan pushed the door completely open, then glanced over her shoulder at Evangeline "Are you feeling up to an appearance?"

"No."

But she headed out into the corridor anyway.

When she entered the Green Salon, she discovered it much as Susan had described it. Stark gray walls. Mold-colored chairs. Fluttering white tapers that failed to cast enough light on the half dozen or so framed paintings to determine their subjects.

Lady Stanton sat on the edge of a tattered chair. Mr. Teasdale slept on the sofa, his head lolling to one side, his cane taking up most of the cushion. Mr. Lioncroft leaned against a tall bookcase. For all Evangeline knew, it was another façade for his network of secret passageways.

"At last." The small black mole shivered above Lady Stanton's pursed lips. "You kept us waiting, Miss Pemberton."

"Mother, don't—"

"She's feeling much improved," Mr. Lioncroft interrupted, his voice low and lazy but his eyes dangerous. "How thoughtful of you to inquire."

Frost coated Lady Stanton's voice. "You dare to correct my manners?"

"You dare to sling accusations of murder while imposing on my hospitality?"

"Evangeline," Susan interjected loudly, causing Mr. Teasdale to start. "Why don't you explain what happened in Hetherington's chamber?"

"Yes, do." Lady Stanton fixed her colorless eyes on Evangeline. "Did 'God' tell you anything?"

"Just that Lord Hetherington was, er, smothered. With a pillow."

"Eh? What's that?" Mr. Teasdale struggled to his feet, relying heavily on his cane. "Smothered with a pillow, you say?"

One of Lady Stanton's pale eyebrows arched. "But *who* smothered him?"

"I don't know."

"Then that's useless. Your mother could often—"

Evangeline's spine stiffened. "Lady Stanton—"

"Can't you strive for more accuracy in your—"

"Lady Stanton, honestly—"

"We're no better off than we were before!"

"We do know how, if not whom," Susan interjected with an encouraging smile toward Evangeline.

"Useless. If 'God' spoke to her through Lord Hetherington, why doesn't she know the killer's identity?"

"Eh," Mr. Teasdale grunted, one pinkie digging in his hairy ear. "Because dead men tell no tales."

Susan straightened her spectacles. "Might the fact that he is dead be a factor, Evangeline?"

"I imagine so. This was the first time I've specifically sought . . . interaction with God through a corpse."

Mr. Lioncroft lifted a brow. "I should hope so. Hardly the favorite pastime of most young ladies."

"How about the living, then?" Lady Stanton turned her glare from him to Evangeline. "Have you tried the obvious?"

"That's right." Susan's eyes widened. "We could know right away."

"Know what?" Mr. Lioncroft demanded.

Evangeline backed up a step.

"I'll ensure your privacy so Mr. Teasdale doesn't suspect anything," Susan whispered excitedly. "As soon as I get him and Mother away, go touch Lioncroft."

"I can't," Evangeline whispered back. "I—"

But Susan had skipped to her mother's side. She tugged Lady Stanton from her seat. "Come, Mother, we've heard enough. Mr. Teasdale, would you be so kind as to accompany us?"

Mr. Teasdale's forehead wrinkled. "Where?"

"Yes, Susan, where?" Lady Stanton stared down her nose at her daughter. "I'm not leaving Mr. Lioncroft alone with Miss Pemberton. *We* don't want *her* to be *compromised*, do we?"

Mr. Lioncroft crossed his arms over his broad chest. "Why does everyone think I'm going to compromise her? I haven't had a rakehell reputation in years."

Mr. Teasdale's cane trembled. "I don't think you'll compromise her."

"Thank you."

"You might kill her. That's your reputation now."

"We'll stay in the hallway." Lady Stanton swept past Mr. Teasdale and into the corridor.

"With the door ajar," Susan added. "Significantly ajar. No killing."

Shaking his head, Mr. Teasdale allowed himself to be tugged from the room.

With that, the threesome pulled the door mostly shut and left Evangeline and Mr. Lioncroft quite alone.

Splendid. Abandoned in pursuit of visions from the one man who couldn't provide her with them.

He did not look pleased.

"What the hell just happened?" Mr. Lioncroft demanded.

"I don't know," she hedged. "They're mad as hatters?"

"Undoubtedly." He prowled forward, until the meager candlelight tossed his shadow over her skin. "But something bizarre just took place beneath my nose. Why are the Stanton women lurking in the corridor? What do they expect you to do?"

Evangeline sighed. "Chat with God."

"Now? About me?"

"Apparently."

"Why?"

"They think God will confirm you killed Lord Hetherington."

"Hmmm. Although I'm unconvinced heavenly hearsay will do much in a court of law, the lot of you have me all but convicted already. Well, except for my nieces."

"Your nieces don't know you killed their father?"

"They don't know he was killed. Rose told them he died in his sleep."

"Is she packing them up to go? What will you do when they learn the truth?"

"I don't know." He hooked his fingers in his waistband. "I'm just concentrating on being an uncle while they're still here."

She tried not to look skeptical. "Do you know much about being an uncle?"

"Not one whit."

"Then what are you doing to be uncle-ish?"

"Keeping my promise of a party for Jane's birthday."

"A party for Jane's—that's very kind of you, but her father died last night."

"He was worthless." Mr. Lioncroft fell silent, then regarded her with an odd expression. "From the moment I first saw you, Miss Pemberton, I knew you were different."

Evangeline's heart thudded. "What—what do you mean?"

"Typical young ladies are simpering ninnies, wilting beneath false smiles and trembling in their jewel-encrusted gowns and whispering about each other behind their fans. 'Accomplished' and portrait-perfect, straitlaced and silly, thoughtless and tedious. You, on the other hand . . ." He advanced closer until she could feel the heat from his body through the thin silk of her gown. "You're stubborn. Intelligent. Passionate." His voice turned husky. "Beautiful in a far better way."

"I . . ." She fought the urge to reach for him, to touch him, to close the gap between them. "Oh."

"But perhaps I have a blind spot." Mr. Lioncroft stepped backward. A cool draft sliced across her body. She took a hesitant step forward, caught herself in motion, and froze. His words were no longer complimentary. "Perhaps you've entranced me merely to throw suspicion from yourself."

"From *myself*?" Evangeline sputtered. "Suspicion of what?"

"Perhaps you are the mysterious murderer. You are not even an invited guest. What brings you to Blackberry Manor?"

"I—the Stantons invited me. I'm a friend of Susan's, not a murderer."

"So you say. But you are as much an outsider as I am, if not more so in this circumstance. The killer was someone capable of lifting a pillow. You are capable of such strength, are you not? The killer roamed the passageways alone last night. You roamed the passageways alone last night." A small self-deprecating smile tugged at the corners of his mouth. "Much as I would like to believe otherwise, I'm well aware you stumbled upon my presence by accident. The killer lied about his whereabouts at the breakfast table this morning. You, madam, lied about your whereabouts."

"Everybody lied!" She cast a nervous glance toward the cracked salon door, wondering if the three persons hovering outside could hear the hushed conversation within.

"Ah. But although everyone seemed content to agree Hetherington died by strangulation, you were the one who pronounced him suffocated to death. How would you know, if you were not the one to do so?"

"I-I—" She had been accused of many things in her life, but murder? The audacity! She'd never have come within eyesight of Lord Hetherington's corpse had her goal not been justice. Evangeline pushed at Mr. Lioncroft's chest in frustration. He remained immobile.

"Perhaps you merely stood in the shadows and watched," he continued, his words low and relentless. "Perhaps you orchestrated the event from afar. I saw you speaking to a strange maid right before dinner. Later I discovered that same maid in Hetherington's employ. Beaten. And then he ended up dead."

This time when she shoved at his chest, he caught her wrists in his fists and trapped them against the faint beating of his heart. She tried to pull away. He would not let her.

"Why would I instruct a servant to do such a horrible thing?" She struggled to free herself and failed. "That makes no sense."

His head bent until the tip of his nose was but a hand's width from hers. "I have no way to know your motives, madam. The Lord does not speak to me." He paused. His faintly tea-scented breath tickled her forehead, her cheek, her eyelashes. "You agree the maid could have wielded the pillow?"

"Any servant could've done so," she bit out, "but not on *my* orders."

"If *any* servant could've done so, you agree dozens of individuals other than myself may have been the villain." And he smiled at her. Satisfied.

Evangeline jerked her wrists from his grip as she realized he had never once thought her guilty of such a horrible crime—he was merely illustrating that whatever evidence the party believed they had against him was based on superstition and supposition rather than fact.

"Fair enough," she muttered.

His lashes lowered. "You believe me innocent?"

"No," she said. "But I don't *not* believe you."

"An improvement."

His face lit with an astonished grin, as if she'd presented him with a pirate's treasure rather than a begrudging concession. Had he truly believed he'd never find someone willing to at least consider the possibility of his innocence?

If so, that made two of them. Evangeline had fully expected him to live up to his reputation as an irredeemable, soulless villain. Instead, he stood before her a man. A man asking for her help. He appealed to her not as a "witch" with psychic visions, but as a woman with a logical mind. When was the last time *that* had happened? Never.

Just like he was the first man she could respond to as a woman. Couldn't *help* but respond to as a woman.

She brushed her fingertips across his forearm, reveling in the ability to touch the dark hairs on his arm, the warm skin beneath, the coiled tension of muscle. She glanced up at him, embarrassed to be caught enjoying the simple pleasure of contact and unable to explain her action. She sought for a safe topic.

"Who do you think killed him?" she ventured.

Rather than respond with words, he claimed her mouth in a hard, bruising kiss. She half-expected to find her spine up against the closest wall, but he surprised her by gentling, by ending the kiss completely, by pressing his cheek against hers.

Evangeline blinked at the unexpected sensation of rough male stubble, and shivered to find it not at all unpleasant. If she turned her face a mere fraction, the sensitive skin of her lips would rub against the coarse hair, the line of his jaw, the pale scar marring its surface.

Before she could do anything so foolish, however, he lifted his head.

His fingers smoothed the flyaway tendrils from her face and tucked them behind her ears. His palms caressed the flushed heat of her cheeks, down the slope of her bare neck, along the curve of her shoulders. He squeezed her arms briefly, as if wanting to hug her but unable to make the attempt, and then his hands fell back to his sides.

Evangeline wasn't sure if she should flee or embrace him. Without his touch, she was chilled, aching, uncertain. She stood there, staring up at him, sharing his breath, wishing she knew the right thing to say.

"I hate to blame anyone unfairly," he confessed, his voice soft. "I was hoping your objectivity would shed some light. Have you no second choice? The new lord, perhaps?"

"Benedict Rutherford?"

Mr. Lioncroft nodded.

"I don't know . . . He doesn't seem to have a strong enough constitution to murder anyone."

"Surely he's strong enough to lift a pillow. A child can lift a pillow."

"So can a woman scorned," she said slowly.

He frowned. "You're not suggesting—"

The door to the Green Salon flew open and Edmund Rutherford lurched in. "You are here," he said. "I thought they were jesting."

Evangeline glanced behind him at the empty doorway. "They who?"

"The Stantons."

"In the corridor?"

"Nobody is in the corridor." He unscrewed a small flask and sniffed the contents.

"So they sent you to watch us?"

"To fetch you and beg your assistance in a matter. That is, unless . . . Were you about to affect a compromising position?"

"No," Evangeline said.

"Bother." He sipped from his flask. "I enjoy watching."

"Where did they go?" Mr. Lioncroft asked, ignoring the taunt. Evangeline fought to do the same. "When did they go?"

"A few minutes ago, when that mousy maid with the bruised cheek came barreling down the corridor, blubbering about Rose being hysterical over the children."

"The children? What's wrong with the children?"

Edmund shrugged and recapped his flask. "They're missing."

Chapter Twelve

While Edmund remained in the Green Salon with his flask, Evangeline joined the others in the search for the missing children.

Or rather, she didn't join anyone at all, because everyone had decided to split up and search separately in an attempt to cover ground in the quickest manner possible, considering the missing children were the two youngest girls.

Benedict Rutherford and Mr. Lioncroft tore outside in case the twins had somehow wandered from the mansion without any of the staff members noticing. Susan and Lady Stanton took the ground floor wing with the library and the salon used for dancing. Francine Rutherford took the opposite wing, with the kitchen and scullery and servants' area. The servants scattered indoors and outdoors to hunt for the girls.

Evangeline headed upstairs to search the guest wings. She stopped by the nursery, where Lady Hetherington was slumped on a sofa, Nancy and Jane cuddled to either side.

According to almost-thirteen-year-old Jane, she'd left the room long enough to find a chamber pot, and when she returned, the girls were gone. According to Nancy, twin five-year-olds could be anywhere, and there was no predicting where. Lady Hetherington was trembling too hard to do more

than murmur that her fervent prayer was that they'd disappeared on their own, and not by the hand of the unknown killer.

Evangeline tugged off her gloves as subtly as she could
before offering all three of them her deepest sympathies and
giving each a heartfelt hug in the hopes of allaying some of
their fears, and gaining insight into the girls' mysterious disappearance.

The only thing she gained was a headache so intense that
for a moment she couldn't see. She winced at the over-bright
shafts of dusty sunlight pouring through the windows, turned
her head too sharply, blinked back tears at the explosion
raging within her skull. Ever since the terrifying encounter
with Lord Hetherington's dead body, even the briefest of
human contact had her cringing at the pain and gasping for air.

Once Evangeline's headache abated enough for her to open
her eyes more than a squint, she made her way to the hallway running alongside the guest wing. She headed down the
corridor, thrusting open doors and calling for the girls.

She heard nothing but the cracking of her own voice. She
saw no one in the unused chambers but the occasional startled servant peeking behind doors and bureaus.

Dare she hope the girls had hidden on their own? Thanks
to men like her stepfather, Evangeline had learned to hide at
a very young age. However, she'd never managed to hide
from servants. They were too observant, too inconspicuous,
too omnipresent. Which could only mean the girls couldn't
have gone far undetected. Not outside, not downstairs, not to
another wing. They had to be near the nursery. But where?

After reclosing the last of the guest-room doors in an adjoining corridor, she slumped against a wall, the wainscoting
digging into her hip, the side of her still-pounding head resting between two framed paintings. Something scurried behind
the serpentine paper, the eerie scritching and scratching echoing in what Evangeline knew to be a larger-than-necessary
crawl space between the walls. Hopefully not rats. She'd hated

the vile creatures from the first time her stepfather had locked her in their old pantry.

She glanced down the long corridor toward where she recalled the secret access door to be. Already she could hear the noises getting louder, moving closer, sounding as much like fingernails against rotting wood as tiny claws from horrid little rodents. Her breath caught. What if the noises *were* fingernails?

Evangeline knocked on the wall. The noises stopped. She pressed her ear to the wall. Was her imagination coloring her perception?

A soft thud thumped near her feet. Could the girls be on the other side? Evangeline kicked the mopboard, striking her toes against the molding three times in quick succession.

Once again, the silence fell for a few seconds before three quick thuds clunked near her feet, making the unmistakable sound of a return knock. And then—thank heavens—a soft, muffled voice.

"Mama? Jane? Nancy?"

Evangeline froze for the briefest of seconds before tearing down the hall, tugging each frame in search of the false painting. One landscape fell with a bang, startling a maid carrying a tea tray from the connecting passage.

"Fetch Mr. Lioncroft!" Evangeline shouted to the wide-eyed maid. "Now!"

The tea set shattered to the floor in a jumbled puddle of spilt tea and broken china. The maid set off down the corridor at a dead run.

Evangeline skidded to a halt before a wide gilded frame as tall as she was. Was this the painting? She jerked on the frame, managing only to set it askew. How had she forgotten which canvas was the façade? Had she not been so desperate to flee the suffocating confinement of the secret passageway, she would've paid more attention to something other than escape.

She tried the next painting, then the next, then the next.

By the time she had the correct frame flung open, Mr. Lioncroft's footfalls thundered fast and heavy down the corridor, the maid dropping behind him to collect the broken tea service.

"What the hell are you doing?" he demanded the moment he reached Evangeline's side.

"The twins," she explained, pointing a trembling finger at the unrelenting blackness. "They're trapped inside."

Without pausing to ask more questions, he brushed past her and vanished, hurrying sideways in the opposite direction from which she'd first heard noises. His disappearance was so sudden and so complete, her breath tangled in her throat.

"No," she called into the dark, standing at the junction between candlelight and shadow, with one hand gripping the open frame and the other splayed against the corner of the wall. "The other way. Go back the other way. They're—"

"Mama?" came a small terrified voice from the undulating gloom to Evangeline's right.

"No, it's Miss Pemberton," she called back, fighting to keep the tremor from her voice. "Come this way."

"Where are you?"

"I'm in the corridor. Follow my voice, darling."

"I can't . . . It's—it's too dark," came the small broken voice of a child. "Can you come get me?"

"I—" Evangeline gulped for air. Could she voluntarily enter such a dark confined space? She slid a slipper forward and shuddered when the tip of her foot disappeared into the inky murk. Her lungs hitched and her limbs melted. Oh, Lord. She couldn't. She couldn't. She *couldn't*.

"Rachel? Rebecca?" came Mr. Lioncroft's deep voice, followed by the shuffling of his large booted feet as he edged back into view.

"Down that way," Evangeline said, panting with terror but pointing in the right direction.

"Why didn't you go to them?" The shadows were too dense

to read his expression, but there was no mistaking the anger in his tone.

"I—" she said again and faltered, unable to complete the thought even to herself.

He was already gone, slipping down the narrow passageway toward a child's soft whimpers. After several long heart-stopping moments, he returned with a dusty blond moppet clinging to his neck.

"Rebecca?" Evangeline asked.

"No. Rachel. She was alone."

"Oh. Where's Rebecca?"

"I don't know. Rachel says she doesn't know, either."

"They weren't together?"

"Rachel, were you and Rebecca together?"

Rachel's head dipped in a wretched nod. "But I don't know where."

Mr. Lioncroft's tone gentled. "That's all right, sweetheart. We just need to know how to find her."

"She's lost. Like I was lost."

Evangeline stood there, feeling stupid and cowardly and useless.

"You weren't lost together?" she asked.

"We were, but then Rebecca dropped her dolly and wouldn't come back without it. I couldn't find the dolly and then I couldn't find Rebecca and then I couldn't find my way back out."

Tears streamed from Rachel's dirty cheeks to Mr. Lioncroft's cravat. He made no move to set her down, and instead only held her closer. "Is she in the same section where I found you?"

"No. I made lots of turns. Lots and lots of turns. I think."

"Do you remember which ones?"

Rachel shook her head miserably.

"Damn it." Mr. Lioncroft's jaw flexed.

Evangeline swallowed her panic as best she could. Ignoring the still-raging tempest storming in the back of her skull, she reached for the little girl.

"Come here," she coaxed softly. "Let me hold you. Just for a second."

"I've got her." Mr. Lioncroft's eyes were cold, hard. He was no doubt disgusted with her cowardice, her inability to go after Rachel instead of standing dumb at the entrance, her apparent apathy about the welfare of his nieces.

"No. I mean . . . please. Just let me touch her."

"Miss Pemberton, I don't have time for this. A five-year-old girl is lost. If you have no wish to help locate her, then just go back to your—"

Evangeline threw her bare arms around both man and child, and squeezed.

Where is Rebecca? Where is Rebecca? Where is Rebecca?

Darkness surrounded her, smothered her, crushed her. She couldn't see. She couldn't breathe. At first she thought she managed to swoon after all, proving herself a coward beyond all redemption. But then, through the unrelenting shadows, came the unmistakable sounds of childlike voices.

> *"Give it back!"*
> *"It's mine!"*
> *"Jane said I could play with it!"*
> *"Jane's stupid!"*
> *"You're stupid!"*
> *"Huh-uh. I've got the dolly, and you d—Oh!"*
> *Something hard clatters against a wall and falls to the floor. Kicking and scuffling sounds fill the subsequent silence, followed by the rip of torn hair and the wail of a hurt child.*
> *"I hate you!"*
> *"Good! I'm going back without you!"*
> *The small, quick footfalls pad down the passageway, go straight through the first intersection, speed up, falter, turn left at the second intersection, stumble to a stop just past the third.*

"Rebecca?"

No response.

"Rebecca? I'm lost."

No response.

"Rebecca? Can you hear me? I'm sorry I threw your dolly."

No response.

"Rebecca?"

Small fists bang against the wall.

"I want out! I want out! I want out!"

A flutter-thump sounds, as though Rachel trips, then tumbles to the floor. The banging at the wall increases and then fades, followed only by the occasional scritch of fingernails looking for purchase in the cracks of the dusty wall.

And then the noise of Evangeline's foot colliding with the other side.

Evangeline gasped and jerked away, reeling so hard at the agony in her head she stumbled against the wainscoting and crumpled in a heap.

"Miss Pemberton?" came Mr. Lioncroft's hesitant voice from somewhere high above her head. "Miss Pemberton? Are you all right?"

"To the right," she managed, still sprawled on her back with her eyes squeezed tight. "You have to go to the right, then right again at the first intersection and straight through the second. Hurry. She's just a dozen meters past, looking for her doll."

"What?"

"I told you Rebecca was looking for her dolly," Rachel put in. "I told you."

Despite the fury of her headache, Evangeline forced her eyes open. "You said she dropped the doll," she corrected her with a stern smile, "not that you took it from her and threw it."

Rachel's jaw dropped open. She closed it with a snap,

shoved her nose in the air, and turned back to her uncle. "Can you find Rebecca? And the dolly?"

Brow furrowed, Mr. Lioncroft glanced from Rachel to Evangeline and back again. "I'll try my damnedest."

He set the little girl down and disappeared into the fathomless shadows.

Gavin rushed along the no-longer-very-secret passageway between the walls. Usually his movements through the lightless corridors were exact, designed for efficiency and speed yet careful not to brush his skin or clothing against the narrow walls. Today, however, his only concern was a lost little girl.

Right at the first intersection, he reminded himself. Straight through the next.

At least that's what Miss Pemberton had said. But how would she know? Short answer: she wouldn't. Not unless she'd been the one to lure his nieces into the branching shadows herself. And how had she known about the swinging access panel in the first place?

"Rebecca," he called, the darkness swallowing his words whole. "Rebecca, can you hear me?"

Was that a whimper up ahead? He hurried faster.

The children had been the only individuals present who treated him without suspicion or fear. After being lost in the forgotten crevices of Blackberry Manor, however, he suspected both he and his home had lost any remaining appeal.

He'd barely careened around the final intersection before his boot crashed down onto something melon-sized and porcelain. The whimpering ceased, then started anew. Apparently, he owed his niece a new doll.

"Rebecca?"

"Papa?"

Gavin closed his eyes, realized he couldn't see either way, and reopened them. "No, sweetling. It's Uncle Lioncroft."

"Oh." She sniffled. "I think you broke my dolly."

"I think so, too. Where are you?"

"Over here. Where are you? It's too dark. I can't even—is this your hand?"

"Yes."

"It's very cold."

Yes, he imagined it was. The thought of her trapped between the walls continued to chill his blood. Her hand, however, was over-warm. And a bit moist—he hoped due to tears or sweat or some other non-nasal fluid.

He pulled her to her feet. She stood readily. Her hand wrapped around his largest two fingers. He stooped for the broken doll and then made his way back toward the corridor where Rachel and Miss Pemberton waited. Miss Pemberton, whose directions had been uncanny at best. Suspicious at worst.

"How did you get stuck back here, Rebecca?"

"Rachel threw my dolly."

"But how did you get back *here?* Did—did Miss Pemberton drop by the nursery?"

"No."

An odd feeling of relief settled across his skin, as though he had not wished to discover Miss Pemberton at fault. Well, of course, he hadn't wanted her to be at fault. He didn't want anything more sinister afoot than children up to mischief. Nonetheless, her performance in the hallway coupled with the accuracy of her instructions left an unwelcome taste coating his throat.

"So," he said presently. "You got stuck because Rachel threw your dolly."

"Yes."

What the hell did that mean? Gavin wished he could see Rebecca's face. Her explanation made no sense. "Where, exactly, did Rachel throw your dolly?"

"Behind the drawing board."

"Behind the—oh." He'd completely forgotten about the

access door in the schoolroom adjoining the nursery. Until the week before this laughable catastrophe of a party, neither he nor his staff had reason to visit the nursery, or even the guest quarters in general.

"Where's Rachel?" came Rebecca's small voice.

"In the corridor with Miss Pemberton."

"Why?"

Ah. Wouldn't he like to know what Miss Pemberton had been up to. When he'd first seen her peering into the blackness beyond the wainscoting, his first thought had been—had been—well, he wasn't sure he'd been able to think much at all. His mind had been on the missing girls. But now that they had been found, there were several questions he'd like to ask the wide-eyed and wild-haired Miss Pemberton. The flickering of candlelight up ahead indicated he would be able to do so in very short order.

When he and Rebecca reentered the hallway, Miss Pemberton was on her feet instead of the floor. She leaned against the opposite wall, fingertips massaging her temples, eyes squeezed shut, face twisted in a grimace.

"Where's Rachel?" he demanded.

Miss Pemberton opened her eyes. Sort of. But she didn't stop rubbing her temples or push away from her slump against the wall.

"Nursery," she said, squinting at him as though the meager sconce light burned brighter than the noonday sun. "I took her to her mother."

"Stay here."

Without pausing to see her reaction to the terseness of his command, Gavin led Rebecca to the nursery as well. Once the door opened, Rebecca tugged her fingers from his and flew across the room to her weeping mother.

"Rachel broke my dolly," Rebecca cried as she hurled herself into Rose's outstretched arms.

"Did not," Rachel yelled from her position at Rose's feet.

Gavin laid the now-headless doll on a small table near the doorway. "I'm afraid I did."

"I'm afraid of everything about this house," Rose murmured.

He stiffened. Everything meaning what? Meaning him?

"I'll purchase a new doll for her."

Rose looked away.

"It's not the doll," Nancy cut in. "It's . . ." She glanced at her mother, then the girls, then at Gavin. "It's everything."

"She means Papa." Jane sat on one of the twins' small chairs, her gown puddling on the floor. "We know she means Papa, Nancy."

Although a spineless worm, Hetherington had been the children's father. For this reason, Gavin nodded gravely and said, "I am very sorry about your loss."

Rose's head snapped up, forehead lined, eyes narrowed. She said nothing. Perhaps she was not sorry. Or perhaps she had nothing left to say.

If any other words threatened to escape the dry confines of his throat, Gavin swallowed them.

What did Rose's expression mean? Did she think him insincere? True, he didn't lament Hetherington's death. Merely the girls' loss of a father. Was he that transparent?

Or did she suspect him of causing the incident in the first place? If so, such suspicion poked a sharp hole in Miss Pemberton's theory that Rose herself might have contributed to her husband's death. But then, there were plenty of holes in the things Miss Pemberton said, and plenty more holes in the things she did not say.

"I am sorry," Gavin said again, when it seemed no one else felt the inclination to speak.

"Sorry?" Rose echoed, scooping both twins into her arms. "As if the loss of my husband was not enough—" She *did* blame him! Gavin fought to keep his expression neutral but could not prevent a slight wince. "—getting my children lost in your walls where they might easily have hurt themselves and, God forbid, never been found . . . Sorry is no substitute for safety. We're leaving tomorrow."

A horrible silence fell.

Then, from Jane: "But tomorrow is my birthday."

All gazes cast in her direction.

"I don't wish to travel on my birthday," she insisted. "Uncle Lioncroft promised kite-flying and pall-mall."

Rachel's eyes widened. "What's pall-mall?"

Rebecca sat up so fast she knocked Rose's chin with the back of her head. "I want to fly kites."

Holding silent, Gavin returned his focus to Rose.

Nancy knelt next to her mother. "I suppose it wouldn't hurt to stay until after Jane's birthday, would it, Mother? We do not have kites or pall-mall at home."

"Nor will we," Rose said bitterly, "Now that Monsieur Lefebvre is no longer a secret."

"Teasdale isn't the only man with money, Mother. And Pierre—"

"Would have been more than merely sacked, had I not distracted your father while he made his escape. You did quite enough *to* your family, young lady, when you should've been doing something *for* them."

"I'll marry well, Mama," Jane put in. "I think love is stupid."

Gavin ran a hand through his hair. He had no idea how to join the conversation, as he had no idea what the conversation was about. Who was Pierre Lefebvre? And why was the Hetherington household permanently without simple activities like kite-flying? That is, unless . . .

"You mentioned you hoped Nancy would make a match with Mr. Teasdale," he said. Rose started, as if she'd forgotten he still stood just inside the doorway, and then her head dipped in a quick nod. "Do you have reason to believe him uninterested?"

Nancy blushed and looked away. "He's old."

"And rich," Jane added.

"And displeased," Rose said with a sigh. "I cannot blame him."

Nancy rose to her feet and glared down at her mother. "I'll marry someone else."

Rose stood as well, returning her daughter's gaze. "You'll marry no one else, as we can no longer afford to put in appearances."

Nancy's chin lifted. "Then you should've let me marry him!"

Rose's reply was gentle, but firm. "He didn't offer."

"He would've!"

"Yet he did not."

"He loved me!" Tears filled Nancy's eyes. "He wrote me poetry!"

"You are too young to understand." Rose reached out to touch Nancy's arm.

Nancy jerked away. "I understand Papa ruined it. Papa ruined everything!"

"Papa's dead," Rachel put in.

Rebecca nodded. "Like my dolly."

With a groan, Nancy spun away from them and stormed past Gavin and out the door. Jane hesitated a second before sprinting after her. Rose sank back onto the sofa and refused to meet Gavin's eyes.

Why, he had no idea, since their conversation had only grown more confusing with each hurled phrase. The female mind was unfathomable. Nancy had *wanted* to marry Teasdale, the deaf old codger? Who had apparently scratched out love letters in his spotted, palsied hand?

After inclining his head to the women, Gavin slipped out of the nursery and back into the corridor. Miss Pemberton still stood about ten meters away, if one could call slumping bonelessly against wainscoting "standing."

When a footman stepped from the guest room across the hall, Gavin motioned him over.

"A favor," he said, careful to keep his voice low. "I'd like the staff to keep an eye on Lady Hetherington, Miss Hetherington, and Miss Pemberton. Discreetly."

The footman nodded and resumed his duties.

Gavin approached Miss Pemberton with soft, slow steps. Although his footfalls were soundless, her eyelashes lifted as if she sensed the minute shift in the shadows.

She did not smile to see him. The pulse in her throat suggested she was waiting for him to pounce.

He hooked his thumbs in his waistband. "You stayed."

"You told me to."

"So I did."

She rubbed her forehead. "Are the girls all right?"

"I believe so. Their mother seems to be the most affected."

"Such is often the way."

"How did you know?"

She shrugged. "I often sequestered myself as a child."

"No," Gavin said, "I mean, how did you know where to find them?" Although, now he very much wished to know where and why she'd sequestered herself as a child.

"I heard noises in the walls."

"Which you immediately assumed to be a five-year-old girl?"

"I immediately assumed rats."

"There are no rats in Blackberry Manor."

"Perhaps not literal ones."

He chose to ignore the barb. "How did you discover the swinging painting? Another lucky guess?"

"Another accident. It was my escape path when I found myself in the walls earlier this morning."

"When you—" Gavin broke off and stared at her, remembering his earlier bafflement at her odd, disheveled appearance. "How does one accidentally find oneself in the walls?"

She arched a slender eyebrow. "By tumbling through one's false bookcase."

"Did you lure the girls in after you?"

Her eyes flashed. "Of course not. I was with you belowstairs, was I not?"

"But you knew precisely where I would find Rebecca. How is that possible unless you were with them when they got lost?"

"Did they say I was with them?"

"No."

"Then blame your own cleverness. If you didn't have an abundance of cunning façades disguising access panels to secret passageways, none of your guests would have found themselves caught between the walls. Had something horrible happened to one of those little girls, you would have only yourself to blame."

He stepped forward.

She recoiled. "Please—please don't kiss me again."

Without waiting for a rejoinder from him, she turned and stalked down the corridor and out of sight. Which was for the better.

He hadn't been about to kiss her. He'd been about to throttle her. He was friendless, soulless, dangerous.

Even his house was capable of evil.

Chapter Thirteen

Before Evangeline progressed even half the distance to her bedchamber, Susan Stanton strode forth from a connecting corridor, linked her arm with Evangeline's, and tugged her off in a new direction.

"May I ask," Evangeline ventured, "where we are going in such a hurry?"

"You may ask," Susan returned, "but do not blame me if you succumb to a fit of vapors upon learning."

"Has something happened?"

"Of course something's happened. You were there when the something that happened was busy happening, while I was stuck scouring the scullery with my mother, who has now decided my sensitive female constitution must be in such a state of excitement over the loss and subsequent discovery of the girls that only one activity remains which might calm my tender nerves." She took a deep, shuddering breath. *"Sewing samplers."*

"But you know I—"

"No, no. None of that." Her arm trapped Evangeline's closer. "I refuse to sew alone."

And in short order, Evangeline found herself in a large rectangular room decorated with a smattering of sofas and chaises, gold-papered walls, a small crackling fire, and an overstuffed wicker basket teeming with threaded needles and bits of cloth. No windows filtered light into the stuffy interior. Instead, oil-on-canvas landscapes filled the walls, just as they did in almost every other room.

Susan flounced over to the sofa nearest the basket of samplers, yanked a half-finished pattern from the pile, and hurled herself lengthwise across the worn cushions. She closed her eyes. She placed the wrinkled cloth across her face like a death mask. She moaned as if in bitter agony. And then she bolted upright, not bothering to snatch at the small square cloth when it fluttered to the floor.

"Stop toying with me," she huffed. "As you cannot embroider, you must know I've engineered your company so that you may recount all details regarding the missing twins. The countess is only saying that they are returned safely to the nursery. Lionkiller is saying nothing at all. As is his wont. I swear, the moment we wed I shall demand regular sessions of interactive conversation. Nothing less than fifteen minute segments will do."

Evangeline settled at the edge of a chaise near the fire and tried not to imagine Susan in long postmarital conversation with Mr. Lioncroft. "I thought you weren't looking forward to the match."

"I changed my mind."

"What?"

"He may portray himself as a taciturn recluse, but in the few days we've spent in his company, I've now come to realize where he goes, trouble follows."

"And that's a good quality?"

"That's a fascinating quality. Life with Mother is dreadfully dull."

Evangeline wasn't sure which horrified her more: that Susan was utterly convinced Mr. Lioncroft was an unrepentant killer who would strike again at any moment . . . or that danger to herself and others seemed a diverting source of entertainment. Evangeline had seen Mr. Lioncroft's face when he'd heard the girls were missing, heard his rapid-fire footfalls as he ran from out of doors to the secret passageway, felt the burning heat of his disgust and disappointment when the best she could do was hover nearby and offer feeble directions.

Susan did not know him at all. She feared him, judged him, dismissed him. And yet she would marry him. Because she found the idea amusing. Acid coated Evangeline's gut—a strange, horrible, desperate feeling she was determined not to name.

"Well?" Susan demanded. "Where were they? Had he put them in danger?"

"He did not." The words came out short, choppy, the final word enunciated too clearly. "Why would he?"

Susan shrugged. "How should I know how an animal thinks? But if you say they are safe from him, I believe you." She shoved her spectacles up her nose and fixed Evangeline with a sudden stare. "Do you believe I should be safe from him when we marry?"

Although Evangeline's mouth opened, neither words nor breath escaped. Good fortune, that, because she was quite sure she'd regret speaking aloud any of the rejoinders that instantly sprang to mind.

If Mr. Lioncroft had killed Lord Hetherington, he had done so to avenge the violence done to his sister. He held his sister's well-being—and that of her daughters—in clear regard. He had not spent the rest of the evening wandering about his mansion smothering the rest of his guests. He appeared in possession of a quick and violent temper, to be sure, but only when provoked.

Susan, Evangeline couldn't help but decide, was quite provoking. If Mr. Lioncroft smothered her with that stupid sampler, any mutual acquaintance would deem such an act justifiable. The very fact that she would question her safety with a man she intended to marry . . .

If Evangeline said, "Yes, I'm quite sure he'd murder you within moments of exchanging vows," perhaps she could sway Susan from the bridal path. The thought of preventing such an undesirable marriage eased the clenching of Evangeline's gut.

However, two problems presented themselves with this line of thought.

First, while she often had to keep the truth about certain things to herself, Evangeline tried very hard not to out-and-out lie. To frighten Susan away from Mr. Lioncroft by confirming the volatility of his nature, Evangeline would be perpetuating rumors she already knew to be exaggerated.

Second, to what purpose would such deception serve? Mr. Lioncroft was hardly likely to offer for *her*, and even if the stars aligned in just such a way to provoke such a turn of events, she would not be able to accept without her stepfather's permission. Which he would never grant.

So she mumbled, "Of course you'll be safe with him, goose," and turned to face the fire. The roiling in her gut increased exponentially.

"Excellent." Susan jabbed her needle through the tattered cloth. "And I shall be good for his circumstances, as well. Father doubled my dowry after last Season's scandal. If it weren't for these infernal spectacles, Mother is convinced I would've been an Incomparable from my very first ball. Our family has connections from London to the Continent, and bloodlines that intertwine with royalty. I'm accomplished in every way that a proper young lady ought to be. I am quite gifted when it comes to—"

Evangeline allowed her ears to go deaf.

Yes, yes, Susan was perfect *ton*. She had two living parents, enviable blood, and more money than Midas. Splendid. If her point was that any machinations to finagle the initial compromise would more than pay out to Mr. Lioncroft's advantage in the end, then huzzah for her. Evangeline paid lip service to her role in the stratagem simply to keep in Lady Stanton's good graces, and held no interest in playing make-believe about what a wonderful life Susan and Mr. Lioncroft might have together.

The door swung open and the one person Evangeline held even less interest in conversing with glided into the room.

Lady Stanton harrumphed. "I'm glad to see Susan minded my instruction for once. I hope you did the same, Miss Pemberton."

"I—" Evangeline's gloved hands twitched in her lap, quite devoid of samples to embroider. "You wished for me to sew?"

"I wished," Lady Stanton bit out, "for you to take advantage of opportunity when we left you in the Green Salon to secure a vision about the murder from Mr. Lioncroft. Pray tell me you did so."

Evangeline jerked her gaze from Lady Stanton to Susan and back again. She had confided in Susan about her visions only that morning, and already Lady Stanton was discussing them freely before her.

She turned to face her. "You told your mother I confided in you?"

Susan frowned, cocked her head to one side, and frowned some more. She stabbed her needle into the center of her sampler, threw it atop the basket, and glared at Evangeline through narrowed eyes.

Blinking, Evangeline recoiled.

"Are you talking about your silly visions?" came Lady Stanton's sharp, cutting voice. "Susan knew about those before we left the house. How else could I get her to cooperate with my stratagem to ensnare Lioncroft? Which is only to her benefit, the ungrateful chit."

Evangeline's jaw fell open. "You . . . didn't tell me," she said to Susan.

Susan jerked one shoulder up, then back down. "And you didn't tell me about your visions until today. I wanted us to be friends. And I figured you'd confide on your own when you felt you could trust me."

Evangeline closed her jaw with a snap. Of course, Susan would already know about the visions. Why would Lady Stanton, of all people, keep Evangeline's secret? Whatever friendship Mama thought she'd shared with that woman had clearly been one-sided. And whatever friendship Evangeline had almost begun with Susan, she'd managed to ruin herself.

"I apologize," she said, the words coming out soft and urgent. "I—"

"Poignant," Lady Stanton interrupted, "but not the topic of conversation. Did you or did you not ascertain Lioncroft is in fact Hetherington's murderer?"

Evangeline's hands fisted in her lap. "I did not."

Lady Stanton stiffened. "You are fed and clothed on my good graces, young lady. Do not forget that. I demand you do so the next time you meet. I demand—"

"Technically," Susan cut in, "we're all fed on Lioncroft's good graces. And those are my cast-off clothes, not yours."

Evangeline glanced at her, hoping her interjection meant she'd forgiven Evangeline for her assumptions. Susan's focus, however, was on her mother, not Evangeline.

"In any case," Lady Stanton continued, "the important detail isn't whether he did it, but whether he'll be caught. Are your visions always of done deeds?"

"They can be any time, past or future, but I told you— I didn't see the killer strike."

"You're going to have to do better. How else will we solve the mystery?"

"Perhaps we won't, Mother. Just like his previous mystery."

Lady Stanton sniffed. "That's not a mystery. Everybody knows he did it."

"He didn't hang for it, did he? Lioncroft has a knack for escaping the gallows."

"It could be the case," Evangeline put in hesitantly, "that Mr. Lioncroft is innocent."

"*Innocent!*" Lady Stanton exclaimed.

Even Susan goggled from behind her spectacles. "What about the blow to the head? Or the handprints about Hetherington's neck? Did he do those himself right before he popped off?"

"Of course not . . ."

Lady Stanton arched a brow. "Lioncroft specifically said he was angry enough to strangle Hetherington."

"And I've no doubt whoever did so intended for Lord Hetherington to die," Evangeline agreed. "But he did not die by that manner, which would suggest whoever attempted to strangle him was incapable of seeing the job done, and so resorted to the closest weapon at hand, which turned out to be a pillow. And I am certain, had Mr. Lioncroft truly wished to strangle Lord Hetherington to death, he would've had no difficulty achieving that goal."

"Brilliant," Susan breathed, finally meeting Evangeline's eyes again. "You're right—he's easily the strongest man here. There'd be no need to resort to bed pillows. I suppose it's possible he didn't do it after all."

"Humph." Lady Stanton's blue-veined fists settled on her hips. "Of course he did. But he's volatile, not stupid. And he's been down this road before. I should not be surprised to discover Lioncroft planned his actions to engender just such a line of reasoning, in the hopes of deflecting blame from himself."

Susan clapped her hands together. "That would be diabolical, Mother. Imagine. Who would ever guess?"

"We don't need to guess. We have Miss Pemberton, who will discover the future for us so we can determine whether or not to proceed as planned."

"Actually," Evangeline admitted, "I cannot. As it turns out, I—"

"As it turns out," Lady Stanton interrupted, "either you help us as promised, or you will find yourself back in your stepfather's possession. I neither want nor need another dependant underfoot when I am trying to marry off the one I already have."

At that moment, the door to the sitting room swung open, and the footman from last night's visit to the library strode into the room with a folded piece of parchment upon a small silver tray.

"Yes?" Lady Stanton snapped.

He paused. "Message for Miss Pemberton."

"I'll take it." Lady Stanton snatched the paper from the tray, using the folded parchment to make shooing motions toward the footman's nose. "Now, go. Go. We value our privacy."

Evangeline rose from the chaise. "Here. I'll—"

"You'll do nothing unless I allow it to be so. Besides, who would possibly be sending missives to a common fluff like you?" She tore open the parchment and scanned its contents. "Lioncroft! I should've known."

"What's he say, Mother? Er, that is . . ." Susan colored slightly. "Shouldn't you hand it to Evangeline?"

"He asks her to meet him in his office to discuss a matter of some import. What matter is that, Miss Pemberton?"

"I—I'm sure I don't know."

"Well, you're to find out immediately. And while you're finding out, you're to do whatever it takes to secure a vision that will put to rest any concern over my daughter's marital future once and for all. Is that clear?"

"I apologize, Lady Stanton, but I—"

"Today, Miss Pemberton. You resolve this today, or you will be returned to your stepfather. Is that understood?"

Understood? How was she supposed to discover the truth from the one man whose touch brought her fever, but no visions? Fingers clenched, Evangeline swallowed her retort and nodded.

"Good. Susan, you are to accompany her."

"I don't wish to go near him unless I know for certain—"

"You are to wait in the hallway for Miss Pemberton to give you a signal as to which way the wind blows. If he is to be hung, we leave on the morrow. If he is to escape justice yet again, we shall move forward with the compromise. Immediately."

"Mother, I'm not *ready* to be compromised. Can't we wait at least until after Jane's birthday celebration tomorrow?"

"No. If he is innocent, you are to take Miss Pemberton's place in his office, and she will remove herself to the corridor, where she will shout for you as though she has no idea where you have gone. And then I shall come from the opposite corridor and surprise the two of you alone. Jane's birthday tomorrow can double as an engagement ball, as far as I'm concerned."

Susan sighed dramatically and dragged herself up from the sofa. "Very well. Off I go." When she reached the doorway, she paused to glance over her shoulder at Evangeline. "Ready to trap me a rich husband?"

No, Evangeline was not.

She glanced at Lady Stanton, whose brittle smile frosted the air around them.

"If you prefer your stepfather's company to ours," Lady Stanton said, "I can arrange for you to get your wish."

Evangeline's muscles twitched as though preparing to flee for safety. She preferred death over her stepfather. Which meant somehow, some way, she would have to do the impossible.

For the first time since Evangeline's arrival at Blackberry Manor, the worst thing about being alone with Mr. Lioncroft in his office had nothing to do with his propensity for violent outbursts or drugging kisses. No, the worst thing about being alone with Mr. Lioncroft in his office was the knowledge Susan Stanton lurked outside in the corridor, ready to burst in and ensnare him for herself.

Not that Evangeline was jealous, of course. She considered herself a reasonable woman. Reasonable women did not begrudge an accomplished young lady marrying an attractive bachelor. Especially if she had no desire for the altar herself.

However, she wasn't feeling reasonable at the moment.

Not with her spine pressed against the closed oak door, her skin flushed, her palms damp—and him just sitting there behind his desk, calm as you please, scratching a pen across parchment without so much as glancing up to see who had entered his domain.

"Whom are you writing now?" her traitorous voice queried. "Summoning your mistress?"

He glanced up, his eyes dark, intense, heated. "I find myself between mistresses at the moment."

"Don't expect me to fill that role," she blurted out, then blushed. Curse her tongue.

He replaced the pen, leaned back in his chair, smiled. "You are the one who brought up the topic. Did you come here for an assignation?"

Oh, Lord. Had she?

"No," she snapped, arms crossing beneath her bodice. "Why did you call for me?"

"Why did you come?"

She glared at him. "Do not play games with me."

"Ah," he said, still tilting backward in his chair. "Now I know you're not saying what you mean. You've done nothing but play games since you arrived."

"I . . ." She faltered. What was he talking about? He was the one who skulked through secret passageways, who kissed her senseless in dark corners of his mansion and then scowled at her when her limbs refused to—oh. "Surely you don't think

I had anything to do with the twins becoming trapped between the walls."

"No," he agreed, "I do not."

Despite his words, the edge of suspicion never faded from his expression. And despite the ignominy of being suspected—of what, precisely, Evangeline could not guess—the greater humiliation came from him remaining seated behind his desk, apparently unaffected by the unwilling attraction that had her clinging to the office door for fear she'd throw herself in his arms and tilt her face up for more kisses.

She was not jealous of Susan. She was *not*.

How could she be? Evangeline had known all her life she would never take a husband. Marriage had destroyed her mother twice over, first in spirit, then in body. The affliction—blessing, rather—of her Gift was a dangerous, double-edged thing. If Evangeline wanted to live, to be useful, to be whole, she could become the legal property of no man.

Especially not one like Mr. Lioncroft. Despite the Stantons' machinations, Evangeline strongly suspected he of all men was not the marrying sort. Even now, in the middle of an argument, he'd returned all four legs of his chair to the floor and resumed his efforts with pen and paper rather than bother to continue discourse with her.

After a moment, her arms fell back to her sides. "To whom are you writing?"

In the twenty years of Evangeline's life, she had never before encountered a man who failed to take advantage of an opportunity to prove his mastery, his superior strength, his ability to be "right" whether or not it was so. She knew she was acting out-of-sorts, obstinate, contradictory. And Mr. Lioncroft merely nodded, allowed her to do so at her leisure, and returned to his correspondence. Maddening, unpredictable man. She had no idea what to make of him.

"A toymaker." He re-inked his pen. "I shall commission

the finest dolls from London for the girls. They should arrive quickly."

She blinked at him for a moment, then stepped away from the comfort of the door and closer to the front of his desk. "Dolls?"

"I'm afraid my boot shattered the original's porcelain face. The least I can do is replace it."

"With two?"

"The twins are two, are they not? And they should have two dolls. I am ordering an identical pair, each with a different-colored bow, so there will be no cause for future rows on that score. The girls would not have gotten lost today had each possessed a plaything of her own." He franked the parchment, placed it in the corner of his desk, returned his writing implements to their proper locations. "How lucky you were able to help me find them."

There it was again—an edge of suspicion. Evangeline could barely concentrate on the undercurrent in Mr. Lioncroft's voice, however, because he was rising to his feet.

What was he going to do? Why had he called her here if not to punish her for her inability to reenter that horrible dark passageway, even to rescue a small girl?

She took a step backward, grateful to have the width of the desk between them.

Rather than come around the wide teak surface toward her, he leaned his broad shoulders against the rear wall and hooked his thumbs casually in the waistband of his fawn-colored breeches in what Evangeline had come to suspect was his favorite pose, whether he realized it or not. He crossed one black leather boot atop the other and smiled. He looked powerful. Rakish. Devastating.

As usual. Damn him.

Dark hair fell forward across one of his eyes. He made no move to shove it from his face. Although his cream-colored waistcoat was crisply pressed and the creases of his cravat white and perfect, the faint stubble along his jaw had grown longer, thicker. If he kissed her again, she would feel it scratch against her skin.

Evangeline swallowed, shivered, sought for a safer topic than the rough texture of his cheek against hers.

To her right was the crackling fireplace. Being more than hot enough already, the last thing she needed was to get closer to its flames. Behind her was the door, but she could not quit Mr. Lioncroft's company just yet. To her left was an oil painting in a large gilded frame, tilted slightly to one side as if recently jostled. Something was different about this painting than the other oils on canvas adorning the rest of the walls throughout his home. Something missing from the rest of the mansion . . .

"People," she breathed.

Mr. Lioncroft stood. "What?"

"The rest of your artwork is landscapes. This is the first portrait I've seen."

She gestured at the painting, strode forward, inspected it.

Three laughing children posed before a river. A slender blonde perched atop a large gray rock, a basket of flowers in her lap. A tall skinny boy with a fishing pole in one hand and a bucket in the other stood to one side behind her. A dark-haired little boy crouched in front, paying more attention to ruffling the golden fur of a panting dog than to his siblings or the painter.

"My family," Mr. Lioncroft said gruffly. "Rose in the middle, David behind her, me with Wilson."

"Wilson?"

"My dog. Named after the Welsh landscape painter, Richard Wilson."

"Your favorite artist?"

"My father's favorite artist."

"Did he paint the landscapes hanging throughout Blackberry Manor? They all seem to be of a similar style."

"No." He leaned against the wall, arms crossed.

Well. Clearly he didn't wish to discuss landscape artists. Evangeline turned back to the painting. "You look happy."

"I was."

"How old were you?"

"Ten."

"Do you have other family portraits?"

He shrugged. "At Meadowbrook, where my brother lives."

His brother, the gangly teenage boy with the fishing pole. How lovely those days must've been. Evangeline had always wanted siblings. "Do you visit?"

"Never."

"Has he visited you?"

"He would rather die."

"Does—oh."

Evangeline turned from the painting of a small laughing child to consider the large serious man he'd become.

Mr. Lioncroft's gaze was dark, inscrutable. Although he remained in his usual pose, his muscles seemed tense, his posture less casual, as if answering her questions about his family was the last thing in hell he preferred to be doing.

"Rose," he said at last, "may not visit again, either. My proximity has a distinctly abortive affect on the longevity of her family members. I shouldn't be surprised if this is the last time I see my sister or my nieces."

His jaw locked and he swiveled his gaze back to the painting, as if he regretted being so candid.

Mr. Lioncroft, Evangeline was beginning to realize, had a lot of regrets. He was not the cold-blooded, black-hearted beast rumor made him out to be.

"To be fair," she ventured, "it is not as if you forced the girls into the passageway. Perhaps you ought to have locked the access doors a bit more securely"—his eyes flashed at this admonition, but he said nothing to defend himself—"but I, too, remember what it was like to be a child. Children get into mischief."

"And her husband?"

"What of him?"

"He didn't get into mischief on his own." He stepped closer, blocking the meager sconce light. "Everyone believes I killed him."

She shook her head. "Not everyone."

The words were scarcely out of her mouth before his lips crushed hers. His fingers gripped the sides of her face, bruising her with passion. The stubble of his jaw chafed deliciously against her skin, just as she'd imagined.

Evangeline's hands barely had the chance to grip the hard muscle of his upper arms before he pushed her from him, as though he had not meant to kiss her, and sorely regretted the impulse.

She stood, wanting, trembling. Waiting for some explanation— why he'd kissed her, why he'd stopped, why he'd thrust her from him.

He said nothing. Tensed. Turned away.

"I'm not convinced Rose believes you a murderer," she said at last.

He smiled, a horrible, humorless mockery of a smile. "Yes, she does."

"I mean," Evangeline corrected herself, "of *this* crime."

"And why wouldn't she?"

"Because anybody could've done it. Including her. Perhaps her suspicion is mere affectation. An attempt to lessen her own guilt and deflect blame onto you."

"If that is what you suspect," he said, his voice low and cruel and terrible, "why don't you find out?"

She blinked. "Why don't I . . . what? I can't just *ask* her."

"No, you can't, can you. Not if you want the truth. But you can find out a different way, isn't that right?"

"I—" Evangeline faltered. She'd meant her speech to be

reassuring, but the earlier mistrust was back in his eyes with a vengeance. "What do you mean?"

"What do you think I mean? I am many things, Miss Pemberton, but I like to think stupid is not one of them. As I told you before, I don't believe for a moment you have little chats with God."

"You think I was lying about Lord Hetherington being—"

"No, Miss Pemberton. That's just it. I don't. I'm sure he did suffocate, exactly as you claimed. In fact, I believe," he said, snapping out each carefully enunciated word like thrusts from a dagger, "you get your information not from the Lord, but from everyone around you. Dishonestly. Surreptitiously. Secretly."

"I—I don't know what you're talking about," she said, but the denial sounded weak even to her own ears.

"I don't think you do any 'talking' at all," he continued relentlessly. "I think you reach over and *take* the information you want. It's why you laid your bare hands on Hetherington's cheeks, is it not? It's why you wanted to hold Rachel, upstairs in the hallway when Rebecca was still lost. It's why you use your kisses and your body against *me*. A soulless murderer like myself must have countless lurid memories for you to steal. Tell me: just now, what did you see?"

"No," Evangeline said, shaking her head violently. "Nothing. You've got it wrong. I swear to you, I—"

"I don't believe you." He strode past her, brushing her aside as if she were less than nothing. He threw open the office door. "I need a maid," he called. "A footman. A—Miss Stanton? What the devil are you—oh, it doesn't matter. You'll do. Come."

He tugged a wary-looking Susan in by the wrist and thrust her before Evangeline.

"Now," he said. "Do you mean to tell me you don't 'see things' from others' touch? Take off your gloves, Miss Stanton. Put the backs of your fingers against Miss Pemberton's arm."

"Er . . ." Susan stammered, clearly at a loss as to how to

react to a conversation that had obviously taken a less than desired turn.

"No," Evangeline said. "Please don't."

Even without Susan's touch, a warning headache brewed at the back of Evangeline's skull. She had no wish to see another vision, to have her head split open by the ever-worsening aftershocks, to faint from pain in the middle of Mr. Lioncroft's office floor.

"You confess it to be true?" he demanded, arms crossed, eyebrows raised.

She took a deep breath, nodded. Heaven help her.

"Go," he said to Susan. "You do not wish to be present while I tell this *liar* exactly what I think about her deception."

Susan's eyes widened, but she remained otherwise both motionless and speechless. Her gaze flicked from Mr. Lioncroft to Evangeline, back to Mr. Lioncroft, back to Evangeline, as though she couldn't decide which desire was greater: to flee from Mr. Lioncroft's obvious rage, or to not abandon Evangeline to suffer his wrath alone.

At that moment, the footman who had earlier delivered Evangeline's summons strode through the door.

"You called for a servant, my lord?"

Mr. Lioncroft's forehead furrowed, then cleared. "I'm sorry, Milton. I no longer need your assistance. Miss Stanton helped me confirm what I needed to know about Miss Pemberton."

The footman glanced at Evangeline, then back to his master. "You . . . know?"

Mr. Lioncroft's voice rose. "*You* know?"

Susan raised her hand. "*I* know."

Evangeline closed her eyes. "Who *doesn't* know?"

"I want to know why my *staff* knows." Mr. Lioncroft faced Milton. "Explain yourself."

"It seems . . . She's done witchery for a few servants, my lord. Missing items, and the like. News of such feats travels fast."

"It's not witchery," Evangeline muttered. "I'm no witch."

"You," Mr. Lioncroft bit out, "are a . . . witch."

But she got the distinct impression he'd been about to call her something even worse.

She cleared her throat. "I wasn't going to—"

"Be quiet," he interrupted, his voice low, edgy, dangerous. "Or I'll burn you at the stake myself."

A hysterical titter escaped Susan's mouth. She clapped both hands across her face in horror and flushed a deep red.

Mr. Lioncroft didn't seem to notice.

"Your 'witchery,'" he said, "appears to be common household knowledge. I do not appreciate being the last to know."

"You're not," Evangeline assured him. "That is, some of the staff may know—and I'm a *woman,* not a witch—but the only guests aware of my visions are those of us in this room and Lady Stanton." At least, she hoped so. "I would much prefer to keep it that way."

"You would, would you? Did it occur to you I would prefer not to be *spied* upon every time you touch me?"

Before Evangeline could respond, Lady Stanton swept into the room.

"Well?" she demanded to Evangeline. "Yes or no?"

Mr. Lioncroft's eyes narrowed. "'Yes or no' what? Has this something to do with her witchery? Let me guess: the sole purpose of your visit was to peer into my mind without my knowledge."

Evangeline blushed, shook her head, motioned for Lady Stanton to speak no further.

Lady Stanton ignored her.

"Yes," she said matter-of-factly. "Miss Pemberton was to discover whether or not you will hang for Hetherington's murder. And as I have just overheard you mention she touched you, I am now expecting confirmation one way or the other. Miss Pemberton?"

"Yes, Miss Pemberton." The slow laziness in Mr. Lioncroft's

voice was unable to mask the hard edge of coiled danger beneath. "Seeing as how the only reason you suffer my presence is to pry my secrets straight from my flesh, I, too, am curious as to whether my neck will survive the fortnight. Care to apprise me of my future at the gallows?"

To be honest, Evangeline felt like vomiting.

If she lied and said, "No, you'll escape punishment," the expression on Lady Stanton's face indicated she was more than ready to move forward with the ill-advised compromise, which meant in seconds Mr. Lioncroft would find himself saddled with both a new bride and a new scandal, and Evangeline would no doubt (rightfully) bear the brunt of his rage.

If she lied and said, "Yes, you'll swing," the Stantons would head out at first light and abandon her at the first roadside inn . . . if she survived that long and avoided being committed to an asylum for her witchery.

And if she confessed the truth with a murmured, "I have no idea and will never have any idea," she would lose her usefulness to Lady Stanton altogether, giving the baroness no reason not to return her directly into her stepfather's custody as threatened.

All the potential outcomes were less than desirable. No matter which path she chose, her future would take a quick turn for the worse.

Unable to conceive of a plan of action that would appease all parties and ensure her continued safety from her stepfather, Evangeline did the only thing she could think of to do.

She faked a swoon.

Chapter Fourteen

Having witnessed Miss Pemberton topple over in a lifeless, graceless heap after her encounter with Hetherington's corpse, Gavin suspected her sudden sigh, fluttering eyelashes, and slow sinking to the floor were all affectation.

But why? Had his touch shown her a vision of him stretched on a gibbet, and she found herself not wishing to admit it?

He had made more than his fair share of mistakes in the eight-and-twenty years of his life, but he had no interest in being put to death for another man's crime. If he found out who was standing silent, content to let him swing in his place, he'd kill the son of a bitch with his bare hands.

Unless it was his sister, as Miss Pemberton seemed to believe. In which case . . . God, he didn't know what he would do.

"Evangeline!" the Stanton chit gasped, nudging her slippered toes against Miss Pemberton's shoulder. "Is she dead?"

It was on the tip of his tongue to say, "She's not dead; she's playacting," but since he wasn't 100 percent sure of that fact, Gavin ignored the question altogether and motioned for Milton to fetch smelling salts.

The footman sprinted out the door in his eagerness to obey Gavin's command, whether because Miss Pemberton looked a mere breath from death's door or because the servants of

Blackberry Manor lived in perpetual fear of the infamous Lioncroft temper, Gavin wasn't sure.

With a sigh, Lady Stanton flipped open a painted fan. When she directed its breeze at her own face instead of Miss Pemberton's, Gavin gave up on the idea of assistance from that quarter.

He knelt to the ground, knees spread, and sat back on his heels. Miss Pemberton's shoulders brushed against his calves and her unruly mass of rich brown hair pooled against the fall of his breeches. He eased both hands beneath her shoulders, palms up. His fingers curved against the soft silk covering the skin above her ribs. Slowly, carefully, he pulled her limp body toward his lap, sliding her warm torso up over his thighs until her head lolled against his chest.

"Miss Pemberton?" he asked quietly.

She said nothing.

"She *is* dead!" exclaimed the Stanton chit, wild-eyed.

Lady Stanton harrumphed and continued fanning her cheeks, as if the threat of perspiration was a much larger concern than human life.

"Bitch," he muttered under his breath.

Miss Pemberton flinched.

Gavin stared at her. She was feigning. He *knew* she was feigning!

He dropped his head forward until the side of his mouth rubbed against her temple.

"From this angle," he breathed into tendrils of flyaway hair, so softly only she could hear him, "I happen to have an excellent view of your nipples. May I touch them?"

Several things happened at once, none of which involved him touching Miss Pemberton's nipples.

First, the allegedly unconscious lady drove a sharp elbow directly into his crotch. Second, his footman shoved smelling salts beneath Miss Pemberton's nose. Third, the collision of Miss Pemberton's elbow with Gavin's cock caused him to double over at the very moment the smelling salts caused her to jerk upright, thus cracking his jaw against the top of Miss Pemberton's head with enough force to shatter teeth.

And then more people arrived.

Francine Rutherford first, looking ill. Then her husband Benedict stepped into the room, took in the scene with one glance, and began coughing into a frayed handkerchief. Edmund Rutherford, on the other hand, immediately burst into laughter.

"I say," he said over what appeared to be a glass of Gavin's port, "you always seem to have the Pemberton chit sprawled across your lap. She seems so prudish whenever *I* try."

Gavin was pretty sure he heard Miss Pemberton mutter, "Kill him."

Tempting.

"Hold this." Edmund shoved his now-empty goblet at the Stanton chit, who was apparently surprised enough to accept it. He stuck out one sweaty hand toward Miss Pemberton, who still reclined on Gavin's thighs with her hand rubbing the top of her head. "Allow me to help you up."

To say Miss Pemberton recoiled from Edmund's touch would be to make an understatement of the most grievous kind.

She recoiled her way right up Gavin's chest until her bottom rested against his crotch and the back of her head once again knocked against his jaw. Then she blushed, rolled off his lap, and sprang to her feet without anyone's aid.

"What the hell was that about?" Edmund demanded.

"Evangeline," the Stanton chit said as she shoved the empty goblet back into his hand, "doesn't like to be touched."

Edmund snorted. "What the devil was she doing with Lioncroft, then? She lets that profligate pull her onto his lap whenever he wants."

Miss Stanton shrugged. "He's Lioncroft."

Francine cast him an appraising glance, as if suddenly rejudging his worth.

Gritting his teeth, Gavin rose to his feet. Yes. He was Lion-croft, man of scandal. But he was not going to be relabeled a murderer thanks to someone else's actions.

"First of all," he began, then paused as he realized he couldn't start with a "first of all" regarding Hetherington's killer when his uninvited guests were busy gawking at the miraculously reconscious Miss Pemberton. "Are you all right now?"

She responded by crossing her arms over her bodice.

"Excellent." He turned to face the footman. "Milton, would you fetch that slip for me? Thank you." Gavin sat against the front edge of his desk. "While a few of us are together, I'd like to take this opportunity to point out any given guest could have killed Hetherington." Their blinking stares indicated he might've been better served with some kind of segue between the two topics. Deciding to forge ahead now that he'd broached the subject, he continued, "We're all in agreement on how he died, correct?"

Francine arched an eyebrow. "Strangulation?"

"Smothered," the Stanton chit corrected her.

"Oh, right." Edmund fished a flask from a pocket. "Miss Pemberton chatted with God about that."

The lady in question froze, then placed her fingertips to her temples. She very carefully did not look at Gavin or either of the Stanton women, no doubt terrified any one of the three would divulge the truth of her visions to Edmund, Benedict, and Francine.

How could Miss Pemberton claim not to be a witch? Gavin now *knew* her to be a liar and the worst sort of spy, and still he ached to crush her to him and claim her mouth with his. What other explanation could there be?

He forced himself to turn in such a way as to face the others without also facing her. Perhaps if he couldn't see her, she couldn't bewitch him.

"What did God say, again?" Francine asked, one hand cradling her belly.

"Said Hetherington was smothered to death." Benedict tugged a fresh handkerchief free from his pocket. "With a pillow."

Edmund sniffed the contents of his flask. "Did God send proof?"

"Actually," Gavin said as his footman returned to the room, "He did. Thank you, Milton. That will be all."

"What," Lady Stanton said, her fan beating double-time, "is that?"

"A pillowslip, Mother. A much stained one."

"From the Hetheringtons' guest chamber," Gavin confirmed.

The Stanton chit peered closer. "Killers often use a weapon of convenience. And what could be more convenient than a feather pillow, when the victim lay sound asleep in his bed?"

"Look." Gavin held the damaged silk by the corners and shook the wrinkles out as best he could. A few flakes fell from a scab-colored splotch in the center. "Blood."

Miss Pemberton tucked a stray curl behind her ear. "Lord Hetherington's forehead was wounded, was it not? The blood must have transferred to the slip when the killer placed the pillow atop the earl's injured face."

Edmund refilled his empty goblet with the amber contents of his flask. "How do we know Lioncroft didn't smear Hetherington's blood on there himself, right after Miss Pemberton chatted with God?"

Gavin bared his teeth at him. "While I appreciate your unfailing belief in the extent of my audacity, I could not have done so."

Francine raised a thin eyebrow. "Why not?"

"Because," Miss Pemberton answered slowly, "when we got to the bedroom last night, the blood had already dried. Remember? The front of the bandage was dark and crusty, and the bit trailing down the side of his nose was kind of scabby-looking, with a tinge of—"

"Miss Pemberton, enough." Lady Stanton's painted fan closed with a snap. "You've made your point. The blood had to have been transferred from cloth to cloth while Hetherington was still alive."

Gavin laid the pillowslip across the desk, blood side up.

"Pah," Benedict scoffed. "We can see blood, but it could be anyone's blood."

"Yes and no," Miss Pemberton countered. "If it were someone else's blood, what would it be doing on Lord Hetherington's pillowslip unless it came from the killer himself? I am uninjured. Lady Stanton and her daughter are uninjured. *Mr. Lioncroft* is uninjured."

In the space of a heartbeat, Gavin decided his very favorite female trait would forevermore be the ability to reason. He grinned at Miss Pemberton, who was busy glaring at Benedict. She'd not only pointed out the flaw in the new lord's logic, she'd made sure to intimate Gavin's potential innocence. Perhaps now the focus could finally be on finding the true killer.

"We're *all* uninjured," Francine put in with a sigh.

"So it seems," Benedict agreed. "Therefore, it must be Hetherington's blood. I see no other explanation for—" His handkerchief flew to his face as Benedict erupted into another fit of vicious, hacking coughs.

"Seems to *me*," Edmund slurred, "you do a fair bit of bleeding yourself, old boy. Your handkerchief is fair covered in blood. Maybe you suffocated the selfish rotter last night and then coughed on him."

Benedict froze.

"No." Miss Pemberton shook her head. "The blood on his handkerchief is minimal compared to the pillowslip, and covered in mucus besides. There's no mucus on the pillowslip."

"Miss Pemberton, really." Francine shoved a fist to her mouth, her narrow face looking more than a little wan beneath the layers of rouge.

Edmund swirled his goblet. "So we're back to Lioncroft, then, are we?"

"No," Miss Pemberton said again. "We're back to 'it could have been anyone.'"

"Although we did agree that Lioncroft seems the most likely," the Stanton chit put in helpfully. "He had the motive to do so, the means to do so, and the opportunity to do so. We all saw the two of them argue at the supper table, and Lioncroft himself admitted being more than angry enough to— Ow! Bloody hell, Evangeline, did you *step* on me?"

Miss Pemberton shot Gavin a nettled look. He could've kissed her.

Lady Stanton rapped her daughter's shoulder with the closed fan. "Watch your mouth, young lady."

"I'm just saying—"

"—what the rest of us are thinking," Francine interrupted. "My apologies, Lioncroft, but you know it to be true. We might as well put it to words."

Gavin's jaw clenched. He did know it to be true—they'd all assumed his guilt from the moment Hetherington turned up dead. And from their current expressions, they'd never expected anything different from one such as him.

The only reason they descended onto his home in the first place was because of their relationship with Rose, and the only reason they continued to linger beneath his roof was because they were all selfish scandalmongers more interested in exploiting his pocket than quitting his company.

Were he poor and ill-connected, not a one of them would be present. But with the abundant food and endless drink and the generous solicitude of his servants at their disposal, the present company were more than willing to overlook so vexing an interruption as murder . . . for now.

However. Even they, fashionable parasites though they were, must have their limits.

"Well," Edmund began, as though reading Gavin's mind.

"If we're putting our suspicions into words, ought we also put them into action?"

"Action?" Gavin repeated, unrepentant that the danger in his voice caused even the drunken Edmund to recoil a few steps backward. "And what action might that be?"

"I'm sure he means the gallows," the Stanton chit piped up. "In fact, I'd wager—Ow! Bloody hell, Evangeline, if you do that again, I'll—Ow! All right, Mother. You don't have to bruise my shoulder. I'll mind my tongue." She crossed her arms and glared at the company.

Gavin rose from his perch against the desk and stretched himself to his full height. "There can be no conviction without proof. And you have no proof."

Lady Stanton cast a pointed glance toward Miss Pemberton. "We'll unmask the murderer quite soon. I have no doubt."

The Stanton chit edged closer to her mother. Francine and Benedict exchanged a knowing look. Edmund smirked behind his goblet. Which could only mean the party had long since decided upon the culprit, and now the only thing in want was evidence to hang him.

Gavin's cravat felt suddenly too tight.

After dining alone in his chamber—for he had no wish to renew conversation about the likelihood of his guilt in the late earl's death—Gavin began to feel restless. Typically at such times, he would spend the evening in the library with a book, or while away the hours outside strolling the land behind the manor or perhaps riding to the nearest pugilism club. But any one of his skittish, suspicious guests might be within the library, no stars lit the night sky, much less his fields, and he had no wish to explain why he'd left a "party" to go fighting in a neighboring town.

When his desire for motion at last outweighed his desire

for solitude, Gavin exited his bedchamber via the primary door instead of his hinged mirror, and strode into the hall.

Shadows teemed along the deserted corridor, but enough candlelight flickered within the sconces for even the most casual of observers to note the content of the oil paintings framed along the passageway.

Miss Pemberton was right. Not a smiling face among them. No faces at all.

Landscape after landscape swirled across the many canvases. Here, a dark river, frothing with rage beneath leafless trees twisting in the wind. There, a lifeless chasm, filled with dirt and rock and ice, smothered with a layer of murky fog. And, ah, this one, a torrent of sleet slashing across a desolate highway, snapping the fragile stem of a single frost-tipped flower protruding from the muck.

He was not, it seemed, overfond of portraiture. And why would he be? Of whom would he commission portraits?

As if appearing before him merely to spite his thoughts, one of his nieces stood at the crossroads between his wing and the guest wing. With both pale hands gripping the banister, Nancy stared dully over the ledge to the marble vestibule below. She leaned forward, Closer. Lower. Her pink ribbons and blond ringlets dangled precariously before her.

Within seconds, Gavin reached her side.

"Please tell me you've no designs on jumping," he said softly, placing a tentative hand across her white knuckles.

"I—no." She straightened, swallowed, blushed. "Fantasy. That is to say, folly. I could never . . . Mother's been through enough without me worsening things further."

His breaths once again came easy now that he no longer feared she might tumble over the edge. And with the return of air to his lungs came the return of doubt. Gavin imagined himself the last person she'd hoped would discover her in such a position, and he had no inkling of how to proceed now that he had. Although Nancy had made no movement to remove her fingers from beneath his, Gavin shoved his hands in his pockets, leaned against the railing, and tried to guess at the thoughts of a seventeen-year-old miss.

He suspected whatever had Nancy contemplating the shortest path down the long spiral staircase had to do with something even greater than Hetherington's death. The son of a bitch *was* his niece's father, and the last thing Gavin wanted to do was belittle the death of a family member. Without that straw to grasp, however, he was at a loss as to discover the cause of her anxiety. He hoped like hell her distress had nothing to do with a romance between herself and Mr. Teasdale. He considered his niece far too young to have to leg-shackle herself to a man old enough to be William the Conqueror's grandfather.

Having thus done away with the topics of death and marriage—neither of which were desirable states in Gavin's estimation—what subjects were safe to discuss with one's estranged niece? She seemed in desperate need of cheering up, but at seventeen, he could offer her neither porcelain dolls nor Irish whiskey.

"After . . . things return to normal," he ventured, hoping he'd found a reasonably bland topic, "will you be heading to London for your first Season?"

Nancy's cheeks paled. Her eyes welled with tears.

"No," she choked out, as if the words were ripped from her soul. "I shall never have a Season, Jane shall never have a Season, the twins will never have a Season, and things will never, ever return to normal again."

And with that, she ripped herself from the banister and tore down the corridor toward the guest chambers in a flash of ribbons and ringlets and tears. With a muffled, hitching sob, she careened around the corner and out of sight.

That . . . had not gone well. Gavin turned to face the burnished cherry railing. Death by spiral staircase suddenly seemed as viable an option as any.

Except there, at the bottom, came his footman. Milton plodded up the curved marble stairs, one hand bearing a small silver tray with a franked parchment atop.

Gavin met the footman halfway, thanked him, and broke the seal on the missive. Its contents read as follows:

Dear Mr. Lioncroft,

It has come to my attention that you are harboring a runaway, namely, my stepdaughter, Evangeline Pemberton. Because she has not yet reached her majority, she belongs at home and I must request her immediate return.

As we are both gentlemen, I shall expect to receive confirmation of your intent to facilitate her prompt departure. To that end, my man is waiting for your reply. If she is too much trouble to deal with easily—and I am quite aware of how much trouble Evangeline can be—it is of no consequence whatsoever for me to come fetch her myself.

I am sure you are a reasonable man who will not allow a simple family matter to escalate to dramatic proportions. My stepdaughter belongs in my custody.

Please inform me of your expenses during the time you housed her, and I will ensure you are properly reimbursed.

Yours, &c.
Mr. Neal Pemberton

Gavin read the letter three times before any of it made sense. Once it did, he crumpled the entire sheet in his fist.

Miss Pemberton, it seemed, was an even greater liar than he'd first supposed.

Here by happenstance, as a special friend of Miss Stanton's, was she? Ha. Yet another bloody parasite, here to take advantage of his roof and food and pockets. How had she talked Lady Stanton into allowing her to impose upon a house party? As silver-tongued as she was bewitching, no doubt.

"Beg pardon, my lord," murmured the footman. "But there's a messenger waiting belowstairs. Should I . . . ?"

"Ah. Right." Gavin's fist tightened around the crumpled missive. "I shall pen an immediate reply."

One neither Mister nor Miss Pemberton was likely to enjoy. For he was not yet ready to give up his beautiful liar. Considering she sought to use him for his money and shelter, she could not object to Gavin using her particular attributes in return.

After all, she possessed the singular ability to prove his innocence by uncovering which of the ingrates below his roof was responsible for Hetherington's murder. That was the least she could do in repayment for her hypocrisy. He had thought she was the one person capable of logic, capable of seeing beyond the rumor, capable perhaps of trust—but, no.

Miss Pemberton was capable of nothing but lies and pantomime, suffering his kisses not out of passion, but out of a gossip-hungry desire to steal through his memories, spy upon his innermost thoughts, and hunt down his weaknesses.

No more.

Neal Pemberton could certainly have his duplicitous step-daughter back—but not until Gavin finished with her first.

Chapter Fifteen

The next morning, wet paintbrush in hand, Gavin turned to face the footman hesitating in the doorway to the studio. "Has something happened?"

"Only that the packages you ordered are here. Where shall we store them?"

"I suppose you can deliver them directly to—no, I prefer to do it myself." He stepped away from his easel. "Where are they now?"

"Belowstairs. They've only just arrived."

A familiar, pungent stench enveloped the room as Gavin uncapped the jar of turpentine in order to clean the bright oils from the coarse hairs of his paintbrushes. He had thought to paint dawn instead of dusk. Something new, different, cheerful. He had failed. The sun lilted drunkenly in the sky, its effect garish, its rays overbright, illuminating the muck splattered across an abandoned cottage and the dirt crusted on the cracked windows.

"And Madame Rousseau? Has she responded?"

"Yes, my lord. She leaves immediately."

"Excellent." Gavin recapped the turpentine and laid his brushes across a paint-stained cloth to dry. "Anything else?"

"No, my lord."

"Very well. Thank you."

The footman bobbed and left.

Gavin replaced his paints, latched the door to his studio, and strode down the corridor. He wondered what Mr. Pemberton thought upon receiving Gavin's no-doubt unanticipated response. Promising to return her "soon" instead of "immediately" was not at all the norm, but most likely a small delay would be of little concern. After all, she was fed, chaperoned, and entertained, and Mr. Pemberton—who claimed his step-daughter a nuisance—had no cause for alarm. Aside from old rumors, that was. Gavin's reply had failed to mention the more recent murder. Or his intention for Miss Pemberton to solve it.

When he reached the vestibule below the spiral staircase, a pair of maids handed him his packages. The two large boxes contained the twins' new dolls. The smaller, part of his birth-day gift for Jane. He fervently hoped thirteen-year-old girls liked jewelry.

He turned to climb the stairs just as the two Stanton women sashayed from around the corner. Damn.

Upon catching sight of him, the Stanton chit froze in place, as if her yellow hair and pale skin and pink gown might somehow blend undetectably into the gray marble surrounding them. Her mother, however, pursed her lips—setting that horrible mole to wriggling—and strode forward, clearly intending to cut him off at the pass.

"Lioncroft," she said, her close-set eyes as colorless as her skin. "Imagine running into you."

Gavin shifted his hold on the packages. "I live here."

"And what a lovely home it is. Susan was just saying so. Weren't you, Susan?"

The Stanton chit was too busy pretending invisibility to respond. Very well. The better for him to pounce.

"Miss Stanton," he said, his unexpected address startling

her into a squeak. "Would you say you've been friends with Miss Pemberton for very long?"

She shoved at her spectacles with the back of her hand. "Er . . ."

Lady Stanton's eyes narrowed. "Why?"

"Why?" Gavin leaned one hip against the banister and stared into her colorless eyes. "Because I've just received the oddest letter. A fellow by the name of Neal Pemberton claims her to be his underage runaway stepdaughter, and demands her return."

"I'm not surprised. Every word you spoke is truth. I sent Mr. Pemberton a letter informing him of her whereabouts."

"Mother, you didn't!"

"Of course, I did. I told her I would do worse than that if she couldn't be bothered to aid us in our cause, and I am a woman of my word."

Gavin placed one foot on a higher step to better balance the packages on his thigh. "And in what cause, may I ask, was Miss Pemberton to aid you?"

Lady Stanton's smile cracked like glass breaking in two. The Stanton chit had the grace to look mortified. Which could only mean one thing . . .

Damn. *He* was The Cause.

Not only was Miss Pemberton a lying, spying charity case, her actions were somehow designed to interest him in the Stanton chit, of all people. Unbelievable. He bit back a groan. Whether by the noose or parson's trap, every single guest beneath his roof aimed to ensnare him.

"I see," he said, although they hadn't spoken. He rose from the banister and climbed a few steps toward the next floor. "I'm afraid I'm uninterested in matrimonial pursuits."

"Is it Evangeline?" the Stanton chit blurted out. "Are you interested in her?"

The chill in Lady Stanton's voice frosted the stale air. "He's not interested in her as a *wife*, Susan. Didn't you hear him?

Gentlemen never marry common sluts. The best that girl can aspire to is a mistress, and I have my doubts she will find success even in that."

Gavin halted his ascent, turned, stared down at her. He wished he was armed with Hetherington's swordsticks instead of the twins' dolls, so he could leap from the stairs and beat Lady Stanton with them.

"You would be wise," he said, the words ricocheting like bullets against the bare walls, "not to disparage Miss Pemberton within my hearing if you wish to remain welcome in my home. I allow your presence as a courtesy to her, not she as a courtesy to you."

Lady Stanton's narrow mouth fell open, for the first time at a loss for words. Her daughter, equally speechless, was rapidly turning an even more frightening shade of pink than her gown.

Gavin inclined his head, turned, and resumed his trek upstairs. They made no effort to stop him.

Within a very few minutes, he reached the nursery door. Being ajar, he was able to nudge it open with one shoulder without dumping the packages to the floor.

Rose sat in the center of the small sofa reading a story aloud, one of the twins snuggled against either side. Jane stood just behind them, attempting to affect boredom and peer at the pages over her mother's shoulders at the same time. Nancy was nowhere to be seen.

"Uncle Lioncroft!" Jane rounded the sofa and rushed up to him, her younger sisters scrambling behind her. "Are all those for me?"

"Jane," Rose admonished from the sofa. "Show some restraint."

"But it's my birthday." Jane grinned up at Gavin. "Who else would they be for?"

Who else, indeed. He swallowed. Replacement dolls for

the twins now seemed to have been an exceptionally ill-timed purchase.

"Actually," he began, and winced when her smile dimmed. "You are half-right. These two boxes are for Rachel and Rebecca, to substitute for the doll whose face I broke yesterday."

"Oh." Jane stepped aside as the twins squealed and tore at the paper. "*Oh*," she said again. "Dolls."

"Yes, dolls. Because they are children," he told her gravely. "You are thirteen now—very nearly an adult."

"That's right," she said, spine straightening. "I'm almost a woman."

"Just so. And instead of commissioning toys for you, I thought you'd appreciate grown-up gifts more suited for a young lady."

"Grown-up gifts? But you've only one package left, and it's the smallest of the lot."

"The other wouldn't fit in a package. Her name is Madame Rousseau."

Jane goggled at him. "The most famous modiste in London?"

He nodded hesitantly. "It will take her a few days to arrive, but if you will still be here, she will be glad to outfit you with new gowns."

She squeezed his waist in a quick, breathless hug before dashing to her mother's side. "Oh, will we, Mother? Do say yes. This is the best birthday *ever*."

Gavin held his breath. As before with his letter to Mr. Pemberton, here he was again, manipulating the travel plans of others. He hoped if he could just convince her to stay another week, Rose might stop thinking of him as a villain long enough to think of him as her brother. He would have his sister again, he would have his nieces, he would have family—if only for a few more days.

Rose closed the book in her lap and sat very still.

Disappointment dampened his palms. She did not want to

stay. She did not want to be in his company. But why? Was Madame Rousseau not enough of a lure? Perhaps Rose did suspect him of killing her husband. Or perhaps, as Miss Pemberton suggested, Rose had done so herself and wished to escape discovery. Gavin could hardly blame her, if she had. He would've killed the son of a bitch long ago. He wouldn't have blamed the murder on a *sibling*, however, and he prayed Rose would not either. Which meant—hopefully—some third party had been the villain, and now stood idly by as Rose's children lost their father . . . and Gavin lost his sister all over again. He refused to let that happen.

"I don't know," she said slowly, her gaze not meeting his. "We'll see what happens."

Jane sighed and turned back to Gavin. "She'll come around."

He wasn't so certain.

Jane cocked her head. "What is in the other package? The one that's for me?"

Gavin's fingers clenched around it, suddenly too embarrassed to hand it over graciously, and beginning to doubt he should hand it over at all.

She pried it from his hand and ripped open the brown paper to the jewelry inside.

"Ohhh," she breathed, eyes wide and shining. "Mother, look! A beautiful, beautiful necklace, with the most cunning little portrait-locket I've ever seen." Her fingers pried open the clasp. She glanced up at him, brow furrowed. "It's empty!"

"I know." The words came out so garbled, he had to clear his throat and begin anew. "I know," he said again, jamming his hands in his pockets. "I thought . . . If you like, that is, while we're waiting for Madame Rousseau to arrive . . . I would paint a miniature for you. Your portrait, I mean. If you'd like to sit for me."

"I'd love it!" She clasped the locket to her chest, the chain dangling between her fingers. "Oh, Mother, say yes! Say yes, say yes, say yes."

Rose said nothing.

Gavin shifted his feet.

"I suppose," she said at last. "But afterward, we're leaving."

Jane squealed and danced about the room, oblivious to the finality in her mother's tone, and the blankness in Rose's eyes.

Gavin, however, was not. Her careful tone, her tense posture, her guarded expression all combined to say the words she hadn't spoken aloud, to confirm his worst fear. All the gifts in the world couldn't keep them indefinitely. In less than a week's time, she and her daughters would leave him.

And they wouldn't be back.

With the gifts delivered safely to his nieces and his discovery of Lady Stanton's matrimonial plan souring both his appetite and his muse, Gavin avoided the breakfast room and his studio alike in favor of his office.

His steps quickened as he strode away from the nursery. A few hours solitude would not come amiss before a flurry of birthday activities. Having already dispatched his response to Miss Pemberton's stepfather, Gavin now needed to confront the duplicitous woman herself. Not outside her chamber, where anyone in the guest quarters might overhear. Not in the middle of Jane's birthday party, either, where curious eyes would be on them at every moment. He needed her now. He needed her alone. He needed her—Good Lord, what the devil was the woman doing outside his office door?

Gavin stood in the shadows and waited. Miss Pemberton gave no indication of having heard him approach from a connecting corridor.

She raised a gloved hand and poised her fist a few inches from the door's surface, as if to rap her knuckles against the wood. She paused, frowned, lowered her hand without knocking. She tugged off her gloves and shoved them in a pocket. No pocket. The crumpled kidskin fluttered to the floor. She bent to retrieve them, unwittingly presenting Gavin with an unexpected view of the perfect derrière.

As she swiped for the gloves, pins flew from her hair. The longer she stayed bent over to retrieve the lost pins, the more gravity worked on her heavy mass of coiled hair. What might've once been a chignon slid from the back of her head to off-center of her crown, and then exploded in a jumble of tangled curls.

Miss Pemberton sighed, righted herself, shook her head. Any lingering pins tumbled to the floor. She allowed them to remain there. After dumping the handful of pins she'd managed to collect into one of her gloves, she returned her attention to the door. Once again, she made as if to knock, then seemed to think better of the movement. She used her raised hand to comb through her unruly curls instead, as if belatedly realizing a lack of hairpins might well portend a lack of style. Locks tamed as much as they would ever be, Miss Pemberton lifted her chin, straightened her shoulders, and reached directly for the doorknob.

Gavin stepped forth from the shadows. "You wanted to see me?"

She squeaked and spun to face him, hands clutched to her throat. This action dislodged both gloves and hairpins, sending the entire collection on a return journey to her feet. She muttered something that sounded suspiciously like a curse before fixing Gavin with a blinding smile. He didn't trust blinding smiles.

"Er, yes. Good morning, Mr. Lioncroft."

Without returning the greeting, he retrieved her gloves and swept past her into his office. He circled his desk, placed the gloves atop its neatly organized surface, and dropped into his chair.

Miss Pemberton hesitated only a moment before inching into the room.

"Close the door."

"I don't know if that's a wise idea," she mumbled.

"Of course it's not," he said briskly. "Neither was coming to see me unchaperoned. As that's never stopped you before and I was hoping to catch you alone in any case, we may as well make the most of a fortuitous situation. Close the door."

She did, and promptly plastered her back against it as if already planning her escape. "You were hoping to catch me alone?"

"As were you me, I daresay, or you wouldn't be here now. Shall we spend a few more minutes informing each other of the obvious, or shall we cut directly to the point?"

"The point," she agreed faintly, resting one hand on the doorknob. "I . . . don't want to be missed."

"No?" Gavin leaned back in his chair to study her. "No, I suppose not. Although, some would say a chit who steals away from her legal guardian should surely *expect* to be missed. Would you not agree?"

She blanched. "I . . . Legal guardian?"

"Let's see, I have it right here, a Mister . . ." Gavin shook the folds from the missive he'd long committed to memory. He produced an unnecessary quizzing glass from his desk drawer and positioned it between his eye and the parchment just to make her sweat with fear. Even though Miss Pemberton was no longer in his direct line of sight, he could *hear* her anxiety, as the trembling of her hand was fierce enough to rattle the doorknob. "Ah, yes," Gavin said above the rapid intake of her breath. "A Mr. Neal Pemberton demands your immediate return."

"*No,*" she burst out, abandoning the door to tremble before his desk. "No, you cannot. I—I cannot. I refuse."

"Legal guardian," Gavin repeated, enunciating each word

clearly. "Surely you do not suggest we hold ourselves above the law?"

"*Yes.* Yes, a capital idea." She slapped a bare palm against the surface of his desk. "Let's hold ourselves above the law."

The quizzing glass fell atop the parchment. "What?"

"I don't wish to return. I don't wish to lay eyes on him ever again, nor he on me. How did he find me so quickly? How did he know I was here?"

"You don't deny having run away from your stepfather?"

Miss Pemberton closed her eyes and shivered. When her gaze again focused on his, a hollowness had replaced the usual spark. "What point would there be? You've a letter from him right before you."

"A letter demanding your return."

"A demand with which I have no intention of complying. He . . ." She paled, shook. "He thinks only of himself."

"Yet you find no fault in complying with others' self-centered demands, do you not?"

She stared at him. "I do what?"

"If you expect me to collude with you outside of the law, the very least you could do is be honest with me."

"I am honest with you!"

"You said you were a friend of Miss Stanton's, not a girl on the run from her stepfather."

"I am both those things."

"Are you? Are you simply the bosom friend of Miss Stanton's as you would have me believe, or are you perchance a manipulator and a liar, presenting me with one face while conspiring behind my back to compromise me against my will to a chit I have no desire to be leg-shackled to?"

"Lady Stanton . . . is very single-minded."

"Lady Stanton," Gavin corrected, "is a bitch. What makes her a better ally than your stepfather?"

"Not *being* my stepfather."

"Were you aware she wrote a letter to inform him of

your whereabouts because you failed to fulfill your half of the bargain?"

Miss Pemberton gasped. "She *is* a—I cannot believe—well, unfortunately, I can believe—but the party hasn't even concluded! How would she know what I will or won't do before we leave?"

"I have no intention of marrying the Stanton chit even if falsely compromised, nor do I appreciate your complicity in Lady Stanton's stratagem."

Miss Pemberton rose to her feet. Although still unnaturally pale, her chin tilted at a stubborn angle. "I respect that. I had no wish to make any progress in that regard. However, I would do anything to escape my stepfather."

"I surmised as much." Gavin nodded toward a chair. "Sit."

She regarded him warily, as if half expecting him to pounce. "You're not angry?"

"I'm furious. *Sit.*"

Miss Pemberton sat.

"Whether you wish it to be so or not, I have the power to send you home to your stepfather."

"You do not," she gasped.

He raised a brow.

"I could run away again," she insisted, eyes wild. "I've done it before."

"To raging success, I see." He returned his quizzing glass to its drawer. "Have you any money?"

"No."

He refolded the missive and replaced it on its pile. "Transportation?"

"N-no."

His fingers steepled. "Lodging? Food? Protection?"

This time the word was a whisper. "No."

He lifted a shoulder. "Then I find running away to be a very foolish alternative, to say the least."

She blinked slowly, as if forcing him into focus. "Alternative to what?"

"Staying here until my brother-in-law's killer has been brought to light."

"But my stepfather demanded my return—"

"And I penned a very pretty apology because I am unwilling to give you up until you've helped me prove my innocence. You begin today."

"I do? Does that mean if I do not, you intend to throw me from your house?"

"If you do not, I intend to return you to your legal guardian."

Her knuckles whitened in her lap. "You're extorting my help. Temporary freedom in exchange for assisting your personal goals."

"Was that not your arrangement with Lady Stanton?"

"It was a horrible arrangement. I should've chosen a penniless life on the streets of London." Miss Pemberton stared at him in disbelief. "You're no better than she is."

Gavin shrugged. "I never claimed to be better than anyone, merely innocent of this particular murder. I intend to prove this fact before being hung for a crime I didn't commit. And I need your help to do so. Do we have a deal?"

"What do you wish for me to do?"

Ah. Progress.

"The last time we were alone, you admitted Lady Stanton orchestrated just such an event so you could touch me and spy inside my mind, did you not? You, Miss Pemberton, have an invaluable talent. I would rather it be used to my benefit than hers."

"Everybody does," she muttered.

"You willfully spied on me. Inside my brain. Without permission. Against my will. Surely I can ask for restitution to such a trespass."

"I did not spy on you." Miss Pemberton crossed her arms and sent him a baleful stare. "I literally cannot. Besides, you have no call for indignation. Aren't you asking me to do the same to others?"

"I . . . I suppose I am." Unease soured Gavin's stomach briefly before his desire to escape the gallows returned to the forefront. "Then you agree? You'll help me prove my innocence in exchange for temporary freedom?"

"No." Her arms tightened below her breasts. "If we're negotiating terms of the arrangement, then I should like permanent freedom in exchange for my help."

"Mr. Pemberton is your legal guardian," Gavin reminded her. "I cannot keep you here forever."

"I do not wish to *be* with a self-centered extortionist like you a moment longer than necessary," she bit out. "Once I've done my part, I should like enough money to take the mail coach anywhere I choose."

Gavin stared at the angry young woman on the other side of his desk, surprised that she'd caught him off guard with her response. Of course, she had no wish to stay. She wanted to leave him. Forever. Just like everyone else. How could he have imagined otherwise? Guilty of murder or not, he did not deserve her—or, likely, anyone. After all, he was in fact the self-centered extortionist she proclaimed him to be. And worse.

So, he nodded.

"Fair enough," he said softly. "But I am not so cruel as to send you off in a mail coach. I will provide a carriage, and if you will not accept that, then at the very least you will allow me to hire a hack for wherever you plan to go. And you must also take enough money to assure me you will have a roof and a bed until you get . . . on your feet."

His blood iced as he looked at her. The most common source of income for a young girl living alone in the streets required her to remain on her back, not her feet. What kind of a man was her stepfather that she would willfully choose such a life over returning home?

Miss Pemberton slumped, defeated. "That is, *if* I live through the worsening aftereffects long enough to prove you innocent."

Her words instantly called to mind the image of her pale form lying unconscious after the terrifying experience in Hetherington's chamber. Rose had reached out merely to offer support, and Miss Pemberton . . . Miss Pemberton had dropped to the ground as though struck by a bullet. Gavin swallowed. He had no idea how serious her condition might be. Could he be asking her to risk her life to save his? Did it even matter?

"Yes," he said aloud, unsure which question he was answering. Perhaps neither. Perhaps both.

Miss Pemberton nodded, rose, and crossed the room.

"Wait," he called. She paused, her back to him. "You never said why you sought me out this morning."

When she glanced at him over her shoulder, her gaze was shadowed and unreadable. "Ironic as it now seems, I came to apologize."

He stood, began to go to her, stopped. "For what?"

"For my role in Lady Stanton's contrivances. I came to tell you I was against it from the beginning, and that I never intended to compromise you to Susan against your will—or hers. I came to tell you I'd paid lip-service out of desperation, and that I was delighted to find I couldn't follow through even if I wanted to, because I think secretly using visions for the sole purpose of spying on or deceiving others is the worst kind of cowardice, and wholly reprehensible. I see now that such an apology would've been a wasted effort, as you are cut from precisely the same manipulative cloth as my stepfather and Lady Stanton. Although I do not get visions from your touch, my lord, I would prefer in the future for you to keep your hands to yourself. Good day."

This time when she turned to leave, Gavin made no move to stop her.

Chapter Sixteen

Evangeline stormed back to the guest quarters in a high fury.

What was it about her that attracted arrogant, violent, self-centered men? Did she have the appearance of someone easily cowed? Angels above, even her *hair* wasn't easily cowed, so why would the rest of her be? Her stepfather had spent the past twenty years trying to beat her into a pathetic submissive state and failed every time. She might have followed his dictates more often if he'd commanded with words rather than with his fist.

And Mr. Lioncroft! He was no better. He could've simply *asked* her to help him prove his innocence. She'd gone to his office to apologize, for heaven's sake. She would've fallen all over herself in her eagerness to make amends. But, no. A man like that doesn't ask for what he wants. He orders. He demands. He extorts. Much like Lady Stanton, a creature of worse evil than Evangeline had imagined. The harridan penned a note to her stepfather on the grounds of a single day's ineffectiveness at getting Susan into a compromising position? Evangeline was clairvoyant, not a saint. Miracles were quite outside her ability.

Solving the mystery of Lord Hetherington's murder might likewise be outside her ability. But she had to try. And she had to be fast. Her home in the Chiltern Hills wasn't more than a single day's drive from Braintree and Bocking. If her stepfather received Mr. Lioncroft's response today, he could arrive by tomorrow evening. Why hadn't she thought to ask when Mr. Lioncroft had sent his reply? Or how he'd sent it? Ah, yes. Because the thought of Neal Pemberton coming to fetch her from Blackberry Manor had struck fear into her very bones. Perhaps she shouldn't bother confronting Lady Stanton. Perhaps she should pack her things—what things? She had nothing!—and leave this very moment.

But . . . on foot? With no food, no clothes, no money? As Mr. Lioncroft had pointed out, such an action would be borne as much of foolishness as desperation. And autumn was cruel. She had no wish to flee, only to die from the elements. Then again, she had no wish to live to be one hundred, bound and beaten in some corner of the Pemberton cottage.

Nothing for it. She would have to solve the murder *today*, accept Mr. Lioncroft's guilt money, and be gone at first light.

Thus resolved, Evangeline found herself once again standing outside a closed door. This time, she had no gloves to remove. As far as she knew, those scraps of cloth still resided on Mr. Lioncroft's desk. Nor did she make any attempt to tame her hair. The pins were lost forever, and besides, her looks had never been palatable in Lady Stanton's eyes anyway. Why bother attempting to please the unpleasable?

With a twist of the handle, Evangeline thrust open the door and charged inside.

Lady Stanton shot up from a cushioned seat before a small vanity. Her lady's maid started, hairbrush in hand, at Evangeline's unexpected countenance in the mirror.

"How dare you enter without permission!" Lady Stanton's words cut across the room like glass.

Evangeline strode forward. "How dare you pen a letter to my stepfather."

"I don't have to respond to such peevishness, Miss Pemberton. Barging in here like you own the place." Both Lady

Stanton's tone and expression turned glacial. "Such behavior is the height of rudeness."

"That's why I did it," Evangeline returned. "What excuse do you have for your actions?"

"I need not excuse myself to a ragamuffin like you, in any case. Just look at you. Dolled up in Susan's castoffs and you still manage to look like the grubbiest urchin alive. Be gone from my room. I'll summon you if and when I feel we have matters to discuss." Lady Stanton sat back down on the cushioned seat before her vanity. "As you can see, my maid is attending to my hair. I suggest you find a servant to attempt something with yours."

Evangeline's jaw tightened. "I don't care about my hair."

"Well, you should. It's a right mess." Lady Stanton swiveled back to face the glass and motioned for her lady's maid to continue.

"I want to know why you corresponded with my stepfather."

"You showed no interest in complying with my stratagem. What use had I of you?"

"What use? I would have been happy to peel potatoes in the larder until you returned to Stanton House. I came to you for safety. For shelter. For—"

"For a handout, you mean. No doubt you took one look at Lioncroft and decided his pockets were deeper than mine. And you're right—they are. But you shan't have him. Despite his many flaws, he was born a member of our class, not yours. You have no class at all, just like your mother. Blood will tell, I always say. She was a tatterdemalion like no other. Looked every inch the gypsy."

"Leave my mother out of this. She was a better woman than you'll ever be."

"Is that right?" Lady Stanton's brittle laugh was like shattered glass. "Then why, in the years I knew her, did she spend the majority of her evenings locked on the wrong side of the attic door? Because she was a witch like you, that's why. Her husband would never have married so far beneath him had he not been convinced of her talents being an asset at the gaming table."

"What?" Evangeline stared at Lady Stanton's reflection. "The Gift doesn't even work like that."

"As he learned, Miss Pemberton. As he learned. If your mother had been honest with him up front, she might've escaped confinement by avoiding the altar altogether. I advise you now to drop whatever designs you think you have on Lioncroft. He deserves better than the likes of you, just as your father did. He deserved a woman, not a witch. Your mother was the worst wife he could've wed. He never did live down the humiliation of having to keep her locked up at home. I'm convinced pure shame is what killed him in the end." She turned to her lady's maid. "I think the pearls should be threaded through today, not the strands of gold. You'll have to start over."

Evangeline's fists tightened until her nails drew blood from her palms. "What about my mother? Wouldn't it be more truthful to say *he* was the worst possible husband for *her*?"

"Piffle. She brought it on herself by overreaching her station. Just like you. Whether you realize it or not, Miss Pemberton, you bring about your own consequences with the actions you choose. I offered you an arrangement. You did not follow through. End of arrangement."

"You asked for the impossible." Evangeline crossed her arms over her chest, clutching herself tightly so as to prevent her from launching into Lady Stanton and clawing out those cold, colorless eyes.

"No, not those pearls. The others. Yes, those." Lady Stanton's gaze met Evangeline's through the glass. "I asked you for a simple compromise."

"Even Susan said she isn't ready."

"That's irrelevant. You'll recall I also asked you whether Lioncroft would hang for his crimes."

Evangeline took a breath. "He didn't kill Lord Hetherington." *Probably.*

Lady Stanton arched a thin brow. "Did you see that in a vision?"

"No."

"Then you don't know that, do you? That was another agreement unfulfilled. We are running short on time, but Susan will wed Lioncroft with or without your help."

"You don't even know if he's a coldhearted killer," Evangeline pointed out.

Lady Stanton lifted a dainty shoulder. "You just said he wasn't."

"You don't believe me!"

"Miss Pemberton, do try to view the world as an adult. Susan has ruined her chances with respectable gentlemen, and I refuse to allow her to grow into an old maid, like you'll undoubtedly become. Lioncroft is the rich, attractive, intelligent son of a respected viscount. He'll have to do. Another strand of pearls, girl. I'm to be the mother of a bride."

"You are not," Evangeline snapped. "He doesn't want her."

Lady Stanton's smile could freeze lava. "That hardly matters."

Evangeline threw out her hands. "Of course it matters. He's in charge of himself, and he's quite determined to remain a bachelor."

"I'm even more determined that he shall wed my daughter." Lady Stanton frowned. "Look, you've dirt on Susan's gown. I have never *seen* such a ragamuffin—"

"You don't understand." Evangeline resisted the urge to peer at her reflection. "He knows about your stratagem and is unimpressed. Mr. Lioncroft refuses to marry Susan, with or without a compromise."

"And how would you know this if you weren't sneaking around with him unattended, you little strumpet? If you had a reputation to ruin, you would've done so long ago. Don't look at me like that—it's true. You are a nobody, and shall remain so until you die. I know it; you know it; Lioncroft knows it. Why else would he be sniffing around you, but to rut without fear of the parson's trap? You're practically servant class, Miss Pemberton. I'm sure he entertains himself with the maids whenever he pleases, so why should you be any different? You are not the sort of chit a man of noble blood marries. True gentlemen—those who belong in Polite Society—settle down with young ladies like my Susan. She is beautiful, well-bred, well-educated, lineaged, and rich. You are none of those things. You are nothing."

"I am nothing?" Evangeline advanced forward until she loomed behind Lady Stanton and the perimeter of the vanity's looking glass was filled with her dirtstained gown. "I am Evangeline. I am a woman. I am a daughter. I am a person. I've spent my entire life helping other nothings like me improve their lives. You've never helped anyone but yourself."

"And my daughter. She and I are my primary concerns, and we should be yours as well. Those of your class should seek to enhance the lives of their betters, not selfishly dwell on your own lot. If you had a thoughtful bone in your body, you would cease being so impertinent and start helping me match Lioncroft with Susan. I command you to do so."

A choking laugh escaped Evangeline's throat. "You command me? In penning a letter to my stepfather, you've long since compromised whatever leverage you might've once had. I owe you nothing."

"Except the clothes on your back."

"I owe them to Susan, not you. However, if you so choose, you can have them."

"What are you going to do, run about naked? I suppose you might catch Lioncroft's eye that way, slattern that you are. Mark my words, in his eyes you're nothing more than a temporary outlet for his passion—if that. How anyone can look at you and see something besides a pathetic guttersnipe is beyond me. Perhaps Lioncroft is afflicted with excess virility. You'd better continue wearing Susan's clothes for the duration. Unfashionable

as they are, I daresay you've never worn anything half so dear.
You ought to be kissing my toes."

"Kissing your—"

A knock interrupted a bout of spluttering Evangeline had
meant as an outraged tirade. She stalked across the room
and flung open the door without asking Lady Stanton's permission.

Carefully avoiding casting his gaze about the frozen coun-
tenances of the persons within, the footman handed Evangeline two squares of paper and quickly took his leave.

"Well, you meddlesome creature, what is it?"

Evangeline tossed the missive marked "Lady Stanton" to
the floor and unfolded the one bearing her own name.

DEAR MISS PEMBERTON,

JANE HETHERINGTON CORDIALLY INVITES YOU TO JOIN IN
THE CELEBRATION OF HER THIRTEENTH BIRTHDAY. WE SHALL
MEET OUTSIDE THE FRONT GARDEN FOR A PICNIC AT ONE
O'CLOCK, FOLLOWED BY KITE-FLYING AND PALL-MALL.

YOURS SINCERELY,
JANE

"Maid," Lady Stanton ordered. "Fetch me that paper."

The lady's maid flashed Evangeline an inscrutable look
before placing pearls and hairbrush atop the vanity in order
to retrieve the fallen paper. Evangeline imagined she'd strangle her mistress with those pearls if she could.

"One o'clock," Lady Stanton exclaimed. "But that's barely
an hour from now. I must finish my toilette. Make yourself
useful for once, Miss Pemberton. Go see that Susan is looking her best. She has a husband to catch."

Evangeline shook her head. "I won't help you."

"Fine." Lady Stanton sniffed. "I'm sure we don't need you.
Susan can ensnare him entirely on her own."

Probably so. And for some reason, that made Evangeline feel . . . ill.

At first, Evangeline had no intention of visiting Susan. But as her fury was at the mother and not the daughter, her desire to speak to a friend outweighed her desire to spite Lady Stanton.

First and foremost, she needed to change into fresh garments. She selected the most flattering gown in the dressing room. Not because Lady Stanton had called her a ragamuffin incapable of catching Mr. Lioncroft's eye. Because she wished for a fresh gown, that's all.

As to Evangeline's hair, well . . . as usual, there wasn't much that could be done with it, but she spent the better part of an hour sitting stock still so Molly could give the tangled mass her best effort. Not because Lady Stanton had called Evangeline an urchin useful only as a receptacle for Mr. Lioncroft's excess virility. Because her chignon had disintegrated earlier in the day and she happened to have time to fix it before the picnic, that's all. Well, somewhat fix it. Her hair managed to look . . . chignon-esque. Most of the pins were even staying put.

After thanking Molly for repairing her unruly locks twice in the same morning, Evangeline squared her shoulders and stepped out into the hall.

Susan glided directly toward her, looking every inch the well-put-together figure of Quality her mother had proclaimed her to be.

"There you are!" She fell into step alongside Evangeline. "Did you see Jane's invitation? I looked for you after breakfast and couldn't find you anywhere."

"I was . . . chatting with your mother," Evangeline hedged. "I did receive the invitation. It was darling. Are you on your way to the picnic now?"

"I was hoping we would both be." Susan linked arms with

her. "You know how I am with directions."

"The front gardens mean the front lawn," Evangeline explained, careful not to smile. "It's the first thing we'll see when we exit the house."

"Yes, well, easy for you to say. And what were you discussing with Mother? Please don't say I'm to be compromised during the picnic. She already informed me today was The Day, come hell or high water, but honestly . . . I should like to eat a sandwich or two before linking my name with Lionkiller's forevermore."

So today really was The Day. Evangeline forced her teeth to unclench. "Please stop calling him Lionkiller. I doubt he's the murderer."

"Truly?" Susan gaped at her. "Did you have a vision? Or are you just saying that because you've made friends?"

Friends? Evangeline bit back a humorless laugh. Did friends plaster each other against the nearest wall and melt into each other's kisses? Did friends demand services from each other in exchange for boons; visions for freedom, vindication for coach fare? She shook her head. Her relationship with Mr. Lioncroft might be indefinable, but whatever they were—they weren't friends.

Susan's spectacles bumped Evangeline's ear as she leaned over to whisper, "Do you think he'll be a gentle lover?"

Evangeline stumbled to a stop. *"What?"*

A violent blush crept up Susan's cheeks. "It's just, the thought of bedding a husband is daunting enough, without having the husband be a vicious blackguard. When I think of our wedding night, I . . . Don't scowl at me so, I didn't say 'Lionkiller,' I said 'vicious blackguard.' You cannot deny his temper—he admits the flaw himself." Susan's voice lowered even more. "I have heard there is pain under the best of circumstances, and I cannot imagine the lovemaking skills of a recluse like Lioncroft being the best of anything."

"I disagree," Evangeline muttered, leaning one shoulder against the nearest wall and closing her eyes tight.

She didn't have to imagine Mr. Lioncroft being the best of anything. She well knew it from experience. The very thought of his kisses weakened her limbs and heated her flesh. And the thought of him sharing those selfsame kisses with Susan . . . for the rest of their lives . . . Angels above, it was enough to make a woman scream.

Not because of Susan's blithe comments, exactly—she was a friend, and as such, Evangeline wished the best for her. And not because she wanted Mr. Lioncroft for herself; there were any number of reasons why they could never be together, and not a single reason to suggest they could. But . . . oh, very well.

A part of her *did* want Mr. Lioncroft for herself, despite him being an arrogant rogue with little to recommend him as husbandly material. But he was the son of a viscount and she was the daughter of a—of a—tatterdemalion gypsy, who had passed down to her daughter untamable hair and a so-called Gift. And a streak of independence, and twenty years of unconditional love, and a value system requiring her to use her talent to better the lives of those who did without, who judged each other on their own merit rather than a hierarchy of inherited titles as prescribed in *Debrett's Peerage*.

Yes, despite her shameless complicity in Mr. Lioncroft's intoxicating kisses, he was unquestionably the wrong sort of man for a woman determined not to have *any* man, for fear she relive her mother's mistakes. And, Evangeline hated to admit, Lady Stanton was probably also right in pronouncing Evangeline likewise the wrong woman for Mr. Lioncroft. Especially when compared to someone like Susan Stanton.

Who now poked Evangeline in the shoulder and sang out, "I'm still waiting . . ."

Evangeline opened her eyes. "For what?"

"For an explanation, of course. I said I could not imagine Lioncroft's lovemaking. You said, 'I disagree.' A more intriguing phrase has never been spoken. Do continue."

"I said that?" Evangeline pushed off from the wall and

started walking again. "If so, that's all I meant to say. In fact, I'm fairly certain I didn't even mean to say that much."

Susan rushed to keep up with Evangeline's increased pace. "Well, if you won't be forthcoming on your own, I shall be forced to ask questions based on your response. *Do* you think about Lioncroft's lovemaking?"

"I—what?"

Prurient curiosity laced Susan's tone. "Have you and he . . ."

"No!" Although this lack owed more to his gentlemanliness than to Evangeline's guardianship of her maidenhood. "I've—I've only even been kissed by one man."

Susan huffed, as though disappointed. "So his style of lovemaking was supposition on your part."

"I . . ." Evangeline stared at her for a moment before facing forward once again and striding down the hall with a vengeance.

Within seconds, Susan re-linked her arm with Evangeline's and slowed the pace to a more manageable saunter. "While we are admitting suppositions, I will admit I don't imagine him to be a gentle lover. He is a publicly acknowledged brute, and brutes are not known for gentleness. Do you suppose otherwise?"

Evangeline supposed she'd vomit all over her nice clean dress if she was supposed to discuss in lurid detail the mechanics of Mr. Lioncroft disposing of Susan's virginity. "If I'd had any idea you wanted to have this particular conversation, I would've . . ."

"Would've what?"

"I don't know." Evangeline sighed. Better to finish with this topic now than to have it creep up again and again. "No, I don't suppose brutes are known for gentleness. On the other hand, I don't consider Mr. Lioncroft brutish."

"You think him *gentle?*"

"Hardly." Evangeline paused to consider what she truly felt about the gentleness or lack thereof in Mr. Lioncroft's manner. The very thought of those stolen moments increased the beating of her traitorous heart. "Gentleness isn't always preferable, is it? I mean, surely passion takes a middle ground. What if . . . what if a man desires you, despite himself? Despite yourself. What if a man wants you so much and so badly, he can't help himself from . . . from touching you, from grabbing you, from shutting up both of your weak objections by pressing his body to yours and kissing you senseless? Hypothetically speaking."

Susan shuddered. "Sounds horrible. Precisely how do you define 'brutish,' Evangeline?"

"Unwanted force," Evangeline responded promptly. "If you're screaming and crying and fighting back and he forces himself upon you anyway, that's brutish and wholly unacceptable under any circumstance. But if you secretly kind of *like* finding yourself up against the wainscoting when he can't keep his lips from yours a moment longer—"

"Who in the world would *like* something like that?" Susan laughed and shook her head. "Consummation is supposed to happen in the bedroom, Evangeline. Lying down. At night. With the candles unlit. You close your eyes, he does his bit, and if you're lucky enough to bear heirs right away, he leaves you in peace. Then you go shop or something. Perhaps take tea."

Evangeline rounded the next corner, steering Susan into the marble tiled anteroom. "I'm not sure it works exactly like that."

"Of course it does. Mother told me so. And she has more experience with marriage than you and I combined."

"That may be, but . . ." Evangeline bit her lip. As ill-suited as she and Mr. Lioncroft might be, he and Susan would be an equally disastrous match if Susan flung herself into a binding contract with a husband who terrified her. Evangeline didn't want either of them locked into an unhappy marriage. "What I'm saying is, I don't think he's as bad as you think. I don't think he's really bad at all. He may have a temper, yes. But from what I've seen, his temper gets the best of him when he's protecting those he cares about. Like his family. And if you"—Evangeline choked on the word—"marry him, you will also be family. Which would mean he would use his strength to protect you, not hurt you. I imagine him to be the sort who would fiercely cherish a wife. If a woman could get him to want one."

"But he won't want me!" Susan blocked Evangeline from opening the front door. "Mother plans to force him. I won't be cherished. I will be quashed."

"Nobody will be quashed. Mr. Lioncroft isn't the sort of man to be forced into anything he doesn't want to do, false compromise or no." Evangeline hoped. "Your mother knows he doesn't plan to marry unless he *chooses* to marry."

Susan's shoulders slumped. "Then how am I to trap him?"

"You cannot trap him," Evangeline blurted out. "That is to say, you oughtn't trap him. Or any man. You can only . . . You can only"—angels above, how could she have this conversation without retching?—"entice him."

A frown creased Susan's brow. "Entice him how?"

"By being yourself. By letting him be himself. By *talking* to him. Getting to know him. And seeing if you like the person who he is inside." Evangeline tugged on the door handle. "And vice versa."

"I don't know." Susan stepped aside. "Sounds complicated."

Evangeline pushed upon the front door and led the way from the porch to the front garden.

Jane Hetherington bounded up to them, face flushed and eyes sparkling. "Just in time! Uncle sent me to fetch you. We're four to a blanket. Five if you count the twins as two people, which nobody ever does. I'm afraid you must mingle separately, however, as one remaining seat is with me and Uncle Lioncroft, and the other with Mother. The third blanket is already full with Lady Stanton and the Rutherfords. Did you see my jewelry? Look!" She beamed at them both while pointing toward her neck. "A cunning little portrait-locket. There's no portrait yet, but there will be soon. And I'm to have a new wardrobe as well. I'll look just as smart as you, Miss Stanton!"

Evangeline tried not to be wounded at being excluded from this last statement. She couldn't deny the truth of it, having left such a trail of hairpins from her bedchamber to the front gardens that even someone as directionally inept as Susan would be able to use them as a path back to the guest quarters. So much for looking a fraction as elegant as the ever-coiffed soon-to-be Mrs. Lioncroft. Evangeline's stomach roiled.

"Go on, then." She nudged Susan with an elbow and tried to keep the peevishness from her tone. "Sit with him and Jane and Nancy. I shall sit with Mr. Teasdale, Lady Hetherington, and the twins." Under no circumstance would she sit with Edmund Rutherford, who even now leered at her from behind a silver flask.

"I don't know," Susan stammered, but already Jane was tugging her toward the square of red cloth where Mr. Lioncroft lounged in conversation with his niece Nancy.

Evangeline began a solitary trek to the far corner of the grass where Lady Hetherington was making a valiant effort to wrestle two blond tornadoes onto a picnic blanket. This would be fun. This *would* be fun. She loved children. She'd hardly be missing anything by not sharing Mr. Lioncroft's blanket. And even if she was . . . well, self-sacrifice made her a better person. Wasn't that what Mama always said?

Besides, Evangeline had a mystery to solve. She could begin by questioning Lady Hetherington. With any luck, she'd oust the true killer before the last canapé was eaten and be well on her way from Blackberry Manor, never to be seen or heard from again.

Evangeline smiled grimly as Mr. Lioncroft rose to help Susan onto their shared blanket. By leaving so soon, she'd have to miss the upcoming nuptials.

Pity.

Chapter Seventeen

Why the hell was he picnicking with the Stanton chit instead of Miss Pemberton?

Gavin had purposefully orchestrated the seating arrangements so as to split up Nancy and Father Time, and to have a space available for a certain luscious female. A certain luscious female he sometimes felt like shaking sense into, yes, but first he owed her an apology. An apology for preemptively ruining *her* apology. How he would've loved to have been on the receiving end of an apology! Gavin wasn't sure such an event had ever transpired.

The moment he finished helping the blond disappointment into a seated position, he rounded on his niece, busy frolicking in circles round the group.

"Jane," he said slowly, careful not to appear angry with her as it was in fact her birthday. "Did you deliver my message?"

"Yes, Uncle Lioncroft."

"Exactly as I told you?"

"Yes, Uncle Lioncroft."

"Then what the devil just happened?" His jaw clenched at Jane's startled expression and he belatedly wished he could recall his abrupt words.

"Please sit, both of you," Nancy called from her position on the blanket. "All your looming is making Miss Stanton nervous."

Gavin glowered at them both before sitting. He didn't care if he made the Stanton chit nervous. He was glad he made the Stanton chit nervous. If it would make the Stanton chit nervous enough to get up and trade positions with Miss Pemberton, he'd drop on all fours and snarl like a rabid lion.

His thirteen-year-old niece plopped down across from him and grinned.

"It's my birthday, birthday, birthday," Jane sang under her breath. She opened and closed the locket hanging around her neck with every repeated word. "It's my birthday, birthday, birthday, birthday, birth—"

"Enough!" Nancy threw a piece of crusty bread at her sister. "We've all seen your necklace. Leave it be long enough to let us eat, will you?"

Jane's lips curled smugly. "You're just jealous because nobody asked you to sit for a portrait. We'll be lo-o-o-ng gone before your birthday, birthday, birth—"

"So," the Stanton chit interrupted tentatively, leaning forward to inspect Jane's locket. "A portrait artist is coming to Blackberry Manor?"

"No," Gavin said shortly, hoping to curtail this train of thought before it bloomed into a full-fledged conversation.

Jane dropped a jar of marmalade into her lap and chortled. "The portrait artist lives here, Miss Stanton. It's Uncle Lioncroft!"

The Stanton chit's jaw tumbled open, giving her already-narrow face the impression of a gaping fish. "*You* are a portrait artist?"

"No." He ripped off a bit of bread and shoved it in his mouth, so as to render himself incapable of participating in the topic further.

"He's not usually a portrait artist. You've seen Uncle Lioncroft's landscapes," Nancy prompted helpfully. "They're on every wall."

The Stanton chit reprised her gaping-fish impression. "You are a *landscape* artist? You painted all those . . . paintings?"

He pointed to his mouth and commenced exaggerated chewing. The Stanton chit was clearly a featherbrain. He'd eat ten loaves of bread if it allowed him to escape her pointless chatter.

"Talented all his life, Mother says," Jane added as she spread marmalade atop her bread. "When he wasn't fencing or racing curricles, and the like."

If the Stanton chit gaped at him any more, he feared she would pass out.

"I've a marvelous idea!" Jane's sticky bread fell into her lap as she clapped her hands together. "You should ask Uncle Lioncroft to paint *your* portrait! Uncle Lioncroft, will you paint Miss Stanton's portrait, too?"

Gavin swallowed so quickly he choked on the dry crumbs. "No."

"Oh." Jane returned her focus to the slice of bread now stuck to her stomach.

The Stanton chit found her voice. "What about Miss Pemberton's?" she asked, a certain shrewdness in her eyes belying the innocence in her tone. "Would you paint hers?"

He glared at the Stanton chit until she paled and broke eye contact, which took approximately one second. Of course, he would paint Miss Pemberton's portrait. He had one unfinished in his studio this very moment, did he not? But his private obsession was none of the Stanton chit's damn business. Impertinent fluff.

Where was Miss Pemberton, anyway? Still over there. Seated between the twins. Passing a basket of fruit to Rose. Chuckling at something Teasdale said. Chuckling at something Teasdale said? Had that deaf old codger managed to wake up long enough to be *amusing?* Perhaps he was snoring again, and Miss Pemberton was simply laughing at his adenoids.

Why wouldn't she look this way? Couldn't she feel his gaze on her? If he stared any harder, he might burn holes in the back of her head. Her gorgeous, ever-mussed head. God, had any other woman ever looked so deliciously rumpled, as if just roused from his bed? That slumberous way of lifting her eyelashes ever so slowly, to send surreptitious little glances his way . . . Where were those surreptitious little glances now? He wanted glances! It was the least she could do, with all the staring *he* was doing.

There she was, laughing again. Teasdale couldn't possibly be that diverting. She had to be driving him insane on purpose. Why would she choose an old roué with one foot in the casket over *him?* Was it the botched apology? Or the extortion? Gavin bet it was the extortion. Well, what else could he have done? Underhanded, he supposed, but at least it worked. She was here, wasn't she? As were his sister and his nieces. Everyone was smiling. Laughing. Having fun. None of which would've happened if he hadn't resorted to manipulation. Had he known it would be a sticking point, he would've added "dining with me upon occasion" to his list of demands.

"Right, Uncle Lioncroft?" Nancy's voice came a little too loudly, as though she'd been repeating herself for some time.

"Er, right," he muttered without taking his eyes from Miss Pemberton's head.

Jane erupted into peals of laughter. "I *told* you he wasn't listening! She said the house was on fire, Uncle Lioncroft. Nancy said the *house* was on *fire* and you said, 'Er, right.' She said—you said—" Words dissolved into hiccupping, choked laughter. The Stanton chit was forced to thump Jane on the back until she could breathe again.

Gavin scowled at all three of them.

What had Miss Pemberton meant by saying she was unable to get visions from his touch? Was that typical? That wasn't the only reason she endured his company, was it? Mental immunity? Because he was pretty sure he'd die right here on this blanket if the only thing to recommend his touch was a lack of accompanying visions.

Granted, he could see how lovemaking would be impossible if every touch of mouth or hand or cock sent her off on a vision of the-devil-knew-what followed by one of those hellacious headaches or, worse, blacking out completely. Nothing would kill the mood quite like unconsciousness.

But, still. No man wished to be *settled* for simply because his touch was the lesser evil. Gavin preferred his lovemaking to be a product of mutual passion. Surely the tension between them wasn't all in his head.

Or was it? Was that why she was off giggling with that rotter Teasdale again? Did she plan to circle the entire party to discover which other men's touches might be able to bring her pleasure without visions? Gavin wouldn't stand for such an act. He'd put a stop to any other man's attentions right now. He'd—

"Uncle Lioncroft?"

"What?" Oh, Lord. He was on his feet and ten paces from his blanket in the direction of hers. He wouldn't really have planted a facer on a septuagenarian, would he? Damn. He might've. Better sit down and have more bread. And a little less wine. Matter of fact, he better trade seats with Jane so he couldn't see Miss Pemberton at all, or who knew what trouble he'd get himself into. Luckily, Miss Pemberton hadn't noticed him launch up from the blanket and charge in her direction. She was far too busy. Laughing. With Teasdale.

Devil take it . . . This was going to be the longest picnic ever.

No matter how much she concentrated on keeping her face averted from Mr. Lioncroft's corner of the garden, Evangeline was unable to miss him rise to his feet, change places with the birthday girl, and sit back down. Not only was his back to her—and she doubted she overreacted in imagining a personal slight behind the exchange—he now lounged alongside Susan far more intimately than ever, having secured his nieces on the opposite end of the blanket.

Evangeline would never have suggested Susan make an effort to arouse Mr. Lioncroft's interest if she'd thought Susan had a chance in hell of succeeding.

"Aargh." Evangeline ripped her gaze away for the ten-thousandth time. If there was an error here, it was hers. She was the one who thrust Susan upon him. If Evangeline had perhaps taken her place at Mr. Lioncroft's side . . . Oh, what would it matter? The moment Evangeline left—and she would surely make her escape the moment she had the where-withal to do so—Lady Stanton would swoop in and leg-shackle Susan to Mr. Lioncroft before you could say "haughty crone."

"What's wrong?" Lady Hetherington leaned forward, her face lined with concern.

"Nothing," Evangeline muttered, embarrassed to be caught mooning over someone she could never have. She fumbled for her glass. Why couldn't she have slept through the entire luncheon like Mr. Teasdale?

Lady Hetherington frowned. "Is it my brother?"

Evangeline choked on her wine. "Er, what?"

"You are smiling at the twins and conversing with me and appearing perfectly happy and engaged one minute, but the moment you glance over your shoulder—which I can't help but notice occurs every few seconds—the most dreadful gri-mace twists up your features as though sharp needles have been stuck in your skin. It's almost as if he . . . That is to say . . . I cannot help but wonder if perchance you share . . ."

"Nothing," Evangeline blurted out, closing her eyes against the heat engulfing her face and the skepticism in Lady Het-herington's gaze. "Nothing at all."

"I see. Then I suppose it wouldn't interest you to know he glances over *his* shoulder thrice as often."

"He what?" Evangeline nearly broke her neck twisting around to look. She froze when she discovered him doing the exact same thing.

His heated gaze locked with hers until the breath escaped her lungs in tiny little gasps. His lips moved. He was mouthing something. What was he saying? She couldn't tell. She couldn't even think. The sight of his lips brought to mind the feel of his kisses, the kisses she would never again have, the kisses he would soon be sharing with Susan. Perhaps he even glanced Evangeline's way to verify she took note of him nestled in close proximity to his future bride. After spending the noontime with Susan, there could be no doubt he'd realized the vast differences between Evangeline and a lady of Quality.

Horrible to imagine another woman feeling the weight of his body against hers, the heat of his flesh burning through her shift, the scratch of his jawline as he scraped his cheek across her skin in order to—Wait. Evangeline squinted.

He had shaved. This morning his jaw had been shadowed with stubble and his attire unremarkable, but now he looked as clean-shaven and tailored as the most particular of *ton* bucks.

Why? Appearances? Since when did he care about appearances? Since deciding to picnic with Susan? He was Quality and she was Quality and Evangeline was not. Harrumph. He'd looked better this morning. When his jaw was as scratchy and rough and raw as the man inside. When he didn't cage his true self behind a smooth, pretty exterior just to appease the ridiculous dictates of Polite Society.

His kisses wouldn't be the same now, without the warm feel of his lips smoothing away the delicious burn of masculine stubble. Then again, for all she knew, the next person to share his kisses might be Susan.

Evangeline jerked back to face Lady Hetherington. It took

only the tiniest of moments for the countess to unblur and come back into focus.

"If he looks at me again," Evangeline said tightly, careful not to blink. "Don't tell me. I prefer not to know."

If Lady Hetherington found this to be an odd request, she gave no sign. She spoke not another word on the topic and allowed Evangeline to spend the rest of the picnic lunch focusing on the rambunctious twins.

Not for the first time, Evangeline wished she'd had a sister. Someone with whom she could play and laugh and tease. Someone she could've run away with, rather than flee her stepfather on her own. The solitary life was, well, solitary.

She glanced over her shoulder despite herself and cringed to see Susan and Mr. Lioncroft deep in conversation. They didn't look solitary. Why, oh, why hadn't she taken the empty seat herself, if she wanted it so much? Because self-sacrifice made her a better person? Bah. Self-sacrifice simply for self-sacrifice's sake didn't make anyone noble—it made her lonely. And maybe stupid. Bearing the Gift was a lonely enough curse on its own, before she'd gone and ostracized the one man she could interact with as a woman, not a witch.

Oh! He was turning his head. Evangeline snapped her gaze back to the twins and threw all her focus and willpower into their entertainment until the servants came to clear away the picnic miscellany.

"It's time, it's time!" Jane danced from one blanket to another, clapping and grinning. "Come away from the flowers and trees, everyone. It's time for kite-flying!"

Susan approached the blanket just as Evangeline rose to her feet.

"Well?" Evangeline heard herself ask sourly. "How did it go?"

"Boring."

"Boring," Evangeline repeated in disbelief. "In what way? Weren't you talking?"

Susan lifted a shoulder. "I suppose."

Evangeline's fingers clenched. She waited until it was clear no further information would be forthcoming before bursting out with, "Well, what did he say?"

"'No,' mostly." Susan rolled her eyes. "I believe it to be his favorite word."

"You didn't . . . take my advice? And learn more about him?" Evangeline held her breath.

"Hmmm." Susan cast her a calculating look. "I learned he's an artist, and painted all the landscapes in Blackberry Manor."

Evangeline's mouth fell open.

"You *didn't* know! I was certain you already knew."

"How would I know such a thing?"

Susan's forehead creased. "I don't know . . . something in his eyes when I asked if he'd paint your portrait."

"If he'd paint my—good heavens, Susan. What a question."

Susan's lips curved into a catlike grin.

After another moment of silence, Evangeline could withstand the suspense no more. She could barely withstand the urge to throttle her. "Susan. What did he say?"

"Nothing."

Evangeline frowned. "Nothing?"

"I suppose that's better than 'no,' which is what he said to every other query, including the question of whether he'd paint mine."

"Oh." He'd said no to Susan, but he hadn't said no to her. Interesting. Evangeline bit back a relieved smile.

Susan's eyes narrowed. "Are you sure you don't have a tendre for him?"

"I—what?" Evangeline shook her head vigorously. "No, I . . . I'm leaving soon."

"That's no kind of answer. You can have a tendre for him even if you don't marry him, just like I can marry him even without a tendre. Oh, don't make that face. I know you believe in marrying for love. But if this is what I must do to escape Mother and rejoin Society, then this is what I must do.

If there were some other recourse, believe me—I would not be pursuing him."

"Why not?" Evangeline glanced at Mr. Lioncroft from the corner of her eye. Who wouldn't want a man like that to call her own?

Susan sighed. "I don't imagine for a second Lionki—Lioncroft is interested in me. In fact, I've come to suspect thirty years of marriage wouldn't change that fact. If I thought for a second I'd ever be welcome in Society again without sacrificing myself to such an arrangement, I'd—"

"Touch me." Evangeline held out her hand, palm up.

Susan blinked. "What?"

"Give me your hand," Evangeline insisted. "Now."

"But you'll get a—"

"Yes, I know. Just try it. Perhaps I'll see you in Society. Meeting a man you do like, who loves you madly." Someone other than Mr. Lioncroft. *I want to see Susan in Society without Mr. Lioncroft. Susan in Society without Mr. Lioncroft. Susan in Society without Mr. Lioncroft.*

Tentatively, Susan placed her fingertips atop Evangeline's palm.

Dozens of expensively dressed ladies and gentlemen mill about an ornate lobby, some sipping wine, others checking fobs or polishing opera glasses.

Francine Rutherford's gloved hand connects with Susan's face, sending her spectacles flying.

Susan claps her own gloved hand to her cheek and leaves her spectacles, broken, on the ground. "I-I—"

"Liar," Francine announces. The crowd hushes, turns, gawks. Francine balls up the paper and tosses it at Susan's feet. "Miss Stanton, I simply cannot condone such ill-bred behavior. Now that I know you for the sneak and scandalmonger you are, I am certain no one of any import shall appreciate your presence either."

With her nose thrust high, Francine pivots and stalks off through the parted crowd.

Susan removes her trembling hand from her reddened cheek and turns to the closest neighbor. The young lady glances down, unfocusing her eyes as if she doesn't register Susan's presence. Susan appeals to the next person, then the next, and the next.

One by one, they each turn away.

Evangeline jerked her hand back to her side. Susan's face fell. "No more parties?" she asked dejectedly. "I told you Lioncroft was my last chance."

"Inconclusive," Evangeline said weakly. "Please tell me the horrific set-down you received from Francine Rutherford was in the past, not the future."

"Was it at an opera house? Then, yes." Susan turned and started across the grass. "That would be the start of the little gossip scandal I mentioned. I'd glimpsed her cavorting with someone other than her better half. And then I told people who it was."

Evangeline ran to catch up. "Angels above, Susan. It looked like you ruined lives."

"I know. I even managed to ruin my own." She walked faster. "I don't really wish to discuss the bad behavior in my past. I'm not like that any more. Shall we fly kites now?"

After a moment, Evangeline nodded and followed Susan to a patch of grass where a few kites remained unclaimed.

"You know," Evangeline said as Susan picked a yellow one from the pile. "I imagine Mr. Lioncroft doesn't enjoy the constant reminders of the bad behavior in his past, either."

Susan whirled to face her. "I said I *know*. And you know what else *I* don't enjoy? The constant reminders of how much better you think you are than everybody else, and how you always think you have the right answer and forever know to do the right thing. If you think you'd be the perfect wife for

Lion*killer,* you can have him. He's heading right for us, anyway. And I'm bloody sure he's not hunting *me.*"

"He doesn't see *me,*" Evangeline said, palms outstretched. "He just sees my Gift. Everybody does. As soon as they learn the truth, I cease being Evangeline and start being The Girl With The Visions. I will never get to be a normal person. You had it all, and you just—"

But Susan had already stalked off, kite in hand, without another word.

Chapter Eighteen

"Why didn't you sit with me?"

Damn. That wasn't what he'd meant to say.

Miss Pemberton turned, slowly, slowly, until at last she stared up at him from under those dark curling lashes. It was all Gavin could do not to shake her, kiss her, then toss her over his shoulder, and escape into his house.

"That is," he began, then stopped. There was really no way to unsay what he'd just said, so what use was artifice? "I saved the spot for you," he admitted. "I had hoped for your company."

A strange look flitted across her face. "Didn't you enjoy Susan's?"

"What *is* it, today?" Gavin demanded. "You ask about her, she asks about you—"

"Susan asked about me?"

The question was innocent enough, but something in Miss Pemberton's expression was off.

"When I said I wouldn't—oh, never mind." Gavin knelt before the few remaining kites. "It's not important."

She knelt beside him. "About the portraiture, you mean?"

His jaw clenched. "Why did you ask me, if you already knew?"

"Why did you say painting was unimportant?" She slanted

him a sideways look. "If you filled an entire mansion with canvases of your own creation, it's clearly important."

"Fine. I like landscapes. Pick up a kite." Gavin rose to his feet.

"What?" She tilted her head toward him, still kneeling, her upturned face even with the buttons of his fall.

"Choose a kite, Miss Pemberton." He swallowed. If she leaned forward any closer, her lips would graze his suddenly uncomfortable breeches. "Please."

"Why?"

Devil take it. He could swear he felt the heat of her breath through the layer of cloth. "So we look like we're kite-flying, not . . . arguing. For God's sake, woman, are you always this difficult?"

An impish smile curved across her face. "I think so, yes."

"Bloody hell." Gavin forced himself to back up so that his cock was at least a few inches from Miss Pemberton's face. She leaned closer.

"I thought you'd want to sit with Susan."

Gavin bent down, snatched up a kite, and stalked several feet from the pile. "Why the hell would I want that?"

Miss Pemberton sifted haphazardly through the remaining kites. "She's rich, she's beautiful, she's Quality, she's—"

"She's not like you."

Her shoulders slumped. "No. She's nothing like me."

Gavin dropped his kite. He stalked back over to Miss Pemberton, hauled her to her feet, and grabbed her by the shoulders. "No. I mean, *she's not like you*." He dropped his voice and leaned into her, until he was sure she knew exactly what he meant. "If we were alone, I'd show you precisely how you affect me, in ways the Stanton chit never could."

She blushed, leapt away from him, busied herself with the kites. "We can't be alone."

He laughed. "Put down that kite and I'll take you somewhere very alone."

"Stop making me think about . . . *that*."

"Mmm. I'm thrilled to know I make you think about 'that.' Care to define 'that' for me? Perhaps we can act it out."

She tossed him what was no doubt supposed to be a glare, but the passion darkening her eyes told a different story. "I will never confess aloud the sort of thoughts you put in my head." Her gaze dimmed. "What would be the point? I'll be leaving soon, anyway."

"All the more reason," he said, infusing his voice with as much husky rakishness as he could muster.

She shook her head, unmoved by his best attempt at charm. A terrible seriousness replaced her earlier teasing look. "I'd like to leave today."

"Today?" he choked, then cleared his throat. If she'd rather talk leaving than loving, fine. He could accommodate her either way. He gestured toward the fashionable coats and pelisses dotting the wide expanse of his front lawn. "Did you figure out which one of these ingrates wishes me to hang in their stead?"

"It could be anyone." She stepped in front of him, presenting him with her back. "Except us."

"Except us," Gavin agreed softly. She was so close . . . It would be nothing to reach out, wrap his arms around her, tuck her body against his. Nothing but scandal. He stepped aside. "And the children. And Rose."

She turned, handed him a bright orange kite, frowned. "I'm not entirely sure."

"I told you—I can't picture my sister murdering her own husband." Gavin began to unwind a few feet of twine.

"Plenty of women would kill to escape their husbands. You cannot discount it." Miss Pemberton squinted at him. "But that wasn't who I meant."

He stopped unraveling twine. "Not one of my *nieces*. They're innocents!"

"Probably," she agreed. "But can you swear it?"

"What do you think happened? The twins clubbed the

rotter over his head with their doll?" He shook his head, laughed, ran forward a few yards until the brisk autumn breeze caught the orange fabric of the kite and lifted it into the air.

She ran with him for a while, watching the kite soar across the sky. And then: "Not the twins . . . Nancy."

He stopped running. *"Nancy?"*

"Think about it." Miss Pemberton plucked the twine from his hands, allowing the spool to bob and unroll with the will of the wind. "She'd want to hurt her father for the same reasons. He struck her mother. And what about the French tutor?"

Gavin hooked his thumbs in his waistband. "What French tutor?"

"The French tutor Lord Hetherington sent away for stealing his daughter's heart." Miss Pemberton darted forward to steady the kite. "And kisses."

He chased after her. "That better be all he stole from her, or I'll hunt the *salaud* down myself."

"Precisely how Lord Hetherington reacted," she called over her shoulder. "How well do you think *that* was received by a young woman in love?"

"But to kill him for it?" Gavin reached for her, curved his hands around her shoulders, turned her toward his niece. "Look at her. She's flying a kite. Just like us." He plucked the spool from her hands. "Admit it . . . Nancy hasn't been acting guilty."

But as soon as he said this, he remembered the scene on the staircase.

Miss Pemberton cocked a speculative brow. "Hasn't she?" She paused, lifted a hand to his chest. "Susan saw her," she murmured. "That night. Creeping into her room."

He slid away from her touch. "Not a single one of us was abed as we claimed. It proves nothing."

Then again, he'd seen her tempting fate at the top of the stairs . . . but surely that was an innocent farce, and just as easily explained.

Miss Pemberton stepped closer, placed her fingers against his forearm. "I overheard her the next day. Talking to the girls. She said if anyone should ask where she'd been, they were to claim she'd been in the nursery all evening."

Gavin tugged on the twine, jerking the kite against the breeze. "She was just scared."

Miss Pemberton inclined her head. "Of what?"

"I don't know! But I don't think she's a killer." He released more twine. The kite dipped and fell, causing him to run several yards before the wind once again whipped it skyward. When he stopped running, Miss Pemberton was still at his side. "Neither is Rose," he informed her. "Rose looks at me like she thinks *I* did it, for God's sake."

"Does she?" Miss Pemberton asked softly. "Or is she trying to deflect suspicion from herself or her daughter?"

"None of your speculation is helping," he snapped. She flinched, but didn't move away. "Why don't you go find out who really offed the blighter and be done with it? I saw you touch the Stanton chit a moment ago. I assume it wasn't her."

Anger flashed across her face. "What do you expect me to do—skip from kite to kite, touching all the fliers?"

Gavin unwound more twine. "If it works, yes. Tell them I made you do it. They think I'm mad anyway." He tugged on the kite. "And unless we uncover the true villain, the crime will no doubt be pinned on me."

"It's unfair," Miss Pemberton muttered after she tired of scowling at him. "Virtually everyone here has motive."

"Perhaps, but I'm the only acknowledged killer."

"Stop it." She shoved him. She actually *shoved* him.

He held up his hands in surrender only to have the spool of twine tumble to the grass. He scooped it back up and adjusted the line before the kite had a chance to fall. "Stop what?"

"Referring to yourself as a killer." She glared at him for a long moment before turning away. "It's not helping."

He shrugged and turned to the sky. "What should I say instead?"

"What did you say to me during the picnic? When I caught your eye. You were mouthing something I couldn't make out."

"You didn't—Oh. Nothing."

Her eyes narrowed. "What?"

"Nothing." If she hadn't caught it then, there was no way he'd admit now that he'd mouthed, *Save me from the Stanton chit*.

Miss Pemberton bumped her shoulder into his. "It had to have been something, or you wouldn't have been trying to tell it to me."

"I told you." He grinned at her. "I'm a madman."

She rolled her eyes. "I'm beginning to believe it."

"Is that why you're so eager to leave me?" he asked, then immediately turned his attention to the dips and whirls of the orange kite. Devil take it, what kind of question was *that?*

Several heartbeats passed before she responded with, "Escaping my stepfather is my primary goal."

"And your secondary goal?" He held his breath.

"Using my Gift."

Always the bloody Gift. Either she had no idea it was killing him to stay away from her, or she simply didn't care. He wasn't sure which was worse, but both thoughts soured his mood. "Then why aren't you using it right now?"

She shot him an annoyed look. "First of all, my head is still pounding from having touched Susan. Secondly, the Gift isn't for spying and crime solving."

"Then what's it for?"

"Helping the less fortunate."

"Won't it be unfortunate when I hang for a crime I didn't commit?"

"The *truly* less fortunate."

"The truly less fortunate?" This time when the kite began to dip, he shoved the spool of twine into her hands. "Who told you *that* horseshit?"

"My mother," she said, then sprinted a few feet to regulate the kite's flight.

"Well, mothers aren't always the brightest stars in the sky," he called out, not bothering to chase after her.

She turned and scowled at him. "My mother was an angel!"

"Fine, so now she *is* the brightest star in the sky." He pointed heavenward when the kite began to dip again. She raced back toward him, frantically coiling twine. He caught her before she collided with his chest. "That doesn't mean I understand how 'helping the less fortunate' precludes helping *me*."

Her eyes widened. "I am helping you."

"You're talking about helping me, but you're not actually helping me. And I want to know why. According to my staff—and yes, I did interview them once I realized they knew more about you than I did—you've helped a few of *them* when they wanted something. Retrieving lost articles and so on." He wasn't sure whether her guilty expression made him feel vindicated or defeated. "Then what's wrong with *me?*"

"What's wrong with you? You're coercing my help by threatening me!"

"Oh, so if I would've just *asked* you to prove my innocence, you would've done so with alacrity?"

"Yes!"

"I don't believe you."

She shoved the spool of twine into his chest. The kite careened from the sky, spearing into the earth a few yards from their feet and splintering on contact. "Are you calling me a liar?"

"I'm calling you naïve. And a liar." He tossed the spool to the ground, grabbed her by the shoulders, and leaned forward until his nose brushed against hers. "There's something you're not telling me, and I want to know what it is," he insisted quietly. "Why do you use this Gift of yours more freely with some people than others?"

Miss Pemberton glared up at him, stony-faced, but did not twist from his grasp.

He leaned closer until his words breathed against the side of her cheek. "All right, then, answer me this: Why do you use it at all?"

"Because," she bit out, "I can't separate myself from it. No matter how I might wish it otherwise, I *am* the cursed Gift." She jerked her head away from his, then pounded his chest with her fist. "I cannot link hands or tend the ill or coddle infants or anything else that requires touching. Which means I cannot do anything *but* use the Gift, whether I want to or not." She took a deep, hitching breath and shuddered in his arms. "To use it on purpose, for people of my choosing, for reasons of my choosing—my freedom of choice is the one thing that makes it tolerable, the one thing that makes living with such an affliction worth it. My only sliver of free will."

"Er . . ." came a nervous female voice. "Am I interrupting?"

God *damn* that infuriating Stanton chit!

"*Yes,*" Gavin roared. "Yes, you're interrupting. Go away."

The Stanton chit reeled backward, but the damage was done—Miss Pemberton spun out of his arms and fled.

While Gavin organized the collection of the kites and ushered everyone to the side lawn bearing the pall-mall wickets, Miss Pemberton cloistered herself well out of speaking distance. He hadn't been able to catch her attention, much less catch her alone. And with his guests in such high spirits after an hour of kite-flying, it was impossible for him to break away from their shining eyes and flushed faces and incessant chatter about the perfect breeze and cunning kites.

That was when Gavin realized a shocking fact: they weren't just blathering at him, they were smiling at him. Including him. Complimenting him. Welcoming him into their circle quite literally, as they surrounded him while bubbling over with which color of kite looked most stunning against the blue of the sky and who had managed to keep theirs up the longest and did everyone witness Edmund tumble over that stone and get himself tangled up in twine?

Benedict Rutherford laughed himself into a coughing fit, then clapped Gavin on the shoulder with a jovial "What sport!" before falling back into animated conversation with his wife and Mr. Teasdale. Even Lady Stanton had unfrozen long enough to smile at her daughter.

Before Gavin had an opportunity to assimilate this new turn of events—much less join his voice with the others—a chest-high blonde launched herself into his arms, squeezed him tightly, then seized hold of his hand to drag him forward through the crowd.

"Thanks ever so much, Uncle Lioncroft! This is the best birthday! Ever! Oh—look! Are those the mallets we're to use? Such colors! May I pick any one I want? I want the pink one. No, the yellow. Which one is yours? If yours is the yellow, I'll take the pink. Unless yours is the pink, in which case I'll take the—"

"Jane," he managed to interject at last. "I have no claim on any particular color, as this is the first time the set has been used. You may use any mallet you wish."

"Oh! Truly? I'll take the pink one, then. It's lovely. This is so exciting! I've never played pall-mall before. May I be on your team?"

"No," cried two small voices. The twins ambushed him from behind and clung to each of his legs. "We're Uncle Lioncroft's team."

"You are your own team," he explained, attempting quite unsuccessfully to continue walking with a five-year-old attached to each thigh. "There are no teams in pall-mall. Everyone gets a wooden mallet and a ball, and everyone takes turns knocking them through the wickets."

"What's a wicket?" the twins chorused.

"The iron hoops sticking out of the grass." He pointed them out. "See the little metal arches? Those are wickets. May I have my legs back now?"

No sooner was the question out of his mouth before the

twins were off and running toward the mallets. They tugged the topmost colors from the pile and lurched back toward him, dragging the mallets behind them and leaving a trail of displaced sod in their wake. His gardener might be less than pleased, but Gavin found himself, for the first time in years, tempted by the uncontrollable urge to throw back his head and laugh. Rather than make a spectacle of himself, however, he knelt down to eye level with the twins before shaking his head and chuckling.

Nonetheless, the sound did not go unnoticed.

Miss Pemberton glanced at him, then just as quickly away. The Stanton chit stared at him as if he'd grown another head, which was pretty much how she regarded him on a regular basis. Benedict and Francine Rutherford looked from him to the ruined grass to the twins and started laughing themselves. Rose gazed at him with a little half smile and a wistful sheen to her eyes.

Gavin stopped smiling. No one with such a tender motherly expression could've murdered the father of her children. Miss Pemberton didn't know what she was talking about. He'd have to show her she was wrong.

He rose to his feet, gave the girls a brief overview of the game, and then steered the twins to the first wicket so they could have the first shot.

"Remember," he reminded them as he bent to help each twin swing, "Just because I'm helping doesn't mean I'm on your team."

They dropped their mallets and raced across the grass, using their booted feet to aid their balls' forward momentum.

"You're too nice to them," came Nancy's wry voice from behind his shoulder. "They'll go home spoiled now."

He grinned. "What are uncles for?"

Nancy snorted and adjusted her stance. "Be forewarned— you're in for it now that you've gained *favorite* uncle status."

He stared at her, speechless, as she took off after her ball.

Favorite uncle? Him? All he did was—was—*talk* to them. Tease them. Play with them a little. He glanced around the laughing, joking melee with dawning horror. Was it possible that he had caused his own ostracism? That perhaps his peers might've tolerated him years ago if he'd bothered to make himself, well, tolerable?

He searched the crowd until his gaze fell upon a familiar lopsided chignon. He should go to her. Apologize for leveraging his knowledge of her Gift to extort favors when he ought to have tried asking first. Tell her he—

"Mooncalfing again, Lioncroft?"

Gavin started to find Edmund smirking at him over the top of a silver flask.

"I do not mooncalf." He hoped.

"Tell that to anyone who laid eyes on you during the picnic. Oh, right, that was everyone. I'd wager if we weren't about, you would've turned up the Pemberton chit's skirts right there on the grass."

Gavin knocked the flask from Edmund's hand. "Mention her skirts again and I'll erase your smirk with this mallet."

Edmund dropped to the ground and grappled for his open flask. "Easy, easy." He fumbled to close the lid. "I didn't know it was like that."

"Now you do."

Gavin turned, smashed his ball through the wicket, and sauntered off in the direction of Miss Pemberton.

If she registered his impending arrival, she gave no sign. Instead, she pivoted toward her ball, lined up her shot, and swung back her mallet.

"I apologize," he called.

Miss Pemberton's mallet came flying backward toward his face. He caught it just before it knocked his teeth out, then stepped forward and handed it back.

She stared up at him. "What did you say?"

"I apologize," he repeated. "You're right. I should've asked you. *Will* you help me prove my innocence?"

She frowned, blinked, blinked again. Her forehead cleared. "Yes."

"Thank you." He moved aside while she took her shot and then followed after her as she tracked her ball. "Have you any other suspects? I mean, besides my sister and my niece."

She cast him a don't-be-ridiculous look. "Everyone?"

"I meant, specifically. I was thinking about the reasons you gave—which, I admit, are as sound reasons as any—and my belief that they didn't do it. And I was thinking . . . What if someone else did it for them?"

She arched a brow. "Hiring a killer is less evil than killing someone yourself?"

"Of course not." He stepped closer and lowered his voice. "I was thinking more like, what if a servant took matters into her own hands, without consulting Nancy or Rose? A servant who, perhaps, found herself frequently on the receiving end of Hetherington's indiscriminate violence?"

Miss Pemberton leaned on her mallet. "Ginny?"

"Why not? She could be avenging her own injustices, as well as those of her mistresses."

She stared at him. "You think a servant killing her master makes more sense than a subjugated wife doing so?"

"Be serious." He glanced at his married guests. "All wives are subjugated to some degree."

She harrumphed. "Exactly why I shall never become one."

For some reason, this declaration fired his temper.

"Fortuitous," he responded, "because nobody's asking you. Do you or don't you think the lady's maid might be involved?"

A moment passed while she frowned and bit at her lower lip. "It's possible," she said at last. "But if Ginny did do it, it's also possible she was acting on orders. Are you prepared for that possibility?"

He glared at her. "I don't think—"

"Uncle Lioncroft," Nancy called from across the grass. "Come on, it's your turn!"

"I will be back," he warned Miss Pemberton before jogging over to his ball and taking a swing.

Nancy tucked her mallet beneath her arm and clapped. "Good shot, Uncle Lioncroft."

"I do better than your intended, anyway," he teased, quirking an eyebrow toward Teasdale. "What happened to his mallet? Did he forget where he left it?"

She giggled. "I believe he's striking his ball with his cane. Is there a rule against that?"

He leaned on his mallet. "There ought to be a rule against little girls marrying doddering fools four times their age."

Nancy scowled at him. "I'm not a little girl."

"But Teasdale is in fact a doddering fool?"

"Well, yes." She rolled her eyes. "Look at him."

He glanced at Teasdale and gave an exaggerated shudder. "Then why did you pick him?"

"I didn't pick him," Nancy protested. "He turns my stomach."

Gavin raised his brows. "But I heard you talking about him to Rose. In the nursery. You said he wrote you poetry, was about to offer—"

"Not *him*." Nancy let out a deep sigh. "Monsieur Lefebvre. My . . . French tutor. It was nothing. Papa overreacted."

Her French tutor. Just as Miss Pemberton claimed.

"The night your father died," he asked her carefully. "Did you go straight to your bedchamber after dancing?"

"No, I . . ." She blinked, broke eye contact, looked away. "I stopped by the nursery to visit the girls. I-I have to go. It's my turn."

After his niece fairly fled from him across the grass, Gavin made his way back to Miss Pemberton's side.

"She told me about the French tutor," he said. "Sort of. Said it was nothing and Hetherington overreacted."

Miss Pemberton nodded slowly, hefting the weight of her mallet, but all she said was, "Hmmm."

"Hmmm?" Gavin repeated incredulously. "Go—go touch her! I want to know if that blackguard ruined her. I hope Hetherington sent him packing with both eyes blackened. She's seventeen, for God's sake. Make sure Teasdale hasn't touched her either. Go see if—"

"So much for your grand apology." Miss Pemberton said, fingers clenched around her mallet as if she considered braining him with it. "You're already back to ordering me around. Here's some free advice, Mr. Lioncroft. People are far more eager to help those they wish to, not those who command them to."

She snapped her mallet up beneath one arm and stalked off.

Wonderful. He'd managed to alienate his sole ally yet again.

"If you ask me," came Rose's dry voice from behind him, "you need to work on your wooing, Romeo."

"If you ask me," Gavin shot back without thinking, "you wouldn't know a good match if it slapped you in the face like your rotter of a husband. What's Nancy doing torn between a decrepit bag of bones and a vagabond French tutor, of all people? She should be in a London ballroom, taking her pick of eligible young bucks with educated accents and all their teeth."

Rose's mouth fell open. "You don't know anything about it!"

"And why's that? *You* returned *my* letters, not the other way around. And then you show up here and expect me to help match her up with *that* ancient lecher? Where's the wedding going to be, by his plot in the family cemetery so he can tumble right in when the ceremony concludes?"

"You're an ass." Her hands fisted on her hips. "I should never have come to you."

"So I'm an ass," he scoffed. "That's not news to either of us. Hetherington was one, too, and he finally got what was coming to him. Need I fear the same fate?"

"I didn't kill my husband," Rose hissed, "but I'm definitely considering killing you!"

"I wouldn't doubt it." Gavin raked her with a speculative glance. "What *were* you doing before you discovered his body? Wandering the halls alone?"

"No, I . . ." She hesitated. "I was with Nancy."

"Where?"

Her eyes narrowed. "Did you just ask Nancy? I saw you talking to her a moment ago."

Gavin crossed his arms. "Actually, I did. And if you were together, you'll tell me the same thing. Where were you?"

"The nursery?"

"Are you asking me or telling me?" His voice rose so loud his sister backed up a step. "God damn it, Rose, be honest! I thought you thought *I* offed the rotter."

Her eyes filled with tears. "Did you?"

"No!"

"Well, neither did I!"

"Er, excuse me," came the Stanton chit's unwelcome voice. "You're standing in the path of my ball."

Gavin kicked it out of his way.

"Er, fair enough," the Stanton chit mumbled. "I'll just hit it from here, then."

"You'll never change," Rose snapped before sweeping off in the opposite direction without a backward glance.

No?

He stalked over to where he'd kicked the Stanton chit's ball, swiped it from the grass just in time to avoid having his knuckles shattered by her swinging mallet, and tossed it to its original location a few feet to the left. She stumbled at the sudden lack of resistance. He caught her by the shoulders, righted her, and aimed her toward her ball.

"Sorry," he muttered, earning an even more startled glance. "I have a feeling I'm going to become fairly adept at apologizing before this party concludes."

The Stanton chit shot him a wary look before rearranging herself behind her twice-displaced ball.

Gavin sighed, stepped behind her, and placed his hands over her wrists. "Not like that. Like this." He kicked at her feet until her stance improved. Somewhat. "Now swing."

"I made it through the wicket," she cried, turning to flash him a brief grin before chasing off after her ball.

There. He'd spent at least thirty seconds not being an ass. That should count for something.

He spun to track down his own ball and found himself face-to-face with Miss Pemberton. The expression she wore indicated she'd just caught him very much being an ass, not the other way around.

"Nice of you to help Susan," she said evenly. Something in her eyes suggested she planned to aim her ball toward his crotch, not toward the wicket.

"She's a featherbrain," he said quickly. "I hated every moment of it. May I help you?"

"No."

He took a deep breath. "I'm sorry I ordered you around again after just apologizing for ordering you around."

She gazed at him for a moment, then nodded. "Accepted."

He leaned for her mallet. "May I—?"

"No." She jerked it out of his reach. "I don't need you."

"Fine."

He glared at her. She glared right back.

Then: "Why did you shave?"

He faltered. "Why did I what?"

"You've appeared every other morning as though you couldn't be bothered with your toilette unless the mood struck you otherwise. So why now? Today? To look like Quality? To show off the scar along your jaw? To impress Susan? To—"

He grabbed her by the shoulders and hauled her to his chest. Their mallets tumbled to the grass, ignored. "To impress *you,* if you must know. If I seemed careless with my appearance before, it was because I had no reason to be careful." He tilted his face forward, gentled his tone. "I treated you badly this morning. I wished to make amends, and I thought—foolishly, it now seems—if I looked better on the outside, perhaps you'd think I was better on the inside."

"I already liked you on the inside," she whispered, brushing the tips of her fingers against his recently-smoothed cheeks. "I liked your outside, too. But now if you kiss me, it won't feel the way I remember it."

"*If* I kiss you?" he echoed disbelievingly. "Woman, it takes every ounce of my willpower not to bend—"

"Um, Uncle Lioncroft?"

"Jane. Yes." Gavin cleared his throat, set down Miss Pemberton, and turned to his niece with a forced smile. "I'm sorry. Was I in the way again?"

"No, I wondered if you could help me like you helped Miss Stanton. I can't make my ball go through the wicket unless it's up close, and look at it—the pink ball is really far. It's impossible. For me. Can you help?"

"Yes. Yes, I'd love to help you. One second. Miss Pemberton, I—" But she was shaking her head and backing away, her reclaimed mallet already in hand. "Never mind." He turned back to his niece. "Now, stand with your feet like this. No, like—yes, exactly. Bend just a little. Not that much! Yes, better. Put your hands here and here. Mind your grip. Now pull your arms back and swing."

Thwack. The ball sailed several yards past the wicket. Unfortunately not *through* the wicket, but with considerably more force and accuracy than previously witnessed.

"Excellent shot," he assured her. "Next time, you'll get it."

She grinned. "Thank you."

"By the way," he began casually, almost unable to make himself ask the question. "On the night your father died, you were in the nursery?"

"I'm always in the stupid nursery. Except today! Pall-mall is grand. And the kites, oh! All my friends will be so jealous. The picnic was excellent, too, even if I got marmalade all over my dress. But that hardly matters when I've a new wardrobe to look forward to anyway, right, Uncle?"

"Er, right. But that night in the nursery, Jane. Who were you with?"

"The twins, of course. I'm always with the twins."

His heart skipped a beat. "Just the twins?"

"Yes." She paused for the briefest of seconds. "Oh, wait, no. I forgot. Also with Mother and Nancy. Right. All of us. Can I go after my ball now?"

Gavin nodded and let her go, frowning as she danced across the grass. Had she really been in the nursery with her mother and sister? Or was Miss Pemberton right, and that was simply the story the girls had been instructed to tell if questioned?

Chapter Nineteen

By the time the game ended, Gavin had no more answers than when he began.

He had, however, helped the twins to "win" the pall-mall game, and managed to stay as far away from the Stanton chit and her mother as possible while still remaining within shot of the wickets. The guests were now drawing nearer, with questioning looks in their eyes. He'd no sooner motioned a few servants to begin collecting the mallets and balls when his thirteen-year-old niece hurled herself into his arms, wailing as though she'd lost a limb to enemy fire.

"No, no, no," she cried into his waistcoat. "This has been the very best birthday and I do not wish for it to end! You said there would be picnics, and there were picnics, and then you said there would be kite-flying, and then there was kite-flying, and you said we would also have pall-mall, and we did, and the twins won even though I'm pretty sure I really won, or maybe Aunt Rutherford because she never snuck in extra hits for her ball, but now all the things you said we could do are over, which means my birthday is over. But I don't *want* to return indoors and resume an ordinary day when my birthday started out so extraordinary!"

"Jane." By gripping her about the forearms, Gavin somehow

managed to pluck her off his chest. He removed her to arm's length, bent to eye level, and did his best to ignore the growing crowd. "What else do you wish to do? Kite-flying and pall-mall are the only amusements I have, and I must confess—I only have them because you requested them of me."

"Not true!" She wiggled in place. "You have the maze! May we explore the maze? Say we can! The twins saw it, too. Didn't you, girls?"

He glanced over his shoulder at two nodding, giggling five-year-olds. Was hysteria contagious?

"Jane," he said again. "I do not have a maze. Nor do I have any idea what you're talking about."

"A huge maze! Behind the manor. All those hedgerows, taller than my head. I'm sure I saw the roof to a gazebo in the center. May we play in the gazebo? And race between the bushes?"

After her words sank in, Gavin straightened to his full height. "You want to play in my blackberry farm?"

The Stanton chit affected her fish impression again. "You have a *blackberry* farm?"

He shot her a pitying look. "Why did you suppose my home was called Blackberry Manor?"

She froze, blinked, and exchanged a glance with Miss Pemberton before muttering, "Better you not know."

"So, *can* we, Uncle Lioncroft? Can we? Can we?"

"All right, but—wait!" He grabbed Jane by the arm and the closest twin by a blond braid. "This is important, so please listen very closely. You must be careful not to touch the plants. The brambles are sharp and will scratch you."

Rebecca peered up at him. "Will it hurt?"

"Yes," he answered solemnly, releasing Jane's arm and Rachel's plait.

"Why do you keep plants that hurt people?" Rebecca asked with a frown.

He hesitated, then dropped to one knee, mostly to give himself time to think of a way to explain his ownership of a blackberry farm. All of his nieces stared at him expectantly, as did a fair number of his houseguests.

"Well," he began, half-wishing he'd inherited money or won his home on the turn of a card so he wouldn't have to explain his choice to a crowd. "You may not think much of them, to look at the fields now. Lots of spiny shoots and arching stems and those prickly brambles I warned you about. But in the springtime, those branches are full and green, and covered in beautiful sweet-smelling flowers."

Jane clapped her hands to her chest. "What color?"

"Er, white ones." What was *with* her and colors? Gavin did his best to stay on topic. "Then, over the course of the summer, the flowers fade away to give the berries room to grow among the leaves."

Rebecca's eyes widened. "Are the berries tasty?"

"Very much so. And by late summer, the ripened berries smell heavenly. They're delicious and sweet, but sharp and prickly when you try to pick them. It's important to wear gloves so they don't scratch you."

Rachel nodded sagely. "They don't like to be picked."

"Perhaps not. Even in the summer with all the flowers and berries, the hedgerows are beautiful but dangerous. Blackberry bushes like to grow wild and are very difficult to tame. You must stay on the paths and not touch the plants."

"Even if we see berries?" Rebecca asked.

"Especially if you see berries. We don't pick them after Michaelmas—September twenty-ninth. They become very bitter and can make you ill."

"Even I wish to see these mysterious hedgerows," came an amused female voice.

He glanced up in time to see Francine Rutherford looking surprised by her own admission.

"As do I," rejoined her husband, and offered her his arm.

By the time Gavin rose to his feet, his guests were already en route to the rear of his property, with the twins scampering several feet ahead. He loped forward until he reached Miss Pemberton's side and was inordinately pleased when she accepted his proffered arm as well.

"You are wonderful with children," she said after a moment. "I imagine you will make a marvelous father."

Gavin nearly took a header into the stone siding of his house. "A what? Me?"

She laughed up at him. "Surely the thought has occurred to you before." Her smile turned wry. "I'm sure the thought is occurring to Lady Stanton even as we speak."

He slowed to a stop, allowing the chattering guests to continue forward and disappear behind the house before he turned to face Miss Pemberton.

"For the devil's sake, any thoughts that woman has about me have nothing whatsoever to do with reality. Look at me. Truly look at me. I'm—I'm—" He ran a hand through his hair hard enough to hurt. "I'm not the marrying sort. I can barely hold a civil conversation with the guests of my own house party. I would be the worst husband. I can't even manage to be a good son or a good brother. I—" He turned away and resumed walking, increasing his pace with each stride. "I don't wish to discuss my many shortcomings. I'd rather show you the blackberry fields. I wish you could see them in the spring, before the berries bud when the flowers are in full bloom. They're beautiful."

He swept her around the corner of his house to the rear of his property before she could comment on his inability to participate in successful, caring relationships.

"My kingdom awaits." He used his free arm to encompass the whole of his fields with a mocking, sweeping gesture, and then turned to grin at Miss Pemberton.

She had frozen.

Not the good kind of frozen, such as frozen in wonder, with eyes shining and lips parted and hands clasped and cheeks flushed with excitement.

The bad kind of frozen.

Her eyes were painfully wide, her skin devoid of color and sheened with perspiration. Her shallow breaths escaped from parted lips with a faint but unsettling wheeze. Farms were not for everyone, but the normally staid Miss Pemberton didn't tend to overreact. In fact, the only other time he'd seen her in such a state was after she'd laid her hands on Hetherington's corpse.

"Miss Pemberton?" He stepped forward and around, blocking her view of the blackberry bushes with his chest. He tilted her chin up until her gaze met his, and tried not to blanch himself at the terror in her eyes. "What is it? Tell me."

"I can't go in there. I can't go in there. If I go in there, he'll get me. Where is he? Is he here already?" She shuddered. "No. I won't go in there."

What the devil did *that* mean?

"All right," he said aloud, retaking her arm and steering her away from both the blackberry fields and his house. "We'll save the farm tour for another day. See that little cottage ahead? It's a summerhouse. I never had a reason to furnish it, so I apologize in advance for its lack of seating arrangements, but we'll be close enough to the other guests without actually joining them"—good Lord, he was babbling as bad as Jane—"and we'll be able to talk privately. Come. Just a few more feet."

He half-carried her up the last three steps and into the summerhouse, and kicked the big white door closed behind them. There really wasn't any furniture. Damn.

He backed against a window facing away from the fields, leveraged himself against the sill as best he could, with his feet spread wide, and pulled Miss Pemberton into his lap. Well, more like he pulled her into his embrace, as he'd tugged her to him face-forward. He smoothed down the sides of her gown until his hands curved over her hips, securing her between his thighs. Her palms settled atop his forearms.

After a moment, she gave a little half sob, half laugh

and toppled forward, smashing directly into his cravat, and mumbled something that sounded like, "I apologize."

"For what?" he asked the top of her head. He dipped his chin until his lips pressed against the softness of her hair. "I have no idea what just happened. Did you have a vision?"

She nodded without looking up. "Earlier. Days earlier. With Susan. She was running through what I now know to be your fields, screaming for me. And then my stepfather burst through one of the paths, with me limp in his arms. He tossed me in his carriage and took me away."

"Over my dead body," Gavin said, and then paused as a horrible thought struck him. "Do your visions always come true?"

"Yes. No. I think so. I don't know. I've never known of them *not* coming true—they seem to be memories, even the ones that haven't happened yet—but I thought . . . I thought if I just didn't go *in* the fields, he couldn't take me *out* of them."

"Logical enough." He tilted his face until his cheek rested against the top of her hair. "We'll do our best to keep you as far from the fields as possible. When was this capture to take place? Today?"

She sighed against his chest. "I don't know. My visions tend to be simultaneously useful and useless."

"All right. Well, let's keep being logical. We were just to the side of my property, were we not? And before that, in the front garden. The front garden is an excellent vantage point of the only means by which a carriage may come anywhere near us, and there were none. Trust me, I've been glancing over my shoulder ever since the Stanton woman first threatened to summon the constabulary."

"It'll be a race," she mumbled with a hiccupy laugh. "Which one of us gets taken away first."

"Not amusing," he returned gruffly, pressing his lips to her hair again. And then suddenly it wasn't enough. He threaded his fingers through what was left of her chignon, cradling the back of her head so he could gaze into her eyes.

Then he bent his head and kissed her.

He meant it to be a small kiss, a dry kiss, a chaste kiss. The merest brushing of closed lips against closed lips. The briefest of illicit contact.

But the moment he captured her breath with his own, her fingers dug into his biceps and she matched him kiss for kiss.

Her mouth opened beneath his. Tempting him. Teasing him. She suckled his lower lip until he gave her his tongue, and then she suckled that, too. He hauled her against his body, not caring if he destroyed her hair, if she destroyed his cravat, if his cock throbbed against those maddening layers of fall and gown and chemise.

He had to have her. She was his. His to have, his to kiss, his to protect. No one could take her from him. And whether she wanted Gavin the man, her body wanted *his* body, and that was enough for now. It would have to be. He was dying for her. Whether or not she was truly his—he was hers.

She gasped into his mouth, ground her hips against him. He was moving too hard, too fast, bruising her with kisses. He had to be. But she pulled him closer, tighter, wrapped her arms around his neck and clung to him.

He deepened the kiss. What choice did he have? He could do nothing but succumb to desire. Succumb, and force her surrender as well. He slid his hands from her hips to her derrière, nestled her more firmly between his thighs, made love to her with his mouth and tongue as he rubbed his aching cock against the softness of her body.

She did not recoil. She did not push him away. She wriggled against him, met his tentative thrusts with a whimper and her own rocking hips. She dug her fingers into his shoulders, his neck, his hair.

"Gavin," she moaned against his mouth.

He almost came.

He tilted his head back long enough to grin at her, with

eyes that drank in her beauty, with lips that yearned for the touch of her mouth.

"I knew you'd first-name me eventually," he teased. Or meant to tease, but the words came out so low and so husky, he barely recognized his own passion-strained voice.

She smiled back at him, the slow sensual smile of a woman who had a man by the balls and well knew it, the smile of a woman swept up in the furor of her awakening body, the lilting, teasing, touch-me-kiss-me-love-me smile of a woman who wanted *him*. Unbelievable. And unutterably arousing.

"I welcome you to call me Evangeline." The smile in her eyes took on a knowing, suggestive edge. "I welcome you *to* Evangeline."

And then her mouth was upon his. Her arms tightened around him, twined, then loosened just enough to unplaster her breasts from his shirt, to rub them against his chest.

God help him. He swore he could feel her hard nipples through his waistcoat. And just in case that wasn't possible, just in case the only thing feeling her nipples was his frenzied imagination, he slid one of his hands from her rear to her hip, from her hip to her waist, from her waist to her ribs. His thumb brushed against the underside of her breast, then his index finger coasted upward, then his palm, and yes, an erect nipple definitely crowned that perfect breast.

Her breath hitched as he rubbed the tips of his fingers against it, rolling, teasing, gently tugging. He longed to feel her, skin to skin. Curse whoever invented clothing! He'd get rid of it in under two seconds. Maybe. Where the hell was the bottom of her skirt? He had to touch her. Now. God damn frustrating mess of silk and—

She tore her mouth from his. "Why did you stop? Don't stop. I liked it. I—"

"I didn't stop," he promised. "I'm about to do something better, just as soon as I get my hands underneath this infuriating ream of—"

"Inside the summerhouse?" came an overloud female voice from outside the thin walls. "Are you sure he's in there, Mother?"

Damn, damn, damn. He was going to kill that Stanton chit one of these days.

Gavin gave up trying to get under Miss Pemberton's gown and instantly set about righting it as best he could.

"Oh, no," she breathed, her eyes now wide with horror instead of heavy-lidded with passion. "It's Susan."

"I know. I'll kill her later. Stand up straight and let me look at you." He cocked his head and shrugged. "You look fine. Well, mostly fine. Your hair is doing something interesting, but other than that, you're as ravishing as ever. I mean, non-ravished-looking. I hope."

She eyed him and giggled. "You, on the other hand, look like somebody clutched fistfuls of your hair and smashed her breasts into your cravat."

He lunged for her, grabbed her, then forced himself to let her go. "Woman, if you keep talking like that, I will *give* the Stanton chit something shocking to see."

As if on cue, the Stanton chit's whiny voice grew even closer. "But I don't *wish* to be compromised today. I told you I'd rather wait until the end of the party. Besides, Evangeline says he won't marry me anyway."

"He'll have to," came Lady Stanton's cold response. "Or his honor will be forever impugned."

"Ha," he whispered to Evangeline. "My honor was impugned ages ago. I haven't had a reputation to uphold in years. You, however . . . Turn around."

"What?"

"Quickly. Turn around." He spun her backward, steadied her, scooped up her curls. "My apologies in advance. I've seen Rose do this to the twins about once an hour, but you seem to have lost the majority of your pins."

"You're fixing my *hair*?"

"Attempting to, my lady. No compliments just yet." He twisted that gorgeous mane into a long, thick rope until it began to buckle and coil. He scrunched the mass into as boringly normal a chignon as he could, and affixed it with the few remaining hairpins. Not too bad for a first attempt. Lopsided, yes, but when was it not? And the tendrils escaping at the temple and nape only added to her beauty. As if she needed anything to add to her beauty. He wanted to shake her hair free and make love to her until their muscles were too weak to do more than tangle together. He wanted to—

"Step lively, Susan! We haven't all day. I'll be back in five minutes to 'accidentally' come upon you just as soon as I fetch another witness. There's Mr. Teasdale; he'll have to do. Go on, now, before Lioncroft leaves. Lord knows what he's doing in there. And don't let him *truly* ravish you. I'll only be a second."

Before Gavin had a chance to do more than leap to the opposite side of the room, the summerhouse door opened. The Stanton chit stumbled inside as if shoved, and the door shut just as quickly behind her.

"Good afternoon, Susan," Miss Pemberton said evenly, her tone and manner remarkably calm considering the arch glint in her eyes.

The Stanton chit gulped, grimaced, swung her gaze from Miss Pemberton to Gavin and back to Miss Pemberton again.

"Now is not the time for manners, Evangeline. We have to hurry. Mother's fetching Teasdale."

Gavin propped a shoulder against the wall. "Hurry and what, may I ask? Is this the moment where I get to ravish you both?"

The corner of Miss Pemberton's mouth quirked.

"I assure you," the Stanton chit said through clenched teeth. "This is not my idea."

"We know." Miss Pemberton jerked her head toward the window, dislodging another pin. "We could hear everything. Come, before your mother returns."

The Stanton chit shot him a suspicious look over her shoulder before following Miss Pemberton outside. Gavin closed the door behind them and they all headed toward the side of his house, away from where Lady Stanton's bonnet and Mr. Teasdale's beaver were just visible atop a row of blackberry bushes.

"How did your mother know where to find me?"

"The twins told her." The Stanton chit slid a half-reproachful, half-impressed glance toward Miss Pemberton. "She neglected to inquire as to whether he was alone."

"Susan? Susan, darling, where have you gone off to?" came Lady Stanton's glass-shattering falsetto from beyond the hedgerows. "Mr. Teasdale, would you be so kind as to help me locate my daughter?"

"Your mother," Miss Pemberton whispered, "is terrifying."

"I know." The Stanton chit blanched. "She's coming! What are we to do?"

"Nothing. We're out of the summerhouse and wandering about like everyone else." Miss Pemberton affected an exceptionally awkward stance. "Look natural."

One of the side doors to Gavin's house swung open. A footman stepped outside and shaded his eyes from the late afternoon sun. As soon as he caught sight of the trio he strode forward, reaching their side in seconds.

"My lord," he said when Gavin inclined his head. "You have a . . . guest."

Something in the slight hesitation sent alarm skittering across his skin.

"Who?" he demanded. "The constabulary?"

"No," Miss Pemberton breathed, backing up until her shoulders bumped against the gray stones of the outer wall. "Please, no."

The footman handed Gavin a small white card. No matter how many times he read it, the name inscribed therein remained the same.

NEAL PEMBERTON

Chapter Twenty

Evangeline plastered herself against the side of Mr. Lioncroft's house, wishing the stones scratching at her hair and clothes could swallow her whole.

Mr. Lioncroft hadn't said as much, but the way he stared at the calling card instead of meeting her eyes spoke volumes. Volumes about how she didn't have until tomorrow after all, how those stolen moments in the summerhouse had now become farewell kisses, how she should've been running away instead of flying kites, for heaven's sake. She should've fled as fast as her feet could take her, until she wore clean through her boots and her feet bled over the dirt and rocks.

And then run some more. Run until her lungs ached, until her knees buckled, until she died of exhaustion if that's what it took, because if her stepfather caught her, she'd never escape again. He was here. He *had* caught her. He would strike her, he would take her, he would lock her up . . . but he wouldn't kill her yet. No, not yet. Not until he was done with her. Not until death was the more favorable option, not until she was begging for him to let her go or let her die, anything but hold her down and— heaven help her. He was *here*.

She should've run.

Strong hands seized her by the forearms. Mr. Lioncroft. Gavin. Too late.

"No," he said to her, his voice low, urgent, determined. "Whatever you're thinking: *No*. Trust me. I know it's impossible, but do it anyway."

"I have to leave," she whispered. "I have to run. I have to—"

"Wait." His knuckles caressed the side of her cheek, softly, briefly, and then he turned to his footman. "Where is he?"

"Doyle showed him into the Yellow Salon to await you, my lord."

"Well, show him out."

"My lord?"

"Show him to the porch. He can wait for me there. He's not welcome in my home. Porch. Go." The moment the footman disappeared, Mr. Lioncroft's gaze was upon her again. He reached out, slightly, subtly, to brush her fingertips with his own. His neck was corded, his muscles tensed, his jaw hard. He cut his gaze toward Susan. "Take Evangeline inside. Now. Use the servants' side entrance."

"I-I won't know how to get back to the guest quarters," Susan stammered.

"You don't need to. Stay in the servant quarters."

"With the *servants?*"

"As a precaution. It's the last place anyone would look for you two." He hauled open the side door. "Go. Keep her safe."

Susan nodded, nudged Evangeline forward and through the darkened doorway. Evangeline stepped inside, turned, gazed at the man still standing outside the cracked door.

"He'll take me," she said, unable to keep the bleakness from her tone.

"He won't."

"He'll hurt me, and then he'll take me. That's his way."

"He *won't*."

"He will. He owns me. There's nothing you can do."

"I'll do it anyway. I—" He broke off, blinked, shook his

head as if startled by whatever he'd been about to say. "I'll be back. Stay safe. I . . . I'll be back."

Then he shut the door and was gone.

"Come." Susan curled her gloved fingers around Evangeline's wrist. "We oughtn't to stay by the door."

Susan tugged Evangeline forward by the wrist. They headed away from the door, made their way down the shadowed corridor and around a corner. A small maid raced to meet them.

"Underbutler sent me," she said by way of greeting. She paused, bobbed, motioned hurriedly. "This way."

They followed her to an oblong room with a lit fireplace and a dozen or so mismatched chairs. A lone candelabrum flickered atop a short bookcase, casting its glow on the worn cushions and dark paintings.

"This is the servants' relaxing room," the maid explained. "Not much to do in here, 'less you know how to read, which those of us as don't are trying to learn, seeing as how the master makes sure we have time for ourselves, but there's a fire to keep you warm and seats as cozy as any, and if you don't mind my company overmuch, I'll be back frequent-like to relate as what's going on out-of-doors."

"Back?" Susan repeated when the maid paused for breath. "Where are you going?"

"To watch, of course. I've been here six years this December, and this is the first week we've had guests of any sort, much less those that dance and fly kites, and now here comes a man with a card and a cane looking smart as you please, and the master has him tossed outside like so much filth? I'd wager there isn't a servant in the house without an eye to a window or an ear to a door." She paused for breath. "You want me to come back regular, and tell you what's what?"

"Yes, please." Evangeline sank onto the closest chair and dropped her head into her hands.

The maid bobbed and fled.

"That," Susan said slowly, "was the oddest maid ever."

"That was Bess," Evangeline said without taking her head from her hands. "Younger sister to the enceinte parlor maid. She means well."

"Do you talk to all the servants?"

"Yes."

"Why?"

Evangeline groaned into her hands. "I don't know, Susan. Do we have to discuss this?"

"What do you prefer to discuss? What you were doing alone with Lioncroft after I told you today was the day for my compromise? Or perhaps when he became such an intimate friend as to first-name you within my hearing? How intimate is intimate, Evangeline?"

This time, Evangeline lifted her head. "You say that as if you have some claim on him."

"My mother—"

"Your mother has no more claim on him than you do. When will the two of you realize that he's his own man and immune to your stratagems? He doesn't wish to marry you." Her voice rose. "He will not marry you."

"And why is that?" Susan flounced into a chair across the room. "Because he's pledged to you?"

Evangeline shook her head. "He's not pledged to anybody. Leave him be."

"If he's not pledged to anybody, then you have no more claim to him than I do. Yet *you* are not leaving him be." Susan's chin lifted. "If he doesn't marry me, it will be because you got in the way."

"So?" Evangeline snapped. "You don't even want him."

"What does that have to do with anything?"

"Everything!"

"Marriage isn't about wanting the other person, Evangeline." Susan's voice took on a lecturing quality, as though repeating a lesson she'd learned by rote. "Marriage is about bettering your position, making alliances, moving upward. Lioncroft is my chance to escape Mother and reenter Society."

"Ha." Evangeline leaned back and crossed her arms. "What does he get from the bargain, but a disgraced scandal-monger and a crone for a mother-in-law?"

"He gets a wife worthy of his station, that's what he gets. One with education and poise and accomplishments, and the ability to manage a house of this size in a manner befitting our class." Susan gestured toward herself then motioned at Evangeline. "What would he get from you?"

"Nothing." Evangeline glanced away and pretended she didn't care that Susan was right, was born superior, was raised to be exactly the sort of woman a gentleman of Quality would want. "He'd get nothing, because I'm not marrying him. Nor has he offered. He *won't* offer because he has no wish to marry and neither do I, so your questions are as stupid as your views on marriage. *Ton* matches may be about bettering positions and bartering for upward mobility, but love matches are about caring for another person as much as you care for yourself and putting their needs and desires on a par with your own."

Susan snorted. "Balderdash. You've been reading too many novels."

"And you've been listening to your mother too much," Evangeline returned.

They were still glaring at each other from opposite sides of the room when the maid burst back in.

"I can't stay long," she warned, "because I think it's going to come to fisticuffs at any moment and I shan't miss *that,* but what has happened so far is this: After my master had the handsome gentleman shown out to the porch—"

Susan started. "Handsome?"

"They're both right handsome, my lady, but as I don't know the name of the one with the light blue eyes, he's to be 'the handsome gentleman,' while the other is to be 'my master,' for the sake of storytelling. In any case, the handsome gentleman is waiting on the porch as pretty as you please until my master comes around the corner—for he was out-of-doors, as you know—and says, 'Why are you here?' Just like that, with no polite words of greeting at all. And the handsome gentleman says, 'Are you Lioncroft?' And my master says—"

"Bess," Evangeline interrupted. "The main points, if you please."

"Right. So my master lounges against a column in that way that he's got—where he looks like he's relaxed, but really you see he could pounce on you at any moment—and he says to the handsome gentleman, 'I told you not to come here.' And the handsome gentleman says, 'No, what you said was that you'd send my property onto me when you was done with her—' Oh, good Lord, my lady, are you quite all right?"

"I'm fine," Evangeline managed. "Pray continue."

Bess hesitated for only a second. "Well, once he says he came to see if my master could be trusted, I thought there'd be brawling right then and there, but my master just smiles as if to say, of course, he can't be trusted, and he pushes off from the column and kind of prowls closer to the handsome gentleman who, to his credit, doesn't back up none, although he did glance around shifty-eyed for a moment as if taking careful note of the paths to escape. So my master says, 'What property is that?' and you'll never believe what the handsome gentleman said in return."

Evangeline slumped back in her chair. "Let me guess. Me."

"Just so," the maid crowed. "That's just what he said. And my master says, 'She's not here,' which is as bold a lie as any, since you're sitting right afore me, and the handsome gentleman says, 'That's right odd, as I got a letter from you and a letter from the Stanton woman both yesterday, and yours said I couldn't have Evangeline yet and hers said to come straightaway and fetch her.'"

Susan made a strangled sound in the back of her throat. "My mother said that?"

Evangeline sat up straight. "But if he just got Lady Stanton's letter, how did he know I'd be here in the first place?"

"Very good, my lady." Bess nodded. "That's just what my master asked, as well. And the handsome gentleman said he'd known enough as to guess you might be wherever the Stantons were, and he checked with Lord Stanton, who said he didn't know a thing about any Pembertons but that his wife and daughter were over at Blackberry Manor for a spell, and the handsome gentleman put two and two together and come by to get you. Said he'd take you home where you belonged and chain you there if he had to, and that there wasn't a dern thing my master could do about it, as the law was the law and you was the handsome gentleman's legal property."

Evangeline's shoulders slumped. "It's true."

Susan crossed the room and dipped to kneel before her chair. "I am sorry about the letter. I didn't know Mother would do something like that." She glanced over her shoulder at the maid. "Where is she now, do you know?"

"There's nobody who doesn't know. She was tearing through the guest quarters like a madwoman, looking for you near as I can tell, but I'm pretty sure as now we've got her abed or close to it. Had some idea you was with the master in the summerhouse and when neither of you was there, she got the idea you was either ruined or killed and she wasn't sure which was the worse, and my master's sister had to pour laudanum down her throat just to get her to settle down." Bess shook her head as if amused by the whole tale. "As to everyone else, they're still out back in the blackberry fields, none the wiser to your mama's hysteria or to my master and his visitor. Except the old gentleman, with the white hair and the cane. Far as I know, he's still asleep on the summerhouse floor."

"In that case . . ." Evangeline brushed Susan out of her way and rose to her feet. "Is there someplace we could go to overhear? You said every servant in the house was watching."

"Well . . ." The maid twisted her hands uncertainly. "My

master's orders were for you to stay hidden in the servant quarters, my lady. He's just on the other side of that wall over there, the one with the bookcase and the big paintings. Doubt you can hear through the wall, though. Please just stay in here. Safe-like. I'll be back soon to keep you informed."

She fled the room before Evangeline had a chance to protest further.

Susan shoved up her spectacles with the back of her hand. "Are you afraid of what Lioncroft might say to your stepfather?"

"Not unless my stepfather's carrying one of his knives. He's the very soul of determination. And he owns me. I don't want Gavin to get hurt."

"I don't want either of you hurt. I . . ." Susan sighed. "I don't want to fight with you. I want us to be friends."

"I'd like to be friends, too," Evangeline said after a moment, "but a good portion of that depends on whether or not I'm returned to my stepfather."

She strode over to the far wall and pressed her ear against the smooth paper. Bess was right. Nothing. So much for listening through walls. Unless . . . She sprinted to the bookcase and jerked books from every shelf.

"Evangeline!" came Susan's startled voice. "What the dickens are you doing?"

"Looking for something."

Susan paused. "A book?"

"A door."

Evangeline stepped back, surveyed the room. Nothing but chairs and books and paintings. Paintings! She yanked on the first frame and barely jumped to safety before the canvas crushed her toes. She tugged on the second frame more gingerly—still nothing. The third frame, however, swung toward her with a groan. Both dust and muffled voices rolled out from the wall's dank interior.

"Bring me a chair," Evangeline hissed.

"A what? Did you just open the *wall?* How did you do that?"

"A chair," Evangeline repeated. "We've got to prop the passageway open so we don't get trapped inside. Trust me."

Susan dashed for a chair. Within moments, they had the access panel propped wide and two more chairs stuffed inside the passageway. When they climbed atop the seat cushions, Susan was still the only one tall enough to peek through the porthole-shaped window high up on the wall. Words, however, filtered through.

"I told you," came Mr. Lioncroft's low, steady voice. "She's not here."

"You're lying. She's mine and I want her."

"You dare accuse me of lying?"

"I'll accuse any liar of lying. I know how valuable the little bitch is. One touch and—Ow! Damn you! I ought to—Goddammit!"

Scuffling sounds ensued. Evangeline elbowed Susan in the ribs.

"Oh," she whispered, tearing her gaze away from the porthole long enough to cast Evangeline a chagrined grimace. "Sorry. Lioncroft planted him a facer. Your stepfather tried to return the favor, but Lioncroft ducked and your stepfather ended up striking the column. He's got a bloody hand and what'll probably be a black eye, and now they're scowling at each other from opposite sides of the porch."

"Not that kind of touch," came Neal Pemberton's voice at last. "Although she's old enough for me to break her in, now that her mother's gone."

More scuffling.

"Another facer," Susan confirmed. "He's going to look like a raccoon. Now Lioncroft's got him by the neck. He's turning purple."

"She gets visions," Neal blurted out. "She sees things. Just like her mother. That's a useful talent to possess, and she belongs to me. Don't think you can use her for yourself, if that's what you have in mind. I will summon every authority, write to every paper, thrash you myself if need be, until you hand that witch—"

Scuffling. Shattered wood. A thud. More scuffling.

"Your stepfather isn't doing very well with his thrashing. He got in a couple lucky jabs, but that wood breaking was Lioncroft throwing him through a balustrade. Lioncroft tackled him before he had a chance to get up, and now—oh, no!" Susan rose even higher on her toes and stared out the window in horror.

"What?" Evangeline demanded, her skin going cold. "Tell me."

"You were right. He has a knife. He got Lioncroft in the side."

Evangeline swayed against the wall. *"What?"*

"Oh! One of the footmen snuck up and hit your stepfather in the head with what looks like the pink pall-mall mallet. It's got red bits now. I think he's dead."

Silence.

Once Evangeline regained her breath and her balance, she glanced up at Susan. "Really?"

"Yes. No . . . wait, he's breathing. Lioncroft kicked him to make sure. He's got one hand over his wound and the other hand motioning toward your stepfather's carriage. Ah, they're putting him back in. Not Lioncroft—He tried, but there's too much blood coming from his side. He keeps staggering and wincing."

Evangeline's heart stuttered. "No," she whispered.

"He's standing mostly upright again. The footmen have your stepfather stuffed in his carriage. Lioncroft's saying something to the driver. Something with a lot of hand gestures. And now they're going. Evangeline, they're going!"

Evangeline scrambled down from her chair and shot out of the passageway and across the room.

"Evangeline," Susan shouted. "Wait for me. You know I can't find my way out!"

"Bess will show you back," Evangeline called over her shoulder as she wrenched open the door and hurtled into the hall. Gavin was hurt. Her stepfather had stabbed him. For trying to help *her*.

If he died from the wound, she'd kill her stepfather herself.

Chapter Twenty-One

The slash in Gavin's side didn't start stinging until Miss Pemberton flew out the front door, launched across the porch, and threw her arms around him. He forced himself not to flinch when her trembling arms squeezed the tender flesh above his injury. He'd never admit it to anyone if asked directly, but he'd discovered over the past week that he rather liked hugs. When there wasn't a four-inch knife wound slicing him from waist to hip.

The good news was, the cut was long but shallow. At worst, give his valet a few minutes with a needle and Gavin would be good as new.

The bad news? He and his decimated porch were soaked in blood, Miss Pemberton was squeezing his torso with rib-shattering strength, and the murmur of concerned party guests was getting louder by the second.

"Come." Gavin wrenched her from his chest, hauled her against his good side, and hustled her back indoors before the party guests caught sight of them. "You can hug me inside."

She allowed him to lace his fingers with hers and pull her across the anteroom and down the hall before glancing up at him with those wide brown eyes.

"Where are we going?"

His steps faltered. Where the hell was he dragging her? Away from potential scandal should curious houseguests stumble upon them, yes, but aside from that . . . Where would nobody look for him?

"Yellow Salon."

Miss Pemberton listed sideways, apparently trying to walk in a straight line whilst bent at the waist inspecting his wound. "Should we send for a surgeon?"

"No surgeon. I promise to live." He smiled at her reassuringly. "For now."

She did not look reassured. "But he stabbed you. There's . . . there's . . ."

"Blood?" Gavin shouldered open the door to the Yellow Salon and ushered her inside. "Nothing a needle and thread can't fix." She stopped so suddenly he tripped over her and sent them both sprawling into the back of a sofa. "What? No needles?"

She rounded on him as if discovering he kept an army of circus performers hidden behind the chaise. "No snakes. No snakes upon the paper, no trolls grinning from the wood, no dark flickering shadows. There's a window in here. A bay window. With a yellow cushion. Gorgeous ivy-colored furniture. And yellow walls. Bright, bright yellow, like daffodils in sunlight."

He glanced around the familiar room. "Yes. That's why it's called the Yellow Salon."

Her hands jutted forward as if about to shove him in the middle of his chest. But when her gaze flickered to his blood-stained side, her palms turned skyward then slapped down against her hips. "What in heaven's name is the matter with you?"

Gavin took a subtle step backward. "You don't like yellow?"

"I love yellow!" She glared at him. "I love yellow, and green and blue and pink and white and—"

He reached behind her to shut the door. His servants did not need to overhear Miss Pemberton's spontaneous recital of her favorite colors. "You sound like my niece."

Her jaw clenched. "I sound like a woman forced to sleep in a bedchamber occupied by snake-inhabited walls and a troll-infested bed."

Ah. That. He tried for a slow, sensual smile. "You can sleep in mine, if you like."

Her lips pursed. Pursed lips couldn't be a good sign. "I would like to know why we weren't shown in here when we arrived, if this is the proper receiving room. It's beautiful."

"*Because* it's beautiful."

He strode past her to the window and pulled the curtains closed. When he turned back around to face her, she hadn't moved. If anything, her pursed lips had gotten pursier.

"You don't like beautiful things?" Miss Pemberton asked at last.

Since she seemed content to stand there squinting at him as though he were the strangest specimen of male she'd ever encountered, Gavin crossed over to a sofa and eased onto the cushion, careful not to bump his injured side against the armrest.

"I like you," he reminded Miss Pemberton once he'd arranged himself as comfortably as he could, "and you're beautiful. But I was angry about having unexpected guests. I wanted everyone to leave as quickly as they came, and they wouldn't hurry off if they enjoyed their stay." He flashed his most devilish smile. "So I didn't show anybody into any receiving rooms."

Her arms crossed below her breasts, plumping them above the dipping neckline. "And the guest quarters?"

"Have not been renovated since I purchased the house. I haven't had guests in over a decade." He widened the spread of his relaxed legs, lounged one arm along the back of the sofa, gazed up to find Miss Pemberton staring at him as if he exuded more danger injured than uninjured. "A few weeks notice was hardly enough time to commission new suites, should I have had the inclination to do so."

She bit her lower lip, suckled it, freed it. Gavin would've liked to do the same.

Her gaze dipped from his eyes, to his mouth, to his ruined clothing. "Why didn't you do it?"

"Do what? Die?"

She came closer, first one tentative halting step, then another. "No. Why didn't you hand me over to my stepfather?"

"Hand you over to that cretin? Why would I?"

"You had to."

"Yet I didn't."

"But he's my stepfather." She paled, shivered, swallowed. "He owns me."

For now, Gavin almost added. Where had that come from? He was in no position to change her legal status. Even if he wished to marry her—which he neither admitted nor denied—he couldn't protect his own neck, let alone hers, too. Plenty could happen between now and whenever he might have the opportunity to petition for a license. If he couldn't promise to stay alive for the wedding, then he could promise her nothing.

"I don't care if he owns you," Gavin said instead. "I sent him away."

"He'll be back."

"Not until he recovers from those black eyes," Gavin assured her with as much flippancy as he could muster. How long would a blackguard like her stepfather stay away, when she was right—he was her legal guardian. How long before he did write his letters, make good on his threats, summon the magistrate? A month? A week? "We'll make sure you're gone by then," he said, hoping she couldn't detect the bleakness in his tone. Not because he feared her worthless scab of a stepfather, but because in order to rid herself from one man, she'd have to rid herself of them both. "Shall I summon you a carriage?"

She started, as if assailed by the same thoughts. "Now?"

He forced himself to say the words. "It's yours when you wish it."

She fairly leapt the distance between them until she was but an arm's breadth before him, his boots on either side of hers. "But I haven't determined the murderer's identity."

"Nor will you be able to help under your stepfather's captivity. I prefer you safe somewhere unknown than unsafe somewhere known." He rubbed his face with one hand, cursed himself for its smoothness. Had he the slightest inkling she preferred his kisses the way he'd been giving them, forceful, scratchy, rough, he'd never have put razor to chin before the picnic. Now their farewell kiss—for surely she would allow him a farewell kiss?—would be inadequate, disappointing, unsatisfying. And, oh, how he longed to satisfy her. Her safety, however, was his primary concern. "Given the choice, I admit to disliking the thought of you going anywhere at dusk. Twilight is a dangerous time to begin a journey. Can you wait until morning?"

She edged closer, her gown brushing against the inside of his calves, his knees, his thighs. "But . . . but I haven't determined the murderer's identity."

"So you've reminded me."

"If I fail to help before I go, will—will you hang?"

Probably. Then again, he might hang even if she stayed. Gavin lifted a shoulder as if the thought held no sway. "Would you miss me either way?"

Her breath hitched. Her palms cupped his face. Her forehead touched his. "I would. You know I would. I miss you already."

As did he. Knowing she felt the same seemed to worsen the feeling of dread, to tighten his already tight muscles, to speed up his already racing heart. Gavin pulled her into his lap, clutched her to him, breathed in the sweet scent of her hair. Her hip curved against his uninjured side. Her knees tucked between his legs. The side of one silk-covered breast pressed against his chest.

She would have to leave him.

He would have to let her.

But not yet.

She tilted her face up at the exact moment his slanted down. Their breath came together first, then their mouths, then their tongues. She tasted like fear, like loneliness, like desire. Or maybe that was him. Maybe that was both of them. She, the woman who couldn't risk touching, who couldn't risk loving, who couldn't outrun her past.

And Gavin, the man who . . . what? Was he any different? He either didn't know or didn't want to know, just like he didn't want to stop kissing her, just like he didn't want to let her go, to put her in a carriage and send her away where he'd never see her again, smell her hair, taste her mouth and tongue and skin. But what else was he to do? What else was she to do? Her stepfather would be back, and the law would side with him.

Gavin wrenched his mouth from Miss Pemberton's.

"Tell me," he said, brushing his lips across the soft skin of her forehead. "Why did you run from him?"

She shuddered, but remained silent.

At first, he thought she wasn't going to answer. But then she leaned the side of her head against his shoulder and let out a long, slow exhale.

"First," she said, "I'll tell you why my mother didn't run. Me. A woman of her position—which is to say, none—can't even aspire to become the lowliest of scullery maids or the cheapest of prostitutes. Not without suffering visions and their consequences. Add to that limitation a child who showed every sign of the same affliction, and she was trapped."

He hated the pain in her voice, the anger, the self-loathing.

"You didn't trap her. You didn't. She married that dilberry maker of her own free will."

"No." Her head fell against his shoulder, her forehead against his neck. "She did so because of me. Had she not been with child, she would've taken her chances as a beggar on the street rather than be wife to Neal Pemberton. But she wouldn't have had to. She had education, if not family; beauty, if not money. She had been a lady. She could've been a fine governess or companion. She would have been. Had it not been for me."

He cradled her in his arms. "Had it not been for the visions, you mean."

"Had it not been for *me*. Even without visions, what could a woman in her position do, but marry? She was to be a mother. Her child needed a father. She took the first man to offer and regretted it ever since."

"Marrying a blackguard like Pemberton?"

"*Having* to."

He hated the unshed tears choking her voice.

"Nonetheless," Gavin insisted, "it was hardly your fault. Surely she didn't blame you for a situation outside anyone's control."

"How could she not?" Miss Pemberton lifted her head to fix him with her steady, bloodshot gaze. "Can you say you've never resented someone for something outside their control?"

"No," he admitted. "I cannot make that claim. But I try to focus my energies on that which I can control."

"I can't control anything. Not even my own skin. The visions come, regardless. Not even myself. I belong to my stepfather. He will come after me, as well. What did he say? He would drag me home and chain me there."

"A figure of speech."

"Hardly."

His grip on her waist tightened. "He would chain you?"

"He would do anything." She paused, shivered. "Every-thing."

Something in her tone chilled his blood. "He's your step-father," Gavin heard himself protest lamely. "Your guardian. Surely he would not—"

"My mother's presence protected me from his baser de-sires, if not from his fist. She couldn't even protect herself from the latter. She couldn't sew a straight enough seam, he said. Neither . . . neither can I." Miss Pemberton's voice cracked. "When he shoved her down the stairs, he meant to hurt her, not kill her. But it was too late."

"I won't let him touch you," Gavin snarled.

He hoped.

After claiming her mouth in the briefest of kisses, Mr. Li-oncroft gently eased Evangeline from his lap and rose to stand beside her. She would've preferred to remain wrapped in his arms all evening.

"We can't stay hidden any longer," he explained softly, as if her reluctance to leave him shone on her face. "They'll be looking for someone to explain why the porch is a shambles of blood and splintered wood."

"Hmmm," Evangeline murmured. "I can see how that might catch their attention. As might you, Mr. Lioncroft, dressed as you are in ripped and ruined clothing."

"Mr. Lioncroft?" he repeated with an arched brow. "What happened to Gavin?"

"My stepfather stuck a knife in his side," she answered. "For protecting me."

"I'd do it again." His eyes flashed down at her. "Let him stick me with a thousand knives."

"Let us hope not." She couldn't suppress a shiver at the thought. The idea was not as far-fetched as Mr. Lioncroft might believe. "What do we do now?"

"Now? I don't know." His head cocked to one side as he gazed down at her. "Supper will be ready soon. I'll change into something a little less bloody and then join you in the dining room. Can you avoid the others until then?"

"I don't wish to avoid them," Evangeline said grimly. "I wish to determine which of them is callous enough to let you hang in his place."

He dipped his head in a quick nod before striding to the opposite side of the room. The tilting of a vase triggered an access panel to the passageway between the walls. He glanced over his shoulder, eyes sober. "If you should save me from the noose, I would be in your debt."

"Not 'if,'" she informed him, but he'd already disappeared into the shadows. The panel eased shut behind him. "*When* I save him," she announced to the empty room, her words more confident than both her tone and her posture. "I'll unmask the true villain. Tonight. At supper."

For the cost of failure was Mr. Lioncroft's death.

Unacceptable.

Evangeline turned on her heel and headed to her bedchamber to prepare for battle. She emerged bathed and pressed and somewhat coiffed, but did not reach the dining room before engaging in the first skirmish.

Edmund Rutherford and Mr. Teasdale fell into step beside her as she made her way to the dining room. Much as she despised being in Edmund's company, it would be rude to rush ahead of the elderly Mr. Teasdale. And based on the sluggishness of the latter's ponderous gait, it would be all but impossible to slow her pace enough to lag behind to study them.

Before the silence stretched on for more than a few seconds, Edmund turned his sly gaze upon her.

"Miss Pemberton," he said, his words spraying forth on a gust of fermented breath. "I had no idea you were a trainer of pets."

"A what?" She cast him a suspicious glance. "I've never had a pet."

He laughed delightedly. "Come now. We all saw Lioncroft trailing after you like a gelded lapdog. Mooning after you from his tragically distant picnic blanket, trying to please you with his enormous skill at kite-flying, paying more attention to your bodice than his ball when the rest of us were playing pall-mall . . . Don't be coy, Miss Pemberton. It appears you've managed to break the untamable beast."

Evangeline's fingers clenched. "I've done nothing of the sort."

"I agree," came Mr. Teasdale's quavering voice.

She gave him a grateful look. An ally. At last.

"He's neither tamed nor trained," Mr. Teasdale continued, "but he's certainly following your scent around with the single-minded intensity of a panther after its prey. He's too busy stalking one step behind you to mind propriety. Shameful behavior. Both of you."

Evangeline tripped mid-step. *"What?"*

"I don't mind a spot of shameful behavior every now and again." Edmund fumbled in his coat pocket. "I'd love to see the lovelorn devil and his darling angel perform a public mating ritual for the amusement of the house party guests."

"How unfortunate," came a low voice from around the corner. Mr. Lioncroft strode from a connected hallway, a warning glint in his eyes. "I do my mating in private. That is, unless you meant some other devil?"

"No. I meant you." Edmund took a quick swallow from his flask and edged backward. "Are you planning to keep her?"

Although he made no verbal response, Mr. Lioncroft's fixed gaze never broke eye contact with Edmund's.

"Because if you're not making a mistress of her until you hang," Edmund continued, "let me know when you're through. I wouldn't mind a tup or two before handing her off to the next gent."

Mr. Lioncroft was across the narrow hall so fast Edmund barely had time to gasp before his shoulders flattened against the wall. His flask fell from his fingers. His feet dangled inches from the floor. His face paled, then purpled, held aloft by Mr. Lioncroft's arm anchoring him across the throat.

"Touch her," Mr. Lioncroft growled, "and die."

"Gavin?" Lady Hetherington emerged from the next intersection and gasped when she saw the milieu. "*Gavin*. Unhand Edmund at once!"

"Precisely what I'm talking about," Mr. Teasdale agreed as he gestured toward Mr. Lioncroft with his cane. "Yet another perfect example of impropriety."

A beat of silence passed before Mr. Lioncroft stepped backward.

Edmund fell to the floor clutching his neck. No sooner did he land than he sprang back up, swiping at his backside. "My whiskey! You spilled my whiskey!"

Mr. Lioncroft shrugged. "It's no doubt *my* whiskey."

"But over a chit? You would spill good whiskey over a chit?"

"I would spill your blood if it wouldn't stain my carpets."

"*Gavin*," came Lady Hetherington's strangled voice. "Please don't speak like that. What happened?"

"Nothing. Except this pup was about to give Miss Pemberton an apology."

"For what?" Edmund burst out. "Admitting I find her attractive? You're the one about to ruin her by dangling after her every chance you get."

Mr. Lioncroft's arms crossed. "I won't ruin her."

Edmund snorted and bent to retrieve his empty flask. "Whether you touch her or not, she's already marked. No female reputation can withstand being linked to yours. The maiden and the murderer? If we were in London, the scandal sheets would have a field day."

Mr. Lioncroft's eyebrows lifted. "In case you haven't noticed, we're not in London."

"Nonetheless," Mr. Teasdale put in, "I for one offer to withhold any whisper of untoward familiarity between Miss Pemberton and Lioncroft." He turned his wrinkled face toward Evangeline. "I'll not discuss his reprehensible behavior toward you, my dear, if you discontinue making a spectacle of yourself by encouraging a killer's affections."

Evangeline's shoulders straightened. "He's not a killer."

Mr. Lioncroft stepped to her side, the back of his hand caressing the back of hers before he crossed his arms over his wide chest and glared at Mr. Teasdale.

Neither action escaped Mr. Teasdale's notice. "How do you know he's no killer?"

"How do I know it's not you?"

"Me?" Mr. Teasdale gaped at her. "Haven't we already agreed I could not have snuck up and clobbered him on the head?"

Edmund tipped back his flask to swallow the last few drops. "That may be, but despite your advanced age, I'm sure you're capable of lifting a feather pillow."

Mr. Teasdale harrumphed. "I thought you didn't believe she spoke to God."

"I—" Edmund paused, capped his empty flask, stowed it back in his pocket. "I believe we'll never know what did or didn't happen."

"We might," Evangeline said. "If everyone is honest."

Mr. Teasdale leaned forward on his cane. "It's honesty you want, is it? Very well, then. I'll clear my name right here and now. And since you asked for honesty, don't get angry with me for speaking my piece."

All eyes were on him in less than a second.

"I didn't go straight to my room that night. I'll admit it. I wanted to have a word with Hetherington about his daughter. I knew she was young, but I hadn't realized she was practically a child. And not the least bit interested in me, I might add. I thought to discuss my concerns with Hetherington before signing any contracts. He said love was of even lesser importance than her age. That she fancied herself in love with a French tutor, that the rumors of the two of them being caught kissing were true, that she needed to marry straight-away, and what more did an old man like me want than a pretty young chit like Nancy Rutherford? Well, I'll tell you. Not to take a French tutor's leavings, that's what. I refused to sign the contract."

Lady Hetherington swayed as if suddenly nauseous. "My daughter is, as you intimated, young and impressionable. She was not happy when we sent Monsieur Lefebvre away. But all that you have proven is that you had more motivation to harm my husband than any of us could have supposed."

"I haven't finished." He tightened his grip on his cane. "As I quit the office where I found your husband, who should I glimpse prowling the halls but Lioncroft? Upset as I was, I didn't wish to make small talk with anyone, so I stayed in the shadows. He entered the same office I'd just left."

"Is that true?" Evangeline murmured to Mr. Lioncroft under her breath. A heartbeat passed before he nodded tightly. Evangeline tried not to think what that might mean.

Mr. Teasdale's shaky voice went on. "I would have continued on to my chamber, had their voices not risen to a crescendo. The subject of their conversation, my lady, was you. Hetherington stated, and here I am quoting the precise words used, 'Whatever you do to me, Lioncroft, I can do to Rose.'"

Mr. Lioncroft's muscles tensed.

"Re-e-e-ally," Edmund drawled. "And how did our host re-spond to that?"

"With his usual charm." Mr. Teasdale's gnarled hands pulled his cane against his chest. "Lioncroft said, 'Not if I kill you first.' And then I heard a crash."

"Gavin," Lady Hetherington begged, her expression horrified. "Please tell me you didn't . . ."

Evangeline stayed silent, though she felt much the same way.

"Tell you I didn't what? Didn't order him never to strike you again? I can't make that claim. Nor did he agree to follow my command. A man like that doesn't deserve to live. But I didn't kill him."

Edmund snorted. "Teasdale heard you threaten Hetherington with just that."

A muscle twitched near Gavin's temple. "So I did. But that doesn't mean I killed him."

"It sure doesn't mean you invited him out back for a round or two of pall-mall," Edmund scoffed. "Sounds like we've wrapped up the case to me."

"I did not kill him," Gavin repeated.

"That right? I'll believe that when you prove it." Edmund turned and tossed a suggestive smirk toward Evangeline. "Maybe your bit of fluff can ask God for help with that trick, too."

Evangeline managed to grab the back of Mr. Lioncroft's jacket before he launched himself at Edmund a second time.

"I don't need to," she said softly. All four of them turned to stare at her. "Mr. Teasdale said he overheard them arguing in Mr. Lioncroft's office, that he overheard a crash. An office is not a bedchamber. And pillows do not crash."

Mr. Teasdale gaped at her. "You're defending the honor of a violent man who fully admits to having threatened the life of a man who subsequently turned up dead?"

Evangeline nodded. "I am. There were no pillows in that office for Mr. Lioncroft to smother Lord Hetherington with. And even if there were, he would've had to carry his body down one wing, up the stairs, through the guest quarters, all the way to the Hetherington bedchamber without being seen by anyone. Pardon me if I find that scenario unlikely."

"Unlikely," Edmund scoffed, "but not impossible. How do you know whether or not there were pillows in Lioncroft's office that night?"

"I—"

"Miss Pemberton," Mr. Lioncroft interrupted, latching his long fingers around her elbow. "May I speak to you alone for a moment?"

"No." Mr. Teasdale shook his cane at them. "Of course you may not. This is exactly the sort of inappropriate behavior I mentioned earlier. You expect us to just continue walking to supper while you slip into an unchaperoned room with Miss Pemberton to have a little 'discussion'?"

Mr. Lioncroft kept his hand tight around Evangeline's arm. "Yes."

"I am going to have to put my foot down at that nonsense." Mr. Teasdale slammed his cane against the floor. "I am going to have to—"

"Go," Lady Hetherington interrupted softly. "You and Edmund go on to dinner. I'll stay with them. Nothing untoward shall occur if I am at my brother's side, do you agree?"

Although Mr. Teasdale's expression indicated he felt equally as reluctant to leave Mr. Lioncroft alone with two women as with one, he had no choice but to continue walking to the dining room with Edmund.

Mr. Lioncroft led Evangeline and his sister into the closest room with lit candles, which turned out to be the library. He motioned them into seats while he closed the door behind him.

Lady Hetherington perched hesitantly on the edge of a wingback chair. Evangeline settled on one side of a sofa. Mr. Lioncroft joined her. Not on the opposite side, as would've been proper, but right next to her, so his hip pressed against her hip, his thigh warmed her thigh, his knee brushed her knee.

"Gavin," Lady Hetherington managed. "Honestly."

He ignored her.

"What were you going to do?" he murmured urgently to Evangeline. "Confess you spent a portion of the evening alone with me in my office?"

"I did, didn't I?" she murmured back.

"Much as I hate to admit it, Edmund's right. Attention from me hasn't done your reputation any favors. If you go home ruined because I spent extra time with you in public, how much worse would it be if people knew I spent extra time with you in private?"

"I'm not going home, remember? I'm leaving. I'll never see any of them again, so what does it matter? Besides, I was never part of Society anyway. What do I care about their views of my so-called reputation?"

"*I* care about your reputation. I want to help you, not ruin your life. I want—"

"That's enough whispering," Lady Hetherington called out nervously. "Scoot to your side of the sofa, Gavin."

He hesitated for a fraction of a second before taking her advice. He lounged against the opposite corner, one arm on the armrest and the other along the back, legs relaxed, knees spread wide.

"I was just informing Miss Pemberton," he said at a normal volume, "that I'd prefer not to ruin her life."

"Oh." Lady Hetherington paused. "That seems a worthy goal."

Evangeline glared at him. "You're not going to ruin my life."

He raised a brow. "Trust me, I've had plenty of practice at ruining lives. Ask my sister."

Evangeline cut her glance to Lady Hetherington, who blanched.

"You didn't ruin my life," she protested weakly. "I thought Papa did at first when he forced me to the altar at seventeen, but I've been blessed with four beautiful children I wouldn't trade for the world."

"Score one for Father, then." Mr. Lioncroft paused, as if waiting for his sister to continue speaking. When she did not, his tone turned sardonic. "Are you saying I've never ruined lives?"

Lady Hetherington exhaled a long, slow sigh. "No," she admitted. "You have."

"There you go. My sister confirms it." Mr. Lioncroft refocused his gaze on Evangeline. "I am not a good person. I never have been. But I am trying to do right by you, and by my family. Which means I refrained from killing my sister's rotter of a husband, much as I might've liked to do so, and which also means I will not allow you to sacrifice yourself for me. I will attempt not to make a cake of myself over you in public."

Evangeline tried to lighten the awkward atmosphere. "Just in public?"

His lips curved in a slow, secret smile. "I reserve the right to make a cake of myself over you in private."

Lady Hetherington cleared her throat. "Please do not discuss right in front of me what you may or may not do with Miss Pemberton in private."

"Would you care to leave, dear sister?"

"No. I thought you were trying not to ruin her."

"Oh. Right." He inclined his head toward Evangeline. "See how quickly I forget? Being considerate is a wholly new endeavor for me. For over the past decade I have lived by myself, but for a couple years before that . . ." His eyes shadowed. "I left a trail of bruised pride and broken promises in my wake."

"More like bruised limbs and broken hearts." Lady Hetherington gave a short, wry laugh. "Anyone you couldn't beat in a carriage race, you beat with your fists. And captured the fancy of most of their ladies in the process."

"Yes. Well. I never claimed to be a good person."

Evangeline stared at him. "I can't imagine that behavior endeared you to your friends."

"I never had any friends."

She blinked. "Never?"

He shrugged one shoulder and glanced away.

"You had me," Lady Hetherington said softly.

His smile was humorless. "Not when it mattered."

Lady Hetherington flinched. "That was your own fault."

"I know."

An uncomfortable silence leached the warmth from the room.

Evangeline gazed at the man on the other side of the sofa. He appeared to be trying desperately to appear as casual and unaffected as ever, but the tightness of his muscles belied the posed carelessness in the splay of his long limbs.

Hard to believe a man like Mr. Lioncroft was more like her than unlike her. He'd grown up friendless. So had she. He had one family member he could count on. So had she. That family member had left him alone and hurting. So had she.

But her mother was gone now, forever. And Lady Hetherington was sitting right there across from them, her cheeks pale, her eyes moist, her hands twisting in her lap. She would not be doing so if she truly thought her brother a reprobate beyond all redemption. If he would just go to her, speak to her, surely she would forgive him for whatever he had done.

Why was he still sitting there, eyes narrowed, jaw clenched, staring at an invisible spot on the ceiling with enough force to burn holes in the plaster? Did he truly believe himself so wholly bad as to be unlikable, unlovable, unforgivable? And why was Lady Hetherington not speaking up on his behalf? Because she believed those things, too?

A distant chime shattered the silence.

Lady Hetherington twisted her skirts nervously. "Time for supper. Should we join the others?"

Mr. Lioncroft started, as if he'd forgotten he wasn't alone. The dark expression in his eyes was fierce, wounded, raw.

Deciding she cared more about him than his sister's

chaperonage, Evangeline reached out, gently, hesitantly, and touched his arm with her fingertips. "Gavin—"

He leapt to his feet. "I'm sorry. You'll have to dine without me."

In seconds, he was across the room, out the door, and gone.

Evangeline turned toward his sister, who immediately closed her eyes.

"Please don't say it." Lady Hetherington's voice was harsh, scratchy. "I—I know. I do know. I'm no better than he. I don't think I'm hungry, either. I seem to have lost my appetite." Her eyes flew open. "I'm sorry, Miss Pemberton. Forgive me."

And she struggled to her feet, crossed the floor, and slipped from the room.

Chapter Twenty-Two

Mr. Teasdale barely made it through the first course before nodding off in his chair. How he could sleep through Benedict Rutherford's hacking cough and Edmund Rutherford's drunken ranting, Evangeline couldn't imagine. Both she and Francine Rutherford kept their eyes focused on their plates, so as to dissuade Edmund from inquiring their opinion as to which of the west wing parlor maids was the fairest.

Unlike Francine, Evangeline made sure to eat everything placed before her. Not only was the fare at Blackberry Manor far superior to any she'd had while living with her stepfather, but also, the future loomed uncertain before her. If she accepted Mr. Lioncroft's offer of a carriage tomorrow—and of course she would, for what else could she do?—she still had no idea where she'd take shelter, much less where she'd get her meals.

On the other hand, she was beginning to think going without would be preferable to spending an hour trapped in a dining room with Edmund Rutherford.

"But the ginger-hackled servant heading toward the guest quarters when the dancing ended the other night," he was saying now, fixing his bloodshot gaze on Benedict. "She may be a maid, but she's not a maiden, am I right? Her skirts are as likely to be up as down."

"I don't know," Benedict muttered. "Perhaps we could discuss something else?"

"Those freckles," he continued as if Benedict hadn't spoken. "I'd say . . . *comely* all right. And when I say 'comely,' I mean in five minutes time, we'd both be—"

Francine's fork clattered to her untouched plate. "Honestly, Edmund. There are ladies in the room."

"Pah." He grinned at her unrepentantly. "Ladies are so missish. That's why I focus my attention on maids."

"I didn't notice any maids," Benedict said in a calming voice, as though hoping to quit the topic before his wife stabbed his cousin with a fork. "I didn't wander the halls after dancing."

Evangeline set her utensils atop her plate. "But you did," she said slowly, thinking back to that night. Not long after Mr. Teasdale's cane had come clomping by, she'd heard . . . "Your cough. I heard you coughing from down the corridor."

"Of course you did," Edmund slurred. "The way he coughs, I'm surprised he doesn't rattle the paintings right off the walls. If he was wandering the halls, I'm surprised he didn't run across that maid with the plump set of—"

"If I did," Benedict cut in, "I failed to notice. Why would I? I'm married."

Edmund shrugged. "I don't see what one thing has to do with the other. Do you, Francine? If I were married, I'd still be sure to hire maids I'd like to—"

"What *did* you notice?" Evangeline interrupted, leveling her gaze at Benedict.

"What?"

"You said you didn't notice any maids, so you must've been looking for something else. Something you didn't want us to know about, or you wouldn't have lied about where you were. Something secret."

Francine pushed her plate away. "Have you been keeping secrets from me, darling?"

"I—" Benedict paused, shifted, coughed discreetly into a handkerchief. "Perhaps I simply had no wish to hear conjecture about my presence and Hetherington's death."

"Why would anyone speculate on a correlation if you weren't anywhere near him?" Francine asked reasonably.

Benedict didn't answer.

"You argued with him after dancing," Evangeline guessed. Perhaps she'd unmask the murderer before she left Blackberry Manor, after all! "You went to his room, you argued with him, and you killed him. Then you blamed the crime on Mr. Lioncroft."

"I did nothing of the sort," Benedict snapped. "He was dead when I got there. He—" Benedict paled, as if shocked by his own words.

"He was dead when you got there?" Evangeline repeated, her voice climbing. "He was dead when you got there, and you didn't raise the hue and cry?"

"And be thought a murderer?"

Francine recoiled from her husband. "What were you doing in his bedchamber?"

"I went to confront him," Benedict admitted after a moment. "But like I said, I didn't get the chance."

Edmund swirled his wine. "Confront him about what?"

Benedict hesitated, then turned to his wife. "I didn't want you to know," he said, "but we're in a bit of a financial state."

She blinked garishly painted eyelids. "We are?"

He nodded glumly. "Hetherington had been giving me an allowance ever since he assumed the title, and just this month he cut it off. Permanently, he said." Benedict coughed into the crook of his elbow. "Our estate didn't turn a profit this year. We needed that money. He refused. Just that morning, he—he laughed when I asked him again for the money. Shook his head, and laughed. At me. His brother."

Evangeline stared at him across the table. "Then why visit him again at night? What would be any different?"

"*I* would be different. I—I'm not proud of it, but I planned to force his hand."

Francine's eyes widened. "How?"

Benedict grimaced. "I took a pistol with me. I wasn't going to kill him! The thing wasn't even loaded. I just wanted to show him I was serious. That now was not the time to be high-handed and miserly. And when I saw him there, I . . . I didn't know what to do. I froze for a moment, and then I ran. I couldn't call for help while standing there with a pistol in my hand. Who would've believed I hadn't harmed him?"

Edmund swirled his wineglass. "I'm not sure I do now. After all, you inherited."

"I didn't kill him," Benedict insisted. "Would I have just confessed the truth of that night if I'd killed him?"

"We do believe you." Francine placed her hand atop his. "You may have been desperate, but you will always be a man of honor."

"If he was alive when he left Mr. Lioncroft's office and dead in his chamber when you arrived," Evangeline reasoned, "someone else wanted him dead. Someone else visited his chamber and suffocated him with a pillow."

"Perhaps Lioncroft came by to continue their argument," Francine suggested. "He's always had an unpredictable temper."

"No." Evangeline shook her head. "Someone else."

Edmund gulped at his wine. "The French tutor?" he suggested. "Surely that chap was less than happy to have the object of his affection betrothed to another."

Evangeline considered that idea for a moment. "While I agree that prospect—and being sacked—might have given Monsieur Lefebvre a strong motive, he's not even here. He would've had to journey a full day's ride, sneak unnoticed inside Blackberry Manor, determine the precise location of Lord Hetherington's bedchamber . . . It makes no sense."

"Might he have bribed a servant?" Francine asked. "After all, he was something of a servant himself. He might have befriended someone."

"It's possible." Evangeline didn't find the idea particularly likely, but she was willing to support any theory that saved Mr. Lioncroft from the gallows. If her dinner companions were at last willing to entertain alternate explanations, surely that meant they could be convinced of his innocence.

Francine rose to her feet, one hand on her stomach. "I think I need to lie down."

Benedict stood as well and placed her hand on his arm. "You hardly ate a thing. Are you unwell?"

Evangeline smiled as she watched them leave and wondered for the hundredth time when Francine would share the good news with her husband. No doubt he'd be thrilled to be a father. She kept her thoughts to herself, of course, as the only reason she had any clue of the happy tidings was due to the onslaught of visions she'd suffered during the country dances that first night.

Her smile faded as she caught sight of Edmund leering drunkenly at her over his wineglass. Her stepfather used to leer at her in just such a way when he'd had too much whiskey. Based on the soft snores still emanating from the direction of Mr. Teasdale, she and Edmund were virtually unchaperoned.

She leapt to her feet.

Edmund's blatantly appreciative gaze followed her every move. "Where are you going?"

Evangeline mentioned the first place that sprang to mind. "The nursery."

He gestured to the seat next to him. "Why don't you stay here with me?"

"I'm not hungry."

"Me neither." His lips curved in a smirk.

"I told the girls I'd visit them," Evangeline said quickly, and quit the room before he had a chance to lumber to his feet and follow her.

She had in fact told the girls she'd visit them. She'd said "sometime," and *now* seemed a very good time to make good on her promise.

On her way to the nursery, she kept thinking about Francine's idea of Monsieur Lefebvre bribing a servant. Mr. Lioncroft had suggested a servant, as well. He'd wondered if Ginny had acted on her own, out of revenge for herself or her mistress.

Could the two be connected? After all, Monsieur Lefebvre wasn't the only one whose plans had been upset by the loss of both his position and his would-be paramour. Nancy Hetherington had been equally distraught. And had instructed her sisters to claim both she and her mother had been with them in the nursery all night.

Perhaps Lady Hetherington hadn't been protecting herself. Perhaps she'd been protecting her daughter.

By the time Evangeline reached the nursery, she'd all but convinced herself of Nancy Hetherington's guilt and planned to confront her immediately. That was not to be, however, as only the twins were present. After exchanging greetings, she settled on the sofa, content to watch the two little girls play with their dolls.

Not half an hour later, Jane swept into the room flushed and breathless. Ignoring her sisters completely, she clapped her hands together and skipped directly to Evangeline.

"Oh! Miss Pemberton, you can't imagine where I've been. Remember my locket? This one." She gestured at her throat. "Uncle Lioncroft has been painting my portrait. Two, really. A big one, which he says he'd like to keep himself—he wants to do one of each of his nieces, he says, so we can be with him even when we're not—and a miniature, which will go right inside my locket. See? It'll be ever so cunning."

"I see," Evangeline said, not quite sure how else to respond. "I'm sure it'll be lovely."

"Quite lovely. I'm very nearly an adult, you see. Uncle Lioncroft says my come-out will be here before he knows it. He says—"

"Nancy says," interrupted one of the twins, "Uncle Lioncroft killed Papa."

"He did not," said the other, clutching her doll to her chest. "Nancy's mean."

"I thought," Evangeline said slowly, "your mother said your father passed peacefully in his sleep?"

"Well . . ." Jane twisted her locket. "She did say that, yes. But then Nancy said she only said that so we wouldn't be scared of Uncle Lioncroft. But I'm not scared of him. He's painting my miniature. It's only Rebecca that's scared of him now. Nancy should never have said that."

"Nancy's mean," Rachel reiterated, still hugging her doll tightly. "Uncle Lioncroft is nice. He got us dolls."

"He's very nice," Evangeline agreed. "Your uncle is a good man."

"Did he kill Papa?" Rebecca asked.

"No." Evangeline shook her head. "No, of course not."

"See?" Rachel stuck her tongue out at her sister before peering up at Evangeline. "Who did?"

"I . . . don't know." Evangeline swallowed, then turned to Jane for help fielding questions.

Jane, however, was still twisting her locket and frowning. "Nancy says Uncle Lioncroft will hang either way. She says he can't take portraits of us to prison because in prison, you're not allowed to have anything nice, especially if you're only there until it's your turn at the gallows. Nancy says Uncle Lioncroft hurt Papa because Papa hurt Mother. Nancy says it doesn't matter why Uncle Lioncroft did it—murderers hang."

Nancy, Evangeline thought, needed to learn to curb her tongue.

"Is Uncle Lioncroft going to hang for killing Papa?" Rachel asked, clutching her doll even tighter.

Evangeline floundered for a safe response and found none. She was positive Mr. Lioncroft was innocent of murder, but unless the true culprit was found, Nancy was probably right—the moment someone alerted the magistrate, Mr. Lioncroft would hang regardless of his culpability.

"Why did Uncle Lioncroft do it?" Rebecca asked plaintively. "Why would he hurt my Papa?"

Because your papa was a violent brute seemed an inappropriate answer. The handprint still hadn't completely faded from Lady Hetherington's face. As her brother, of course, Mr. Lioncroft would want to protect her. He wouldn't rob his nieces of their father, but he'd certainly do his best to save his sister from future harm.

"He . . ." Evangeline began, and faltered.

The last thing she wanted was for Mr. Lioncroft's nieces to fear him. But he'd already admitted fighting with their father and being angry enough to kill him. What could she say to mitigate a statement like that, especially if Nancy parroted back to the girls everything he said?

"I hate him," Rebecca cried. "I hate him for killing my Papa!"

She threw her doll across the room. When the porcelain face shattered against the corner of a bookshelf, Rebecca burst into tears.

Evangeline ran to her side and gathered the weeping child into her arms. She ground her teeth against the instant headache brought on by a barrage of little girl visions about biscuits and chocolate. She'd caused more harm than good if Rebecca had interpreted her hesitation as a tacit admission of Mr. Lioncroft's guilt.

"Rebecca," she said softly, stroking her blond curls. "Your father—"

"Was a bloody saint," came a low growl from the open doorway.

Evangeline jerked her gaze up Mr. Lioncroft's tall, tense form to the anger slashing across his face.

"I was just—"

"Allowing my nieces to believe I murdered their father. How kind of you." His voice was tight, his eyes cold, hard, furious, as he took in the scene before him. Jane, twisting her locket. The beautiful doll, lying rejected and ruined on the floor. Rebecca, shivering and sobbing in Evangeline's lap. "I was a fool to hope otherwise."

He spun from the doorway and stalked into the shadows.

"Wait," Evangeline called, struggling to her feet as best she could without dropping Rebecca to the floor.

But he was gone.

If only she could start her visit to the nursery anew. Perhaps she could've said the right things, kept Rebecca from crying, saved the lovely doll from destruction.

There'd been more than rage in Mr. Lioncroft's eyes. There had been pain. He'd taken Rebecca's rejection of his gift as a rejection of himself. And he'd no doubt interpreted Evangeline's clumsy handling of his niece's question as the worst kind of betrayal. He'd trusted her. Trusted her to believe in him when nobody else did. Trusted her to help him.

Instead, she'd made everything worse.

Evangeline pressed her ear against the wall and listened.

Mr. Lioncroft wasn't in his office. He wasn't in the dining rooms, the drawing rooms, or the library. And from the sound of it—or lack thereof—he wasn't even roaming the secret passageways between his walls.

How was she going to apologize, to explain he hadn't heard what he thought he'd heard, if she couldn't even find him?

She'd almost given up altogether when she recalled his studio.

Her knock on the closed door went unanswered, as did her tentative, "Gavin?" and her somewhat more forceful, "Gavin!" Either he was not inside, or he had no wish for her company. Too bad.

Her fingers curved around the brass doorknob. The cold metal sent ripples of gooseflesh along her arms. Or perhaps the gooseflesh was due to her impending confrontation with the man within. If he were within. There was but one way to be sure.

With a twist of the handle, she eased the door open.

Large windows graced the far wall. A maze of tall wooden easels cluttered up the interior. Layer upon layer of canvases tilted against all four walls, some bare, some with breath-stealing landscapes. A thick, pungent smell permeated the air with a sharp, strange scent. Paintbrushes, color-smudged palettes, and half-rolled tubes lay atop a table covered in stained cloths. A jumble of wood stacked in one corner next to an unfinished frame.

On the opposite side of the room stood a lone long-limbed figure, feet at shoulder width, thumbs hooked into his waist-band, gaze fixed at the sprawling view of wild blackberry fields below.

Evangeline cleared her throat.

He remained motionless.

"I know you're innocent," she informed him softly. "I know you've never killed anyone in your life."

He smiled grimly.

"Rebecca heard rumors, that's all," she tried again, taking a hesitant step closer. "I had already told her you didn't do it."

He didn't respond.

"I apologize," Evangeline said. "I didn't mean to hurt you."

He said nothing.

"Do you want me to leave?"

His jaw tightened.

"Do you want me to stay?"

His muscles twitched.

"May I see Jane's portrait?"

He whirled to face her.

"What would be the point?" he demanded, eyes bleak. "It's half-finished. It'll never be finished. Now that they're terrified I killed their father, they'll be too frightened to suffer my company, much less sit for me. Rose will take them away and I'll never see them again. Not even on canvas."

Before she could respond, he strode to an easel facing a small chair. He grimaced at the canvas perched on the crossbar. His hand lifted above his shoulder, then came flying down toward what was no doubt Jane's unfinished portrait.

"No," Evangeline cried and launched herself across the room.

She tried to throw herself between him and the still-wet canvas—and succeeded.

The edge of his palm barely glanced against her, but a horrified expression engulfed his face.

"Oh, my God." His voice was strangled, his face ashen. "I *hit* you. Oh, my God."

"You didn't." She shook her head frantically. "I swear you didn't. It was me. I didn't want you to ruin the painting. You love your niece. She loves you. Don't look at me like that, Gavin. You didn't hurt me. I'm fine. I'm fine."

"I didn't mean to hurt you," he whispered, his voice hoarse and raw. "I would never hurt you."

"I know. You didn't. I swear."

He hauled her to his chest and crushed his lips to hers.

She clung to him and opened her mouth to his. He tasted like shock, like fear, like desperation. She gripped his forearms, dug her fingers into hard muscle. His tongue swept across hers, needing, searching. She licked, bit, suckled. He growled and held her closer, tighter, as if afraid to let her go, as if afraid she *would* go. She welcomed the passionate fury of his kisses, tried to tell him with her tongue and her mouth and her body that she could never leave him alone and hurting, that she couldn't bear to see him in pain. She needed him, trusted him, loved him.

Her breath caught. She *loved* him.

As if she'd spoken the thought aloud, his embrace gentled, his kiss became sweeter, less demanding. After a moment, he gave her lips a final soft kiss and rested his overly warm forehead against hers.

"I'm sorry," he said. "I was . . . scared."

The admission sounded as though it had been tortured from his lungs.

"I'm sorry, too," she said, leaning her cheek against the rapid beating of his heart. "I didn't mean to scare you."

He scooped her up, reached the portrait chair in two long strides, cuddled her onto his lap. He kissed her again, hungrily, urgently, as if he couldn't bear *not* kissing her. She hoped he never stopped. His hands cradled her face, stroked her hair, nestled her closer. His shaft was hot and rigid against her thigh. Her breasts ached above her stays, the nipples chafing against the unyielding cloth.

"Touch me," she whispered into his mouth.

For a moment, she thought he would refuse, that she'd been too forward, that he was shocked at her request.

Half a heartbeat later, he sucked in a deep shuddering breath and slid his hand from the back of her neck to her shoulder.

"Here?" he asked, his voice teasing, his eyes dark with passion. "Should I touch you here, on your shoulder?"

"No." Her nipples tightened in anticipation. "Lower. Please."

His palm slid downward, coasting from her shoulder, to

her forearm, to the side of her ribs. His fingers splayed there, his thumb tantalizingly close to the swell of her breast.

"Here?" he asked. "Is this better?"

"You know it's not." It was all Evangeline could do not to rip her bodice open herself and force his hands to her chest. "I want you to touch my breast."

"Oh, your *breast,*" he said, his rakish grin stealing her breath and quickening her pulse. "I would love to touch your breast."

Slowly, slowly, his fingers slid from her side, the heat from his palm burning through her gown. His hand cupped her, stroked her, caressed her. He claimed her mouth with a hot, wet kiss. His fingers rolled across her nipples until she arched into him, silently demanding more. And when her aching, needing body didn't get everything he could offer, she voiced her demands out loud.

"Touch me," she said, "like you were going to touch me in the summerhouse."

He arched a brow. "Do you know what I was going to do?"

She shook her head.

"But you want me to do it anyway?"

She nodded eagerly.

His eyes crinkled as his mouth curved into a slow sensual smile that left her trembling with need. "Then I would love to."

His head bent over hers, his breath becoming her breath. She threaded her fingers through the back of his hair and kissed him back. His teasing fingers left her nipple, slid down her breast, her ribs, her waist, her hip, her thigh. Cool air tickled her skin as he lifted her gown higher, higher. His warm knuckles brushed against her ankle, the curve of her calf, the back of her knee.

She whimpered against his mouth as his warm palm coasted up her inner thigh. His fingertips brushed against the damp hair hidden beneath her chemise. She was fairly certain she was getting damper by the second. Her entire core heated, moistened, swelled. She shifted, tilting her pelvis toward his taunting fingertips, desperate to feel them against the throbbing ache between her legs.

Ah! She sucked in a breath. There. *There.* The curve of his finger stroked against her flesh. Her thighs tightened around his hand. He did it again, over and over, his knuckle warm and slick against her, forward, backward, rubbing, nuzzling, teasing. Her thighs tightened again as muscles she didn't even know she had began to wake, to tense, to yearn.

She gasped when he nudged the tip of his finger inside her body and stroked her with his thumb. He slid his finger the rest of the way inside, slowly, relentlessly, the entire time making delicious circular patterns with the pad of his thumb against her burning flesh. With one finger fully inside and the other coaxing her to an ever-building pressure, he bent his head to her breast and suckled her through the thin silk of her gown, grazing his teeth across her tender nipple.

Her entire body spasmed. Her muscles clenched around his finger, kneading him. His thumb continued stroking her until the tremors subsided and she fell face forward against his shoulder, panting.

"That," he murmured into her hair, "is what I wanted to do in the summerhouse."

Her muscles contracted again at the thought.

He slid his finger from her gently, smoothed down her gown, cradled her to him. His cheek rested atop her head. Evangeline wrapped her arms around his chest and held tight. His heart was beating as fast as her own. His shaft still throbbed against her.

"May I touch you?" she asked.

He seemed to grow even harder against her thigh.

"Not here," he said. "Too messy."

She lifted her head until her gaze met his. "When can I?"

"Evangeline," he said, his voice hoarse and unsteady, his

gaze smoldering with restrained passion. "You don't have to touch me just because I—"

"I *want* to touch you." She stroked his cheek with her palm, nipped at his mouth. "I want . . . everything."

He swallowed. "Everything?"

She pressed her lips to his and nodded. "Will you?"

His shaft leapt and swelled. She smiled. He may not have realized it, but his body had already given his answer. She opened her mouth and kissed him.

"Tonight," he gasped between hot, demanding kisses. "I'll come to you tonight."

She licked his lower lip. "And you'll touch me again?"

He closed his eyes and shuddered. "I'll do anything you ask."

Chapter Twenty-Three

He came to her through the bookcase.

Evangeline replaced the poker she'd used to stoke the fire and turned to face him. Gavin was in half dress. She wore nothing but her shift. He looked splendid, as always. Dashing. Hungry. Hers.

Thumbs hooked in waistband, he lounged against the now-closed panel. The intensity of his gaze heated her flesh more than the fire at her back. Now that she'd invited the lion into her den, what was she going to do with him?

She took a tentative step toward him. "What are you doing?"

"Waiting."

"For what?"

"You." His mouth smiled, but his eyes suggested he wanted to devour her.

She glanced around her bedchamber. Bookshelf, bookshelf, fireplace, mirror, bed. Yet he continued lounging against the bookshelf, watching her, waiting.

"W-what are you doing?" she asked again.

"I told you." His eyes held wicked promise. "Anything you ask."

She wrapped her arms across her chest. "I have to *ask* for everything I wish?"

He inclined his head. "I'm yours to command."

Her arms relaxed. Hmmm. Put that way, she couldn't help but think of a dozen different things she could ask him to do. Everything he'd done in the studio. And then some.

Perhaps she should start with the "then some."

"Come here," she ordered. Her pulse raced when he immediately prowled closer, his dark eyes never leaving her face.

He stopped just before the tips of his boots brushed against her toes. He gazed down at her, serious, intense, the heat in his eyes betraying barely restrained patience. It was killing him not to take charge, Evangeline realized as she stared up at him. He was the sort of man who knew what he wanted, went after what he wanted, took what he wanted. And yet he did not. He was relinquishing control for *her*.

Her thin cotton shift suddenly felt as thick and heavy as wool. Already she could feel her body responding to the masculine scent of his skin, the dark passion in his eyes, the power in his taut muscles.

She reached out with one hand and skated her fingertips along the width of his shoulder, down the length of his arm. He didn't move. Holding himself in check. For her. Her body thrilled at the knowledge.

"Take off your jacket," she commanded him.

In a trice, he shucked the offending garment and dropped it at his feet. She kicked it away. Still his gaze didn't leave her face.

"May I divest you of your cravat?" She tugged at the snowy white cloth without waiting for a response.

He gave none; just waited, tense, letting her do as she would.

"And this waistcoat," she said. "We must take it off."

Fingers trembling, she fumbled with the first button. When he stood there, strong, silent, unmoving except for his heart pounding beneath her fingertips, Evangeline grew bolder. She tossed him a saucy sideways look through her lashes as she slipped the buttons from their holes. But when his waistcoat joined his jacket and cravat in an unceremonious pile on the floor, she hesitated before touching the last remaining bit of linen covering his chest.

"You . . . don't have to do anything you don't wish to," he said softly, the words coming out gruff and strained.

"I wish," she informed him just as softly, "to do everything."

His lashes lowered. His nostrils flared.

Unable to wait a moment longer, Evangeline pushed up with her toes and wrapped her arms around his neck. He caught her just as she pressed her lips to his.

"Kiss me," she whispered against his closed mouth.

When his teeth parted, she swept her tongue against his. He tasted just like she remembered. Spicy. Masculine. Potent. Leaving him tomorrow would tear her heart in two. At least she'd have tonight.

Reminded of their fleeting time together, she set to work removing his shirt as best she could between long, lingering kisses. Once unbuttoned, she slid the linen sleeves off his wide shoulders, down the hard ridges of his arms. He let go of her long enough to let the garment fall to the floor, and then he pulled her to him. He held her against his mouth, his bare chest, his thick shaft.

When a now-familiar heat began to coil between her thighs, she pulled away just far enough to look at him. Warm firelight flickered across his neck, his shoulders, his arms. Her hands slid across the warm skin of his chest, the strange wiry hairs, the tensed muscles. She rubbed one of his nipples. It hardened beneath her fingertip.

"When do I get to do that to you?" he asked gruffly.

"When I ask you."

He frowned, as if more than half-regretting putting her in control of the evening's activities. "Ask soon."

"I will." She smiled up at him, a large part of her delighting in having the power to determine what and when and how.

She pushed him backward until his thighs bumped against the foot of the bed. "Sit. I want to take off your boots."

He sat.

She knelt before him, tugged his boots from his feet, tossed them aside. Fingers curving around a carved wooden bedpost, she pulled herself upright and then slanted him a suspicious glance.

"You're not the artist responsible for these hideous trolls, are you?"

"You don't like them?" he asked innocently.

"Insufferable man."

He grinned.

Once she'd stripped him of his stockings, she pushed at his chest until he fell back against the mattress.

Legs splayed, he propped himself up on his elbows to watch her. His arms flexed. His grin widened. She ran a finger along the edge of his waistband. His eyes grew serious, intense. Her hand hovered a hairsbreadth above the ridge creasing the fall of his breeches. His shaft pulsed, pushing the material in brief contact with her fingers. She touched him again, gently, tentatively. As before, his shaft jumped against her palm. She cupped her hand over it, stroking down, stroking up.

Gavin collapsed against the mattress.

Evangeline froze, her hand still molded to his heat.

"What's wrong?" she asked nervously. "You don't like it?"

"No," he groaned toward the canopy. "I love it."

She smiled, gripped him a little harder, stroked again. His fingers clenched the bedsheet. She undid the buttons of his fall to caress him again, this time without the cumbersome cloth between his shaft and her hand. It was smooth, hot, throbbing.

"Give me words," she commanded.

"What?"

She squeezed a little as she tugged. "What do you call this?"

"Uh . . . my cock?"

His cock. Yes. It responded to her caresses by swelling

against her palm, just like her body had responded to his caresses by heating and becoming damp.

She tugged down his breeches and paused when she caught sight of a thin red line slashing across one hip. He had gotten that wound while trying to protect her.

"Will it scar?"

He lifted himself up on one elbow, shrugged. "Won't be the first."

She bit her lip. "I didn't mean for you to get hurt."

"I'd do it again." He gazed at her, his expression grave.

Evangeline stared back at him for a moment, silent, wishing he weren't lying down so she could kiss him. Wait. He was hers to command, was he not? She could kiss him anytime she wished.

She tugged him forward until he was sitting up enough for her to cradle his face in her hands and touch her lips to his. His mouth opened hungrily beneath hers, licking, suckling, nibbling. When he slid his hands down her back to cup her closer, she pulled away long enough to yank off his breeches.

Finally. He was naked. And perfect.

She'd seen men in various states of undress before, but only in visions. She'd never held one, touched one, loved one. Everything she knew about lovemaking came from stolen glimpses of other people's lives. At last she would have a memory of her own. She lifted her shift above her head and tossed it to the floor. There. She was naked, too.

Her nipples budded in the cool air. His cock pulsed.

"You're beautiful," he murmured.

She touched a hand to her head. "My chignon fell apart."

"I like your hair curly and loose and wild. The fire gives your silhouette a warm glow. I would like to paint you, just like that."

"Nude?"

"Utterly."

A thrill shivered down her spine. Could she do something like that? Pose naked, exposed, allowing him to commit every curve of her body to canvas? The very illicitness of his proposal only made the idea more erotic.

"Next time," she promised.

His half smile didn't reach his eyes. They both knew there wouldn't be a next time.

"Move up against the pillows," she directed him. "Lie in the middle of the bed."

Never taking his gaze from her, he complied. "Now I'm further away from you."

"Not for long."

Rather than lean his head back against the pillows, he propped himself up on his elbows again to watch her.

At the moment she was standing still, staring at the dark-haired, dark-eyed man reclining nude atop her bed sheets. The fire glinted orange and gold across his bare chest and long limbs. His shaft jutted toward his stomach. The muscles of his bent arms curved hard and strong. His wide lips looked firm, kissable. A hint of stubble shaded the line of his jaw.

The best part, the unbelievable, inconceivable, astonishing part, wasn't merely his presence, but that she could have him without worrying about her cursed visions. She could touch him anywhere she wished, kiss him anywhere she wished, meld her flesh with his anyway she wished. He was a miracle, a gift, an answer to a secret prayer.

And tonight he was hers.

What should she do first? The possibilities seemed endless. The night, however, was not. Evangeline rounded the bed, climbed atop the mattress, lay on her side next to him.

"How long will you stay?"

Another pensive half smile flickered as he muttered, "I feel like I should be asking you that."

She brushed the soft dark hair from his brow. "I mean tonight."

"I know." He regarded her in silence for a moment. Then:

"I told you I was yours to command, and I meant it. I'll stay with you until you fall asleep."

"Then I shall endeavor to stay awake."

"I can help with that." This time his smile reached his eyes.

If it were possible to freeze an image of him in her mind forever, then this was precisely how Evangeline wanted to remember him. His eyes crinkling, his mouth curved in a rakish grin, his body so close every inch of her flesh could feel his heat.

"May I touch you?" she asked.

"Anywhere."

"Thank you."

His grin widened. "I'm fairly certain the pleasure will be mine."

No, the pleasure would be hers. She reached up with one hand, cupped the side of his face, brushed the pad of her thumb against his cheek. She leaned over, pressed her lips hard against his. A brief kiss. She would take her time after she had a chance to explore him.

She ran her hand down his corded neck and along the width of his shoulders. His shoulders were so wide, his skin so warm, his scent so intoxicatingly masculine. She laid her head on his chest. Small wiry hairs rubbed against her cheek. His heartbeat thudded against her ear. She slid her palm from his shoulder to his hand and laced his fingers with hers.

"Gavin?"

He kissed the top of her head. "Yes?"

No. She couldn't say it. To give voice to her feelings would only make leaving even harder. And what if he didn't feel the same way? She couldn't bear to know. Not now. Not yet.

She unlaced their fingers and lifted herself on one elbow. She stroked his face, his shoulders, his arms, his chest, his stomach, reveling in the different textures of his body beneath her palm. Parts of him were smooth. Parts of him were scratchy with tiny hairs. All of him was hard, strong, scalding to the touch. She scooted further down the bed and ran her hand along his thigh, his foot, his toes, then back up the other side until her fingertips brushed against the root of his shaft. It flinched.

"Does it hurt?"

He smiled. "Only in a good way."

She returned his smile, pleased to touch him without the encumbrance of clothing. She curled her fingers around the heat of his flesh, caressed, squeezed, stroked. He grew bigger, hotter, harder. She glanced up at his face. His gaze was locked on the movements of her hand around his cock, his breath shallow, his muscles tense.

"If I keep touching you like this, would I be able to give you the same pleasure you gave me in your studio?"

His eyes flicked to hers. "Undoubtedly."

The naked desire in his unguarded expression filled Evangeline with a strange, glorious sense of power.

"I can do anything I want to you? With you?"

His eyebrows lifted. "I'm yours."

She hesitated, nodded, then rolled atop him. Her breasts flattened against his chest. When she bent her knees on either side of his thighs and pushed herself into a sitting position, the hard length of his shaft pulsed between her legs. Her body responded in kind, becoming moist and swollen. She rubbed herself against him experimentally and gasped at the rush of pleasure to her hypersensitive . . . what? She wasn't sure, but the delicious sensation of her aching dampness rubbing in long, slow strokes up and down the length of his cock had her tingling and trembling just like when he'd touched her with his finger.

"Do you feel me?" She ground her body against his again. "What I'm doing?"

"God, yes."

"What . . . what do you call it?"

He blinked. "Pre-lovemaking?"

"No, I mean the bit of my body rubbing against you." She did it slower, to demonstrate. "'Womanly parts' seems inadequate."

"Uhhh . . . I don't use polite words."

Her breath quickened. "Tell me impolite ones."

"All right." His heated gaze captured hers. "The vision of you astride me, rubbing your hot wet cunny against my cock, is almost enough to make me come right now. I can't wait to bury myself inside you, to feel your body clenching around me, to make you come, over and over, until you take me with you."

She shivered at the passion in his eyes and continued the intoxicating motion for a few moments before scooting upward to kiss him.

The movement swept her breasts over his chest, her nipples hardening as they scraped across the hairs. She sucked in a startled breath at the unexpected pleasure, then did it again. Her entire body responded, heating, moistening, quickening.

His eyes closed briefly, as if in pain. She kissed his lips, his neck, his jaw. Rough stubble scratched at her mouth. She licked him, tasted him, kissed him. And began to wonder what that familiar texture would feel like against her breasts instead of her mouth. She broke the kiss, inched a little further upward, lifted her breasts in her hands. His gaze locked on the display.

"Anything I wish?" she asked again.

"Anything." The word came out strangled.

She leaned forward until her breasts grazed the side of his face. She pivoted slightly, letting the line of his jaw scrape against one nipple at a time. When her body clenched in response, her eyes widened.

"No matter what I rub against you," she murmured, "I feel feverish, aching, needing."

"Thank God," Gavin muttered. "Me, too."

She splayed her fingers on the pillows above his head and leaned over to allow her unfettered breasts to fall against his face as they would.

He grabbed her hips, tilted his head, and suckled a puckered nipple into his mouth. Her legs trembled. Without releasing her breast from his mouth, he slid one hand over her thigh and tilted the pad of a finger against her damp core. She whimpered. He continued his tender assault with his hand and his tongue, teasing, licking, rubbing, nibbling.

When he slid his finger inside, the pressure proved too much. She cried out, tensed, her muscles spasming as the waves of pleasure hit her. When the aftershocks faded, he slipped his hand from her. She fell forward, panting against the pillow, cheek to cheek with him.

"Sorry," he murmured, not sounding the tiniest bit contrite. "I meant to wait for you to ask."

"Somehow, I'll find it in my heart to forgive you."

He chuckled.

"*If*," she began, and lifted her head.

He stopped chuckling.

"If," she repeated, "you make love to me right this second."

"Thank you, God," he muttered.

Before she had a chance to so much as blink, his hands gripped her hips and he rolled them both over in one fluid movement. He trapped her wrists to the pillows on either side of her head and kissed her.

Without lifting his mouth from hers, he nudged her legs apart with his knee, settled himself between her thighs, rubbed his cock against her core just as she'd done when straddling him. Just that quickly, the tingling, trembling pressure returned. Every inch of her body yearned for him.

"I said," she breathed against his mouth, "*right this second.*"

He tilted his hips. A tantalizing pressure nudged her throbbing, swollen flesh, rubbed against her wetness, dipped a little inside. The brief twinge of pain dissipated under the onslaught of amazing new sensations. He slid the tip of his tongue across her lower lip, across her teeth, into her mouth, every thrust mimicking that which he did with his cock until both tongue and shaft were buried inside of her. She gasped into his mouth. Incredible. He cupped the back of her head, kissed her.

She bit him, suckled him. He rocked his hips against hers, urgent, strong, driving himself deeper inside. His pelvis rubbed against her with an almost unbearable pleasure. She bent her knees, gripped him with her thighs, met him thrust for thrust. This must be what it felt like to truly share one's soul. She couldn't have chosen a better man.

His limbs tensed and flexed as he moved inside her. When she bit back a helpless moan, he broke the kiss, panting, the hair across his forehead damp with sweat.

"You're beautiful," he whispered, cradling her to him.

She smiled. "You told me that already."

"Did I tell you I've dreamt of *this*?" A deep, claiming thrust accompanied the last word.

Her eyelids fluttered. "So have I."

"You're perfect."

"So are you."

"Ha." Still buried inside her, he grabbed her wrists and rolled onto his back. "Straddle me."

"What happened to me giving the orders?" Hands splayed on his chest, she pushed herself upright and trembled when his shaft shifted inside her.

"Ride me," he commanded, his gaze dark and heated. "You can control the rhythm. I'll match my movements to yours."

She tensed her thighs, rose up, lowered. He slid his palm from her knee to her hip, then down across her stomach until his thumb circled the area just above their joined bodies. When she fell forward, he captured one breast in his mouth, sucked, bit, licked. He bent his knees so her rear rested against his thighs, angling his shaft even further inside her. His fingers never stopped their exquisite torment of steady circular strokes.

Her body clenched, once, twice.

"Gavin," she gasped. "You're making me . . . I'm going to . . ."

He lifted his mouth from her breast long enough to say,

"Do it." He continued tilting his hips, filling her, stroking her. "Come for me," he whispered.

She couldn't help it. She cried out, shattered against him, gripped his torso with her thighs. His shaft jerked inside her, throbbed against her contracting muscles, filled her with something hot and wet. He took her mouth in a demanding kiss.

Muscles trembling, she collapsed atop his chest. She lay there several minutes listening to his racing heart slowly return to its normal pace. The musky scent of their lovemaking filled the room.

He stroked her hair from her face, kissed the top of her head, wrapped his arms around her, and held her tight.

"I could make love to you for the rest of my life," he murmured into her hair.

She nodded against his chest. "I'm going to miss you."

He paused, tensed, pressed his lips fiercely against her forehead. "If I was ensured of living long enough to follow through on a promise, I would make you one now. You're not the kind of woman a man can just walk away from."

She shook her head, lifted her chin to make eye contact with him. "It's all right. I've never been the marrying kind." At the moment, however, she couldn't remember why that was. "But I don't want you to walk away. Not yet. I'm still awake. I want you to stay all night, and love me again. Will you?"

"Of course." He tilted his neck forward, kissed her. "I can't help it."

"Thank you." Evangeline rubbed her thumb along the edge of his jaw, smoothing the bristly stubble, tracing the line of his scar. "How did you get this?"

"Dueling."

Her eyes widened. "Dueling?"

"Not over anything honorable, trust me."

She kissed the scar, then his lips. "Then over what?"

"A girl. My brother's girl. David caught us kissing and called me out immediately. We couldn't duel with pistols because we were the only heirs and my father would've killed us both. David chose rapiers, said we would fight till first blood. I'll always believe he meant to slice open my neck. I didn't blame him, then or now." Gavin glanced away, as if unwilling or unable to meet her eyes. "I told you I wasn't a good person."

"How old were you?"

"Sixteen, same as the girl. David was twenty."

"What happened to the girl?"

Gavin gave a wry chuckle. "He married her. Not long after, my parents died. I haven't seen my brother since."

"How many duels have you fought since then?"

He finally glanced at her, frowned. "None."

"Stolen kisses from anybody else's fiancée?"

He shook his head. "No."

"Then I don't think you're a bad person. You made a mistake."

"I make lots of mistakes. I'm impulsive. Careless. Selfish."

"You may have been in the past, but you're not now. You're the most selfless, caring man I've ever known."

"That's because you've only managed to be around men who are even bigger pricks than I am." He tried to dispel the shame of his words with a smile, but his eyes were tortured.

"Stop it." She gripped his chin with one hand and crushed her lips to his. "I wouldn't make love to you if I thought you were an irredeemable blackguard. Over a decade has passed since then. You were young. People change."

"Do they?"

"*I* think so. I like you just the way you are."

His cock stirred. "I like you just the way *you* are."

"Just don't duel over me," she teased, pulse racing at the thought.

"I will if I want to," he growled, flipping her over and driving his shaft inside her. "If you so much as think about kissing another man, I swear I'll meet him at dawn."

"I would never," she gasped, locking her legs around his thighs. "Only you. I promise."

"Good." He laced her fingers with his, crushed his mouth to hers, pumped his hips.

She arched against him, hands locked with his. "How much longer are you mine to command?"

Her heart pounded so loud, she almost didn't hear his whispered reply.

"For as long as I live."

Chapter Twenty-Four

Gavin was still in Evangeline's bedchamber when the sun rose. He'd meant to quit the room when she fell asleep, but couldn't make himself leave her earlier than absolutely necessary. So he stayed, stroking her hair, watching her sleep, holding her close.

And realized what a precious gift she'd given him.

Not just her virginity—although that had seemed a miracle, too—but even more precious than that, she'd given him her unconditional trust. He hadn't forced her to do so. He'd somehow earned it.

She would not make love to a murderer. She would not fall asleep in the arms of a man of irredeemable evil. She said so herself, did she not? She believed in him, even when all evidence suggested she should not.

It was a new sensation, being trusted implicitly. He hadn't lied to her—he'd been an incorrigible youth. Amazing that he hadn't been forced to duel on a regular basis. Nor had he lied when he said he'd call out any man who dared to touch her. Sweat beaded on his skin at the very thought. Horrifying.

He pulled her closer into his arms. When she left, he wouldn't have much say over it, would he? He wouldn't even be there. Might never see her again at all.

Unacceptable.

But what could he do about it? They were no closer to solving Hetherington's murder than when they began. Edmund and Francine had flat-out said they believed him responsible. His own family regarded him with suspicion. The way that Stanton woman sent off missives, the constabulary would arrive with a rope and shackles any day now.

Legalities of guardianship aside, he could hardly ask Evangeline to stay with him when he wasn't sure how much longer he'd be able to stay himself. If he truly cared for her, he would have to let her go. Give her a bagful of money. Send her off in his best coach. Hope she thought of him once in awhile.

He should give her something to take with her. A memento of the short time they had together. Something to let her know they would always be together in his heart.

But what? Jewelry? A nice long string of pearls, perhaps. Something that even if she wrapped it thrice around her neck, the longest strand would dip across the slope of her breasts, brushing against the tender skin where the pale curves met with the trim of her bodice.

No. There was no time to order anything. She planned to leave today.

What did he have to give her? Nothing. Neither literally nor figuratively. She deserved better. She should be in bed with a better man than him. She should be . . . but he would die before giving her up to another. Bad enough he couldn't protect her from her stepfather. He could hardly ask her to stay at the very house she'd seen herself being abducted from.

He'd rather her leave him for safety than be taken by force. Maybe she'd even let him join her, wherever she planned to go. He'd promised Jane a new wardrobe when Madame Rousseau arrived in a couple days. He could say his good-byes and slip away in the excitement of new clothes. Perhaps save himself a trip to the gallows in the process. Would Rose let him visit if he were a fugitive from justice? He certainly couldn't visit if he were dead.

Evangeline tilted toward him, snuggled closer, opened her eyes.

"What a grim expression," came her sleep-thickened voice. "What are you thinking about?"

"Death," he answered. "By hanging."

She stared at him for a second, then sighed. "Good morning to you, too."

"I'm sorry," he said, instantly contrite. He should've said "puppies" or "lemon ices." Yet another fine example of the many ways he wasn't good enough for her.

He bent down and kissed her anyway. When he lifted his head, her expression was still pensive.

"If I'm leaving anyway," she said slowly, "I don't see why I can't just admit I was with you in your office. Who cares about my reputation if I can save you from the gallows?"

He shook his head. "Wouldn't work."

"Why not?"

"You weren't with me all night."

"A fair portion of it," she insisted.

"Not good enough. Besides, considering all the . . . mooncalfing I've been doing over you, they'd no doubt consider any alibi you provide to be a fabrication."

"Mooncalfing?" she repeated with a smile.

"Edmund's term, not mine," Gavin mumbled. "Lovesick swain" would've been his words, had he dared to say them. He hoped she couldn't read his true feelings in the lines of his face, in the passion of his kisses, in the urgency of his love-making. Good-bye would be hard enough without adding something so complicated as *love* to the mixture.

"I think I like being mooncalfed over," she said, her voice teasing.

"I'm sure." He planted a loud, smacking kiss on her forehead and tried to smile like an inveterate rake, not a man in love. He was pretty sure he failed.

She reached up to touch his face. He pressed his lips gently against her wrist, then tilted his cheek into the warmth of her palm. He would miss her for the rest of his life, however short that might be. He missed her already.

"It would be so much easier," she said, "if everyone stopped lying about their whereabouts. We might've determined the true villain already if the innocent parties would've just been honest."

"Are there any innocent parties here?" he asked wryly.

Her thumb rubbed his cheek. "Perhaps not. But why must they all cast blame on you? Like Mr. Teasdale, with his ridiculous stories about you fighting with Lord Hetherington in your office. I wouldn't be surprised to learn you argued with him, but it's not as if you throttled your brother-in-law."

Gavin hesitated. "Actually," he said, not wishing to lie to her but even more not wanting to admit the truth. "I did."

Her hand fell away. "You did what?"

"Throttled him, then threw him into a wall." He cleared his throat. "Those handprints around his neck were mine."

She scrambled out of his arms and into a sitting position. The expression on her face could only be described as horrified.

"Bloody hell," he muttered. "I should've lied."

She stared at him, unspeaking.

He opened his mouth to defend himself, to justify as well as he could the rage that overtook him at the thought of that sanctimonious prick continuing to beat Rose—after all, much as he'd wanted to, he *hadn't* killed him—but at that moment, voices sounded from the corridor.

Familiar voices. Female voices. His maid staff, come to open the curtains.

"Damn it." He rolled out of bed, shoved his legs into his breeches, gathered his boots and the rest of his clothes in his arms.

Evangeline watched him, silent.

"I'll be back," he promised, then shook his head when he realized he wouldn't. "Rather, we'll talk later this morning. I'll explain"—the voices grew louder outside her door—"I'll explain everything later. I should leave before a passel of servants stumble upon us."

He pushed open the bookcase, strode inside the passageway, glanced over his shoulder.

She sat there, pale, unmoving, her eyes filled with—disappointment?

The doorknob turned. He ached to go to her anyway, to lay his head on her chest, to beg forgiveness for letting his temper get the best of him yet again.

Instead, he left.

Evangeline almost didn't go to breakfast.

She could hardly remain abed all day, wishing Gavin hadn't told her about strangling Lord Hetherington, wishing Gavin *hadn't* attempted to strangle him, or at least wishing she'd reacted differently to the news. Said something. Anything. Like the fact that a rather large part of her had hoped he'd planted the smirking earl a facer.

Where was the line between a fist to the face and fingers about a neck? Hadn't she told Susan that Gavin was only violent when fighting for those he loved? He'd only raised his voice against Lord Hetherington after the man struck Lady Hetherington. In fact, the only occasions she'd seen him resort to violence at all was when Gavin was protecting his sister . . . and herself.

Heaven help her.

He loved her. He *loved* her. Why else would he have told her the truth? And she'd thrown that love back in his face by being too high-minded to think clearly. What had Susan accused her of during the kite-flying? Ah, yes. Thinking she was better than everyone else, and always knew to do the right thing. She'd certainly done the wrong thing this morning.

While her lady's maid dressed her, Evangeline made furious plans.

She'd have to apologize to Gavin, of course. Tell him she'd been surprised—obviously he'd shocked her, no denying that—but not angry. Tell him she understood his anger, that she'd been angry on Lady Hetherington's behalf, too. Tell him she knew, in her heart and in her soul, that he would never harm an innocent person. *That* would be unequivocally dishonorable. That was left to the most evil of men, like Lord Hetherington, like her stepfather.

Not Gavin. He was a good man. And she'd let him down.

She barely made it halfway to the dining room before being waylaid by her least favorite houseguest. How Edmund Rutherford could be drunk at eight o'clock in the morning was beyond her, unless he happened to still be awake from the night before.

He staggered over to her side. "You look ravishing today," he slurred. "What's different about you? Same hair . . . high color in your cheeks, though. Tup one of the footmen last night?"

Before she'd even made the conscious decision to do so, her palm connected with his cheek. Her ungloved palm. And she found herself once again spying on the activities in Lord Hetherington's bedchamber.

The earl is absent, but his cousin Edmund crawls across the floor next to the bed, one hand rifling under the mattress. Without locating whatever he's looking for, Edmund rises to his feet.

He crosses the room and picks up a small traveling desk. Within seconds, he discovers a secret latch, opens a hidden drawer, and removes the contents. He shoves the papers into his pocket without reading their contents, and places the desk back on the table.

Next, he heads to the dressing room. Edmund fishes through each drawer in turn. In one, he finds a change purse. In another, a snuffbox. Both disappear into his pockets.

Two of Lord Hetherington's fashionable swordsticks lay propped against one wall. Edmund picks one up and hefts it in his hands, turning it over to scrutinize the craftsmanship. As if suddenly realizing it was far too big to fit in a pocket, he kneels to lean it back against the wall.

"You!" comes a sudden cry.

In one startled movement, Edmund tightens his fingers around the swordstick and pivots, swinging upward at the intruder.

Lord Hetherington crumples to the ground. A trickle of blood flows from his temple to the floor.

The swordstick clatters to Edmund's feet.

He stands stock-still for a moment, as if paralyzed. After a sudden, terrified glance toward the open chamber door, he drops to his knees and puts his ear against Lord Hetherington's mouth.

Edmund searches his pockets with shaking fingers and pulls out a crumpled, white handkerchief. He wraps his makeshift bandage around Lord Hetherington's head and drags the limp body toward the bed.

Lord Hetherington doesn't stir.

The sudden headache sliced through Evangeline's skull like thick shards of broken glass. She clapped her hands to her aching head, gritting her teeth against the familiar pain. It was worth any discomfort to have found the murderer at last. She massaged her temples until her brain once again could form coherent thoughts, then cracked her eyes open enough to squint at the man she'd just slapped.

He'd apparently already forgotten the act, for he was slumped against the wall drinking whatever he carried in his silver flask. When he turned to face her, a cruel sneer twisted his face.

"You may not have known this," he said as he pushed off from the wall, "but I like a woman with a little fire in her. I like her even better when *I'm* in her, too."

Evangeline backed against the other side of the hall. "Touch me and I'll scream."

"Like you scream when Lioncroft touches you?" he mocked. "I'd wager I can guess precisely how and when you scream for him. You can do as much for me."

"Touch her," came a low voice from behind them, "and I will kill you here and now."

"Lioncroft." Edmund stumbled backward a few steps. "Should've known you wouldn't be too far behind this one's skirts."

Gavin lunged for him and managed to blacken his eye before Evangeline could tug him away.

"Stop." She threw her arms around his waist, laid her cheek on his chest, hugged him tight. "He didn't touch me. I'm all right."

"Bitch touched *me,*" Edmund spat, eyes flashing.

"Say that word again and I'll—"

"No!" Evangeline tightened her hold around Gavin's torso. "I already slapped him."

He practically snarled. "Why did you have to?"

"That's not important right now. I need to tell you—"

Nancy and Lady Hetherington glided around the corner and stumbled to a stop.

Evangeline dropped her arms from around Gavin's waist. His hand found hers, squeezed, let go.

"What's going on?" Lady Hetherington asked, brows arched.

Edmund covered his rapidly bruising eye with one hand and glared at them with the other. "Besides the Pemberton chit clinging to Lioncroft, as usual? You can't trust him when she's around, and you can't trust her even when he's not. She's a menace."

"No more than you," Evangeline countered. "Considering you killed Lord Hetherington."

"Considering I *what?*"

All gazes swiveled toward Evangeline, who took a deep breath and prayed she was right. "You were, ah, *seen* that night. Sneaking into his bedchamber. Stealing papers, money, a snuffbox."

His hand fell from his eye. "I was *seen?*"

Lady Hetherington swayed back against the wall, upsetting the balance of a framed landscape. "You killed my husband, and then stole from him?"

"Other way around," Evangeline put in once it was clear Edmund planned to continue glaring rather than defend himself. "He had just finished stuffing his pockets when your husband caught him unawares. He clubbed him with a swordstick."

"You can't prove it," Edmund muttered.

"Can't I? You assert that if we perform a search of your chamber, we won't find the papers, the change purse, and the snuffbox?"

"Proves nothing," Edmund insisted. "You might've planted those items in my room yourself."

Evangeline crossed her arms. "Did I plant the handkerchief tied around the wound to his head?"

He blanched. "Er . . ."

"If we look closer, we'll discover it embroidered with your initials, will we not?"

"All right. Fine. I hit him with a swordstick." His gaze flicked from person to person. "But I didn't kill him. He was still breathing when I left."

Gavin's muscles flexed. "Is there any reason we should believe you?"

A silence settled in the shadowed hall before Nancy Hetherington cleared her throat and whispered, "Actually . . . yes."

"Honey." Lady Hetherington reached for her daughter's hand. "No."

Nancy squared her shoulders. "I . . . I went to visit Papa long after the dancing stopped. He had the bandage about his head already, but I didn't even ask how he'd gotten injured. I was too angry. I told him I didn't want to get married to someone who was too old to dance, much less . . ." She colored, coughed, took a deep breath. "I know it's selfish and horrible but I couldn't make myself marry Mr. Teasdale. I'd run away before I let that happen."

"With *Monsieur le professeur du Français?*" Edmund interjected with a sneer.

"Yes," Nancy responded hotly. "At least Pierre has a pulse. And he loves me. He told me so. But Papa said . . . Papa said I was young and foolish, and that I shouldn't put girlish dreams over his dictates as head of the family. That money matters more than love, and I'd been raised well enough to know my duty. And then he said . . . and then he said . . ." Nancy burst into wet, noisy sobs. "He said he'd not only sacked Pierre, he sent him hog-tied on a boat to India."

Shocked silence enveloped the dim corridor, until Edmund's wry voice broke the stillness.

"Well, sweetheart," he said with a relieved smirk. "Sounds like you had more of a motive to kill the selfish rotter than I did."

"My daughter would never kill her father. You're the selfish rotter, Edmund. Stealing from my husband? Leaving him to die?" She pounded her fists against his chest. "Get out. And never come back. You're no longer part of this family."

He lurched away from her. "You can't order me around. It's not your house."

"No," Gavin agreed. "It's mine. Do as my sister says. Return whatever you've purloined, and get out. I'll send some footmen along to make sure you do."

"I didn't kill Papa," Nancy choked out, sobbing into her mother's arms.

Gavin slanted a look at Evangeline. "She didn't do it," he murmured.

Evangeline sighed, unable to deny the truth. "I know."

Nancy and Lady Hetherington headed back toward their chambers. Half a dozen footmen followed Edmund to his room.

Evangeline turned to Gavin, held his face in her hands, kissed him. "I'm so sorry."

"For what?" His arms went around her waist and held her tight. "You caught a thief."

"But not a murderer." She gazed up at him. "And I'm sorry about this morning. I've always been quick to judge, and I know I shouldn't be. If anything, you've taught me to rely on my own intuition rather than the suspicions of others. And I know you. I know you would never harm an innocent person. Whatever you did to Lord Hetherington, he deserved."

An indefinable emotion flickered across Gavin's face. Unease rippled through Evangeline's stomach.

"About that," he began hesitantly, then paused as a new pair of female voices came from down a connecting corridor. When the voices turned out to belong to Susan and Lady Stanton, Gavin dropped his arms from Evangeline's waist and groaned. "Those bloody Stanton women," he growled sotto voce. "I'll kill them yet."

As Evangeline turned to greet Susan, she wondered what Gavin had been about to say . . . and whether she'd be better off not knowing.

Chapter Twenty-Five

Evangeline spent most of breakfast staring at Gavin beneath her lashes and wishing they could've spent more time together. Although he returned her gaze openly, his eyes were hooded, unreadable. When she stood to fetch another piece of toast, she wasn't surprised to find him joining her at the sideboard.

"I already requested a carriage be brought round for you," he murmured. "It will be by the front garden in less than an hour. But first . . . first . . . I can't let you leave without telling you . . ."

Toast in hand, she whipped around breathlessly to face him. "Yes?"

He swallowed convulsively, tensed his shoulders, turned away. He stared at the gleaming silver platters for a long moment before muttering, "I'll miss you."

He'd miss her. He'd told her that last night. Well, what had she expected him to say? Evangeline nodded, forced her fingers to unclench from around the now-mangled piece of toast. She selected a new slice even though she was no longer hungry.

"I'll miss you, too," she said, careful to keep her tone light so he wouldn't be able to hear the breaking of her heart beneath her words.

He grabbed her wrist, eyes intense. "Evangeline, I—"

A hunched shadow fell across them.

"Mind your inappropriate behavior, Lioncroft," came the trembling, reproachful voice of Mr. Teasdale.

Gavin's muscles tensed, but he released Evangeline's wrist. "I shall be as inappropriate as I wish in my own house."

"Then I shall quit the premises at the earliest opportunity." Mr. Teasdale's palsied hand slowly removed each lid until he found the correct platter, slowly lifted the serving tongs above the kippers, slowly poked around for the perfect strip. "I shall leave after breakfast."

Gavin's jaw clenched. "Good."

When Mr. Teasdale set about sifting through a tray of eggs with even less haste, Gavin muttered, "Propriety is for gentlemen; I am not," and tugged Evangeline a few feet to the right.

His voice was low, strained. "Don't leave without saying good-bye."

"I would never." If there weren't a half dozen people in the same room, she'd throw her arms around his neck and kiss him until his eyes lost their desolation.

"I . . ." He paused, grimaced . . . blushed? Surely not. "I have something for you. It's stupid. It's nothing. It's all right if you don't want it. I'll send it to your room. I—if we had more time, I would give you anything. Everything. Clothes, jewelry, whatever you wished."

It was almost impossible not to kiss him, breakfast guests be damned. He looked so embarrassed, so earnest, so endearing.

"Don't worry," she assured him. "I don't want anything."

That was a lie, of course. She wanted plenty of things she couldn't have. But more than that, she wished to ease the anguish in his eyes. So she smiled up at him, trying to infuse her gaze with all the love clutching at her heart.

He sucked in a breath, stared at her with naked hunger, then abruptly turned on his heel and stalked from the dining room without another word.

Her limbs were leaden as she resumed her place at the table.

Benedict Rutherford glanced over with a concerned frown. "What's the matter? Did you have words with Lioncroft?"

Evangeline shook her head. She feared she hadn't had *enough* words with him. Perhaps she should go to him. Now. Wherever he was. The carriage would be here in less than an hour and she had nothing to pack. She should spend her last fleeting moments in Gavin's arms. What if this was the last time she saw him? What if she managed to escape her stepfather until she reached her majority, and returned here only to learn the owner of Blackberry Manor had long since been hung for a crime he hadn't committed?

She shoved her chair back and sprang to her feet. If only she could've identified the murderer! Why was she cursed with a Gift capable of helping villains and strangers, but unable to save the man she loved?

Ignoring the startled expressions of the breakfast guests, she bolted from the dining room and sprinted through the corridors.

When Evangeline reached the anteroom, Francine Rutherford was descending the spiral staircase, one slender hand curved across her belly, the other resting atop the burnished railing. Her slipper slid on the slick marble, pitching mother and unborn child forward.

Evangeline leapt forward to prevent her from tumbling headfirst down the remaining three or four steps.

Francine twisted midair, recoiled, clutched for the banister. "Stay away, you little witch," she hissed, eyes wide, face pale. "Don't you dare touch me."

Evangeline froze, arms still outstretched from her attempt to prevent a fall. Her flesh chilled and she returned her hands to her sides.

A strangled "What?" was the only word her numb lips were able to form.

Francine's eyes narrowed. "Lady Stanton told me about you and your unholy abilities. So much for speaking to God."

Evangeline's spine straightened and her fingers clenched. She was not violent by nature, but she found herself battling an overwhelming desire to plant Lady Stanton a facer.

Nose pointed skyward, Francine eased down the last steps until she was toe to toe to Evangeline, who still hadn't moved.

Francine's arms crossed below her bodice. "Go ahead and touch me if you want to see it firsthand, you little freak. Nobody will believe a commoner over a countess. If you breathe a word, I'll say I saw Lioncroft kill him myself." She shoved past Evangeline, head held high, and sauntered toward the hallway leading to the dining room. "As soon as I collect my husband, we're leaving. Our carriage is waiting outside."

"What?" Evangeline gasped, reaching out to grab Francine's arm.

But Francine had already sailed through the open doorway into the depths of a shadowed passageway.

The new countess seemed to think Evangeline in possession of a dangerous secret. Just as obvious was the substance of that secret. But how could Evangeline prove it?

If Francine followed through on her threat to provide false witness against Gavin—and Evangeline had no doubt she would do so—Francine's prediction as to which one of them would be believed would no doubt come true.

There had to be some way to prove Francine's presence in Lord Hetherington's bedchamber. If not, Evangeline should at least be able to determine a motive so heinous the others would be forced to believe her. Was the simple fact of inheriting strong enough?

Francine was leaving in the next few minutes. Whatever Evangeline was going to do, she needed to act quickly. She needed clues. She needed information. Who would be the most likely to know other secrets Francine Rutherford might be keeping?

Susan.

Evangeline raced up the spiral staircase two steps at a time, dashed down the corridor to the guest wing, and vaulted into Susan's bedchamber.

"Bloody hell, Evangeline. Could you wait until my maid finishes lacing up my gown?"

"No." Evangeline grabbed Susan's gloved hands in hers. "Francine Rutherford killed Lord Hetherington."

Both Susan and her maid stared at her, mouths agape.

Susan found her voice first. "I'm sorry, what?"

"Francine killed him. I need your help proving it. Fast."

"How can I help? I had no idea."

"But you know other things, don't you? She slapped you for spreading lies, but—were they?"

Susan stepped backward and smoothed the lace of her bodice. "No. I stupidly spread the truth."

"Just so. You know her better than me. Why would she do it?"

"How the hell would I know?" Susan began to pace around her bedchamber. "I thought she was still in love with him."

"Still in love with—" Evangeline gaped at her. "But isn't she married to his brother?"

"Biggest mistake of her life. Well, unless you count killing Hetherington."

"Francine Rutherford was in love with Lord Hetherington," Evangeline said slowly, trying to replay the moments she'd seen them interact.

"Madly," Susan confirmed. "Emphasis on *mad*. She made a cake of herself over him for years. Gave him some sort of ultimatum. Should've known better, with a bounder like Hetherington. He responded by turning his attentions to another woman. Rumor has it Francine accepted Benedict's proposal in an attempt to make Hetherington jealous, but as he made no attempt to win her back, she was forced to go through with the wedding."

Evangeline frowned. "This all sounds like ancient history, though."

Susan nodded. "It is. I was a child at the time."

"Then why did she slap you that day at the opera house if her unrequited love and ill-advised marriage were both common knowledge?"

"Because the details of her extramarital affairs were not." Susan's cheeks colored. "Or *affair,* rather. With Hetherington, of course. Her husband's brother. I happened to glimpse him with his hand down her bodice deep inside the Dark Walk one night at Vauxhall. He got rid of her gown faster than any lady's maid *I've* seen."

"You spied on them lovemaking?" Evangeline asked incredulously.

"Of course not. There wasn't time. I ducked behind a bush. Not long after, I heard footsteps approaching, so I had to sneak out of there. But before I did, I heard her tell him if she were lucky, he could provide her with the one thing her husband could not."

"How did she know *you* spread the rumors?"

"The footsteps turned out to be her husband's. He was calling for her, afraid she'd been set upon by footpads. Hetherington went one way, she another. Unfortunately for me, the direction she chose coincided with the bush I was hiding behind."

"Criminy, Susan."

She shrugged. "I wouldn't have stumbled across them if they hadn't been up to mischief."

"What did she mean, provide her with the one thing her husband could not?"

"A *baby,* Evangeline." Susan shook her head with a sigh. "Obviously."

Evangeline's jaw dropped open. "Benedict Rutherford can't father children?"

"Apparently not."

"But Francine's increasing! And he has no idea."

It was Susan's turn to goggle at her. *"What?"*

"That's it! That's why she did it. She could be the mother of the next heir. If she hadn't killed him, he and Lady Hetherington might've kept having children until he fathered a son. It explains everything."

Susan's eyes widened. "What do we do about it?"

Evangeline hesitated. She'd promised Gavin she'd stop jumping to conclusions, and she'd been wrong about the murderer's identity so many times before, but . . . No. She'd rather be wrong yet again than let a murderer walk free.

"We shall stop her." Evangeline threw open the door. "Quick, go after them before it's too late. They've already brought their carriage round. I'll go find Gavin and tell him we've uncovered the murderer's identity."

"Wait. Take this." Susan jerked open the drawer to a portable desk and rifled through its contents before thrusting a folded parchment at Evangeline. "Here's a copy of the scandal sheet that ran the column. I saved all the articles to remind myself what can happen when secrets aren't kept."

Evangeline took the proffered paper and tore off in search of Gavin.

Had Gavin known Evangeline might burst into his studio at any moment, he might've chosen to work on his niece's miniature rather than the portrait of Evangeline he was painting from memory.

As it was, she caught him brush in hand, adding a few more flyaway curls to her gorgeous mane of hair.

"Gavin, I—angels above. Is that me?"

He inclined his head. There was no point in denying it.

She blinked at the canvas. "I thought you wanted to paint me nude."

"I thought if I painted you with clothing, I might hang it in plain sight."

"Oh." She blushed. "Good point."

"This way," he said gruffly, "even if I can't hold you at night, at least I can see your smile. That is, unless I'm hung for murder."

"Never." She thrust a scrap of newsprint at him, eyes shining. "That's what I've come to tell you. I know who killed Lord Hetherington."

He tossed his paintbrush aside and took the paper. "Truly? Who?"

"Francine Rutherford. She's carrying Lord Hetherington's child." Evangeline gestured at the folded sheet in his hand. "Read the article and you'll understand. Benedict's already got their carriage round front, but Susan's making sure she doesn't go anywhere. I came to tell you straightaway."

Francine killed Hetherington and planned to let Gavin hang in her place. That unbelievable bitch. Thank God Evangeline figured it out before he found himself—

Gavin's heart slowed, then raced to a crescendo. Wait. If he needn't fear the gallows, that meant—that meant—

"Stay," he begged, tugging Evangeline into his arms. "Don't leave me. Don't go anywhere. I meant what I said last night. I want—wait for me. I'll be right back. Just let me make sure Francine doesn't escape before the magistrate arrives."

He crushed his lips to hers, then let her go. But only for now. Saints be praised, the moment Francine was arrested he could make Evangeline all the promises he'd longed to make the night before.

"I'll wait until you return," she promised, giving him a

little smile. "To be honest, the thought of leaving makes me want to throw myself in a river."

Gooseflesh rippled up his arms. Without thinking, he found himself saying, "That's how my father died."

She blanched. "Oh! I didn't mean . . . I thought a carriage . . . that is, I knew you had nothing to do with it, but—"

"I had everything to do with it."

"What?" Evangeline backed up a step, crossed her arms.

He winced, and hoped telling her everything was the right thing to do. "You remember when my sister mentioned my love of curricle races?"

She nodded, brow furrowed, eyes frightened.

Devil take it. He didn't want to tell her any of this . . . but she deserved to hear the truth from him, rather than through secondhand visions or thirdhand rumors.

He let out a slow breath. "I was seventeen. Home on holiday. Positive my father's order to 'mind my safety' was yet another of his high-handed attempts to control my life. Ban me from curricle racing, would he? Fine. The first moment his back was turned, I tore off in his conveniently readied carriage. Alone. Reckless. I heard a slow, sickening crack, slowed the horses, leapt to the ground. Amazingly I didn't die right then and there. Another quarter hour bearing my weight, and the front axle would've snapped in two. At the rate I was flying, I wouldn't have had a chance."

Evangeline's head tilted to one side, her expression confused. "By all accounts, you were an incorrigible devil, but I don't see how your personal recklessness makes you a murderer."

"My first mistake was arguing with my father in front of servants and siblings alike, screaming about how he couldn't tell me what to do, that he'd be sorry he tried. My second mistake was ignoring my father's well-intentioned dictates and taking off hell-for-leather in his carriage. My third mistake . . ."

Her warm hand settled on his arm, stroked softly. "What was your third mistake?"

"Not telling him about the broken axle," Gavin confessed when his throat cleared enough to allow the passage of words. "I knew the carriage was in a dangerous condition, and I didn't say a word. I couldn't. I knew my father would be furious."

He closed his eyes to block the memory. It didn't work.

When he reopened them, Evangeline's expression was horrified.

"It was already suppertime," he explained. Or tried to explain. Truly, no explanation would ever be acceptable. "I planned to have the axle replaced first thing in the morning. How was I to know my father planned to dine elsewhere? That he'd promised my sister he and my mother would set out that very night with gifts for her baby? The carriage was waiting. Ready. Had I been thinking, I might've guessed, remembered. But I wasn't thinking." He swallowed thickly. "And now I can never forget."

Evangeline clapped her hands over her mouth, paled, backed against the wall.

"Which is how," he forced himself to continue, "within an hour of our shouting match, my father and mother headed out at twilight in a deathtrap. They were far too disgusted with me to say good-bye, so I didn't know they'd left until I heard the screams." He took a deep, shuddering breath. "My mother was thrown from the carriage. She died in my arms. My father and the horses slid over a curved precipice into the river below. That night, my brother inherited the viscountcy. He never forgave me." Gavin smiled humorlessly. "I never forgave myself. How could I? I'd killed our parents."

She looked like she might be ill at any moment.

"People talk," he continued. Lord, did they. And why not? He'd given them plenty to talk about. "By dawn, the tragedy was common knowledge, as was the asinine threat that preceded it. My brother's first act as viscount was to evict me. I couldn't blame him."

Evangeline shook her head, groped for the door, stumbled out into the corridor.

Gavin's flesh chilled in terror. He'd told her the truth, and now she was as horrified as everyone else. He'd warned her he wasn't a good person. He'd *warned* her.

He shoved the folded parchment into a pocket and sprinted after her. She wasn't far, just outside the door, hugging herself, back to the wall. When he came to stand in front of her, several heart-stopping moments passed before she finally met his gaze.

"Did you tell everyone you hadn't meant for your parents to die?" she asked, her voice wooden, her eyes dull.

"David was too angry to speak to me. I rode to Rose's, to tell her Mother and Father weren't coming, to tell her why. She already knew. Wouldn't let me in." He shrugged. "I didn't care about anyone else's opinion. Didn't realize the gossip would matter. By the time mourning was officially over and I made my first attempt to rejoin Society, it was too late. Even my tailor gave me the cut direct. Everyone. I was an outcast. And I deserved no better."

Evangeline hugged herself tighter. "What did you do then?"

"I went to work. I had nothing else to do, nothing to live for. Then I moved to Braintree and Bocking. Eventually bought a home, turned a profit, remembered my love of art. And then, barely a month ago, I discovered the depth of one's pockets correlates inversely with the length of the *ton*'s memories."

She frowned. "What do you mean?"

"I mean, the sister that spent years refusing my letters decided to come calling with her family. A baroness who hadn't spoken to me in a dozen years suddenly wished to leg-shackle me to her daughter. Even another death couldn't deter the Rutherford clan from eating my food and depleting my whiskey. I wasn't a person. I was a scandal sheet and a pocketbook. An object of derision, wealth, and fear." Gavin hesitated, fighting the sensation of his heart in his eyes. "Then came you."

He reached for her.

She flinched.

Part of his soul died.

"You'd better go." Evangeline stared at him for a moment, then looked away. She motioned down the hall with one listless finger. "Susan can't hold Francine captive forever."

"I promised you a carriage to anywhere you chose, but . . . don't leave me. Please." He reached out, gripped her tense shoulders. His voice trembled with desperation. "I need you."

Her gaze lowered. She said nothing.

He released her, backed up a step, paused just in case . . .

She didn't move.

With a heavy heart, Gavin gave up. He'd known from the start his hopes had been set too high. He didn't deserve her. He didn't deserve happiness. And what was she, if not his source of happiness? Without her, his life would be nothing once again.

He gazed at her for a long moment. At least he would have her portrait. Those impassioned brushstrokes would forever remind him of the short time he had loved her—and those precious moments when he had been loved back.

No matter where she went, she would always be the keeper of his soul. He would love her until he died, and ever after. He couldn't help it. She was everything to him.

Her continued silence was worse than screaming epithets at him, worse than a thousand knife wounds. But there was nothing he could do to change the past. He'd spent over a decade trying, and still remained the worthless cur he'd been at seventeen.

Evangeline closed her eyes.

At least he'd met her, known her, loved her. No matter she

could no longer bear the sight of him, he'd never regret the days he'd lived with her presence.

She'd told him to hurry, to confront Francine. Very well. He could at least do that. He'd do anything she asked. He'd prostrate himself at her feet, declare himself her slave for eternity if only she would forgive him his many, many faults and let him touch her once again, kiss her, hold her.

Perhaps . . . perhaps if he just tried hard enough, he could somehow redeem himself in her eyes. Enough to warrant a second chance. Was it possible? He had to believe there was hope. Hope of a future with the woman he loved. He *had* to believe there was hope.

If there were none, he would die.

After a final glance at her downturned face, Gavin ducked behind the closest secret panel and slipped into the shadowed network of passageways between the walls.

Chapter Twenty-Six

Too late. Why was he always too late?

Gavin forced himself not to throttle the Stanton chit. "Where the devil did they go?" he asked for the third or fourth time. "I thought you were watching her."

"I meant to watch her." She quivered before him, hands wringing, eyes tearing up behind her spectacles. "She was already gone by the time I came downstairs. Mr. Teasdale's gone, too. They summoned their carriages before breakfast."

"I don't care about Teasdale," he thundered, smashing his fist into the closest wall. "I care about that bitch Francine. Where the *hell* did she *go?*"

"I don't know," she cried. "I told you I don't know! Ask your sister. They were talking before breakfast. Maybe—"

He spun away from her and set off in search of Rose. She wasn't in the dining room. She wasn't in her bedchamber. She was upstairs in the nursery, reading stories to the twins. Jane and Nancy perched on either edge of the sofa beside her.

"Number one," he announced by way of greeting. "Where is Francine Rutherford?"

Five pairs of startled eyes gazed his way.

"On her way to one of their country properties, I believe," Rose responded hesitantly. "Why?"

"Number two," he continued without answering her question. "Why the hell did you and Nancy ask the girls to lie about where you were the night your husband died?"

"Wh—what?" Nancy's face paled. "We didn't—"

"You *did*. You forced Jane to lie to my face. And for what? Neither one of you did anything wrong."

Rose and Nancy stared at each other, mouths agape. "You didn't—?"

Gavin glanced at the open doorway. "Oh, for God's sake. Each of you thought the other did it, and you were trying to protect each other's neck? All this time, I was sure you thought it was *me*."

Nancy colored and shook her head.

Rose moved the twins aside and got to her feet. "Even families who love each other can suspect each other of horrible things," she said softly. "Even families who love each other can be wrong. Forgive me?"

"Have you ever forgiven *me?*" he asked and turned to go.

"I wouldn't be here otherwise," Rose said simply. "I'm a mother. I would never leave my children alone with someone I didn't trust. You've been a wonderful uncle to them."

He paused to look back at her. "Not for much longer. Francine killed your husband. But if I don't find her, *I'll* be the one to hang."

"No," Nancy gasped, eyes wide. "Aunt Rutherford mentioned stopping by their London town house before heading home. Don't let her get away with blaming you for Papa's death."

Gavin nodded as he sprinted from the room and down the hall. Within minutes, he was on the back of a horse and tearing down the dirt road to catch a killer.

Evangeline's head was still swimming from Gavin's confession when she finally returned to her bedchamber. She didn't know what to think. She'd been positive he'd had nothing to do with his parents' death.

She closed her bedchamber door and headed to her bed, intending to throw herself atop the mattress and scream into the pillows until she made sense of her life, and decided whether to stay or to go. That plan, however, did not come to fruition.

There, in the center of her bed, sat what appeared to be a brown clay pot filled with dirt.

She stepped closer. Definitely a pot. She stuck her finger in the moist black soil. Definitely dirt. And lying atop was a small card simply reading, "Think of me. Gavin." She blinked, reread, poked the soil again. She'd been unlikely to forget him in the first place, but he'd vanquished the possibility altogether by being the first man to present her with a pot of farewell dirt.

Mystifying.

No matter how much she stared at it, turned it, prodded it, it steadfastly remained a brown clay pot filled with dirt.

She picked it up. Heavier than she expected, but not too heavy to lug around England. Was that what she was supposed to do with it? Lug it around England and think of Gavin? If ever she required a sign from God that she wholly and unequivocally did not understand the world of the *ton,* surely this was that sign. Couldn't he have just given her a locket with his miniature inside?

Having nothing else pressing to do, she balanced the pot on one hip and shouldered through her connecting door to beg an explanation from the resident *ton* expert.

Susan took one look at her, leapt backward against a hanging mirror, and threw up her arms for protection.

"I apologize! I apologize! Please don't throw dirt on me!"

Evangeline paused. "For what?"

"For not finding Francine in time."

"You didn't find Francine?"

Susan peeked through her fingers. "You didn't know?"

Evangeline shook her head slowly. "Where'd she go?"

"I don't know." Susan's hands lowered. "But Lioncroft went to find her. I'd hate to be her right now. He's frightening when he's angry."

"He is not," Evangeline began, then stopped, startled. Her defense of him was automatic. Was it what she believed? Either he was frightening, or he was not. He could not be both.

"I'll be honest," Susan said. "Despite everything you said, I never quite believed he was innocent until today."

"I told you." Evangeline dropped into Susan's chair and settled her clay pot on her lap. "There was no way he could've smothered Hetherington in his office, or even knocked him out and carried him through the entire mansion, sight unseen."

"I might've agreed with that logic had I not witnessed you prying open the wall yesterday afternoon. I imagine it's quite simple to move about unseen when one is secreted within hidden passageways."

Evangeline stared at her. "I never thought of that."

"Of course you didn't. Why would you? You thought he was innocent. You were trying to think of ways other people might've done it. I, on the other hand, was convinced of his guilt, so of course, I was looking for ways he might've committed the crime."

"You'd make him a terrible wife."

"Oh, piffle. We both know he's never going to marry me."

Perhaps she had known, but nonetheless, a blessed sense of relief settled in Evangeline's tense muscles to hear Susan speak the words aloud.

"If you don't mind me asking," Susan said hesitantly, "why are you walking around with a pot of dirt?"

"I was hoping you could tell me."

"How the dickens would I know?"

"I don't know. I thought it was maybe some particular *ton* tradition."

"*Dirt?*" Susan poked a tentative finger inside. "Are you bamming me?"

"Never mind. I'll consider it a new mystery to solve." Evangeline hesitated. "You were right about me being a bossy know-all. I shouldn't have been like that, and I apologize. Still friends?"

"Pah, of course. All women have their moments of being bossy know-alls. Take my mother, for example. Or don't . . . I shouldn't wish her on anybody. Speaking of which, where will you be off to next?"

"I don't know yet."

"What are your choices?"

Evangeline felt her face flush. "My choices," she said slowly, "seem to be Blackberry Manor . . . or somewhere else."

Susan tapped her chin. "Well, Blackberry Manor sounds intriguing. Does this mean Lioncroft asked you to marry him?"

"No. But he did give me a pot of dirt."

"I see." Susan shoved her spectacles up the bridge of her nose with the back of a hand. "Ill-advised attempts at gift giving aside, what's to stop you from staying? Is it that a lack of a proposal rather implies he's hoping you'll stay on as his mistress?"

"No," Evangeline answered slowly. "It's not that. In fact, he somewhat . . . he almost proposed."

"Almost?"

"He implied if he were assured of not hanging, he *would* ask for my hand."

"Oh, Evangeline!" Susan clapped her hands together excitedly. "That's wonderful! Isn't it? Why don't you look happy? Is it the pot of dirt? Men are imbeciles. You must be very specific about what constitutes a proper gift. Tell him no more dirt. Tell him you require jewelry for an engagement gift. Tell him pearls, or perhaps—"

"I don't know if I want to marry him," Evangeline confessed.

Susan gaped at her. "Why on earth not? You've been taken with him from the first. And even Edmund harped on Lioncroft's constant mooncalfing, remember? You yourself said

Lioncroft would only marry if he wished to. He must love you. Wasn't that what you wanted? A love match?"

Evangeline frowned. *Wasn't* that what she wanted? What was her problem?

"And he didn't even kill Hetherington," Susan continued blithely. "So you needn't worry he's resumed any violent tendencies. Well, he did bruise Hetherington up a bit, and he thrashed Edmund once or twice, and he planted on your stepfather a few well-deserved facers . . . but absolutely no killing. That's good, isn't it?"

"I wouldn't say *no* killing. It turns out," Evangeline confessed softly, "he's responsible for his parents' deaths after all."

Susan's brows lifted uncertainly. "Er . . . That's exceptionally old news, Evangeline. He killed them over something trivial, if I recall correctly. I don't remember what . . . Pugilism, maybe? Or his marks at university?"

"Carriage racing," Evangeline stammered. "And he didn't do it on purpose. It was a horrible accident. Well, not an accident-accident, which I think is why my stomach won't lie still, but he didn't mean to hurt anyone."

Susan blinked. "I'll be honest. I heard what you just said, yet I have no idea if you're defending him or denouncing him. Which is it?"

"I don't know," Evangeline groaned. "What would you do?"

"Clearly, I'd meant to marry him regardless. I would've felt my decision even more validated had I known the tragedy was an accident. While I understand it's easier to believe in a past you know than a future you don't, the trouble with the past is it's unchangeable. Much as he might like to, Lioncroft can no more reverse his parents' deaths than I can go back in time to prevent myself from spreading malicious gossip. It happened. Either you love someone enough to forgive them their past mistakes, or you don't."

Evangeline dropped her head in her hands. Heaven help her. Weren't those the exact words she'd used to coax Gavin into forgiving himself for the careless things he'd done as a young man?

"You're right." She glanced up at Susan. "I'm a ninny-hammer."

"Well, yes. It's part of your charm. I can come to the wedding, though, right? Oh, let me help plan it! Lioncroft has enough money to make it the Society event of the Season. Oh, and since you haven't a mother to do so, I can be the one to tell you all about the wedding act."

"The wedding act?"

"You know. Lovemaking. I'll tell you now if you want. Mother says it's not so bad because it's always dark so you can't see what he's doing anyway, and if you lay still enough, it'll be over quick as can be and you can get on with whatever you were doing, and if he doesn't jostle you about too much, you might even be able to compose shopping lists in your head while he—"

"Susan."

"Yes?"

"Promise me something."

"What?"

"If you think you might have the slightest chance of entering into a physical relationship with a man, for marriage or otherwise—"

"Why would I do it otherwise?"

"Listen to me. If you even have a *dream* about kissing, promise me you will write immediately for my advice."

"You have advice?"

"More like a counterargument, yes." Evangeline lifted the pot of dirt and rose to her feet. "But right now, I have to find Gavin before he leaves. I owe him an apology . . . and to let him know he owns my heart."

Before the opportunity to set things right was lost.

* * *

The brisk October wind rifled Gavin's hair, chapped his dry cheeks, destroyed his cravat. He didn't care. He felt suddenly free. Freer than he'd ever been. He had his family again. As long as he didn't swing for Francine's crimes.

He caught sight of the Rutherfords up ahead and overtook their carriage within moments. When their wheels slowed to a stop, Gavin leapt from his horse, strode over, and yanked open the door.

Francine stared at him with barely-concealed horror.

"Lioncroft," she managed, her hands twisting nervously in her skirt. "What a surprise."

He inclined his head coldly. "Isn't it?"

Benedict regarded him with a furrowed brow. "To what do we owe the pleasure?"

"I came to congratulate you," Gavin said, "For your future heir."

Benedict frowned. "I'm not the future heir anymore, Lioncroft. Now I'm the earl. Horrifying as it is, *Edmund* is the future heir."

"Actually, that's not the case at all," Gavin bit out. "Is it, Francine?"

She paled.

"Uh-oh." Gavin flashed a ferocious smile. "You haven't told him? He's going to notice, sooner or later."

Benedict coughed into his napkin. "What the hell are you talking about, Lioncroft?"

Gavin swung inside the carriage and arranged himself atop the rear-facing seat. He lounged back against the squab, knees spread, arms crossed. "Your wife killed Hetherington because she's pregnant with his child."

Benedict froze.

"He's a liar!" Francine clutched her husband's sleeve, hands shaking.

"She's been lifting her skirts to him for years, it seems, and it's finally paid off," Gavin continued relentlessly. "She might very well have the next little Lord Hetherington in her belly."

Francine closed her eyes and dropped her hands from her husband's sleeve.

Benedict stared at his wife, face ashen. "You promised me it was over. When that scandal sheet came out, you promised me it was an exaggeration, a one-time relapse blown out of proportion."

Francine glanced away, lips tight.

"The scandal sheet said more than that," Gavin reminded him helpfully. He produced the very article from his front pocket and unfolded the clipping on his lap. "It claims Francine had to look elsewhere if she wanted heirs. If that's true, she won't be able to deny her condition for more than another month or two before it's obvious to anyone with eyes."

Benedict swallowed, his gaze and tone dull. "Francine . . . ?"

"We both wanted a baby. We talked about it all the time. It's not my fault you couldn't father one. So I found someone who could. I didn't love him, Benedict. I just wanted a baby. For us. Like we dreamed about."

He recoiled and stared at her. "I wanted a child *of my own*."

"It's your baby," she gritted out, "if you say it is. Just think, darling—we'll be raising the new earl!"

"Because you killed the old one?" Benedict slammed his fist against the carriage wall. "My brother, Francine. My *brother*."

Her voice wobbled. "You hated him, too. How many times did you wish for his untimely death?"

"Because he *slept* with my *wife*," he roared. "I wanted to kill him for that."

"I did it for you." She placed a trembling hand on his knee. "I did it for us."

"And now we're all going to the magistrate. I'll follow on my horse." Gavin rapped at the panel to summon the coachman. "Don't kill each other before we get there."

* * *

Rather than drive herself mad waiting for news of Gavin, after she had missed seeing him before he had left to catch Francine, Evangeline decided to while away the hours watching the children play in the nursery. However, the girls were nowhere to be found. Even stranger, she couldn't even find a servant to ask where they might be. Or, in fact, *any* house-guest. Might everyone have gone outside for kite-flying or pall-mall?

Pot of dirt still tucked under her arm, she made her way to the servants' quarters rather than the front porch, as the side door spilled directly into the lawn where the wickets had been set up for Jane's birthday. No wickets. No kites. Dozens of scurrying servants.

Dread began to coil in Evangeline's belly. She had the horrible suspicion the staff of Blackberry Manor was not engaged in a casual game of hide-and-seek.

Jane flew out from between two tall rows of blackberry bushes, caught sight of Evangeline, and burst into tears.

Evangeline ran up to her, stroked her hair with her free hand. "What happened?"

"It's my fault," Jane sobbed. "The twins have been asking to play out-of-doors all morning, and I said I would but I didn't because I wanted to sneak into Uncle Lioncroft's studio to look at the miniature he's painting of me. When I came back they were gone. I was so angry at them for running off again that I told Nancy and Mother they should be spanked, and we all came outside to fetch them. But we couldn't find them, and then we found Rachel, and Rachel was crying, and she said Rebecca was hurt somewhere between the bushes and we can't find her anywhere."

"Oh, no," Evangeline breathed. "Poor thing. Does Rachel know where she is?"

"She's crying too hard to speak. We can't get any helpful information from her."

Evangeline straightened. "*I* can. Take me to her. Hurry!"

Jane took off running with Evangeline right on her heels.

They sped through the rows of towering blackberry bushes, mindless of the occasional brambles tugging at their hair and ripping at their skirts. Just when Evangeline was beginning to think the fields stretched on forever, a smart white gazebo appeared in the center of a small clearing.

Jane stumbled to a stop. "Rachel? Rachel?" She turned to face Evangeline, panic in her eyes. "I don't understand. She was right here. Now I've lost her, too!"

"No," Evangeline choked, catching sight of a too-familiar form stepping out from behind a tall bush. "She's still here."

"Mornin', darling." Neal Pemberton tightened his hold on Rachel's limp body, one large hand clapped over the child's mouth, the other holding a knife to her ribs. "Miss me?"

Oh, God. The blackberry fields. Of course.

"Let her go," Evangeline demanded, wincing at the tremor in her words.

"Now, why would I want to do that?" he drawled, casting a slow, lascivious smile at the top of Rachel's blond head. "She's right pretty. You know how I like pretty girls."

"Let her *go,*" Evangeline repeated, her voice high-pitched and cracking. Yes, she did know. Far, far too well. "Jane, I need you to run. Find your mother, find a servant, find anyone. Tell them Neal Pemberton is here and he's got Rachel." She took a deep breath and tried to look confident. "For now."

"For as long as I want," he corrected softly. "Look at those plump little cheeks and long curling lashes. And just think— there's *two* of these darling creatures. What I wouldn't give to have both . . ."

Jane turned and gagged into her fist before glancing back at Evangeline. "Tell them Neal Pam-pem-what?"

"Pemberton. My stepfather." Evangeline hugged the clay pot to her chest. "Your uncle will know what to do. *Go.*"

"No, no, honey," Neal crooned, grabbing for Jane with one hand. "Stay."

With a gasp, Jane twisted away and took off running.

A chilling smile played at Neal's lips. "I sure hope she comes back with her sister." He sliced off one of Rachel's buttons with his knife. Tears rolled down the child's dirt-stained cheeks. "Two pretty girls are better than one, I always say. And identical ones . . . even better."

"She's five years old," Evangeline burst out. Gooseflesh mixed with sweat as she recalled the predatory looks he'd given her at that age. "Please let Rachel go. We—we both know you're here for me."

"I own you," he reminded her, eyes hard. "Come closer, stepdaughter. I won't let go of this juicy chit until I've got you nice and secure. I know how tricky you are when it comes to escaping. You'll never see the attic again, little witch. From here on out, it's the pantry for you."

Evangeline's vision briefly faded at just the mention of that horrible dark space. God, how she hated that wretched pantry. But she hated the terror in Rachel's eyes even worse.

She inched forward warily, knowing every step toward her stepfather was another step toward her own slow death, even if she managed to gain Rachel's freedom. She was fairly certain she wouldn't survive another night incarcerated in the suffocating blackness of the pantry. And she didn't *wish* to survive a night engaged in the nauseating activities her lecherous stepfather had in mind.

The moment Evangeline was within arm's reach, he snatched the pot from her with the hand he'd previously been using to muffle Rachel's screams.

"What the hell is this?" he demanded.

"D-dirt." Evangeline reached for the little girl. "Can you please let Rachel go now?"

Neal spat at her shoes, reared back, and hurled the pot at the gazebo. The clay vessel shattered on impact, showering damp soil against the side.

A tiny bit of green fluttered to the ground.

Evangeline bit back a hysterical laugh. A seedling. Gavin had given her a *seedling*. Wherever she'd gone, she could've planted her own blackberry bush, and thought of him every time the flowers bloomed and the berries budded. He'd given her a living thing, something that grew, that blossomed, that thrived. Or would've thrived, had her stepfather not thrown it against a wall.

Neal shoved Rachel forward. The little girl scraped her knees on the rough dirt, but didn't cry out. She scrambled to her feet and stared wide-eyed at Evangeline, who now had Neal's hand across her mouth and his knife digging into her side. He didn't cut off a button, however. He sliced through her gown and into her skin. Not enough to kill her—just enough to hurt, to bleed, to terrify. She couldn't go back with him again. She couldn't.

Evangeline lifted one leg and kicked him in the knee.

He cursed and flipped her up into his arms, slicing her anew in the process.

Rachel burst into tears.

"For that," Neal hissed, "I just might visit you *in* the pantry. You're nice and motionless when you're trapped in the dark. It'll be much easier to get what I want."

He tore through a row of bushes, laughing as the brambles scratched Evangeline's exposed face and ripped one of her slippers from her feet.

"Evangeline!" came Susan's panicked voice from somewhere across the fields. "Evangeline! Come back! He's out there! He'll kill you!"

Too late.

Chapter Twenty-Seven

Gavin's relief at seeing the true murderer taken into the constabulary's custody warmed him throughout the long ride home, but his euphoria disappeared the moment Blackberry Manor rolled into view.

His sister, his nieces, the Stanton chit, and quite possibly every single one of his servants crowded the front lawn and ruined porch. As his homecoming never previously heralded an all-hands-on-deck welcoming party, Gavin doubted his afternoon was taking a turn for the better. Particularly since Evangeline wasn't present.

He leapt from the horse a few seconds too early and almost took a header into a clump of rocks. He hauled himself upright and ran toward his porch.

"What happened?" he shouted, trying not to fear the worst. Which would be what? That Evangeline had left forever? That would be the worst for *him,* but surely not cause for his servants and houseguests to await him out-of-doors, hands wringing, faces drawn.

"It's Evangeline," the Stanton chit stammered, eyes watering. No.

"What happened?" he demanded again. Instead of sounding fierce, the words came out . . . scared.

"The bad man cut her," Rachel said, voice quivering. "Then took her."

Gavin's hands convulsed into fists. *No.*

"Neal Pemberton," Jane confirmed. "Her stepfather."

He was wrong. *This* was the worst possible scenario. He'd sworn to protect her. And failed.

"I'm sorry," Rebecca wailed, and threw herself into her mother's arms. "I'm sorry!"

"What happened?" he said again, wishing the blackguard was right in front of him so he could tear the son of a bitch apart with his bare hands.

Jane took a deep breath. "When I went to see my miniature, the twins snuck outside to play hide-and-seek. We hunted for them right away—servants glimpsed them heading to the blackberry fields—but we could only find Rachel. She thought Rebecca was hurt, but Rebecca was just still hiding."

Rebecca's sobs grew louder.

"Miss Pemberton said if she could talk to Rachel, she'd find Rebecca, so I took her to the gazebo. Except when we got there, he had Rachel captive. Miss Pemberton sent me to get help."

"The bad man cut off my button." Rachel's lower lip trembled. "Miss Pemberton made him take her instead of me, and he poked her with his knife two times."

Gavin's lungs seized. Oh, God. Why hadn't he been here to save her?

"He . . ." the Stanton chit began, then faltered.

"Just tell me," Gavin growled.

"She was trying to get away, so he hit her. In the face." The Stanton chit swallowed and pushed up her spectacles. "She stopped struggling and went limp. He shoved her into his carriage, and that's the last we saw of her."

Gavin whirled to face his staff. "Ready my carriage," he ordered his coachman. "We're leaving in ten minutes."

He stalked up the porch steps, pushed through the crowd of people, and headed toward his front door. Neal Pemberton had included his home's exact location when he'd requested Evangeline's immediate return. It was twilight now, but if he rode all night, he'd be able to make it by dawn.

"What are you going to do?" the Stanton chit asked.

Gavin stared at her over his shoulder. "What the devil do you think I'm going to do? I'm going to *kill* him."

"You can't just . . . kill him."

He snorted. "I'm fetching my pistol and a swordstick. One is bound to do the trick."

Rose stepped forward, one hand on each twins' shoulder. "He's her legal guardian, Gavin."

"Not if he gives her to me . . . or dies." He flashed a lethal smile. "His choice."

Evangeline drifted in and out of consciousness during the long ride back to the Chiltern Hills. Every bump, every rut jarred her until the vicious thudding in her skull swallowed her completely into darkness.

She *hated* the dark.

It wasn't until they arrived and her stepfather dragged her from the carriage that she realized, at some point during the journey, he'd bound her at the wrists and ankles. She had to hop from the carriage to the house. Each awkward landing clacked her teeth together and set her brain pounding anew.

Her stepfather laughed and tugged her along faster.

He shouldered open the front door and shoved her inside so hard her chin bounced against the dusty wood floor. She lay there, tongue coated with blood from the impact, and fought the overwhelming sense of helpless desolation brought on by the unwelcome sight of her childhood home. After a moment, she pushed up with her bound fists and struggled to her knees.

Neal ignored her in favor of locating his bottle of whiskey.

Evangeline spat blood on the floor. She watched him until he disappeared from view just behind her.

How could she have ever believed Gavin to be a monster? *This* was a monster. Gavin was . . . Gavin was . . . wonderful. Although he'd made his fair share of mistakes, he'd risen above his past. He was capable of both change and love. Was she? She'd told him once that all wives were subjugated. Perhaps that wasn't so. Perhaps it depended on the men they chose as husbands. She'd lost a very, very good man.

Lost forever, because by trading her freedom for Rachel's, Evangeline had surrendered herself to her stepfather's custody. His legal custody. He'd never let her out of the house again, unless it was in a casket.

His footsteps prowled up behind her. Slow, precise thuds of his leather soles against the wooden floor. The footfalls stopped. His fingers twisted in Evangeline's hair, yanked upward. An involuntary squeak escaped her throat as several strands ripped from her skull.

She clamped her mouth shut tight. She hated to show pain. It brought him too much pleasure.

He let go, smacked her on the back of the head, circled into view. Smiling, of course. He'd always found moments of physical mastery both amusing and arousing. The latter scared her far more than his laughter.

Neal cast a slow, lascivious gaze over her body, beginning at her feet, up the length of her bound legs, lingering on her thighs, her breasts, her mouth. When his eyes met hers, he gave her a deliberate, mocking wink.

"All grown up, aren't you?" He drained his glass of whiskey and grinned. "Lucky for both of us, I'm feeling good enough to welcome you home nice and proper."

Gooseflesh erupted over Evangeline's limbs.

Neal arched a brow. "What's this? No tears? No pleading for me to 'just leave you alone'?"

No. She'd learned the hard way begging him to stop merely

spiked his arousal. If Mama hadn't been there to protect her all those years . . . Evangeline's body tensed. Better not to think about those days. Nobody was here to protect her now.

His legs bent until he nearly sat on his heels, face at her eye level, arms crossed over his knees. He tilted forward, licked her forehead, sniffed her.

She tried not to vomit.

He reached out and fingered the ribbon encircling her ribs. "Pretty dress. Too bad it's all dirty. We'd better get you out of this gown and into my bed."

Evangeline clenched her teeth and glared at him. He'd have to untie her to undress her. The moment her hands were free, she'd gouge out his eyes, and the moment her legs were free, she'd knee him in the bollocks and run out the door. She'd die before letting him touch her.

He rose to his feet, reached in a pocket, pulled out a ring of keys.

"I'd better go unchain a few servants. Cold enough to see my breath. We need a fire in here, a bath for you, more whiskey for me . . . Stay right here, darlin'. The fun will start the moment I come back."

With a smirk, he was gone.

Evangeline struggled to her feet and hopped toward the front door. She was just turning around to twist open the handle with her bound hands when her stepfather strode back into the room, another glass of whiskey in his hand.

"Now, now," he drawled. His brows arched. "What did I tell you I'd do if I caught you trying to escape again?"

Oddly, it took her a long moment before she could recall his threat. She'd no doubt blocked the possibility from her mind. She'd rather he kill her right here and now than lock her up in that godforsaken pantry.

"Ah." He smiled. "I see you remember now. It's not so very terrible in there, is it? So very dark, so very small, so very tight? We'll have to see if you still fit inside. I wager you'll be begging for my company once you've spent a night locked inside. Perhaps two nights. Or three." His fingers squeezed her upper arm as his voice dropped dangerously. "You'll stay in the pantry until you're ready to greet me proper."

"I won't go in there," she whispered. "I can't."

"You will."

When he pulled on her arm, Evangeline's knees gave way beneath her. She thudded heavily to the ground, legs limp, eyes wide with terror.

"Get. Up."

Her lungs wheezed. Her body shook. Her pulse faltered. She couldn't move.

Neal bent down, hooked the fingers of his free hand through the rope binding her ankles, dragged her dead weight across the room feet-first. He hauled her down the corridor to a tall narrow door that haunted her nightmares.

He flung open the door.

An icy draft rippled across her skin. The gaping maw of the long-abandoned pantry yawned blacker than ever in the absence of both sunlight and candles. What if he lost the key? What if he never released her? What if he left her to die?

He tugged her toward the open doorway. "In you go."

"Not again." She shook her head from side to side. "No. No!"

He hauled her forward by her ankles, dropped her legs, kicked her shoulders inside with the heel of his boot.

She thrashed, ready to die before being confined in that tiny slice of hell. When he reached down to shove her face into the darkness, she bit him. Hard.

"Little *bitch*."

He hurled his glass of whiskey over her head. It shattered behind her, sending a pungent spray of sticky liquid and tiny shards against the back wall. He kicked her the rest of the way inside, hard enough to hurt, hard enough to bruise, hard enough to maybe break the bone.

No. He hadn't broken any of her bones this time. She was

lucky. *Ha*. Lucky. If she was lucky, he wouldn't shut the door and lock her inside. If she was lucky, he'd just kill her and have done with it. If she was lucky—

The door slammed shut with enough force to blow strands of damp hair from her face. Keys jangled. The lock snapped in place.

Evangeline opened her mouth, but the darkness swallowed her scream.

It was worse than being lost in the walls at Blackberry Manor. So much worse. The pantry was darker. Smaller. Tighter.

Her limbs were bent. Cramped. She couldn't move. She couldn't breathe. The air was cold, dank, stale. The shadows smelled like sweat and liquor and fear. Or maybe that was her. She was a shadow now, too. She was nowhere. She was nothing.

Cobwebs clung to her cheeks and arms. Were there spiders in her hair? On her face? In her clothes? She yanked at her bound wrists. The twine dug into her skin until blood coated the bindings, but still she could not break free.

Something brushed against her toe. A rat? There. Skittering across the floor. She couldn't see, but she could hear them. Lots of them.

Rats could smell blood. Her wrists and ankles were wet.

They'd be on her soon. Sniffing her. Licking her. Biting her. She couldn't fend them off. She couldn't get away. She couldn't do anything but suck in great panting lungfuls of dry, dusty air and flail her bound limbs against the locked pantry door.

And scream.

Evangeline awoke in total blackness.

She reached out for Gavin and—couldn't reach, hands bound—*pantry*—Gavin just a dream. The back of her head thumped dully against the floor. She writhed in the dark, struggling against the twine that bound her bruised ankles and raw wrists. Strong. Tight. Impossible.

No. Never. She would escape even if she had to chew off her arm. Where were the rats? Perhaps they could chew her arm off for her. She bit back a hysterical giggle. No chewing. Rats must be asleep. Focus.

She rolled to her side. Twisted. Grappled for her ankles. The binding was too tight to slip more than the pad of one finger beneath the cord. Too tight. Too tight. Digging into her skin. Hurt. Pull anyway. *Pull*.

Nothing.

Her heartbeat quickened. She tugged on the twine. Sweat dampened her skin. The shadows shifted. She couldn't breathe. Listen. Wheezing gasps. Her breathing was too shallow. Short, rapid, desperate gulps of air. Calm down. *Try*. No panting. No passing out again. Must escape.

Her ankles throbbed. Her feet were numb. Her wrists were numb. Could she free her hands? Keeping her elbows tight together, she folded her arms until the back of her right wrist grazed her chin. Tight. Hurt. Ignoring the biting pain and the slick, tangy blood coating the cording, she bared her teeth and sawed at the twine, tugging and pulling and yanking and chewing.

She gasped. Recoiled. Spat. What the hell was that? Cobwebs? Hair? No. Thread. A bit of the twine had unraveled. Good. Try again.

Tears streamed down her cheeks when she finally bit through one of the strands of bloody twine. Her teeth tore at the rest of the cording, ripping the rope from her burning wrists. The dusty air stung the open wounds. Free. Her hands were free.

She lay back, arms raised, and rotated her wrists until feeling returned to her fingertips. So dark. The walls were closer, tighter, she was sure of it. Closing in. Suffocating her. No. She freed her wrists, she could free her ankles.

How? She scrabbled at the twine until her fingernails tore. Still tied. Still helpless. Still here.

Days, he'd said. He would leave her locked inside for days. She would go mad.

A faint knocking noise. Someone paying a call? If they came inside, she would scream for help. *If* they came inside. Move closer. Listen.

She lifted her head. Tried to scoot toward the door.

Ouch. Something thin and sharp sliced the back of her calf. What cut her? She flopped around, patted the floor until her fingers closed around a sovereign-sized shard of glass. Smelled like whiskey. A piece of the tumbler her stepfather had thrown. Sharp. Sharp enough to cut her—sharp enough to cut twine?

She sawed at the cording. Her fingers flayed as much as the rope, but at last a strand snapped in two. She yanked the twine free, massaged her tender ankles. A thousand prickles burst along her skin as blood rushed to her numb feet.

Voices. Whose voices? Neal, of course, and . . . Gavin? Here? Could it be possible?

Evangeline leapt to her feet, fell back down, hauled herself back up gingerly with one hand clutching the locked doorknob. It *was* Gavin. It was.

She banged her fists against the unforgiving door and screamed his name.

Noises. Scuffling. Rapid footfalls.

Gavin: "Evangeline! Where are you?"

Neal: "None of your business."

Gavin: "I'm making it my business."

The door handle jiggled.

Neal: "You can't have her. She's mine."

Gavin: "I'm hers. Now open that door."

Neal: "Never. She disobeyed me. She knew the punishment."

Gavin: "What? Get her out of there. Give me the key. Now!"

Scuffling. Fists connecting with flesh and bone. A thud. Cursing. Struggling. A yelp of pain. Keys jangling.

A crash.

"Evangeline, I'm going to get you out of there. Stay strong." More jangling. "Damn it." Hollow clicking. "Not this one either. *Damn* it."

Then the door swung open and Evangeline tumbled out into the hall.

Gavin caught her before she hit the floor, stared at her in horror. "What the hell did he do to you?"

She could only shake her head and cling to him.

"Come on," he hugged her tightly. "Let's get you out of here."

"You can't." Neal hauled himself up from the floor. "I'm her legal guardian."

"Not for long." Gavin swept Evangeline into his arms, carried her to the receiving room by the front door, laid her on the sofa closest to the crackling fire. "Please," he said softly, kneeling before her. "Will you marry me?"

She nodded, touched his hand. "I would love to."

It wasn't until she saw his eyes widen that she realized even now, even under these circumstances, he hadn't been completely convinced she'd say yes.

"Gavin." She smiled up at him. "You *are* a good person. I love you."

He grinned. "I love *you*."

"Touching," Neal drawled as he lounged against the doorway. "But she can't marry you without my permission."

"Then you shall give it." Gavin searched his pockets. He pulled out a pistol, set it on the cushion by Evangeline's feet, then pulled out several sheets of folded parchment.

She stared at the parchment, the pistol, then Gavin. He was so calm, so rational. Not railing at top volume or throwing vicious punches like the murderous madman he'd been made out to be. Which was good. One madman in the room was enough.

Her stepfather stepped closer, knife drawn. "What the hell is that?"

"Marriage contract." Gavin rose to his feet. He held the papers out to Neal, who snatched them immediately.

Evangeline blinked up at Gavin. "When did you have time to draft a marriage contract?"

"I didn't," he confessed. "This contract was supposed to be for Nancy and Teasdale. Hetherington was making copies of it that night in my office. I brought pen and ink in the carriage and changed a few details. Like the bride. And the groom. It'll serve as intent until I can have my solicitor draw up another. By tomorrow, at the very latest."

"Assuming I sign," Neal interrupted. His face twisted in distaste. "Why would I?"

"Money," Gavin answered simply. "I have plenty. If you keep her here, you'll see none of it. So name your price."

"You'd pay for her?" Neal sneered, but his eyes lit with greed. "Like a whore?"

Although his jaw tensed, Gavin lifted one shoulder in a shrug. "I'd give her my life. What's money? Sign."

"Hmmm." Neal cast Evangeline an appraising look. "If I keep her, I can use her as a witch *and* a whore. Perhaps I can rent her out and make more money than whatever you're offering."

"Touch me and die." Evangeline picked up the pistol Gavin had placed at her feet and aimed it at her stepfather. She would never hurt another human being . . . but Neal Pemberton hardly counted.

Eyebrows raised, Neal glanced from Evangeline to Gavin, then back to Evangeline. "Put the gun down."

She kept it trained on her stepfather's chest.

"See here," he said, backing up a step. "I can't sign if I'm dead. I won't sign either copy until it says exactly how much money I have coming. Ten thousand pounds?"

"Done." Gavin gestured toward the papers.

"I meant fifteen," Neal said quickly.

Gavin inclined his head. "Get your ink and I'll sign."

Neal returned with a traveling desk in seconds, dipped his pen, scratched a few lines on both sheets. "There. It says you owe me twenty thousand pounds, payable at the time of betrothal. Nonrefundable."

Evangeline's stomach dropped and the pistol wavered in her sweat-damp palms. Twenty thousand pounds? Did *anyone* have that kind of money?

"So be it." Gavin's tone was bored. "Did you sign?"

Neal did so with a flourish, re-inked his pen, held it out for Gavin.

When both documents had been signed, Gavin left one on the desktop and returned the other to his pocket. He turned toward Evangeline and held out his hand.

"Come, my love. Let's go home."

"Wrong." Neal shook his head. "She's not going anywhere."

Gavin's hands fisted. "You just signed—"

"A marriage contract. She's still mine until the wedding."

"Over my dead body." Gavin scooped Evangeline into his arms and headed for the door. She laced her arms around his neck, careful not to let the pistol fall from her trembling fingers. She stared over Gavin's shoulder at her stepfather's twisted expression. Terror strangled her heart.

Neal slid a poker from the stand next to the fireplace. "As you said. 'So be it.' I'll get my money either way."

"No!" Evangeline cried. Gavin ignored both of them and hurried through the doorway. She beat against his shoulders. "Gavin! He has a poker!"

Gavin strode faster.

Evangeline held tight with one hand and used the other to aim the pistol at her stepfather's arm. Neal leaped toward them, slashing down toward Gavin's head. Evangeline squeezed the trigger.

The bullet burst into her stepfather's chest, sending a tide of crimson pulsing across his waistcoat.

He dropped to his knees. The poker slipped from his fingers. He fell forward and didn't move.

Gavin spun around, his heart thudding against Evangeline's. She tightened her hold around him, buried her face in his neck.

The pistol fell from her fingers and clattered to the floor.

"Is he dead?" she mumbled into Gavin's collar. He held her tighter, kissed the top of her head. She was safe.

"I'll make sure." He set her down, squeezed her hand. She hugged her arms around her chest and forced herself to breathe. He knelt next to the body for a long moment before glancing up. "Yes."

"I didn't mean to kill him," she whispered. "But I'm not sorry he's dead."

"I know." Gavin gathered her in his arms, hugged her, stroked her hair. "It was an accident. You're safe now. I've got you."

"Forever?"

"Forever."

As she traded her village for Blackberry Manor once again, instead of running away, this time Evangeline was finally going home.

Epilogue

A breeze rifled Gavin's hair as he peeked around the canvas.

"Quit hitting your sister, Rebecca," he called from behind his easel.

Evangeline considered switching places with Rachel in order to break up the twins' row before she remembered Gavin had already begun painting them standing in the previous order. Oh, well. He'd figure it out. She held hands with the twins to keep them from fighting, and exchanged a grin with their mother.

Having Rose and her daughters come to live with them at Blackberry Manor had been the best wedding present Evangeline could've asked for. A family. At last.

"Beautiful day, wouldn't you say, Eve?" Rose commented, tilting her face to the sun.

Evangeline nodded. "Absolutely."

Gavin had been right about Blackberry Manor in springtime. The field at their back was alive with thick green hedgerows, delicate white flowers, and the most heavenly scent in the air. Beautiful as it was, Evangeline could hardly wait for the blackberries to bud. It would be her first time picking the delectable fruit. She smiled at the thought of Rose's little girls racing between the hedgerows, hands sticky with blackberry juice.

"Everybody else chose pall-mall and kite-flying for their birthdays," Jane groused for at least the hundredth time that afternoon, "and Uncle Lioncroft picks portraiture. We'd be done by now if he would've just painted a miniature like he did for the locket he gave me on my birthday."

"You were just one person," Nancy reminded her patiently. "We're six. And this portrait's to adorn a wall in Uncle Lioncroft's library, not dangle from his neck."

"We'll fly kites afterward," Evangeline promised. "You can have first pick of the colors."

When the girls immediately began arguing over who would fly which kite, Rose cupped a hand over her mouth and turned to Evangeline.

"Any word yet?" she murmured.

Evangeline shook her head. "Benedict's letter said he was sure the baby's birth was imminent, and he still plans to raise the child as his own when Francine goes to Newgate. Gavin says Benedict's always wanted a child."

"And you?" Rose prompted, arching a brow. "Are you still nervous about motherhood?"

"Gavin isn't," Evangeline admitted, touching a hand to her belly. Maybe someday soon . . . "He says if we have a daughter with visions, we'll be sure to give her as many siblings as she wants so she'll never be lonely."

"And if your daughter doesn't have visions?"

Evangeline grinned. "She's stuck with plenty of siblings either way. Gavin promised."

The twins began poking each other. Nancy rolled her eyes and let them fight. Jane started complaining again about kite-flying and pall-mall.

Rose shook her head. "How could any child be lonely with so many well-behaved cousins to play with?"

"No pugilism in the family portrait," Gavin shouted, poking his head from behind his easel. "What has you ladies so excited?"

"We're talking about families," Evangeline called back. "And having one of our own."

Gavin's eyes crinkled. He tossed his paintbrush over his shoulder, strode into the middle of the melee, and scooped Evangeline up into his arms.

"I think," he murmured into her hair, "I just changed my mind about what I want for my birthday."

She threw her arms around his neck and squeezed.

"Splendid," she whispered back. "That's exactly the present I wanted to give you."

Dear Reader,

There are those who opine that gothic romances routinely feature a dark, brooding, dangerous hero and the helpless, weak (some might say . . . Too Stupid to Live) heroine who loves him, despite the fact that he's a raging dissociative psychopath. If a devilishly attractive dissociative psychopath. With a large . . . ego.

With TOO WICKED TO KISS, I was totally on board with the dark, brooding, dangerous hero (although I hope you'll find Gavin still firmly rooted in sanity) but I wanted an unquestionably strong heroine. A woman with goals, with dreams, with brains. And then I wanted to rip her life apart and make her prove her courage, tenacity, and heart despite everything I threw her way.

Because I am nice, I gave Evangeline a special Gift: psychic visions from skin-to-skin contact. Because I am evil, I made sure this Gift gave her a life of lonely isolation, plagued with debilitating migraines from the slightest touch. Oh, and just so it wouldn't be anything resembling *easy,* I made sure the success and relevance of said visions was a roulette wheel of its own. (And you thought Sleeping Beauty's wicked godmother gave bad gifts!)

What kind of (dark, brooding, dangerous) hero would actually deserve a woman like this, who can rise above all adversity with steel in her spine and selflessness in her heart? Clearly, he would need to be tested, as well. So I made his past come back to haunt him (figuratively) and gave him a few new troubles. Like falling in love. And finding a dead man in the guest room. With Gavin's own handprints laced around the corpse's neck.

I hope you love Gavin and Evangeline as much as I do. (Susan's book is next, so feel free to love her, too.) As a special bonus, don't miss the following sneak peek. Please come visit me at *ericaridley.com.* I promise to be more hospitable than Gavin . . .

All the best,
Erica Ridley

Please turn the page for
a sneak peek of Erica Ridley's
next historical romance,
coming in 2011!

March. The last of the plumed lords and ladies swooped into Town like crows feasting upon carrion. Miss Susan Stanton had escaped the confines of her bedchamber for the first time in six long, dark weeks—only to be bundled in the back of a black carriage and jettisoned into the vast void of nothingness beyond London borders.

To Bournemouth. *Bournemouth*. An infinitesimal "town" on a desolate stretch of coastline a million miles from home. Less than a hundred souls, the carriage driver had said. Spectacular. Thrice as many bodies had graced Susan's London come-out party four years ago, not counting the servants. Being banished from Town was the worst possible punishment for disobedience Mother could've possibly devised. Nothing could deaden the soul quite like the prospect of—

Moonseed Manor.

Susan's breath caught in her throat. Her mind emptied of its litany of complaints as her eyes struggled to equate the stark, colorless vista before her with "town of Bournemouth."

Dead brown nothingness. Miles of it. A steep cliff jutted over black ocean. There, backlit with a smattering of fuzzy stars, a bone-white architectural monstrosity teetered impossibly close to the edge.

Moonseed Manor did not look like a place to live. Moonseed Manor looked like a place to die.

Not a single candle flickered in the windows. As the carriage drew her ever closer, its wheels bouncing and slipping on sand and rocks. Susan's skin erupted in gooseflesh. She hugged herself, struck by an invasive chill much colder than the ocean breeze should cause.

The carriage stopped. The driver handed her out, then disappeared back into his perch, leaving her to make her presence known by herself. Very well. He could stay and mind the luggage while she summoned the help. Miss Susan Stanton was no shrinking violet. Although she wished for the hundredth time that her lady's maid hadn't been forbidden from accompanying her. She was well and truly exiled.

The back of her neck prickling with trepidation, Susan found herself curling trembling fingers around a thick brass knocker, the handle formed from the coil of a serpent about to strike. The resulting sound echoed in the eerie stillness, as if both the pale wood and the house itself were hollow and lifeless.

The door silently opened.

A scarecrow stood before her, all spindly limbs and jaundiced skin with a shock of straw-colored hair protruding at all angles above dark, cavernous eyes. The sharpness of his bones stretched his yellowed skin. His attire hung oddly on his frame, as though these clothes were not his own, but rather the castoffs of the true (and presumably human) butler.

"I . . . I . . ." Susan managed, before choking on an explanation she did not have.

She what? She was the twenty-year-old sole offspring of a loveless titled couple who had banished their ostracized disappointment of a daughter to the remotest corner of England rather than bear the continued sight of her? She nudged her spectacles up the bridge of her nose with the back of a gloved hand and forced what she hoped was a smile.

"My name is Miss Susan Stanton," she tried again, deciding to leave the explanation at that. Mother had written in advance, and what more need be said after Mother's missive? "I'm afraid I was expected hours ago. Is Lady Beaune at home?"

"Always," the scarecrow rasped, after a brief pause. His sudden jagged-tooth smile unsettled Susan as surely as it must frighten the crows. "Come." ·

Susan slid a dozen hesitant steps into a long narrow passage devoid of both portraiture and decoration before the oddity of his answer reverberated in her ears. *Always.* What did he mean by that, and why the secret smile? Once one entered Moonseed Manor, was one to be stuck there, entombed forevermore in a beachside crypt?

"P-perhaps I should alert my driver that your mistress is at home." She hastened forward to catch up to the scarecrow's long-limbed strides. "I have a shocking number of valises, and—"

"Don't worry," came the scarecrow's smoky rasp, once again accompanied by a grotesque slash of a smile. "He's being taken care of."

Normally, Susan would've bristled with outrage at the unprecedented effrontery of being interrupted by a servant. In this case, however, she was more concerned with the rented driver's continued wellbeing. She was not sure she wanted him "being taken care of." Shouldn't the butler have said her *trunks* would be taken care of? She glanced over her shoulder at the corridor now stretching endlessly behind them, and wondered if she were safer inside these skeletal walls or out.

Susan didn't notice a narrow passageway intersecting the stark hall until the scarecrow disappeared within. She stood at the crossroads, hesitant to follow but even more nervous not to. After the briefest of pauses, she hurried to regain the scarecrow's side before losing him forever in the labyrinthine walls.

If he noticed her moment of indecision, he gave no sign. He made several quick turns, passing tall closed door after tall closed door, before finally making an abrupt stop at the dead end of an ill-lit corridor.

This door was open. Somewhat.

A candle flickered inside, but only succeeded in filling the room's interior with teeming shadows.

"Sir," the scarecrow rasped into the opening. "It's Miss Stanton. Your guest."

"Guest?" came a warm, smartly-accented voice from somewhere within. The master of the house? No. "You were expecting guests at this hour, Ollie?"

Ollie? Susan echoed silently in her head. Wasn't Lady Beaune's husband named Jean-Louis? Perhaps she was about to meet a distant relation. A cousin would make a lovely ally.

"All guests arrive at this hour," a deep voice countered. "It's midnight."

Before Susan had a chance to parse that inexplicable response, the door swung fully open and a fairytale giant filled the entirety of the frame.

Her shoulders reached his hips. *His* shoulders reached the sides of the doorframe and very nearly the top as well. His broad back hunched to allow his dark head to pass beneath the edge. Small black eyes glittered in an overlarge square face, his mouth hidden behind a beard the color of fresh tar. Arms that could crush tree trunks flexed at his sides. He did not offer his hand.

"Miss Stanton."

Although her name was more a statement than a question, Susan's well-trained spine dipped in an automatic curtsy as her mouth managed to stammer a simple, "Yes."

He did not bow in kind. Nor was it remotely possible he was a child of Lady Beaune. He was easily five-and-thirty. Had Papa's fourth cousin thrice removed remarried in the unknown years since Mother had last spoken to this distant limb of the Stanton family tree? Did Mother *comprehend* where exactly she'd condemned her daughter to? Or care?

"Move out of the way, oaf," came the cultured voice from before. "I must see this creature that travels alone and in dark of night to visit the likes of you."

Rather than move aside, the giant stepped forward, crowding Susan backward. Her shoulders scraped the wall opposite. Her hands clenched at her sides.

A new figure filled the doorframe. Tall, but not impossibly so. Well-muscled, but not frighteningly so. As smartly tailored as any London dandy, but with an air of barely contained danger more suitable to the meanest streets where even footpads feared to tread. Alarmingly attractive despite the too-long chestnut hair and day's growth of dark stubble shadowing the line of his jaw.

"Mmm, I see." An amused grin toyed with his lips. "My pleasure."

He performed as perfect a bow as any Susan had ever encountered in a Town ballroom. Before her trembling legs could force an answering curtsy, the giant moved back into place, blocking the . . . gentleman? . . . from her view.

The giant's thick arms crossed over his barrel chest. "Carriage?"

"Gone," rasped the scarecrow.

Susan jumped. She'd forgotten his silent presence.

"Driver?"

The scarecrow's terrifying smile returned. "Taken care of."

Satisfaction glinted in the giant's eyes. Susan was positive panic was the only thing glinting in hers. Would she be "taken care of" next?

"Take her to the bone chamber."

Susan's heart stuttered to a stop until she realized the giant had said *Beaune* chamber, not *bone* chamber. Beaune, like Lady Beaune, her father's fourth cousin thrice removed, with whom her family clearly should have kept a much more detailed correspondence. Yet even with this correction firmly in mind, Susan couldn't help but doubt the Beaune chamber would remotely resemble the sumptuous Buckingham-quality guest quarters she'd hoped to find.

The scarecrow turned and headed down the hall without bothering to verify that Susan followed. He was wise not to worry. She had no intention of standing around under the giant's calculating gaze any longer than necessary.

Susan scrambled after the scarecrow without a single word of parting for her host—not that the giant seemed particularly concerned about adhering to social niceties—and rounded a corner just in time to see the scarecrow ascend a pale marble staircase she swore hadn't existed when they'd traveled this exact sequence of corridors moments before.

She hurried to his side before she got lost for good. "That . . . wasn't Lord Beaune."

A dry laugh crackled from his throat, accompanied by a sly glance from his dark glittering eyes. "He seem French? Or dead? That's the new master of Moonseed Manor. It's to him you owe the roof over yer head tonight."

Dead. Her ears buzzed at the news. The news that Lady Beaune had been widowed and remarried was surprising. But the idea that Susan owed anything to anyone—much less her cousin's new husband—was intolerable. She had once been Society's princess! And would be again. Just as soon as she got back to London.

The wiry manservant led her through another complicated series of interconnected passageways. A lit sconce protruded from the middle of an otherwise unadorned passageway, as bleached and unremarkable as all the rest. Orange candlelight spilled from an open doorway, chasing their shadows behind them. Susan wished she could flee as easily.

"Your room," came the scarecrow's scratchy voice.

Susan nodded and stepped across the threshold. When she turned to ask him directions to the dining areas and drawing rooms (and when she might hope to see the lady of the house) he was already gone.

She faced the cavernous chamber once more, doing her best to ignore the uneasy sensation of walking into a crypt. Although the room was as cold as any catacomb would be, a large canopied bed, not a casket, stood in the center. The shadowy figure next to the unlit fireplace had to be a maid provided to ensure Susan's comfort. Thank God. At least there was *some* hint of London sensibilities.

Susan stepped forward just as the cloaked figure swiveled without seeming to move her feet. Long white braids flanked a narrow face hollowed with hunger and despair. Age spots mottled her clawed hands and pale neck. An ornate crucifix hung from a long gold chain. Trembling fingers clutched the intricate charm to her thin chest. She did not appear to be starting a fire in the grate. She did not appear to be a maid at all.

"M-may I help you?" Susan asked.

The old woman did not answer.

Were there more sundry guests in this pharaoh's tomb of a manor? Was this one lost, confused, afraid? So was Susan, on all counts, but the least she could do was help this poor woman find her correct bedchamber.

Before she could so much as offer her hand, however, a sharp breeze rippled through the chamber. She shivered before she realized she could no longer feel the phantom breeze—although it continued to flutter the old woman's dark red cloak and unravel the braids from her hair.

In fact . . . the breeze began to unravel the old woman herself, ripping thread by red thread from her cloak like drops of blood disappearing in a pool of water. The wind tore long curling strands of white hair from her bowed head, then strips of flesh from her bones, until the only thing standing before Susan was the empty fire pit. The glittering crucifix fell onto the hardwood floor and disappeared from sight.

The chamber door slammed shut behind her with foundation-shaking force. Susan didn't have to try the handle to know she was trapped inside.

She wondered what else was locked inside with her.

More by Bestselling Author
Fern Michaels

___	**About Face**	0-8217-7020-9	$7.99US/$10.99CAN
___	**Picture Perfect**	0-8217-7588-X	$7.99US/$10.99CAN
___	**Vegas Heat**	0-8217-7668-1	$7.99US/$10.99CAN
___	**Finders Keepers**	0-8217-7669-X	$7.99US/$10.99CAN
___	**Dear Emily**	0-8217-7670-3	$7.99US/$10.99CAN
___	**Vegas Sunrise**	0-8217-7672-X	$7.99US/$10.99CAN
___	**Payback**	0-8217-7876-5	$6.99US/$9.99CAN
___	**Vendetta**	0-8217-7877-3	$6.99US/$9.99CAN
___	**The Jury**	0-8217-7878-1	$6.99US/$9.99CAN
___	**Sweet Revenge**	0-8217-7879-X	$6.99US/$9.99CAN
___	**Lethal Justice**	0-8217-7880-3	$6.99US/$9.99CAN
___	**Free Fall**	0-8217-7881-1	$6.99US/$9.99CAN
___	**Fool Me Once**	0-8217-8071-9	$7.99US/$10.99CAN
___	**Vegas Rich**	0-8217-8112-X	$7.99US/$10.99CAN
___	**Hide and Seek**	1-4201-0184-6	$6.99US/$9.99CAN
___	**Hokus Pokus**	1-4201-0185-4	$6.99US/$9.99CAN
___	**Fast Track**	1-4201-0186-2	$6.99US/$9.99CAN
___	**Collateral Damage**	1-4201-0187-0	$6.99US/$9.99CAN
___	**Final Justice**	1-4201-0188-9	$6.99US/$9.99CAN
___	**Up Close and Personal**	0-8217-7956-7	$7.99US/$9.99CAN
___	**Under the Radar**	1-4201-0683-X	$6.99US/$9.99CAN
___	**Razor Sharp**	1-4201-0684-8	$7.99US/$10.99CAN

Available Wherever Books Are Sold!
Check out our website at **www.kensingtonbooks.com**

Romantic Suspense from
Lisa Jackson

See How She Dies	0-8217-7605-3	$6.99US/$9.99CAN
Final Scream	0-8217-7712-2	$7.99US/$10.99CAN
Wishes	0-8217-6309-1	$5.99US/$7.99CAN
Whispers	0-8217-7603-7	$6.99US/$9.99CAN
Twice Kissed	0-8217-6038-6	$5.99US/$7.99CAN
Unspoken	0-8217-6402-0	$6.50US/$8.50CAN
If She Only Knew	0-8217-6708-9	$6.50US/$8.50CAN
Hot Blooded	0-8217-6841-7	$6.99US/$9.99CAN
Cold Blooded	0-8217-6934-0	$6.99US/$9.99CAN
The Night Before	0-8217-6936-7	$6.99US/$9.99CAN
The Morning After	0-8217-7295-3	$6.99US/$9.99CAN
Deep Freeze	0-8217-7296-1	$7.99US/$10.99CAN
Fatal Burn	0-8217-7577-4	$7.99US/$10.99CAN
Shiver	0-8217-7578-2	$7.99US/$10.99CAN
Most Likely to Die	0-8217-7576-6	$7.99US/$10.99CAN
Absolute Fear	0-8217-7936-2	$7.99US/$9.49CAN
Almost Dead	0-8217-7579-0	$7.99US/$10.99CAN
Lost Souls	0-8217-7938-9	$7.99US/$10.99CAN
Left to Die	1-4201-0276-1	$7.99US/$10.99CAN
Wicked Game	1-4201-0338-5	$7.99US/$9.99CAN
Malice	0-8217-7940-0	$7.99US/$9.49CAN

Available Wherever Books Are Sold!
Visit our website at **www.kensingtonbooks.com**